W9-CMG-534

THE CARETAKER

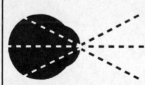

This Large Print Book carries the Seal of Approval of N.A.V.H.

THE CARETAKER

A.X. AHMAD

THORNDIKE PRESS
A part of Gale, Cengage Learning

Detroit • New York • San Francisco • New Haven, Conn • Waterville, Maine • London

GALE
CENGAGE Learning·

LIBRARY OF CONGRESS CATALOGING-IN-PUBLICATION DATA

Ahmad, A. X.
    The caretaker / by A. X. Ahmad. — Large print edition.
        pages ; cm. — (Thorndike Press large print thriller)
    ISBN 978-1-4104-6422-4 (hardcover) — ISBN 1-4104-6422-9 (hardcover)
    1. Squatters—Fiction. 2. East Indians—United States—Fiction. 3. Martha's Vineyard (Mass.)—Fiction. 4. Political fiction. 5. Large type books. I. Title.
PS3601.H573C37 2013b
813'.6—dc23   2013037090

Published in 2013 by arrangement with St. Martin's Press, LLC

Printed in the United States of America
1 2 3 4 5 6 7 17 16 15 14 13

THE CARETAKER

PROLOGUE

At nineteen thousand feet on the Siachen Glacier, there is no longer earth and sky, just an endless mountain of snow.

In this infinity of white are six men, walking in a line, moving in the drunken lockstep of the exhausted.

They wear white snowsuits over their Indian Army uniforms. Heavy assault rifles are slung across their backs. Their lips are split and bleeding, their eyes hidden by snow goggles.

It is quiet up here. The only sound is their ragged breathing.

The soldier at the end of the line is a gangly nineteen-year-old. He hums tunelessly, then begins to sing, his voice growing louder.

"Loaded like a freight train, flyin' like an aeroplane . . ."

The turbaned Sikh captain at the front of the line turns angrily. "Shut up, Private

Dewan."

"Loaded like a freight *traaaain*!" The reedy voice rises to a shout. "Flyin' like an *aeroplaaaane* —"

"For God's sake, somebody shut him up."

The soldier in front of Private Dewan raises his rifle like a club, is about to bring it down when the Sergeant intervenes.

"Let me handle this. He's just a boy."

Sergeant Khandelkar grips the Private by his thin shoulders and whispers urgently. The singing stops and once again there is only the deep silence of the mountains.

Captain Singh calls for a halt. The men drop their packs and slump into the snow.

Sergeant Khandelkar's bony face is dark with worry, and he speaks in a low voice. "Captain, any idea where we are? Have we crossed over into Pakistani territory?"

The Captain shrugs. They'd left the Indian Army base camp, far down the glacier, two days ago. Maps are useless up here. Technically, India and Pakistan are not at war, but the Siachen Glacier is a gray zone between the two countries, a place of armed skirmishes and ambushes.

They've been on tough missions up here, but this one is different: complete radio silence, no helicopter evacuations, no parachute drops of ammunition. Like ghosts,

8

they are to cross high up into Pakistani territory, hit their target, and come back undetected.

The Captain glances at Private Dewan. The boy is staring up into the sun with unseeing eyes.

Sergeant Khandelkar leans in. "Sir, I'm worried about him. It looks like high-altitude cerebral edema. His brain is swelling. He'll be hallucinating soon."

They both look at Private Dewan, who is now giggling to himself. He does a little twirl in the snow, then starts humming again.

The Captain's face darkens. "If he compromises the mission, we're going to have to leave him behind."

"No!" Sergeant Khandelkar's voice rises to a shout, and he makes an effort to lower it. "He's just a kid, we can't do that . . . I'll walk with him sir, I'll keep him quiet."

"All right. But keep a close watch on him. If he's any trouble, any trouble at all . . ."

The corners of the Sergeant's mouth turn down in disgust. "This mission stinks, sir. We've been walking three days to reach a set of coordinates. Why couldn't they tell us what our target is?"

Captain Singh shrugs. "This is how it's done these days, Sergeant. They dream up these missions down in New Delhi, and we do the dirty work."

The Sergeant sniffs indignantly, but keeps his peace.

Private Dewan is smiling blankly now. He begins to hum again, the same stupid tune from some stupid American band.

"Time to move on, Sergeant. Gather the men. And keep an eye on that boy."

The soldiers rise slowly, pull on their heavy packs, and start walking. Captain Singh thinks he hears a noise and looks sharply up the mountain.

There is nothing to see but snow.

■ ■ ■ ■

I
THE ISLAND

■ ■ ■ ■

The times are like drawn knives, kings like
    butchers,
Righteousness has fled on wings.
The dark night of falsehood prevails,
The moon of truth is no longer visible.
    — Guru Granth Sahib, Majh

CHAPTER ONE

The Senator's wife is late. Very late.

Ranjit Singh stands beside his battered Ford truck and squints down the long, empty line of Beach Road. There is no sign of Anna Neals's silver Mercedes. Only seagulls coast through the evening sky, their shrieks drowned out by the waves crashing across the road.

He turns and looks at the gray-shingled liquor store behind him, wondering how much longer it will be open. It is mid-December, and shops close early during the off-season on Martha's Vineyard. If he loiters in the empty parking lot, the Edgartown cops will surely notice him, and that's the last thing he wants.

If anybody else were an hour late, he would have left. But Anna Neals isn't just anybody, she is the wife of Clayton Neals, the longest-serving African-American senator. He has worked for her all summer, trimming hedges and building stone steps down to her private beach. When she called this morning, he heard her warm, melodious voice and instantly agreed to meet her.

But she is now an hour and ten minutes late. *Damn it.*

Ranjit leans against the green flatbed truck, feeling the warm metal against his aching back. Though the gold cursive painted on the door says SINGH LANDSCAPE COMPANY, he's the only employee, and his six-foot frame has been bent over all day, raking piles of red and yellow leaves. Before driving over to meet Anna, he changed into a red turban and his cleanest army surplus sweater — the epaulettes torn off — and even tried to clean his cracked fingernails, then gave up. The long summer of landscaping has seamed them with dirt.

A car speeds down Beach Road and feathers into the parking lot, but it isn't hers, it's a rust-eaten blue Mercury, its front bumper held on with duct tape. In the backseat, caged in by a mesh partition, is a thick-muscled black dog wearing a black leather collar.

The car screeches to a halt and a heavyset man in a red plaid shirt emerges from the passenger seat, mumbling something to the driver. Plaid-shirt walks toward the liquor

14

store with a rolling gait, like a sailor unused to dry land.

Hunters, probably on a day trip from the Cape. Ranjit looks down at his watch: five minutes, no more; as it is, he is late picking up his daughter from her school.

He stares across the road at the cold, angry ocean. When he first came to the island with his wife and daughter six months ago, the water was warm and shimmering, the beaches were lined with parked cars, and long-tailed kites fluttered in the hot sky. All summer and into the fall he'd worked as a landscaper, feeling his unused muscles stretch and harden, feeling the hot sun beat down on him, and felt a kind of peace.

But now winter is upon them and the tourists are all gone. The ice-cream parlors and clam shacks have closed, and the migrant workers — the Jamaicans and Bulgarians and Czechs — have left. Even the sky feels like a gray bowl jammed over the island.

Worse, all the landscaping jobs have ended. For the millionth time Ranjit wonders how he is going to survive the winter months. Food and gas here are so expensive, and lately, the furnace in their old house has been cutting out abruptly. If it dies, he just won't have the money to get it fixed.

He needs to find another job soon, or else he'll have to return to Boston and work in Lallu Singh's cramped, overheated Indian store, and the thought of going back there makes him sick.

An hour and a quarter late. The Senator's dark-eyed wife definitely isn't coming, and hope fades away, replaced by a deep disappointment. *Forget it.*

He strides toward the liquor store for a nip of Bacardi to dull his mind before heading out. At the doorway he slows down, and can't help looking over his shoulder one last time.

Someone slams right into him.

The man in the plaid shirt staggers and clutches a case of beer to his chest. A tall bottle of bourbon balanced on top of it falls and hits the asphalt with a crack. Its neck shears off and it rolls away slowly, the golden liquor glugging out.

The dog in the back of the car barks once, a sound from deep within its chest.

"*Aww,* crap. Look what you've done." Plaid-shirt's voice is slurred with alcohol. Despite his thick stubble, he has the face of a spoiled child, his high forehead framed by long, uncombed blond hair. "That was a thirty-dollar bottle of Jack."

Ranjit stands motionless. "I'm sorry, sir,

16

but *you* walked into me."

The man stares at him out of blue, blameless eyes, taking in his red turban, his mustache and full beard.

"Hey, what are you, some kind of Arab?"

"I'm a Sikh from India. Sir, I said I was sorry."

"Sorry, huh? Well, that bottle cost me thirty bucks. Thirty American dollars."

There is no mistaking the menace in the man's voice. *There must be no trouble. No trouble and no police.* Taking out his wallet, Ranjit counts out a ten and some singles.

"This is all I have."

"This ain't worth shit." Plaid-shirt grabs the bills and turns toward his car. "Hey, you see this bullshit?"

A pale face stares out at Ranjit from the driver's seat, younger, but with the same washed-out blond hair. This man has a blue-black fish tattooed on each forearm.

"I got an idea," the tattooed man says, waving at the broken bottle. "You clean up that mess you made, and we might accept your apology."

His words are followed by the metallic *chuck-chuck* of a shotgun being racked. A blued barrel appears in the car window, pointed right at Ranjit.

Time stops. As it used to in combat, all

noise drains away and the world shrinks to the two men in the empty parking lot. Ranjit is bound to them now by words and actions, bound till something changes.

The tattooed man in the car smiles, showing yellowed teeth. "Come on. Clean it up."

The shotgun doesn't waver. It's a Remington 870 with a twenty-eight-inch hunting barrel, probably loaded with birdshot. At this range the pellets will rip his face to shreds.

There is no choice. Ranjit's hands are shaking with rage as he bends down and reaches for the broken glass. Under his breath he mutters a prayer.

The truly enlightened ones
Are those who neither incite fear in others
Nor fear anyone themselves . . .

Glass shards are everywhere, glinting in the fading light, and the sharp smell of alcohol stings his nostrils.

The tattooed man in the car watches him, finger tensed on the shotgun trigger. The dog caged in the backseat paces and growls. Plaid-shirt places the carton of beer on the hood of the car and leans back unsteadily, lighting up a cigarette.

A sliver of broken glass slices into the ball

of Ranjit's thumb. He gasps as warm blood puddles into the palm of his hand.

Plaid-shirt chuckles. "*Aww,* look at him. He's bleeding."

The tattooed man in the car joins in the laughter, the shotgun barrel wobbling with hilarity.

Ranjit's neck burns with shame.

The truly enlightened ones
Are those . . .

"Come on, towel-head. My beer's getting warm."

Fuck it. Ranjit reaches for the jagged neck of the bottle, calculating his moves. *The dog is caged in, not a threat. Go for the man, grab the shotgun barrel and twist it aside. Jam the jagged glass into his throat, hear him burble and beg.*

He straightens up, the glint of glass in his hand. There is a sudden screech of tires and a car door slams like a rifle shot.

"What the hell is going on here? Ranjit, are you okay?"

Anna Neals's silver Mercedes is parked askew. She takes long strides toward them, her boots thudding angrily against the asphalt. Her dark face is hidden behind blank aviator shades, her straightened, jaw-length hair fluttering in the breeze. She's wearing jeans torn at the knees, a silver down jacket, and thick glass bracelets that clank as she walks.

She is shouting now. "Jeff? Norman? Is there a problem here?"

The two hunters' faces redden. The shotgun disappears from the window, but the dog barks loudly and flings himself at the door.

Anna doesn't flinch. "Control that dog. I said, do we have a problem here?"

"No problem, Mrs. Neals. No problem at all." Plaid-shirt picks up his case of beer and ducks around the side of the car. "Hey, your husband is a hero. Stood up to those damn Koreans. Showed 'em."

"I'll pass on your compliments. Now leave before I turn you in for hunting illegally. Open season for waterfowl is over."

Nodding his head, Plaid-shirt stumbles into the car. The dog's nose is pressed against the rear windshield as the car squeals out of the lot, accelerates down Beach Road, and disappears in a blue haze of exhaust.

The only sounds are the crashing of the waves and Anna's angry breathing.

Standing up, Ranjit squeezes the pressure point below his thumb to stop the bleeding.

He doesn't want the Senator's wife to make a fuss.

"Anna, it was my fault. I bumped into that man, I was helping him clean up . . ."

"I know those two, they're real losers. You don't have to put up with their crap. This is America."

He presses the base of his thumb. People are always saying to him, "This is America." *What the hell does it mean?*

"Please, I'm okay. These things happen. People see my turban . . ."

But the truth is that he had been unprepared. During his two years in Boston he'd been taunted in Southie, almost beaten up in the North End — but on the Vineyard things have been different. Blacks and whites mingle easily here, and a brown man in a turban is smiled at, a sign of the island's easy tolerance.

Anna is shivering, from the cold or from anger, he can't tell.

"Those morons and their pit bull. Let me see that cut."

"It's nothing."

Ignoring him, she grabs his wrist, pushes her shades onto her head, and holds his thumb up to the light. She's almost his height, striking-looking rather than beautiful, her short, boyish haircut emphasizing

21

her long neck and high cheekbones. It is her eyes that draw him in, black as night, so dark that her stare can be disconcerting. Today the skin around them is puffy, and he realizes, with a shock, that she has been crying.

"You won't need any stitches. It's a clean cut."

She pulls a white cotton handkerchief from her pocket, tears off a strip with her teeth, and bandages his thumb, the wrapping tight and professional. Noticing his appraising look, she smiles, and deep dimples appear in her cheeks.

"Surprised? I used to go hunting with my father. He'd get hurt, and I'd bandage him up. I've had a lot of practice fixing up men."

When she's done, the bandage is wrapped so tightly that his thumb throbs like a drumbeat.

A cold wind blows in from the ocean and she shivers and hugs herself. "Ranjit, I'm sorry I'm so late. I didn't think you'd still be here."

He remains silent, waiting for her explanation.

"Clayton arrived this afternoon. Unannounced."

"The Senator's here? But I saw him on television just last night, he was at a press conference in Washington —"

"Yeah, well," Anna says, "he flew in from D.C. a few hours ago. He said he'd had enough of the press."

She stands in front of him like a hurt child, hugging herself tightly. He wants to lean forward and wrap his arms around her. Instead, he doesn't move an inch.

"Anna, why did you want to see me?"

She takes a deep breath. "Look, I wanted to say that I'm really sorry. I owe you an explanation for my behavior that day. I was really upset, and believe it or not, you helped me. But . . ."

He feels the sharp disappointment again. "It's all right. I understand."

"You do? You're kind to say that." There is a silence and then she continues, her tone brisker. "Listen, I was thinking. Are you still staying here through the winter? Or are you heading back to Boston?"

"I'd like to stay here. I hated it in Boston."

"Well, I talked to Clayton, and we need a caretaker for the house. Our regular guy just broke his leg. You can start now, and we'll pay you through next spring. What do you think?"

She smiles and removes a strand of hair that has blown into the corner of her mouth.

He is stunned. It's impossible to get a job

as a caretaker on the island; only old, trusted Vineyarders get to take care of rich people's houses. And a steady paycheck means that he can stay here through the winter, maybe even move to a house where the heating actually works.

"It's not a lot of work. Close up the house, shovel snow, check for leaks. What do you say?"

He nods slowly. "Okay, Anna — thank you. I'll take the job."

She jingles car keys in her coat pocket and looks away. "Go see Clayton tonight, he'll fill you in. I better get going. I'm catching the evening ferry to the mainland."

"You're leaving?"

"I need a change of scene. The last few months have been so . . . taxing. But I'm not going far, just to the house in Boston."

There seems to be nothing else to say. They turn and walk to Anna's car, its engine still purring, the soft wail of jazz coming from inside. Ranjit knows that the silver Mercedes Kompressor costs more money than he has earned during his two and a half years in America.

She stops, a hand on the door handle. "You're sure you want to stay here? It's brutal in the winter. I lived here off-season as a child, almost went mad with boredom."

24

He nods. "I'll be all right. I'm used to the cold."

"I thought India was hot? Tropical?"

"No. We have mountains too, high ones. With snow and ice."

She smiles apologetically, and her cheeks curve into dimples again. "I should have known that. Us dumb Americans, huh?"

She puts a hand on his arm, a touch so soft that it's barely there. She gets into the Mercedes, slams the door, and swings the car out onto the road. The powerful engine growls, and she's gone.

The pink neon sign in the liquor store window suddenly blinks out. An elderly man emerges from the store and begins to chain the front doors together.

Ranjit kicks the glass shards aside and hurriedly climbs into his truck. What had he expected from the likes of Anna Neals? She is a senator's wife, and he is just another servant here. Things might have been different if . . . but there's no point in thinking like that.

The adrenaline rush has subsided. He feels cold and nauseous, and blasts the heater before leaning back and closing his eyes. *If Anna had arrived a few minutes later, he would have killed that man.* He imagines sharp glass entering the man's soft throat, the screams of a butchered animal . . .

Taking a deep breath, he remembers what the doctors back home had said: *The instincts are there, they don't go away. Anything can trigger them: a loud sound, a movement in the periphery, a threatening shadow.* The key is to not follow through, to short-circuit the impulse.

Like the doctors taught him, he breathes deeply and imagines a calm, peaceful place. An image of the Golden Temple at Amritsar gradually takes shape: it sits in the center of the sacred lake, its golden dome burnished by fading sunlight, and from within it he can hear the sound of *kirtans* being sung.

He is a boy again, following his mother down the long causeway leading to it, the marble warm under their bare feet. It is his father's death anniversary, and they have come to the temple to pray. Underneath the threadbare *dupatta* that covers her head, *Mataji*'s face is pale, exhausted from crying all day, but she grows calm as she sings the evening prayers. The words float in the air, old and comforting.

A faint, putrid smell tickles his nostrils, disturbing the image. He tries to ignore it, but it grows stronger, and when his eyes flicker open, there is a shimmer in the seat next to him. No doubt it is a trick of the fading light; closing his eyes again, he tries to return to the place of stillness.

There is the sudden, rasping sound of breathing. *Those bastards are back.* His eyes fly open, and he reaches under his seat for a spanner, then stops abruptly.

Sergeant Khandelkar is sitting in the seat next to him, wearing a white snowsuit, an assault rifle lying across his knees. He is bent over and coughing desperately, his eyes strained and watering.

No, please, Guru, no. It must be a hallucination, triggered by the encounter with the two men. *It will go away soon, he will wake up.*

The Sergeant's head is shaved to reveal his bony skull, giving him the severe look of a priest. As he wheezes, desperately trying to breathe, Ranjit smells again the putrid smell of decay. *Perhaps it's a seizure, they say that people smell things right before their convulsions, almonds or perfume.*

The Sergeant manages to take a deep breath. "What is this place, Captain?" His voice is raspy, as though he isn't used to talking anymore.

Ranjit cannot answer. The doctors said this could happen and had given him a bottle of blue pills, but he'd thrown them away before he left India.

27

"Not much in the way of cover here, is there? We'll have to call for air support." Sergeant Khandelkar shivers, and his face and hands are blue with cold.

Ranjit finds his voice. "Sergeant, is it really you?"

Khandelkar ignores the question. He flexes his bony fingers and stares down at them. "Those men, Captain. You could have easily taken them. Why didn't you?"

"I don't . . . I don't fight anymore."

Khandelkar laughs. "I see, Captain. You don't fight."

"I'm not a captain. I'm nothing here. Everything has changed."

"Nothing changes. Nothing changes, where I am." Khandelkar's hands are lilac, the color that comes before frostbite. "The cold burns like fire, Captain, did you know that?"

"Khandelkar, I'm sorry, so sorry —" Ranjit reaches out to touch the Sergeant, and finds himself reaching through the air.

The seat next to him is empty. Heat gushes out of the vents in the dashboard, and the air smells like burning leaves.

"Sergeant, where are you?"

In the silence Ranjit can hear the pounding of the waves across the road. He rolls down his window and feels the cold air buf-

28

fet his face.

Something is ringing. He fumbles in the pocket of his stained canvas coat and finds his cell phone.

"*Papaji,* where are you? I've been waiting and waiting. My teacher is going home." It's Shanti's nine-year-old voice, rolling her *R*s like an American.

"*Beti,* I'm sorry, I got tied up. Put on your coat and wait in the lobby, okay?"

The truck engine rumbles into life, and he drives quickly down Beach Road, the ocean a dark blur to his right. After a few turns, he reaches Tradewinds Road and arrives at the long beige building of the Oak Bluffs elementary school. Shanti is sitting in the brightly lit lobby, twirling the ends of her long, curly black hair with one hand. Her high forehead and liquid brown eyes are carbon copies of her mother's, but she has his tall, lanky build.

She sees the truck and comes running out, her hair flying behind her. When she opens the door, Ranjit is staring at the empty seat next to him.

"Hello, *Papaji.* What happened to your thumb?" She reaches out and holds his hand, staring at the knotted strip of cotton.

He pulls his hand away, his breathing quick and shallow.

"What's wrong? *Papaji,* are you all right?"

Ranjit cannot speak. He holds out his arms and hugs her, feeling her long, skinny body, her breath warm against his cheek.

"I'm fine," he says, pulling away. "I cut my thumb while working. I'm just glad to see you, that's all."

"Can we drive along the ocean? I want to see if the ferry is in. And if the Flying Horses is open."

He's told her a hundred times that the Flying Horses Carousel will be closed till the next summer, but she always insists on checking. It will take him out of his way, but he hates to disappoint her.

Sighing, he turns back toward the ocean.

He is silent as they drive away. *All these years he has feared this would happen.* He tries to remember the name of the pale blue pills but cannot.

"*Papaji,* are you listening to me?"

"Sorry, *beti,* what were you saying?"

Shanti sighs dramatically. "You need to listen. This girl in my grade, Elena, she's Portuguese, she said that all Indians are short. I said no way, you should see my dad, and she said you just *look* tall because you wear a turban, and I said, my dad is tall even without a turban, but she wouldn't

30

believe me, can you believe it?"

"*Beti,* Americans have strange ideas about us."

"Not all of them. Just some. And, oh, Miss Heather said to ask you if we're staying for the winter. She said that all the foreign kids start school in the fall but then they leave, and she never gets the textbooks back. Are we going back to Boston?"

"We're staying."

"Hector's gone back to Brazil. And Jorge."

He thinks of the two miserable years in Boston, slaving in the basement of Lallu's Indian store. "We're staying, *beti.* Tell your teacher we're not going anywhere."

"Okay, good, I like it here. Hey, I know the capitals of all fifty states. Let's play, okay? Easy one first. What's the capital of New York?"

As the truck turns onto Seaview Avenue, the sick panic in Ranjit's stomach begins to fade.

"New York City, obviously."

"No, silly, it's Albany. Now, California?"

"San Francisco?"

Shanti peals with laughter. "It's Sacramento! Everybody knows that!"

"It makes no sense. They always choose someplace that no one has heard of. In India, the biggest city is the capital. Like

31

Mumbai. Or Chennai."

"*Papaji,* really," Shanti says, dissolving with laughter, and he smiles too; being with her always makes him feel better.

They enter the town of Oak Bluffs and speed past the large green oval of Ocean Park, surrounded by the sprawling bungalows of the African-American elite. They pass the strip of beach nicknamed the Inkwell, and just as the long pier of the ferry terminal appears, Ranjit swerves left into town. The marquee of the Strand movie theater is blank, and the carved wooden horses of the Flying Horses Carousel are motionless, but lights are still on at Jerry's Pizza. Ranjit smells hot cheese and feels a sudden pang of hunger, then remembers that he'd given the last of his money to those two men.

"Hey," Shanti says, "we're pretty late today. I hope Mama isn't mad at us."

Usually Preetam sits at home all day, watching her Hindi movies, and panics if they are even five minutes late. But today she has gone with a neighbor to a sewing circle at the church and shouldn't be back till dinnertime.

"Mama's out, remember? I have to go and talk to Senator Neals for a few minutes. I took you there during the summer — it's the house with all the dolls. He was away, but you met his wife."

"I remember that house. Is he the man who's been on television all the time?"

"Yes, that man. But don't ask him any questions."

"Why?"

"*Beti,* rich people don't like that. If he asks *you* any questions, just answer politely."

"I'm always polite, *Papaji.* You know that."

He nods absentmindedly. They drive through the town and stop at the drawbridge leading to Vineyard Haven. A red light flashes and the middle section of the bridge lifts up to let a yacht into the lagoon. He switches off the engine to save gas, an old habit from India.

He is startled at how much information Shanti soaks up, but Preetam always has the television on, and Neals has been on the news for the last two nights.

The news stations replayed the same footage over and over again, showing the Senator walking briskly up the steps of the flood-lit Capitol. Despite his sixty-plus years of age, he had the quick grace of a much younger man, and his dark blue suit only emphasized his barrel chest and wide shoulders. His shaved head and flattened nose — at some point it had been broken and roughly set — only added to his aura of authority.

Reaching the top of the stairs, the Senator made a speech about freedom and democracy, and then handed over the microphone to a young Korean-American woman journalist. Still pale from her months in North Korean captivity, the woman described in a shaking voice her arrest on a trumped-up charge of spying, and her subsequent death sentence. If the Senator hadn't flown to Pyongyang to negotiate on her behalf, her body would now be arriving home in a plywood box. As soon as she was done, the reporters surged forward, shouting out questions, but the Senator just raised her arm in a victory salute and then escorted her away.

The news stations all called the Senator a hero, and there was even talk of him running for President someday. Earlier that summer, the same news stations had broadcast programs on the Senator's fading popularity and predicted that he wouldn't be reelected. Thinking about it, Ranjit shakes his head. *Opinions change so fast in this country.*

The large yacht slides under the raised drawbridge, only the top of its masts visible. Soon the bridge is lowered, and they clatter across it, skirting the town of Vineyard Haven.

The island of Martha's Vineyard is small — roughly triangular, twenty miles from east to west, and ten from north to south — but it houses many worlds. The WASPS live amid their white picket fences in Edgartown, while Oak Bluffs is the home of the African-American elite, whose bungalows cluster around Ocean Park. Vineyard Haven, with its wide harbor and bustling main street, is the commercial heart of the island. Senator Neals has chosen to live far away, among the movie stars and tycoons of Aquinnah, his custom-designed house perched high on its red clay cliffs.

They drive down State Road, past the scattered restaurants and boutiques that cater to the summer people. Jenni Bick's handmade journal store is closed, as is the Vineyard Glassworks, and there are only a handful of cars parked outside Kronig's grocery store. As the population of the island shrinks from a summer high of a hundred thousand down to fifteen thousand, the Vineyard once again becomes a small town.

The twilight gathers around them and Ranjit flicks on his headlights, illuminating stone boundary walls. Hidden behind these are the summer estates of the millionaires, only their driveways and NO TRESPASSING signs visible from the road; the houses are set far back, facing the water. They're empty now, inhabited only by mice and the blinking lights of alarm systems. If this were India, poor people would cut the power to the alarms and move in, shit in the Jacuzzis, keep goats and chickens in the empty swimming pools. But this is not India, this is the Vineyard, and all these beautiful, perfect houses lie empty for most of the year.

He drives through the exclusive towns of West Tisbury and Chilmark, and soon the road becomes a causeway, cutting between the dark waters of Menemsha and Squibnocket ponds. Reaching Lighthouse Road, they drive along the edge of the island, the jagged cliffs falling away to the ocean below.

Ranjit turns into a graveled driveway that curves down the hillside, and the truck whines around the sharp turns. After one last dizzying twist the road flattens out, and there, beyond the Senator's house, is the ink-black ocean, ranks of whitecapped waves racing to the open horizon.

He turns off the engine and the air is filled with the roar of water. Shanti sits silently, mesmerized by the view.

"Beti," he says, "do you know what ocean

that is?"

"The Atlantic Ocean."

"And what's on the other side?"

"India."

"How come India? Not Europe?"

Shanti shakes her head firmly. "No, it's India. That's what Mama says."

"What do you remember about India, *beti*?"

She takes a deep breath. "We were rich in India and we had a big house and mango trees and many servants."

He nods slowly. Just as he thought: she doesn't remember a thing about India, and now Preetam is filling her head with nonsense.

"Wait in the truck. I have to talk to the Senator."

Crunching over the gravel, he approaches the house, praying under his breath. *Please, Guru, please let me get this job.*

From this level, the house looks deceptively like a modest one-story, its rough fieldstone walls topped by a wide, overhanging roof. The rest of it is hidden on the other side, two lower floors of steel and glass cut into the hillside, ending in a terraced garden with a kidney-shaped swimming pool.

The doorbell chimes deep within the house, but there are no answering footsteps.

Despite the chill, perhaps Senator Neals is out on the rear deck, where the sound of the doorbell will be drowned out by the waves.

Shanti presses her nose against the truck window as he walks toward the high hedges that shield the back of the house. He spent hours during the summer trimming them into perfect cubes, but scraggly branches have broken through, undoing all his hard work.

Pushing through a gap in the hedges, he looks at the rear of the house, its rows of tall windows dark and silent. He takes one step forward.

And almost falls over Senator Neals.

CHAPTER TWO

Clayton Neals is crouched over a deep hole. Dirt streaks his broad face, and the neck of his gray Harvard sweatshirt is ringed with sweat.

"Who the hell are you?" He holds a large shovel, its metal blade as sharp as a knife.

Ranjit steps backward, feeling the sway of shrubbery behind him. He is taller than the Senator, but the man has wide, powerful shoulders, and arms thick with muscle. On television, in a dark suit, he appears both powerful and controlled, but right now his face is twisted into a snarl.

"I'm Ranjit Singh, sir. I worked here this summer. Your wife told me to come and see you about a caretaker's job."

The Senator slowly lowers the shovel. "She said something about a caretaker, but I wasn't expecting you *now.*"

Damn it, there goes the job. "Sir, I drove up here all the way from Oak Bluffs. If you could spare a few minutes . . ." Ranjit glances at the hole the Senator is digging, deep enough for a foundation post. "I have a shovel in my truck. Perhaps I could help?"

The Senator follows his gaze, and the snarl vanishes. "I was just . . . staking down the shrubbery. Thanks for your offer, but I'm pretty much done."

The hole is too far from the hedges to be of any use, but Ranjit has learned never to contradict rich, powerful people.

The Senator wipes his face in his sleeve and flashes a bright smile. "Hey, why don't you come up to the house? We can talk about the job."

Without looking back, he begins to walk across the lawn to the wooden deck.

"Sir, is it all right if I bring my daughter with me?"

The Senator turns and frowns. "Your daughter?"

"She's in the truck. It's just that it's getting cold, and —"

"Sure, sure, bring her in, I'll open the front door."

The Senator walks away, the muscles in his broad back rippling through his worn sweatshirt. Ranjit looks again at the deep hole that the Senator has dug, the layer of dark topsoil giving way to the sandy earth below.

Then he shrugs and hurries back to his truck.

When the Senator lets them in, he has changed into a pale blue linen shirt and crisp white trousers, regaining some of his television presence.

Shanti stands silently in the huge living room, staring through the sliding glass doors at the wide wooden deck and the view of the open ocean. On one side of the vast room is a sunken seating area with gray leather couches and red silk pillows, ending in a prowlike bay window with an oak dining table. On the other side is the kitchen, its gleaming stainless steel appliances separated from the rest of the room by an island of polished black granite.

What captivates her most is a floor-to-ceiling glass cabinet set between two sets of glass doors. Inside, arranged on transparent shelves, are dozens of dolls, their pale porcelain faces glinting in the wash of halogen down-lights. They wear ball gowns of yellowed lace and dark brocade, their porcelain hair swirled into ringlets and glossy buns.

"You like the dolls, sweetheart?" The

Senator points and Shanti nods, her face flushed with excitement.

"Do you have a little girl who plays with them? Why are they in a case?"

The Senator's face darkens. "Oh, nobody plays with them. They're antiques, they belonged to my wife's family. Go ahead and look at them." He turns away. "Hey, Ranjitt, want a beer? I've got orange soda for the little girl. What's her name?"

Without waiting for a reply, he walks behind the granite island and pulls open a sleek stainless steel refrigerator.

"It's Shanti. Thank you, sir."

"Shanti means 'peace,' right?" The Senator's voice is muffled as he busies himself with bottles and cans. "And your last name — Singh — you're from Punjab, correct? Which city? Chandigarh? Ludhiana?"

Ranjit is surprised. "Correct, sir, Chandigarh. You know a lot about India."

The Senator chuckles and hands him a chilled bottle of beer, then goes over to give Shanti a glass of orange soda.

"I've spent years on the Foreign Relations Subcommittee. Even went to India, back in oh-two, when your country almost started a nuclear war. Well, cheers."

Standing on opposite sides of the granite island, they both drink. The beer is dark brown and delicious, and as Ranjit drinks it, he wonders why the Senator is being so hospitable.

The muscles in the Senator's thick neck work as he downs most of his bottle. "Yeah, I went to India as a special envoy, to negotiate between India and Pakistan. And let me tell you, it was tough going, talking some sense into your generals. Your army seems to think it's no big deal to lose a city or two in a nuclear attack." He chuckles. "But I don't suppose any of this interests you."

"Well, sir, actually I was —"

"Right, right. You want to talk about the job." The Senator turns and gestures out at the cliff edge. "Let me ask you something. You did a fine job building those stairs. Yet you were cheaper than the other landscapers. How did you do it?"

The Senator sounds casual, but Ranjit knows that the job interview has begun. He thinks about saying that he bought granite in bulk, or that he saved money through a clever design. Then he decides to tell the truth.

"Sir, I lost money on the job. I was just starting out, I underbid it."

The Senator chuckles. "You're an honest man. Ted Kennedy always used to say to me — I served in the Senate with him, you know — that an honest man is the hardest person to cut a deal with." He gulps down the rest of his beer. "So, Ran-jitt, what's your story? What brings you to the Vineyard?"

"Well, sir, we lived in Boston for a couple of years, but I'd like to stay on here. I mean, I have my own landscaping business here, and people in Boston — it was not easy for us there."

The Senator's deep belly laugh is very different from his polite politician's chuckle.

"I know all about Boston. Another beer?"

The alcohol is making Ranjit light-headed, but before he can decline, the Senator opens two more beers and hands him one, gesturing to him to drink. Ranjit finds himself complying; it is clear that no one refuses the Senator.

The Senator waves at the room. "You may find it hard to believe, but I didn't inherit any of this. I grew up in Roxbury, on Blue Hill Avenue. My father worked in a funeral parlor." He leans both elbows against the granite island and grows expansive. "He used to say it was the best job to have. No matter what happened to the economy, people were always going to die. And I would have joined him, if I hadn't gotten a football scholarship. Yeah, I know all about

Boston."

Ranjit looks away. Any more self-disclosure, and the next time the Senator sees Ranjit, he'll be distant and aloof. That's just how rich people are, their bursts of fellowship followed by a great remove.

"Sir, thank you for the beer. I really must be going, it's late for Shanti, and we have a long drive back."

The Senator sets his beer down with a clink. "Of course, of course. The caretaker position. Anna says you're trustworthy?"

"I can provide references. I built an arbor for Mr. Phillips in Edgartown and —"

The Senator looks at Ranjit steadily, then seems to decide. "No, that's not necessary. Anna speaks highly of you, and I need someone reliable. The island isn't what it used to be . . . there has been a rash of break-ins, people looking for alcohol and prescription medicines and so forth."

"Sir, I can swing by here every day, if need be. I have my own truck. And I see you have a new alarm system. In addition to calling the police, the alarm signals can be forwarded to my cell phone —"

"Good, good." The Senator seems reassured. "You know the rest of the drill? Rake the leaves, close down the house, et cetera? Our housekeeper, Mrs. Green, will clean the house before you close it up. Let me just get the spare keys."

The Senator heads down a spiral stair in the corner, and Ranjit motions to Shanti. She is still peering into the glass case of dolls, the glass of orange soda tilting in her hands.

"*Beti,* please don't spill that soda. Not now. Please."

She carefully holds the glass upright. "*Papaji,* these dolls are so beautiful. That one has a real pearl necklace —"

The Senator reappears, waving a ring of keys and some printed sheets of paper. "Couldn't find the spares. You know how women are, they put things away. How much shall we say? Six hundred a month sound good to you? You just need to sign the standard contract."

Senator Neals switches on a bank of overhead halogen lights and sits at the granite island, uncapping a fat ink pen.

Six hundred a month. Listening to the scratching of the pen, Ranjit feels relief flood through him. *That will help a lot, and if he can get a few other odd jobs . . .*

Ranjit signs two copies of the contract, and the Senator gives him back a copy, along with a stiff white business card, a golden federal eagle engraved in its corner.

46

On its back are scrawled some names and phone numbers.

"Send a monthly invoice to my office in Boston. The address is on my card. And I've written down some other folks who are looking for caretakers. You know Ray Clarke, over at the Red Heron? Call him."

Ranjit is stunned at the Senator's generosity. Clarke started Black Entertainment Network and owns the Red Heron Estate in Chilmark, the place where the President vacationed this past summer.

"Sir, I really appreciate the leads, it's very kind of you —"

"Don't mention it."

Ranjit had wanted to ask for an advance, but there is no way he can bring it up now. He nods and prepares to leave, but just then Shanti wanders over. She stares up at the Senator, her head barely clearing the top of the granite island.

"You were on television," she says. "I saw you. You were in Korea."

The Senator caps his ink pen and beams down at her. "Hey, smart little girl. Yes, I was over there."

"Why did they let that woman go? The one they said was a spy?"

"She wasn't a spy, honey. The whole thing was a flimflam."

"Did you *make* them let her go?"

"It was a negotiation. You know what that means?"

She shakes her head, her large brown eyes fixed on the Senator.

"It means they wanted something, and I wanted something, and we worked it out."

"*Huh.* So what did you give them?"

Ranjit can see that the Senator is getting irritated. "Shanti, enough talk, let's go. Senator, sorry for taking up so much of your time."

The Senator stands up slowly, bracing himself with both hands. "No, no. Smart little girl you have there. She's going to be a lawyer, no doubt."

The Senator accompanies them out to the truck. He leaves the front door open, and light spills onto the tall hedges, casting long, inky shadows across the driveway.

Ranjit boosts Shanti into the truck and turns around. "Sir, I appreciate your trust, I'll take good care of the house."

"Don't mention it. Hey Ran-jitt . . . one more thing." The Senator is half turned away, his voice barely audible above the roar of the ocean.

"Sir?"

"You know, I haven't been around much this summer. I usually spend a few weeks

48

up here at the house with Anna, but with all this North Korea stuff . . . so, anyway . . ."

Ranjit stiffens.

". . . so anyway, while you were working here during the summer? Building the steps and so forth? My point is, did Anna — Mrs. Neals — did she seem okay to you?"

The Senator takes a step backward and is silhouetted against the lit doorway. Ranjit cannot see the expression on his face.

So this is why the Senator has been so hospitable all evening; he wants some information about his wife. *What exactly is he asking?*

"Well, sir, Mrs. Neals seemed fine. From what little I saw of her." He pauses and starts again. ". . . I mean, she spent her days by the pool, from what I could tell. And sometimes she would go running. She seemed fine."

"Hmmm. Did she have any visitors?"

"Visitors? No, I don't think so."

"Good, good." The Senator's voice is businesslike again. "I'm off tomorrow, and Betty will have the place cleaned in a few days. Send the invoices to my office."

He turns and walks abruptly back into the house, his hand raised in dismissive farewell.

As they begin the long drive back to Oak

49

Bluffs, Shanti looks up at Ranjit.

"*Papaji,* did the Senator just give you a job?"

He nods, concentrating on the dark, winding roads.

"Yippee. Can I have a new jacket? I saw a pink one in the L.L.Bean catalog." She gives him a wide-eyed look. "My jacket is too small and it's *blue.* It's a boy's coat, not a girl's."

He glances down at her parka and sees that it is too short, the blue faded and dirty. He remembers finding it at the Goodwill store in Boston, and thinking it was a good deal. *How the hell was he supposed to know that in this country only boys wore blue?*

"I have a job, but he hasn't paid me yet. When I get a check, the first thing I'll do is buy you a new jacket, okay?"

"You won't forget?"

"I promise. And you know I never break a promise."

"That's great. I want the pink one. It has a pink lining, and a hood, and this fleece inside that you can unzip and . . ."

She chatters on for a few minutes, then rests her head on his shoulder and dozes off, tired from her long day at school. He drives on, the dark ribbon of road unfurling in front of him, the shuttered towns passing by, each with their white-steepled church and darkened library.

Six hundred dollars a month seems like a lot of money, but some of it will go to repaying Preetam's uncle, Lallu Singh, for their tickets to America. The rest will be eaten up by gas for the truck, heating bills, and the rent on the house.

But the Senator has given him Ray Clarke's number. Ranjit has heard that Clarke collects buildings the way other people collect paintings, hauling old barns and farmhouses to his estate and converting them into guest cottages. The Red Heron Estate has six buildings, including the main house, and if Ranjit can land a caretaking job there, it will mean a lot more money.

The Senator has been incredibly generous with his contacts and Ranjit feels a hot flush of guilt. *What does the Senator know? Has Anna told him anything?* From the outside they look like the perfect couple, but . . .

He thinks of the first time that he saw them together. It was a Sunday morning at the beginning of the summer, and Linda Jean's coffee shop was full. Ranjit and his family were waiting patiently for a table when a couple by the window caught his eye: a muscular black man in a pastel blue golf shirt, sitting silently across from a much

51

younger woman. She wore a daffodil-yellow cotton dress and her short, boyish haircut emphasized her slender neck. They were clearly not father and daughter — Ranjit could sense that — but he could not understand their relationship.

The man sat with his legs spread apart, cutting rapidly into a pile of pancakes and bacon, and when he crooked a finger, the waitress hurried over to refill his coffee cup. The woman picked at her soft-boiled eggs and smiled apologetically at the waitress, as though to offset her husband's brusqueness.

They made a compelling couple, and as they left the restaurant, many of the other customers stared at them. The air of privilege the woman exuded — the yellow dress was expensive, as was her carefully sculpted hair — was counteracted by her athlete's easy stride, her muscular arms and legs no doubt the product of many hours on a tennis court.

The man beside her was a few inches shorter, thick chested and broad shouldered, walking canted slightly forward on the balls of his feet. She stood to one side as he greeted people on the way out, boisterously slapping high-fives, and only when he was done did they walk away together. Ranjit learned only later that the man was a U.S.

Senator, and the woman — young enough to be his daughter — was his second wife.

The Senator had seemed so youthful then, but the last few months had aged him. Tonight his eyes were bloodshot, his dark skin was ashen, and deep creases had appeared on both sides of his mouth.

Ranjit feels the sick guilt again when he remembers the Senator's halting question, and his own lying response.

The truth was that he had talked to Anna almost every day that summer. At first, she spent the mornings by the empty swimming pool, her face shaded by a large straw hat, staring at the same paperback, its cover illustrated with a golden Buddha. In the afternoons she went running, wearing blue-and-gold running shoes, shorts, and a white tank top. Once, driving into town, he saw her at least ten miles from the house, drenched in sweat, her long legs straining, her arms moving in short, choppy motions. He waved, but she seemed to be in a daze; running, he realized, not tennis, had accounted for her slim, muscled build.

While he was demolishing the rotten wooden steps down to the beach, he passed by the pool three or four times a day, pushing a wheelbarrow of debris. It was mid-August when she finally seemed to notice

53

him, and smiled distractedly.

"Hot day," he said, not knowing what to say.

"Yes, it is very hot," she replied, and later that afternoon — he had just started building the new steps — she brought him a jug of iced tea. He was shirtless in the heat, hacking into the hillside, when he heard the tinkling of ice cubes and looked up.

She was freshly showered, her hair damp, and wore a white halter top and a rustling yellow skirt. Her eyes were hidden behind aviator sunglasses, giving her high-cheekboned face a blank, expressionless air that unnerved him.

"I hope you like it sweetened," she said.

"Why, thank you, Mrs. Neals," he replied, putting down his pickax.

"Mrs. Neals was my mother-in-law. Call me Anna."

"Well, thank you . . . Anna."

She sat down on the last finished step and poured him a glass of tea. When he took it from her, he saw his own reflection in her dark lenses, his face burnt nut-brown by the sun, his long hair twisted into a topknot and covered with a sweat-stained red bandanna.

He was afraid that he smelled, so he stood a few steps below her as he drank the sweet tea, feeling the cool liquid run down his throat and coil into his stomach.

That first day they talked, or rather, she asked him questions and he tried to answer them. She asked about life in India, and what it meant to be a Sikh. She had read a lot of books, and Eastern religions interested her, she said, especially their recurring cycles of life and death, so different from the linear beliefs of the Western world.

He was half dazed by the sun, and at first he stumbled over his own words, but soon her quiet, attentive presence calmed him. He found himself telling her about the Sikhs, how in the fifteenth century Guru Nanak had conceived of Sikhism as a reform religion. Instead of the elaborate caste system of Hinduism, or the fanaticism of Islam, the Sikhs expressed their faith simply, through their everyday life. They believed that work, and not pilgrimages or rituals, was the path to enlightenment. He explained to her how Sikh philosophy had been developed by ten successive Gurus, till finally it was all collected into a single holy book, the Guru Granth Sahib.

He told her how the Sikhs had suffered terrible persecution and developed their own martial ways to survive. It was the duty of each Sikh man to keep his hair long, to wear a special metal bracelet, and to carry a sword. With their distinctive turbans and beards, Sikhs went forth into the world as the embodiment of their religion, ready, if necessary, to fight and die for their beliefs.

He talked, squinting into the bright sunlight, and Anna listened quietly.

"So there is no heaven and no hell in your religion?" she asked. "No original sin?"

"No, there are only the endless cycles of life, which are *maya,* illusion. With enlightenment, one simply breaks free of them."

"You sound like a Buddhist," she said, smiling, and dimples appeared in her cheeks. "Except your people know how to fight."

"After our last Emperor, Ranjit Singh, died, the British conquered us. Ever since then, we Sikhs have been in the army. The rigor, the discipline, suits us."

"You were in the army too?"

"Oh, that was a long time ago," he replied and stared off into the distance.

Anna left that day, but returned the next, and they settled into an afternoon routine of iced tea and conversation. Finding out that he had a daughter, she became very quiet. "You must bring Shanti to visit me," she said. "She sounds like such a remarkable little girl."

56

When he brought Shanti over, toward the end of the summer, Anna made a huge fuss over the little girl and showed her the cabinet of dolls. Anna explained that they came from Germany, Czechoslovakia, and Denmark, and were now prized antiques, each with its maker's mark. Slipping the dress off one pearl-white doll, she pointed out a blue design of crossed swords on its shoulder, the mark of the German Meissen factory, from the 1840s.

"These belonged to my great-grandmother," Anna said. "She found most of them at auctions in Boston and collected them her whole life. My grandmother added to the collection, too. But now they're so rare, I've only been able to find two more."

Shanti listened, entranced, and wanted to return, but Ranjit was terrified that she would drop a doll and shatter it. He promised Anna that he would bring Shanti back, but he never did.

The summer days passed quickly, and he worked longer and longer hours, having badly underestimated the amount of work that the stairs required. Each day he cut a few more steps into the cliff face, laid gravel, tamped it down, measured and cut stone. He worked with care, pushing dirt between the stones so that the new stairs looked as though they'd been there forever.

That final afternoon in mid-September was a blazing hot day. Anna wore a fresh white tank top and a short orange skirt and was silent as she handed him a cold glass of tea. There was something expectant about her, and he could sense a strange electricity between them . . .

"*Papaji.* Are we home yet?"

Ranjit starts. Shanti has awoken, her face reddened with sleep. He is suddenly conscious of the dark road outside and his daughter looking wide-eyed up at him.

"We're almost there, *beti.*"

"I'm starving. Can we get pizza for dinner?"

He remembers that there is no cash in his wallet. "Not tonight, *beti.* Maybe later this week."

"Okay. Don't forget about my new jacket, okay?"

Shanti and her one-track mind. Swearing that he won't forget, he drives through Vineyard Haven, recrosses the drawbridge, and enters Oak Bluffs.

CHAPTER THREE

As Ranjit turns onto Masonic Avenue, the truck's headlights sweep across their house, its white window frames flaking, its gray cedar shingles falling off in patches and revealing the dark wood cladding underneath.

He shuts off the engine and the night is silent.

Just around the corner are the painted cottages of Oak Bluffs, with their fussy wooden fretwork, but on this tiny stub of a street there is only their house with its sagging porch and crabgrass lawn. Across the street is Mike's Tow Yard, a greasy cinder-block garage with an apartment above it, its yard cluttered with rusting, disemboweled cars. Mike's Tow has been bought by a Brazilian brother and sister; Jõao fixes the cars but doesn't speak a word of English, and his sister, Celia, answers the phones.

"Hey there! Ranjit!"

Celia gestures to him from her front steps, the red glow of a cigarette illuminating her platinum blond hair.

"What, you're back already?" Ranjit gets out of the truck, looking confused. Celia was supposed to drive Preetam to the sewing group at the church tonight.

Celia comes clattering across the road in her lacquered red high heels, her lit cigarette in her hand. Her white-blond hair comes out of a bottle, but her smooth tan is real. She's probably in her late forties now, but twenty years ago in Rio she must have been a knockout, and still carries herself like one, wearing skintight jeans and high heels, no matter the weather.

"Ranjit, what can I tell you? We went there for an hour, but then Preetam wanted to come back, so I drove her home."

"Why, did something happen?" Ranjit knows that his wife is conscious of her accented English and hates leaving the house.

"She wouldn't say. You know how she is, so polite, so formal. It's hard to tell."

"Well, thanks for taking her, anyway. I'd better go in and check." He looks worriedly at the house, noticing that the lights are on in the kitchen.

Celia puffs at her cigarette. "Hey, did you hear about the guy who owns the Hibiscus

60

Gallery?" She pauses dramatically. "He's left his wife, run off with a waitress from the Artcliff Diner, the grumpy one with the nose ring. Can you believe it?"

This island is so small, and everyone knows each other's business. "Incredible. Now, Celia, I really must —"

"So how's that piece of junk doing? When are you going to get a *real* truck?"

Ranjit can't help smiling. Every time they meet, Celia teases him about the truck he'd bought from her brother for four hundred dollars. Jõao rebuilt the 1985 Ford using the chassis from one wreck, the engine from another. The flatbed Ranjit made himself, hammering together a wooden box that has since splintered.

"It's running fine. Starter is giving a little trouble, though."

"Ranjit, Ranjit." Celia squints through a cloud of cigarette smoke. "You work all the time, never go out for a drink, but you still haven't saved enough money for a new truck? A handsome man like you should not drive an old, old thing like that . . ."

Shanti jumps down from the truck and regards Celia with bleary eyes.

"*Aiee, quao bonita.* Shanti, you are getting more and more beautiful. Listen, if you want me to take Preetam to the sewing group next week, I can." Waving at them, she sashays back across the road.

He grabs Shanti's hand and they climb the creaky steps onto the porch, passing coils of rope, ladders, and a broken velvet La-Z-Boy chair left by a previous inhabitant. As he pushes open the front door, he's anticipating the cozy warmth of the house, but the living room is freezing cold and empty.

He can hear the rapid swishing of a mop in the kitchen, interspersed with ragged breathing.

"Shanti, why don't you go and wash up?" he says, and after she goes into the bathroom, he walks into the kitchen.

Preetam is in a far corner, her cheeks flushed, mopping the splintered wooden floor with long, wet strokes. She is wearing an old pink *salwar kameez,* her hair is coming loose from her long plait, and her gold bangles clink as she pushes the mop back and forth. He has told her many times that she shouldn't be using water on wood, but he bites his tongue.

"Hello. Doing some cleaning?"

She looks up, her eyes bright with manic energy. "Ranjit, this place is a mess. I've already cleaned the bedroom, but really, this kitchen —" She gestures at the turmeric-stained wooden table and the rows of dented pots hanging from hooks.

"You've done a good job. It's looking great." He pauses. "So what happened at the sewing group? Celia said you wanted to come home."

"Nothing. Nothing happened." She pushes a strand of hair out of her eyes and continues mopping the floor.

"Preetam, please, talk to me." Taking the mop gently from her hands, he puts it down and hugs her, feeling the hammering of her heart, like a bird fluttering in a too-small cage.

"It's just . . . It's just that those women, they all look at me as if I'm so strange. Everybody there was wearing pants and sweaters, and I was wearing this —" She gestures at her *salwar kameez.* "And they don't know anything about India. One woman asked me when I learned to speak English. I told her that I grew up speaking English, that I went to a convent school, but she acted like she didn't believe me, and . . ." She is crying now, her face buried in his chest, and he hugs her tighter.

"It's okay," he says. "It's okay. I know it's hard for you. Those women are nice people, it will take some time to get to know them. You should give it a chance." She continues to cry, and he tries again. "Hey listen, I got a good job today. There's going to be more money coming in."

She steps back and wipes her eyes with the backs of her hands. "A job? Where? In Boston? Are we going back there?"

"No, I have a job *here,* as a caretaker. And I may be able to get more work —"

"We're going to stay in this house? The whole winter?" She waves a hand at the freezing kitchen, the bangles on her wrist jangling loudly.

"I can make good money here. I can pay your uncle back soon, and we can even save some —"

"Pay him back? How?" Her voice rises. "How? He spent ten thousand dollars to bring us here. And he gave us a place to stay in Boston, he gave you a job at his store —"

Shanti sticks her head into the kitchen. "Hey, Mama, are you okay?"

"Shanti, stay in the living room." She vanishes, and Ranjit takes a deep breath. "Preetam, please try to understand. I'm not a shopkeeper. Standing behind a counter, selling things, that's no life for me. At least here I have my own business. I know it's a new place, but Shanti likes it here. No one teases her at school. If only you —"

64

"Can we go back to Boston, please? At least I have my family there, some people I can talk to. But here? You're gone all day, and Shanti is in school. What is there for me here?"

She stares at him. Clad only in her thin cotton *salwar kameez,* she is shivering with cold.

"Can we talk about this later? It's freezing in here, and you'll get sick. Did the furnace stop working again? Did you press the reset button, like I showed you?"

She gestures out of the window at the dark, deserted street. "Do you know, Ranjit, sometimes I sit and just look out of the window. For one hour, two hours, and I don't see anyone. Not a single person passes by. Not one person." Her voice cracks. "I'm going crazy here, but what do you care? You always do what suits you."

Turning on her heel, she storms into the living room and switches on the television. Soon Ranjit can hear the music from an old black-and-white Hindi film: *Chori Chori,* a tale of doomed lovers from 1965. Preetam watches it over and over when she's depressed, her lips moving as she recites the dialogue.

Sighing, he crouches in front of the silent furnace and presses the reset button. Soon warm air belches through the leaky ducts, smelling strangely smoky; he bends and sniffs around the furnace, but there doesn't seem to be an oil leak.

It's a miracle that the damn heating works at all. This house is usually rented out to migrant summer workers, to men who only come home to drink and sleep. When Ranjit moved in at the beginning of the summer, the toilet was backed up, there were thick spiderwebs in the corners, and pictures of naked Brazilian women covered the living room wall. Ranjit unclogged the toilet and took a broom to the cobwebs; he even tried to scrape the pinups off the wall, then gave up and covered them with a map of the world, though a few brown arms and legs still poke out at the edges.

He thought of the shack as temporary, but when the landlord offered it to him at a discount for the winter months, he extended the lease, put sheets of plastic over the windows, and patched the leaky heating ducts with tape. Now he prays that the motor on the burner assembly doesn't burn out.

Standing up, he surveys the gleaming kitchen: it's clean, but there is no dinner.

"Preetam, did you make any food?" he calls out, but there is only the blare of television.

When there is no answer, he washes out a pot, heats some oil and drops in a cinnamon stick, cardamom pods, cloves, bay leaves, and whole black pepper. As the kitchen fills with the hot scent of spices, he adds a cup of rice and two of pink *masoor* lentils, frying them with the spices till they are no longer raw. He then adds boiling water, making *khitchri,* the way they did in the army, a one-pot dish that is hot and nutritious.

The rice and lentils begin to boil, and he quickly peels and chops potatoes. As his knife slices hard through their crisp flesh, he feels a catch in his throat. *Is it his fault that Preetam has become so lonely and bitter? Damn it, how is she going to adjust to this country if she spends all day in the house, watching old Hindi movies and talking on the phone?*

He tosses the cubed potatoes into the pot, adding frozen peas. He throws in a pinch of turmeric, a little salt, and covers the pot with a lid. While the *khitchri* steams and cooks, he slumps down at the kitchen table.

He remembers how excited Preetam had been when they landed in Boston, so eager to experience the glamorous American world she'd seen on television. The third week they were there, they went to Filene's Basement, and not understanding how a department store worked, she stepped onto the escalator leading out of the store, a sweater clutched in her hands.

The store detective — a sour, overweight man — accused her of stealing, ignored her pleas, and took her to a small room at the back. When Ranjit found her, twenty minutes later, she was crying hysterically, so frightened that she was shaking. He begged the store detective not to call the cops, so instead the man made Preetam sign a document saying that she would not return.

After that, she'd refused to go out. Ranjit had seen her sliding into depression, but by then he was working fourteen-hour days at Lallu's store and had no idea what to do.

Yes, Preetam's uncle had lent them the money for the plane tickets and given him a job, but working for that plump, pompous man had been unbearable. All day Ranjit stood behind the counter at Kohinoor Food and Spices in Cambridge, waiting on the college students and the hippies who came in for packets of incense and cheap *samosas.* The worst were the rich Indians, who treated him like a servant: *Yes, madam,* he heard himself saying, *we have fresher cilantro in the back, let me fetch it for you.*

At the end of each month, Lallu gave Ranjit two hundred dollars, making a big show of it, counting out the notes, then stuffing them into his shirt pocket, as though he was doing them a huge favor. Why couldn't Preetam understand that he was just cheap labor for her uncle? He was even more helpless than the illegal Mexicans who worked frying *samosas,* because he was family and had to be grateful.

The final straw came one Sunday afternoon when a prosperous Sikh family came into the store. The father wore a crisp green turban, his plump wife was dressed in an embroidered *salwar kameez,* and two teen-aged daughters wore T-shirts and low-rise jeans.

The man, straight-backed, with a military mustache, spotted Ranjit behind the counter and walked slowly up to him.

"Captain?" the man said. "Is it you, Captain?" and Ranjit recognized a Brigadier from his old battalion.

Ranjit ducked his head and feigned confusion. The man apologized and laughed embarrassedly, but it was too close, much too close. Boston was a big city, and sooner or later, someone else was going to recognize him.

A few days later, taking a break in the alley outside, he heard two Brazilian cooks from the restaurant next door discussing summer work on the Vineyard — high wages, they'd said, and no one checked papers there. They put Ranjit in touch with Jõao, who promised to sell him a truck and help him find landscaping work. Lallu's thick face turned purple with anger when Ranjit packed up his family and left. *This is how you pay me back,* he bellowed. *After I take you in, after I help you? What do you know about America? When you fail, you'll beg me for your job back!*

The *khitchri* bubbles on the stove. When Ranjit checks it, the potatoes are soft, the lentils and rice cooked into a thick stew. He puts bowls and spoons on the kitchen table.

"Shanti! Preetam! Come and eat!" he calls out, but only Shanti arrives.

"Mama says she's not hungry," she says, bending her head to her steaming bowl.

"Careful, it's hot," he says absentmindedly, looking through the doorway at Preetam slumped on the couch. He knows that if he doesn't intervene, she will eat only when they are asleep, and the next morning he'll find her crusted plate lying on the table.

Walking into the living room, he sees the blue light of the television playing across her face. She is lost in the film, and for a second he sees the girl he had fallen in love with, the Colonel's daughter, with her pale face and beautiful long hair.

"Preetam, please come and eat. I made *khitchri.* It's hot."

"I'm not hungry." She doesn't take her eyes off the television screen.

"Come on, please. I know you're angry with me, and I'm sorry. Look, I'll find another place for us to live, okay? Someplace nicer."

"Really?" She looks up at him, her eyes glistening with television light. "How will we afford it?"

"Don't worry. I'll work something out. There are all these empty houses. I should be able to get a cheap rental." He knows that he is lying through his teeth, but he cannot bear to see her like this. "Now come and eat. Please."

When they go back into the kitchen, Shanti looks up from her plate and studies her mother's face. She instantly figures out the situation and rushes to pile a plate with *khitchri* for her mother.

"Oh, so much?" Preetam protests. "I can't eat all this, *beti.* I'll get fat."

"You eat what you can. I'll finish the rest." Ranjit knows that once the food is on her plate, Preetam will eat it all. "And you're not fat. You have a perfect figure. Everybody thinks so, especially Jerry. Every time we go to his restaurant, he can't take his eyes off you."

"Oh gross, Ma." Shanti pretend-shudders, and Ranjit smiles.

Jerry, the dapper seventy-year-old owner of Jerry's Pizza, always makes a huge fuss over Preetam, making her a special pie with hot peppers.

"What? Why shouldn't Jerry have a crush on me?" Preetam tosses her long hair back. "Before I met your father, I had many boyfriends in Chandigarh. *Hanh,* men were lined up to marry me."

Preetam nibbles at her food and tells Shanti, for the hundredth time, the stories of all her suitors: the Sikh businessman from London who flew to India to propose to her; the industrialist from Ludhiana who bought her a diamond "as big as a quail's egg"; the chief minister's playboy son, who saw Preetam in the street and swore chastity if he couldn't marry her.

"So why did you choose *Papaji*?" Shanti asks, playing along.

"I chose your father because of how handsome he was. When he walked up to me at that tea party, I saw how tall he was, and I liked his hands — he had such long fingers. I thought, I'm going to marry this man. You remember our wedding day, Ranjit?"

He nods, glancing down at his bandaged thumb, which she hasn't noticed. She loves to talk about their wedding, but it seems as though she's talking about a ghost from the past.

"Your father arrived on a white horse, in front of five hundred guests. I was wearing a red *ghagra-choli* with real gold embroidery and a gold necklace, and people said to me, Preetam-*ji*, with all respect, you should act in films, you are so beautiful and . . ."

Shanti listens, eating absentmindedly. In three or four years, she will be taller than her mother, maybe as tall as him. It is as though he and she — tall, calm, methodical — are from one tribe, and Preetam is from a completely different one.

Preetam finally finishes eating the portion on her plate, and Shanti notices and quietly puts some more food on her mother's plate.

Who is the child here, he wonders, *and who is the parent?*

After they finish eating, he washes up alone, the music from Preetam's movie filtering in through the rush of water. It's a scene where Nargis, wearing a white sari, simpers coyly

73

in a moonlit garden while Raj Kapoor, dapper in his pencil mustache, serenades her. Preetam must have seen this film thirty or forty times.

Before he leaves the kitchen, he sniffs the air: mixed in with the rich aroma of *khitchri* is that smoky smell. Shanti hadn't noticed anything, and she's very sensitive to smells; maybe he's just imagining it.

Passing by the battered couch, he pauses and kisses the top of Preetam's head. "It's late. Why don't you come to bed?"

She keeps staring at the television. "In a few minutes."

He knows that she'll fall asleep on the couch and spend the night there. They haven't slept in the same bed for months, but he doesn't want to say anything tonight.

Entering the dark bedroom at the rear of the house, he sees that Shanti is fast asleep on the narrow cot at the end of the room, her curly hair spread out across her pillow.

The cotton bandage around his thumb is wet and he unwraps it, seeing the deep gash. He unwinds his turban, undresses, and climbs into the double bed, careful not to bang his thumb and reopen the wound.

The ache in his thumb leads him back through the events of the day. He thinks of the two men in the parking lot, and how the

Sergeant had appeared with his staring eyes and hollow cheeks. *It was in my head,* he tells himself, *I imagined the whole thing.*

He fears that he is going to enter the dream, the one he dreads. He tosses and turns in the cold sheets and tries to get the Sergeant's face out of his mind, but it is still there when he falls asleep.

Darkness washes over him, claiming him.

CHAPTER FOUR

Cold. Very cold. The men on the Siachen Glacier have been walking for five hours before they reach the first rock face.

They slip packets of chemical warmer into their gloves. They check and recheck their Heckler & Koch MP-5K assault rifles, which can fire nine hundred rounds a minute, but jam easily in the subzero cold.

"Private Dewan, you climb lead," the Captain says. "Don't take any chances. Anchor yourself when you reach solid rock, so we can belay you."

The boy can climb like a monkey, with a twisting, unconscious grace, but now he just hums under his breath and looks blank.

"Do you hear me, Private?"

Sergeant Khandelkar steps in. "Sir, the boy is not right. I can lead."

"You?" Khandelkar is the best sergeant in the regiment, but he climbs like a cow. "No, I'll go up. You keep an eye on him."

The Captain flexes his fingers and walks over to the sheer rock face, looking for the first hold.

Soon he finds the old rhythm and time fades away. It is just him and the cold, slippery rock, the stretch and twist of muscles, the search for the next toehold. When he is halfway, he looks up and sees their final destination, three ridges away: in the late-afternoon sunlight the slopes of the Sia Kangri look like sheets of hammered gold. He tears his eyes away and continues to climb.

When he reaches the top of the rock face he is exhausted, every muscle aching, but for one blissful hour he has not worried about his men. Hammering pitons into the rock, he carefully lets down a rope, and the men clamber up one by one. Dewan is last, and Sergeant Khandelkar whispers down encouragement to the boy.

It will soon be dark, and they have to reach the safety of a higher ridge. There is no longer the luxury of a secure, anchored climb. The men rope together and the Captain climbs lead, all joy gone as he feels the rope tugging around his waist: the lives of five men are in his hands.

They are almost at the top when he hears a faint *pop pop pop,* like bottles of soda being opened.

Below him, Private Dewan sighs and leans backward. The rope suddenly goes taut, cutting deeply into the Captain's waist, and he slams his ice ax into the rock face. He looks back, thinks that Dewan has fainted, then sees the red bloom in the chest of the boy's white snowsuit.

Dewan is dead weight now.

A machine gun opens up, the bullets moving in an arc toward them.

If they don't move, they will be dead in seconds, but the weight of Dewan is pinning them down.

"Cut him loose, Sergeant! Do it now!"

Khandelkar looks up imploringly, his face pale.

The Captain's voice is a scream. "Do it, damn you, do it!"

He sees the flash of a knife, turns away, feels the rope go slack.

Freed, the Captain and his men swarm up the ridge. They reach the top and crawl behind a ledge of rock. They fire back till the barrels of their guns are white-hot and then there is silence.

CHAPTER FIVE

For the next week, the nightmare haunts his sleep.

Early the next Sunday morning he awakes with a jerk, his hands scrabbling at his pillow as he calculates angles of fire, shouts unsaid orders to his men.

The red numbers on the digital alarm clock show just five thirty, but he dare not risk entering the dream again. Staggering out of bed, he cracks the window a few inches and lets the late-December air play over his face. When the dream began, the trees outside still had a few red and orange leaves, but a fierce storm has stripped them clean.

He pulls on his beige canvas jacket and walks into the living room.

Preetam has slept all night on the couch again, the television remote clutched in her hand. Gently taking it away, he bends to kiss her pale cheek. Maybe his mustache tickles her, because she mutters and turns her face away. Careful not to wake her, he tiptoes into the kitchen and shuts the door.

The damn furnace has stopped again and a smoky smell hangs in the air. He clicks the reset button, then lights the stove and makes *chai* in a saucepan, army style, boiling tea leaves with milk and sugar. The cut on his thumb has healed, but the heat of the saucepan makes it ache and he rubs the white scar.

Sitting at the kitchen table he drinks *chai* and studies his accounts ledger, filled with additions and subtractions. Thanks to the Senator's contacts, he has taken on four additional caretaking jobs in the last week, and is happy to have the work, but the storm that hit midweek was brutal. He was forced to hire three of Jõao's cousins to help him deal with downed trees and clogged gutters, and paying their wages has set him back badly. He has sent out invoices for the work, but he knows that the checks will take weeks to arrive.

Over the summer he's learned that money seems to be an abstraction for rich people, something with many zeroes, rolling onward and gathering interest. Small sums bore them; they don't make a connection between the checks they write and the food that goes into his family's stomachs. If he's going to survive this month, he desperately needs one or two of them to pay up . . .

"*Papaji,* it's freezing in here. Can I have some *chai*?"

Shanti stands in the doorway, barefoot, her hair falling about her face in a tangle.

"*Aare,* up so early?"

"You were shouting in your sleep, *Papaji.* I'm awake now."

"It was just a dream. Go put on a sweatshirt and socks and I'll give you *chai.*"

When she returns, she sits across from him and drinks *chai,* her face half hidden by a large red mug, imitating his every move: when he slurps his tea, she slurps hers; when he says *Aaah,* she echoes him.

He can't help smiling. "Come here, you," he says. She climbs into his lap and he inhales the sleepy, warm smell of his daughter.

She shivers. "It's freezing in here, *Papaji.* What happened to the heat?"

He looks, annoyed, at the silent furnace in the corner.

"And what's that smell? It really stinks." She wrinkles up her nose.

"I'll fix it, *beti,* just a minute."

She climbs off his lap, and he goes to press the reset button again. It clicks, but there is no whoosh of air, and he groans with exasperation, then remembers the tank in the basement — could they possibly be out of heating oil? Grabbing a flashlight from the counter, he opens the door to the basement and walks down the rickety wooden stairs, the beam of light playing over broken beds, beach chairs with no seats, and an old-fashioned rolling lawnmower.

The oil tank is in the corner, and as he walks toward it, he feels his feet slip and slide. Turning the flashlight downward, he illuminates a puddle too viscous and shiny to be water. Bending down, he smells the high-octane stink of heating oil.

There is a leak in the tank. All this while oil has been puddling onto the floor, and the furnace has finally cut off. There is a lake of oil down here, and one electrical spark will set it on fire.

Turning off the flashlight, he stands in the darkness and desperately tries to think. A leak like this will cost hundreds — perhaps a few thousand — to fix, and the landlord has made it clear that he doesn't want to sink another dime into this house.

Could Jõao help him clean up the oil and patch up the tank? He turns on his flashlight again and sees the thick yellow puddle spreading across the basement floor, all the way to the far corners. This isn't like cleaning up a flooded basement, this is highly flammable oil; he's fooling himself if he thinks he can fix this.

Maybe he could find another place to stay, but where? The summer people won't rent out their houses in the off-season, all the cheap motels have shut, and, unlike the Cape, there are no trailer parks on the Vineyard. At this time of the year, finding another place is going to be impossible.

His shoulders sag in defeat. There is only one thing to do: pack what they can, get onto the ferry, and drive to Boston. His attempt at freedom is over: he'll have to ask Lallu, Preetam's fat uncle, to give him his old job back.

He suddenly becomes aware of the heavy bunch of keys in his jacket pocket. Keys that unlock the five houses under his care, houses with good heating systems and comfortable beds. He thinks of one house in particular, perched on a cliff in Aquinnah, far from prying eyes. Maybe they can live there for a few days, perhaps a week, while he figures out what to do.

He is still thinking it over as he walks back up to the kitchen.

Shanti sees him and screws up her nose. "Did you fix it? You really smell. What happened to your pants?"

Looking down he realizes that the hems of his jeans are soaked in heating oil.

Preetam stirs in the living room. "What's that noise? What time is it?"

He walks into the living room and crouches next to the couch. "Listen. The oil tank is leaking, and the furnace has stopped working. The basement is flooded with oil."

"Oh my God. Ranjit." She sits up, her long hair loose and disarrayed. "I've been telling you all this time, this house is useless. We should go back to Boston."

He thinks about returning to his job at the Indian store. Back to hauling up sacks of lentils from the basement and cleaning out the weevils. Back to frying *samosas* in the stifling kitchen, the hot oil spattering his arms. Back to Lallu saying, *Well, Captain, here you are not commanding a regiment. It is my shop, and you will do what I tell you.*

He takes a deep breath, slows the thudding of his heart, and reaches a decision. "Just listen a moment," he says, his voice calm and reasonable as he lies to her. "It's not that bad. We can get it fixed in a few days. And I just called a friend." He reaches into his pocket and shows her his cell phone. "This friend says we can stay at his house, no problem."

"Friend? What friend? I'm not staying with that Jõao and his sister in their filthy place."

"We're not staying with the Brazilians, *jaan*. This is my high-up client. His house has got three bedrooms and a swimming pool. I mean the swimming pool is empty, but it's like a five-star hotel."

Preetam looks at him suspiciously.

"It's beautiful. Huge beds. Better than a hotel. You wait and see."

"You're sure they will let us stay?"

He senses that his description appeals to her. "Yes, of course. Just pack quickly, take some clothes. I can come back for the rest of the stuff later."

She shrugs off the blanket and stands. "Maybe we should just go back to Boston —"

He holds her shoulders. "For once, just trust me, okay?" He turns to Shanti, who is hovering in the doorway. "I need your help. Code Red."

Her eyes widen. "Code Red? Really?"

He nods. It is a game they have played since she was little, rehearsing an emergency drill in case of danger. "Find the duffel bag in the closet. Take your clothes and don't forget your school things. Fast."

She runs into the bedroom, and he hears

the thump of drawers being opened and closed.

Walking past the couch, he joins Shanti in the bedroom and pulls out an old suitcase from under the bed, the Air India tags still on it. He throws in a red pouch containing their passports, along with clean clothes and turbans. Shanti is busy packing, and she doesn't notice as he slips his hand under his mattress, pulling out a long sheath made out of layers of duct tape. Inside it is a knife he has constructed, taking the blade from a kitchen knife and replacing its plastic handle with a piece of wood, wrapped in coarse rope for a better grip. It's not much of a weapon, but is razor sharp and slips easily into his boot.

Shanti finishes packing and runs outside. By the time he carries out the duffel bag and suitcase, she is already sitting in the driver's seat of the truck. As he taught her, she has turned on the engine, and is swinging the steering wheel back and forth and pretending to drive.

"I warmed up the car. What happened? Where are we going?"

"Scoot over." Ignoring her questions, he throws the luggage into the flatbed and climbs into the truck. Preetam gets into the back, her hair unbraided, falling loose around her shoulders.

He is about to release the brake when she turns to him. "Did you bring the wedding album?"

"Why do we need that now? I mean —"

Her mouth becomes a thin line. "I'm not leaving it behind."

He returns to the darkened house and finds the leather-bound album lying next to the couch. After all these years, it still smells of incense.

When he returns to the truck, Preetam puts the album into her lap and looks straight ahead. Shanti is bouncing around in the front seat.

It is a foggy morning, and the mist blankets the trees, turning the road into a dark smear. Flipping on the headlights, he backs the truck onto the road and heads in the direction of Aquinnah.

They are halfway down Vineyard Avenue when Jõao's huge truck appears through the fog, towing a shattered car behind it. Ranjit pulls over parallel to it and Celia's tanned face peers down at him, her eyebrows arched in surprise. As always, the burly Jõao smiles shyly, showing gold teeth, and lets his sister do the talking.

"Hello, Preetam. Where are you off to so

early, Ranjit?" Celia must be on her way to church, but her lacy, low-cut white blouse is more suitable for a nightclub.

"We're having problems with the heating. Going up-island for a few days, to stay at a friend's place."

"Heating is broken? Maybe Jõao can help you with it. Where are you going?"

"Thanks, but it'll be fixed in a few days." Changing the topic, he gestures to the old Buick hanging behind the tow truck. "Bad wreck."

"*Ooh,* Ranjit, terrible, no? Some teenager again. Always drinking and driving." She aims a thumb down her throat, making a glugging sound. "And then —" She smacks a fist into her open palm and smiles again.

He is conscious of Celia staring at him, and Preetam looking curiously at both of them.

"So, you're off to church?"

"Yes, and afterward we take this wreck to the junk dealer on the mainland, in Mashpee. And I will have my hair done there." She pats her streaked, shoulder-length blond hair. "Nobody on this island knows how to do Brazilian hair. Maybe one day I open a beauty parlor here. You will let me do your hair, no, Preetam?"

"Well, Celia, we have to go. Nice talking

to you."

"Wait . . . Jõao says to tell you . . . to be careful. Some people they are once again — *roubar,* how do you say? Thieving? Yes, thieving the summer houses. And yesterday, they break into this old lady house, they think she is gone, but she is there." Celia pauses dramatically. "They hit her on the head. Dead."

Ranjit is stunned. There are robberies on the Vineyard, but there hasn't been a murder here for years.

"Are you sure? She's dead?"

"Jõao's friend is police. It will be in the newspaper, later."

"Thanks for telling me," he says. "I'll be careful."

"Okay. Hey, Preetam, if you want to go to the sewing circle, you call me, okay?"

Preetam smiles a stiff smile, and as they drive away, she turns to Ranjit. "Did you see what she was wearing? What kind of a church does she go to? And this house we're staying in, is it safe? I don't want to be alone there."

"Don't worry. It's very safe. There's an alarm."

The fog is so thick that he has to strain to see the road. Saying a prayer under his breath, he drives away carefully.

CHAPTER SIX

The three of them stand stock-still in the living room of Senator Neals's house. The fog outside obscures the view, and the glass doors on the far side reflect their silhouettes.

Ranjit switches on all the lights. Halogen spots shine down on the kitchen, and the glass case lights up, revealing rows of pale porcelain dolls. Preetam gasps in astonishment.

"Oh, that," he says. "It's a hobby of theirs. They're rich."

"I know, Ma, aren't they beautiful?" Shanti walks over and presses her nose against the case.

Ranjit motions to her. "*Beti,* you're not to touch them. Remember, this is not our house. We can't break anything."

"Whose house is this?" Preetam demands.

Shanti turns to her mother. "It's Senator Neals's house. I came here before with *Papaji.*"

"I told you, Preetam, it's all right. We can stay here for a while, they're away for the winter."

Preetam frowns at him, but he can tell that the house is working its magic, and before she can say anything else he jumps in.

"Come on, I'll give you both a tour."

They walk down the circular stair in the corner, their footsteps echoing on its steel treads. On the level below is a wide hallway lined with bookshelves and they walk down it, passing the Senator's study, till they find themselves in the master bedroom.

"Cool." Shanti peers in, then rushes off in the other direction, but Preetam pushes past him and stands by the bed, fingering the cream bedcover. He notices with a shock that the yellow walls are hung with framed charcoal sketches of nudes. *He hadn't remembered those from the afternoon he was here . . .*

Preetam opens a closet, and he sees Anna's yellow dress hanging there. The smell of her musky perfume fills the air, and he turns away, hoping that Preetam hasn't noticed the expression on his face. Luckily by then she's in the bathroom, examining the circular Jacuzzi and smelling the shampoos made of papaya and mango.

"I didn't know people lived like this," she

says in a soft voice. "Are these people very rich? This woman just left all her things here."

"Yes, well . . ." He cannot bear the thought of sleeping in this room. "Maybe we should stay in the bedroom on the lowest floor, so that we don't disturb their things."

They both descend another twist of stairs to the lowest level, emerging into a large room with brightly colored yoga mats and a treadmill, its mirrored back wall reflecting the dark ocean outside. Off to one side is a suite of rooms, probably intended for a maid: a tiny bedroom with a twin bed and a dresser, and a small bathroom off to one side.

"We'll sleep here. Where did Shanti go?"

They hear her yelping in delight and find her in a small corner bedroom on the floor above. It has bubblegum pink wallpaper, a child's bed with a pink comforter, and tall built-in shelves full of well-loved dolls and stuffed toys. Ranjit feels very confused; he had assumed that Anna and the Senator were a childless couple.

"It's a little girl's bedroom!" Shanti is dancing around the room, pirouetting ballerina style. "A pink bedroom! Fantastic!"

"*Chee,* what's that? It's so ugly!" Preetam points to a doll sitting on the bed.

It is as big as a newborn baby, its barrel-like body clad in faded petticoats, a red-checked kerchief wrapped around its dark head. Its face is a caricature of an African-American woman, with a flattened nose and thick red lips; he can tell that it is very old from its yellowed porcelain, crisscrossed with hairline cracks.

"Where did you get that, Shanti? From the display case?"

She shakes her head, her dark curls flying. "No, *Papaji,* it was lying here, on the bed."

"It doesn't look like a toy. Remember, we can't break anything." He takes the doll from the bed and puts it on top of a high shelf.

"I wasn't going to break it," she says indignantly. "Can I sleep here, *Papaji, pleeeese*?"

"Your mother and I will be in the bedroom below. As long as you're okay with that. You're not going to get frightened, are you?"

She sniffs. "*Papaji,* I'm nine now. I'll be fine."

He carries down the luggage and Shanti instantly unpacks, throwing her clothes into the closet.

She turns to him. "I'm done. Can I go and explore outside?"

Seeing her so excited, he smiles. "Okay,

but don't go far. It's foggy."

He leaves Preetam to unpack and wanders through the quiet house, looking for a family photograph to explain the child's bedroom: perhaps the Senator had a daughter by his previous marriage. The hallway is hung with bright abstract paintings, but there are no photographs, and he wanders into the Senator's study and pulls open the heavy drapes. He can see Shanti on the deck outside, leaning over the rail, and he waves to her. She is singing to herself, and her high, sweet voice makes him smile again.

Turning, he looks around the study, taking in the banker's desk with its green felt top, the wine-colored leather armchairs, and the wall hung with framed photographs and newspaper clippings.

In one yellowed clipping, the Senator is a young DA with a full head of hair, shaking hands with a man identified as Boston Mayor Kevin White. Another black-and-white photograph shows him as a three-term State Senator, wearing a suit with wide lapels and posing on the steps of the Boston State House. In a color photograph, he sits in a darkened Washington restaurant with Ted Kennedy — not the liberal lion of the Senate, but an earlier, bloated version — with an inscription in thick marker that reads "To Speedy Neals, the best wingman I ever had."

Ranjit is confused by the nickname, but under the photograph is a framed front page of the *Harvard Crimson* from 1968, its headline blaring HARVARD BEATS YALE, 29–29. Ranjit reads on, learning how "Speedy Neals," Harvard's running back, scored a touchdown in the last few seconds of the final game, tying both teams, and breaking Yale's six-year winning streak.

There are other group photographs, yearly pictures of the Senator's staff party, all with Neals at their center, his tie loosened and sleeves rolled up. The styles change — lapels get narrower, and the women's Afros give way to weaves — but the dynamic in each picture is the same: the attractive young men and women jostle subtly to be close to the smiling Senator. And there, in a photograph dated ten years ago, is Anna Neals.

Correction. She's listed as "Anna Williams, Intern." She was younger then, and heavier, with curly hair falling to the shoulders of her little black dress. Even in the confusion of faces and limbs, he can see that Anna's hand is resting on the seated Senator's shoulder, and that his smile, in response, is even more high-wattage than usual. The photograph causes Ranjit's heart to ache;

he's never seen her smiling like that.

The other walls hold inscribed photographs from Presidents Bush and Clinton and framed awards from Senate committees, but there are no pictures of a daughter.

Ranjit is suddenly aware that he cannot hear Shanti singing anymore. He looks out of the window, but the deck is bare, and the fog muffles his view. Returning to the lower level, he sees that Preetam is still hanging up her clothes.

"Have you seen Shanti? She was outside on the deck."

"Hmmm? Did you know they have lavender soap in the bathroom here? It smells fantastic . . ."

Walking across the room, he pulls open the sliding glass door and steps out onto the lower deck. He calls Shanti's name, but there is only an echo, followed by a deep silence.

Where could she be? Stepping from the deck to the brown grass of the lower terrace he peers down the slope of the hill, but the fog is too thick. Beyond the terrace is the abrupt edge of the cliff, and the granite steps that zigzag down to the cove below. On a day like this, they will be slick and very slippery.

Entering the fog, he walks across the terrace, and then he remembers the empty, kidney-shaped swimming pool ahead. He'd been meaning to clean out all the fallen leaves and cover it, but hadn't gotten around to it. It has high, slippery sides, and a deep end of twelve feet. *Oh, Guru, if Shanti has fallen in —*

His heart beats faster as he reaches the kidney-shaped crater. It is empty, except for a few inches of rainwater, and he sees a reflection of himself, outlined against the white fog.

Shanti has to be on the steps, then, and he hurries to the edge of the cliff. Looking down, he catches a flash of her blue coat: she is standing on a landing halfway down. Hurrying down the slippery stone steps, he reaches her, and hearing his footsteps, she turns around.

"What the hell are you doing down here? If you fell, you'd break your neck." His relief is mixed with anger, his voice harder than he intended.

"I'm not going to fall. *Papaji,* look." Her eyes are shining with excitement, and she points down at the cliff face.

At first he can see nothing: just the empty beach below and the Senator's yacht, its sails lowered, riding at anchor. Then there is a flash of movement, and he sees a huge winged shape riding a downdraft. As he watches, it soars up into the sky and vanishes into the fog.

"It's an osprey, *Papaji*. They were almost extinct. They've just returned to the island, after many years. We've been learning about them at school."

"That's great, but I don't want you coming down here, understand?"

"Okay, sorry, but —" Holding his hand, she climbs up the stairs, chattering on about ospreys. She says that the giant birds pass through the Vineyard every fall, and use it as a final stop on their migratory path to South America. This particular bird must have missed the window to migrate, and now must winter on the island.

He listens, nodding, and feels his fear subside. Maybe he overreacted, but those stairs are so steep. Returning to the house, he keeps an eye on Shanti, but she doesn't venture out again. He can hear her in the pink bedroom, playing with the old doll, but this time he doesn't tell her to put it away.

That night, after dinner — they eat a frozen pizza found in the Senator's freezer — Ranjit takes Shanti down to the pink bedroom. He brings her nightclothes and watches as she brushes her teeth, the foam covering her mouth and hands. When she is done she slips into her teddy-bear pajamas and climbs into the bed, which is already made up with clean-smelling pink sheets.

"It's an upside-down house," she says happily, and he understands what she means. It's strange to enter the house at the top of the hill and travel downward, but he likes the way it is tucked into the earth. It feels safe here.

"*Papaji,* whose room is this? A girl my age?"

"Maybe, *jaan.* Now go to sleep. It's been a long day."

Shanti's eyes close, but she struggles to stay awake. "I bet it's a girl my age. Maybe I can . . ." Her breathing slows and her eyes close. ". . . find out tomorrow . . ."

For a few minutes he watches her sleep, her long eyelashes casting shadows on her cheeks. He will have to talk to her tomorrow about staying here; she can't mention it to anyone at school.

Downstairs, Preetam has changed into a faded pink nightgown, almost translucent after many washes. He lies back on the narrow bed and watches her undo her long plait and brush out her waist-length hair. There are gray hairs, as bright as wires, running through her dark hair. *How come he hasn't noticed them before?* He wants to ask her to leave her hair open, so he can bury his face in it, as he used to, but she plaits it deftly, wrapping the end tightly with a rubber band.

It is his turn to use the small bathroom, and when he emerges, he thinks that she is asleep, but then hears her rapid breathing. As he slides under the feather duvet, her voice comes out of the darkness.

"This is a nice house, Ranjit. Very nice house. Where does the owner work?"

"I told you, he's a senator, he's in D.C. most of the time. This is just one of his houses — he has others, in Boston and Washington."

"I could live in this country, if we had a house like this . . ."

It has been so long since they've slept in the same bed. He reaches out and touches her arm, but she shrinks away.

"Not now. It's so late, and I'm so tired . . ."

He takes his hand away, his desire curdling, and the bed suddenly seems impossibly small.

His thoughts are all jumbled together as he lies in the darkness and listens to the crashing of the waves below.

Anna's perfume still lingers in his nostrils, and he thinks of the yellow dress hanging in her closet. He knows that he mustn't let his mind go there, but he can't help it.

Anna wore that yellow dress when she brought him iced tea on that last September afternoon. The yellow was vivid against her arms and shoulders, which were burnt dark brown from all her running, and she was thinner too, her legs hard and muscular.

Her eyes were hidden, as usual, behind her mirrored sunglasses. As though reading his mind, she pushed them up onto her forehead and looked at him. Other women's eyes revealed their emotions, but her raven-black eyes were hard to read.

"Mind that step you're sitting on," Ranjit said, looking away. "The edge is sharp. I cut the stone this morning."

"I like the feeling, it makes me feel alive," she answered, running her fingers along the sharp stone.

Not knowing what she meant, he said nothing, and just thanked her for the iced tea. She sat on the step above him, squinting as she formulated a question in her mind.

"It must be strange for your daughter," she said slowly, "to come all the way from India to this little island, and to think of it

101

as home."

He took a sip of cold tea and wiped his mouth before replying. "Shanti's fine. She loves the Vineyard. This is her world now, she doesn't remember anything about India. Some days *I* wake up in the morning and don't know where I am." As soon as he said that, he felt embarrassed.

"I know that feeling." She nodded slowly. "Every single morning I wake up and wonder what I'm doing here. I've been reading this book on Buddhism, and it says . . ." She paused, and beads of sweat dripped from her temples. "It says that all life is suffering. We have to accept that. Do you think that's right?"

Not knowing what to say, he took another sip of tea. "Mrs. Neals . . ." he began.

"Anna. Please call me Anna."

"Anna," he said, softly. "I know something is wrong. You don't have to tell me. But as long as you believe in a higher power, a god, then there are reasons —"

"Your god is here? On this godforsaken island?" Her voice quivered.

He quoted a verse from the Guru Granth Sahib to her.

God has his seat everywhere
His treasure houses are in all places.

She half listened, tears welling up in her eyes. "There is no god," she said. "Your god or anyone else's."

Before he could tell her that god included pain, included loss, she rose to her feet and nodded absently at him. As she started up the steep stairs a sudden wind flattened her thin cotton dress against her legs.

He put down his glass and hurriedly followed her.

"Anna, wait. What's the matter? What has happened?"

She stopped, her calf muscles tensed in mid-step. Turning, she pressed her palm flat against his bare chest, as though for support.

He felt the warmth of her palm against his skin. The ocean beyond them was green and empty that day, no boats or kayaks, just the shimmering water, stretching away to the horizon.

She reached down and slipped her fingers through his, pulling him alongside her. They walked up the steps together, and she let his hand go only after they entered her darkened bedroom. Its curtains were drawn, but the sun shone through a gap and made a slice of brightness on the yellow wall.

The room still smelled of her shower, of steam and shampoo, and the large bed was unmade. Her running clothes lay in a heap on the floor, reeking of ammonia, her blue-and-gold running shoes lying on their sides.

She closed her eyes as she pulled off her yellow dress, the cotton rustling like tissue paper. Reaching for him, she undid his jeans, and his belt buckle clanked as it hit the floor.

Naked, he didn't dare to touch her. Her body was perfect, slim-shouldered and high-breasted, a flare of hips before her long legs began. Looking down, he saw black blood blisters on the back of her heels from all her running.

"Anna," he whispered. "I really smell. Perhaps I need to take a shower —"

She stood on her toes and kissed him, her soft breasts pressing into his chest. Soon he was kissing her back, feeling something shockingly fierce inside, a feeling that he had long forgotten.

She led him to the bed and he lay next to her. His mouth moved down her neck to the slope of her breasts, then moved lower. He kissed the pale stretch marks that marked her hips and thighs, realizing that she had hewn this hard body out of older, more pliant flesh.

When he slipped a hand between her legs she was wet already, and she whispered into his ear, urging him on. Hearing her hoarse words, he moved between her legs, stretching out her long, dark body under his. She wrapped her long legs around his lower back, her hands pushed down on his shoulders, and he was lost in the heat and sea-smell of her.

Her breath came out in gasps, and at first he thought she was moaning in pleasure, but then her lips trembled and he realized that she was crying, tears flowing silently down her cheeks.

"What's wrong?" he asked, stopping.

She just bit her lip, wrapped her legs tighter, and urged him on in a choked voice.

"Anna, you're crying. Is it me?"

"No," she managed to say. "No. It's not you. Keep going." But she cried harder, and turned her face away.

"I . . . I can't go on like this," he whispered. He pulled free and lay on the crumpled sheets beside her. When he reached out to hold her she hid her face in his chest and sobbed, her crying unbridled now. Not knowing what to do, he held her, rocking her gently, as though she were a child. After a long time her breathing slowed, and then she fell fast asleep.

He held her as she slept. The minutes ticked by, and jumbled thoughts raced through his brain: confusion at what had just happened, and fear at being discovered here. He thought of his wife, alone halfway across the island, lost in front of her television set, and felt the first sickening pang of guilt.

It felt like forever before Anna jerked awake. She sat up groggily and walked naked to the bathroom, and when she returned, her face was washed and her short hair carefully brushed. As she pulled on her yellow dress her face was peaceful, all the tension drained away, replaced by the blankness of a sleepwalker.

He wore his own sweaty jeans, and she walked him out to the deck, wordlessly touching his cheek before turning back. The glass door slid shut, and she was gone.

He walked, dazed, back down to the half-finished steps.

The afternoon outside was still the same. The green summer ocean still ebbed and flowed, and a few sailboats were now tacking across Vineyard Sound. His hammer was exactly where he'd dropped it, one wooden peg half sunk into the earth. It was all the same, but he felt the way a dreamer does upon awakening, when the mood of the dream colors everything.

Except that it hadn't been a dream. He

could still smell her strong odor on his fingertips, feel her muscular, yearning body under his.

He looked at a pile of cut stone, the strings and pegs he'd laid out earlier, but he could not bear to keep on working. He gathered up his tools and drove away in the truck, and before he went home he stopped at the liquor store and sat in the truck and finished a small bottle of Bacardi.

When he came back to Aquinnah the next morning, the iced-tea glass was gone from the steps. He cut stone, his hands feeling the touch of her fingers even as he handled the sharp edges. All afternoon he waited for her, listened for the tinkling of ice cubes. When she didn't come he walked up to the house, but the chair by the pool was empty. The sliding glass doors were locked, and the curtains were drawn tight.

Anna didn't appear that afternoon, or the next. Most days her silver Mercedes was gone. Sometimes there was a white van parked outside the house, like those driven by construction workers or plumbers, though this one was pristine, without a logo or a name painted on it. She must have been having some new appliance installed, but he never saw anyone going in or out of the house.

He willed her to appear again, but the days passed, and when he finished the job, he slipped a bill under the front door. She mailed him a check, and he did not see her again till she called him nearly three months later.

CHAPTER SEVEN

A week passes in the Senator's house, and then a few more days. It does not snow, but the island settles down into the stillness of winter, the ground hard and frozen, the ocean gray and dull.

Ranjit wakes early one morning, Preetam lying next to him, blissfully asleep under a thick down duvet. For a second he does not remember where he is, then he hears the waves crashing below and it all comes back: they are still at the Senator's house, and today is the day before Christmas.

When he showers he sees that Preetam is using a bottle of Anna's expensive mango shampoo. Walking up the stairs, he passes Shanti's room and sees her fast asleep, an arm around the large, dark-faced doll. *Damn it, both his wife and daughter behave as though this is their house.*

In the kitchen he boils water for *chai,* and feels a pang of fear: sooner or later, someone will figure out where they are living. This island is too small for secrets.

The problem is finding another place to live. The only other apartment that he has found is a cramped flat above a Chinese restaurant in Vineyard Haven, at twice the rent of the old shack.

And Preetam is so happy here: she has finally stopped watching television and instead cooks dinner each night, using Anna Neals's copper-bottomed pans. Ranjit has heard her on the phone, talking to her relatives in Boston, saying, "*Hanh,* of course this house is temporary, but you should see it. They have two freezers, all stainless steel appliances, and you should see the view. Yes, yes, Ranjit is doing very well, soon we'll be moving into a house like this one."

Tonight is Christmas Eve, he tells himself. *Let them be happy for a few days more. We'll move in the New Year.*

He fills his travel mug with *chai* and drives out to check on his houses. He has drained all the heating systems and cleaned out gutters, and now all he has to do is check for mice. He should be done by noon, in time for him to swing by the Oak Bluffs Post Office. A few payments have come in, and he's used the money to order Christmas presents for Shanti and Preetam.

His first stop for the day is the Red Heron Estate. He stops at its high iron gate, flanked by stone pillars and an alarm box. Security was beefed up for the President's visit, and there are now alarms and cameras everywhere. It is hard to remember all the alarm codes, but last week an alarm had malfunctioned three times, and the alarm technician, tired of making the trip out to the island, had given him the master override code. Now he punches in BLUESKY and the gates swing open.

Driving up to the main house, he walks past the wide front porch with its rows of colorful rocking chairs, imagining the President of the United States sitting here last summer, smiling his wide, toothy smile. The African-American elite of the island must have congregated here, men in pastel-colored polo shirts, and women like Anna, with sleek figures and big sun hats. Something of that event remains, caught in the angles of the rocking chairs, and the rings on the wooden tables made by wet beer bottles.

He carefully punches in BLUESKY again and the front door swings open. Shanti has asked him to look through the house for traces of the President, and see if he can find her a toothbrush with the presidential seal on it, or perhaps one of his daughter's toys, but the house is clean and impersonal, all the furniture draped with white dust cloths. He wanders from room to room, looking for leaks or mouse droppings, and completes his check quickly before rearming the alarms.

His next stop is half an hour away, in Oak Bluffs, a gray-shingled mansion that faces Ocean Park. It belongs to an African-American doctor, and has been in his family for generations.

Noticing the dark droppings of field mice, he sets mousetraps throughout the house, spreading each with a gob of peanut butter. As he wanders from room to room, the urge to pry, once ignited, does not go away. He opens drawers and closets, and on a high shelf finds a large tin box. Opening it, he sees an old stethoscope, along with rolls of bandages, disposable syringes, and even vials of antibiotics and morphine.

Clearly the doctor likes to be prepared, and that is not all. Lying on the floor to put a trap under a bed, Ranjit sees a dusty, rectangular leather case. Dragging it out, he clicks open its heavy brass locks and peers into its red velvet interior. It is a disassembled shotgun, and not just any gun, but a hand-crafted twelve-gauge Holland &

Holland, decorated with ornate silver scrollwork. Without thinking, he picks up the walnut stock, slips the long barrels into place, and screws on the side latch.

He inhales the familiar tang of gun oil and can't resist lifting the gun to his shoulder. There is a black crow sitting on a branch outside the window, and he aims at it. *Bang, bang,* he says under his breath, *you're dead.*

Perhaps the crow hears him, for it suddenly caws and flaps into the sky. Laughing, he quickly breaks the gun down and replaces the case under the bed.

All this fooling around has made him late, but he gets to the post office in Oak Bluffs before it shuts. He waits patiently in line, relieved to find out that his three large boxes have arrived, sent express delivery from L.L. Bean. He has spent two hundred dollars on presents, money he can ill afford, but it will be worth every cent just to see the expressions on Preetam and Shanti's faces.

He signs for his packages and is about to leave when he hears a high voice behind him.

"So how are things at the Senator's house?"

Has he been found out? Heart hammering in his chest, he turns and sees an elderly woman in a wool hat, her swollen ankles bulging over thick-soled shoes. He sighs in relief as he recognizes Betty Green, the Senator's housekeeper.

"Oh, I haven't been up there in a few days, but so far, so good."

"The field mice are going to get in. Ah, what a stupid place to build a house, in the middle of nowhere. But that Anna Williams, she never had any sense. Her father had a hunting shack up there, and then she goes and builds that big house."

Betty pauses for a breath, and he sees his chance. The native Vineyarders he meets are normally a closed-mouthed bunch.

"So, you've known Anna — Mrs. Neals — for a long time?"

Betty chuckles, ending in a long, hacking smoker's cough. "Known her? Known her? Her mother died when she was just a baby. I practically brought up that girl. Oh, she was a handful even then, no sense in her. Still, I blame the father. Old Mr. Williams, he was a strange one. Black man — as black as me — but went off to Ha-vahd and thought he was white. Always wearing those ridiculous hunting clothes, tramping around, drinking, shooting animals.

"Other people, they built houses, they farmed their land, but not Mr. Williams. Prime land all along the coast, given over to

114

the skunks and the birds. Can you imagine it? All that land, just sitting there. Well, this was a sleepy place back then, not like now, the whole island owned by . . . outsiders, foreigners."

She glances at him and smiles sweetly. "No offense, I didn't mean you, Ranjit, I mean all those stuck-up mainlanders."

"No offense taken." He looks at his watch and sees that it is getting late, but he has to ask. "When I was up at the house, I noticed a child's bedroom. Does the Senator have a daughter, I mean, from his previous marriage?"

Betty gives him a sideways glance, and her voice drops to a whisper. "You haven't heard? That was Anna's daughter. Died in an accident, three years ago. Anna never recovered, but who would? Losing a child is unnatural, they aren't meant to go first. Oh, I shouldn't gossip, it isn't right."

She turns around abruptly and heads for the post office doors. "Well, Merry Christmas," she says over her shoulder. "And be careful. There's been three more break-ins after that old lady was killed."

"Yes, thanks," he says, but his face burns with shame when he thinks back to that afternoon; had he tried to take advantage of a grieving, mixed-up woman? No, she had taken him by the hand, led him into the house . . .

Forget it, he tells himself, *that's all over.* Holding the large packages, he hurries to his truck.

His last house is on the way home, in Lambert's Cove. It belongs to a retired character actor and is his least favorite, with cigarette burns on its dark furniture, its lace curtains fumed brown with nicotine. If he's quick, he should be out of there in ten minutes.

Lambert's Cove is silent and the houses he passes are all shut for the winter, their shades pulled, their driveways empty of cars. He parks the truck on the street and walks up to the front door, turning the key with one swift motion. Then he stops dead.

From the kitchen beyond comes the murmur of men's voices. *Someone is in the house.* He remembers Betty Green's warning and pulls the knife from his boot, the rope handle rough in his hand. As his eyes adjust to the darkness, he sees that the plaid sofa in the living room has been overturned and the long wooden bar is littered with empty bottles of liquor.

There is sudden, raucous laughter in the next room, then heavy footsteps, followed

116

by the creak of the screen door opening and the back door being unlatched. The intruders are leaving.

He has to find out who they are. Crouching low, he crosses the living room, the knife blade held downward. Holding his breath, he peers through the kitchen doorway.

The refrigerator is open, its dim blue light filling the room, and the men are gone. If he hurries to the back window, he can catch a glimpse of them. He lowers his knife and steps into the room.

A growl. Out of nowhere, a dark shape springs at him.

Hits him, hard and fast, high on his left shoulder. He spins aside, feeling his canvas jacket rip. A large black dog hurtles past him, slams into a cabinet, and turns, its canines bared.

The Pakistanis had attack dogs at the border. Without thinking, he unbuckles his thick leather belt and whips it free.

The dog's hind legs tense, and it launches into the air, going for his throat.

His belt cracks in the darkness, its brass buckle smacking the dog's nose. Distracted, it lunges for the belt and sinks its teeth into the leather, trying to jerk it away. Ranjit pivots, bringing the knife down, aiming for the spot right behind its head.

The long, thin blade pierces flesh. The dog howls and twists, letting go of the belt, its teeth snapping. Ranjit drops the belt, both hands on the knife handle now, and pitches forward, bringing his two hundred pounds of dead weight down onto the blade.

Dog and man fall to the floor. The dog's back feet skitter and scrape; it is dying, but slowly, too slowly, and its teeth are still snapping, close, too close.

Help me, Guru.

He pushes the blade deeper, cutting through thick muscle, feeling a warm liquid flow over his hands.

The dog gasps, its breath hot and meaty. With one final shudder, it goes still.

Over. It's over. Letting go of the knife, he falls backward against the cabinets. Near his feet the pile of black, bulked muscle twitches convulsively, and he watches the life fade from the dog's yellow eyes.

Only when it is completely still does he try to rise, slipping in wet blood. His shaking hand finds a switch and a bright fluorescent light floods the room.

The dog lies on the worn linoleum floor. Bubbly dark blood leaks from its open mouth and stains its velvet muzzle.

A dog. Almost killed by a fucking dog.

Outside there is the sound of a car engine

starting. He runs to the back window, but all he sees is a blue car vanishing down the road, its bumper held on with duct tape.

He turns and stares at the thick black collar around the dog's neck. *He knows this dog. It belonged to those men outside the liquor store, Plaid-shirt and his brother.*

Pulling his knife free with great difficulty, he wipes it in the dog's thick black fur. He leaves the house and leans against the truck, gulping in the cold air, his eyes shut, thinking of the dog's dying eyes.

Unbidden, a memory surfaces from Siachen. All the firebases high in the mountains were re-supplied by strings of mules, and Ranjit's favorite was Rajah, a gray pack mule who unhesitatingly led each convoy around the crevasses hidden below the snow.

One bright, sunny day, Ranjit was leading a convoy high up on the glacier when the Pakistanis found their range. The clear blue sky suddenly rained artillery shells, and Rajah panicked, tore the reins out of his hands, and bolted blindly away. He sprinted after the beast, just in time to see it plunge through the snow into a deep crevasse.

Rajah somehow survived the fall. He could hear the animal's frightened screams from deep in the crevasse, as though it was begging for mercy. He fired down into the blackness, but the bullets just ricocheted against a thick lip of ice.

He knelt by the crevasse. "It's okay, boy," he called down. "It's going to be all right," and for a moment the screaming died down.

He pulled the pin on a grenade and dropped it into the crevasse. He was already walking away when he felt the muffled boom under his feet. *Rajah was the first to go. The first betrayal.*

"Yes, the mule, Captain. It really upset the men."

Ranjit's eyes snap open, and Sergeant Khandelkar is leaning against a tree, his white snowsuit hanging off his emaciated frame. The skin on his face is pulled tight, and he seems to have shrunk, as though all the water has evaporated from his muscles.

"Private Dewan was most upset about Rajah," Khandelkar continues. "He loved that animal. Always stealing potatoes and feeding it. Do you remember?"

"Yes." Ranjit's voice is a whisper. "I remember everything."

"Remember that terrible American band the boy liked? Guns and something — yes, Guns and Roses." Khandelkar laughs, and a blue vein pulses in his forehead. "He still sings, you know. I hear his voice on the wind. He is a terrible singer."

120

The Sergeant's sunken eyes bore into Ranjit. "Something strange is happening to us, Captain. The snow is melting. Soon it will no longer provide a covering. And the crows know it, they sit on my chest and peck and peck, their beaks as sharp as little knives. I will not exist much longer, Captain. But Dewan is still buried deep. Keep your promise. Bring him down."

Ranjit's voice comes in a rush. "Sergeant, there is nothing I can do for you. I am a servant now, I look after houses —"

He is talking into the air: the space where Khandelkar had stood is empty. He leans back against the truck and holds his head in his hands. *The dog has triggered this hallucination. The Sergeant's words were gibberish: snow does not melt on the glacier in December.*

This logic calms him, and he takes a deep breath, and then another, and gradually the reality of the situation reasserts itself: the house is wrecked, and he knows that he should call the police and file a report. But what if they ask for his papers? He looks down at the driving license he had bought in Boston. *Will it pass muster?*

No choice. He takes out his cell phone and dials, and the West Tisbury police say they're sending a car out right away.

121

By the time the dark blue cruiser pulls up, he has left messages on the character actor's answering machines in New York and Los Angeles.

A thick-trunked police officer with a lined face gets slowly out of the cruiser. His peaked cap is pushed back on his head, and his blue uniform shirt is tight over his midriff. Peering at Ranjit, he unbuttons his holster with one flick of his thumb.

"Don't move. I need to see your hands, now."

Looking down, Ranjit realizes that the shoulder of his jacket is ripped open, its beige canvas spattered with dark blood.

"Wait." Ranjit's words come out in a rush. "I didn't do anything, it's dog blood —"

The officer's hands are a blur and his gun slides out of the holster. "Shut up. Do it."

Ranjit backs up against his truck and raises his arms high. He takes a deep breath and speaks slowly. "Look, I'm the caretaker for this house. I'm Ranjit Singh, my client is Mark Allston. I have a contract with him, I have the keys to the house —"

The officer steps forward slowly, squinting at Ranjit, and a look of recognition passes across his broad face. "Hey, you the guy who lives next to Mike's Tow? On Masonic Avenue? The Indian guy?"

Ranjit nods, making sure his hands are in full view.

"Yeah, I get my car fixed at Mike's, I seen you before. I'm Officer Gardner." The man slowly lowers his weapon, and the deep lines in his forehead disappear. "Now, what happened in there? You called in a burglary in progress. The intruders attack you?"

Ranjit shakes his head. "No, they're gone. Their dog attacked me. A big dog."

"Dog? Wait here, okay?"

The officer approaches the back door, cautiously peers in, and then walks into the kitchen. There is a muffled cry and he bursts out, breathing heavily.

"Mary mother of God." He stares at Ranjit, who is still standing by his truck. "What the hell happened to that pit bull?"

"I killed it." Ranjit suddenly feels very calm. "It attacked me. I had no choice."

"Jesus Christ. How did you do that?"

"I was in the military. We were trained to deal with dogs."

The man takes off his cap and runs a hand over his crew cut. "Those pit bulls will tear your throat out. I've seen it. You better tell me what happened in there."

Ranjit tells him about hearing voices in the kitchen. The intruders must have heard him come in, pretended to leave, then loosed their dog on him.

"They were two men. I can't be sure, but I think I've seen them before. They drive an old blue car, a Mercury. The rear bumper has duct tape on it."

The officer's face turns red with excitement. "An old Mercury? Did one of them have tattoos?"

Ranjit thinks back on the parking lot outside the liquor store. "Some sort of fish." He gestures at his arms. "One on each arm."

"Son of a bitch." The officer runs to the cruiser and begins to talk excitedly on the radio. "Hey, Gardner here. You know those two guys we busted for illegal hunting? Yeah, yeah, in the fall. I got an ID here on the burglaries. Put out an APB on those guys. Yeah, thanks."

Ranjit remembers that Anna had known their names, but he can't remember them. Most American names sound the same to him. "Officer, you know who those two men are?"

Officer Gardner's thick face lights up with a smile. "Yeah, I think we have a pretty good idea. Now don't leave the island for the next week, okay? We're going to need you to ID those guys. You're still at Masonic Avenue, right?"

Ranjit pauses. "Yes, sir."

"And get that shoulder looked at. The dog in there looked pretty sick to me." The officer shakes his head in disgust, and the lines in his forehead reappear. "Those guys breed pit bulls, they keep them hungry and mean."

Ranjit nods, feeling relieved. "Yes, sir, I will. Can I go now? It's Christmas Eve, and my family is waiting —"

"Ah, there's one thing. Any chance that those two recognized you? It's a small island, and you stand out, for sure."

Ranjit's face darkens, and the officer puts a reassuring hand on his shoulder. "Hey, no need to worry now, we'll pick 'em up in a day or two. Just be careful. I tell you what. I'll swing by Masonic Avenue now and then and keep an eye on things."

Ranjit forces himself to speak. "Well, I don't want to put you to any trouble, Officer. I know it's Christmas, and you must be busy . . ."

The cop beams. "No trouble. No trouble at all. Merry Christmas."

Getting into his truck, Ranjit realizes that he's shivering. *What happens if the cop drives by Masonic Avenue and sees that the house is empty?* They could easily be traced to the Senator's house, and then he'll be arrested for trespassing.

He gets into his truck, blasts the heater,

125

and begins the long drive to Aquinnah. Whether Preetam likes it or not, they're leaving the Senator's house. *He'll have to talk to her soon, but not tonight, not on Christmas Eve.* He glances over his shoulder at the large boxes lying on the backseat.

No matter what, his family will celebrate this Christmas.

CHAPTER EIGHT

It is dark by the time Ranjit gets back to Aquinnah. He parks outside the house and unbuttons his shirt to check for scratches: his shoulder is bruised, but, thank the Guru, his skin is unbroken, the thick canvas jacket having absorbed the impact of the dog's assault. The jacket is ripped and useless now. Taking it off, he stuffs it into his toolbox before entering the house.

He expects Preetam to be on the phone, but instead it is quiet, and he can hear the low murmur of voices.

Standing in the entryway, he sees Preetam sitting on the gray leather couch, with Shanti on the floor below her. He watches as Preetam gently combs through the tangles in Shanti's long, curly hair, then pours oil from a bottle and massages it into her daughter's scalp. The sickly sweet fragrance of coconut oil fills the room.

He slips into the room. "Hey, you two.

Shanti, you look so . . . different."

Shanti looks up at him with beseeching eyes. Her hair is gleaming with oil and she is dressed in a too-short pink *salwar kameez,* her nails painted a matching color.

Ranjit chuckles, knowing that she hates having her hair oiled, and would rather wear jeans and a sweatshirt.

Preetam misses the whole exchange. "See, Ranjit, how beautiful your daughter looks now? Like a proper girl. These days she's always running around in those dirty jeans, like a tomboy."

"Yes, indeed. She looks very nice."

With the heat cranked up, Preetam is wearing a thin white cotton *salwar kameez* and her feet are bare, just as she would dress on a hot day in India. He knows that in this house, she has forgotten about America.

He sniffs the warm air. "What are you cooking? It smells delicious."

"Well, it's Christmas and all. So I thought I'd make that chicken that you like, and rice. Why don't you wash up, and we can eat?" She stares into his face. "Are you all right, Ranjit? You look pale."

"Oh, I'm just a little tired. It's been a long day."

Preetam nods and goes back to combing Shanti's hair. "Okay, dinner's ready. I'll

128

reheat the chicken while you wash up."

He walks quickly down the stairs and notices that a light is on halfway down the corridor. Entering the Senator's study, he sees that the wooden swivel chair is askew and a desk drawer is open. Lying half-made on the desk is a necklace of paper clips. *Damn it, Shanti must have been in here — he'll have to give her a stern talking-to.*

He starts to close the drawer, but can't help peering in. In the front is a tangle of rubber bands, ballpoints, and paper clips, but behind them is a page torn out of a notebook and folded over. He reaches in and unfolds the paper, seeing a drawing in vivid crayon. It is crudely done, but there is no mistaking the outline of this house, the blue sea beyond, seagulls like check marks flying above it. In a wobbly child's handwriting is written "Jojo."

So Anna's daughter was called Jojo. What is that short for? Johanna? Josephine? He replaces the paper and gently closes the drawer. He imagines a girl younger than Shanti dancing into this room, imagines the Senator lifting her up into his lap, taking the picture and admiring it, then placing it carefully in the back of his drawer.

From upstairs he hears the clink of plates on the table.

"Ranjit! The food is hot!"

"Coming, Preetam," he says, but lingers on in the silent room for another moment. It seems strange that the pink bedroom has been left intact, but there are no photographs of Jojo anywhere in the house. *Stop it,* he tells himself. *This is too morbid.*

He walks to the bathroom and takes a quick shower, seeing that his shoulder is bruised a dark blue. He scrubs his beard and mustache and soaps his hands over and over, trying to wash away the smell of the dog.

For once they eat at the oak table in the bay window, laid with the Senator's fine china. Ranjit takes a big helping of steaming *rajmah* beans from a tureen, heaping it over a mound of basmati rice. There is also chicken curry, redolent with onions and the rich aroma of saffron.

Preetam watches him eat, smiling indulgently.

"This is fantastic. Where did you get the saffron?" he asks, his mouth half full.

"Oh, there's a cupboard in the kitchen full of Indian *masalas.* There's even mustard seed and cumin. Whoever owns this house must like Indian food."

He thinks of the peanut-butter-and-jelly

sandwiches he'd seen Anna eating during the summer, but doesn't correct her.

Shanti's face is beaming as she eats. "*Papaji*, have you seen Ocean Park? They took us on a field trip. It's so beautiful. There's a Christmas tree in the bandstand, and sparkly reindeers, and a green fountain made out of lights."

He smiles back. "They really take Christmas seriously here. Out by the Radio Shack, I saw two tractors decorated with Christmas lights."

She stops eating and sighs. "I love Christmas, *Papaji*. Too bad we don't celebrate it."

"What do you mean, *beti*?"

"Well, Mama told me that we're Sikhs, so we don't get presents . . ."

Preetam looks down at her plate, and he can see the strain in her face.

"Well," he says, "actually, Santa got here early. Some packages arrived in the mail."

Shanti's eyes widen. "Really? You're not kidding?"

"No, I'm not. Finish your dinner, and we'll see what he sent."

Preetam looks up at him and raises her eyebrows. He nods, *Don't worry, I've got it under control,* and starts to get up. "This food is so good, I'm going to get a second helping."

"No, no." Preetam takes the plate from him. "I'll get you some food. You're tired, you sit." As she passes his chair she gently squeezes his shoulder.

Shanti just stares when he brings in the boxes from the truck. Two are wrapped in shiny, striped-pink paper, and the third is a flat purple box with a turquoise bow.

"*Papaji,* we're not supposed to open presents till Christmas morning . . ."

"That rule doesn't apply to Sikhs. We can open our presents any time we feel like. The pink ones are for you."

Ranjit and Preetam sit on the couch, watching Shanti unwrap the first box, sliding her small fingers under the pieces of tape and carefully setting aside the shiny paper.

"Oh. Oh." She opens the box and lifts out a hot pink L.L.Bean parka wrapped in crackling white tissue. She rubs her cheek against the fabric, inhaling its new smell. "It's exactly the one I wanted, it has a fleece liner and everything. Thank you, *Papaji,* thank you."

She plants a wet kiss on his cheek and runs to the hall mirror to try on the jacket.

"The other box with the bow," he says softly, "is for you, Preetam."

"Me? Why did you spend your hard-earned money on *me?"*

"Open it."

Preetam tears open the wrapping paper, and inside is a black wool coat with a fur-lined hood, two pairs of pants, and three colorful wool sweaters.

"You can wear the pants when you go out," he says. "I know you didn't like wearing *salwar kameez* to the sewing group."

Preetam's eyes are sparkling. "They're beautiful, and the coat is so warm. I can go outside in this." She puts on the coat and pulls the hood over her head, so that only her nose protrudes.

"You look like an Eskimo, Ma," Shanti shouts.

"Don't listen to her. You look beautiful."

Preetam drops the hood and suddenly looks stricken. "And you, Ranjit? You didn't get anything for yourself? All you have is that dirty old coat . . ."

"Both of you are my presents. You are all that I need."

They come over and hug him and he's suddenly enveloped in a crush of wool and shiny acrylic.

The boxes have been stored in a corner, the ribbons and paper flattened and put away.

133

Shanti has taken her other present, a matching pink backpack, and gone downstairs to her room. Preetam starts to clear the dirty dishes, telling Ranjit to put his feet up and rest.

"*Papaji,* tuck me in, please." Shanti appears at the top of the stairs in her pajama bottoms and her new pink coat.

They go downstairs and he sits on the edge of her bed. "Hey, you can't sleep with that on. You'll get all sweaty."

She reluctantly pulls off her coat and snuggles deep into her blankets. There is a lump next to her, and he reaches under the blanket, drawing out the old, dark-faced doll. It is heavy and reeks of musty old cloth.

"I told you not to play with this. It's old, and it might break."

"*Papaji,* please, Rosie keeps me company when I sleep. I don't have bad dreams when she's with me."

"Rosie?"

"Yes, that's her name. She told me so."

Ranjit sighs. "Okay, but just for tonight. And put Rosie back on the shelf during the day." He bends and kisses her warm forehead. "Now go to sleep. I'll sit here for a few minutes."

"Merry Christmas, *Papaji.*" She sighs and turns onto her stomach. Soon her breathing slows and she's deeply asleep.

Upstairs in the kitchen Preetam is washing the dishes by hand — she is suspicious of the dishwasher — and he dries, standing next to her. He sneaks a glance at her as he wipes the last plate, careful not to crack the thin bone china. Her face is bright with happiness, and seeing her like this, it frightens him to even think of leaving this house.

When they are done the sleeves of her white cotton *kameez* are wet and there is a damp patch on her stomach where she has leaned against the sink. She looks at him, and he meets her gaze.

"Is Shanti asleep?" she asks in a whisper.

He nods, and together they walk down the stairs to the bottom of the house.

They sit on the side of the small bed, holding hands like teenagers, her soft, moist palm in his.

"How hard you've been working, Ranjit, your hands used to be so smooth, but now . . ." She turns her face to his, and he leans in to kiss her.

It has been so long that he has forgotten everything: the feeling of her small mouth on his, the scent of her hair, the soft skin at the back of her neck.

How could he have forgotten? He starts to

unbutton her *kameez* but she says, "No, no, turn off the light," and slips off the bed.

In the darkness he watches her pale silhouette as she lifts the *kameez* over her head. He pulls off his own clothes and unwraps his turban. Her skin feels cool — she was always cold, he remembers, even in the heat of summer — and he buries his face in the hollow between her neck and shoulder, inhaling her scent. *I'm home,* he thinks, *take me home,* but she stiffens in his arms.

It has been a long time, he tells himself, *she's nervous, be patient.*

Stroking her back, he feels her relax and lean in to him. This time, when he kisses her, her cool lips press back. He traces the contours of her breasts, her stomach, and her hips, his touch awaking hidden memories: the first time she had taken her clothes off, looking solemn as she stepped out of her red wedding sari. The years before Shanti was born, when each Sunday afternoon they would explore each other's bodies, then drowse together in the heat, their bodies stuck together with sweat.

He kisses her till she is ready, and then they are rocking together on the small bed, the ocean close by, its waves rising and falling.

When they are done, he remains on top of

her, inhaling the rich, clean smell of her hair. But she has been using Anna's shampoo, and he finds himself remembering how fiercely Anna had kissed him in her bedroom, the way she had felt under him, her strong arms locked around his back . . .

No. Don't think about that. That was one afternoon, an aberration. His life is here, with his wife and child.

Preetam must sense his mind drifting, because she whispers in the darkness. "What are you thinking about, Ranjit?"

He rolls off her and holds her hand. "Nothing. I'm just so happy that you're happy here."

"Thank you for the presents, Ranjit. I know how hard you've been working, and I know that I . . . I have been so cranky all the time. I'll try to do better —"

"Shhh. No need to apologize. It's been hard for all of us. I have a feeling that this next year will be better."

"Yes, I think so, too. Hold me."

She cuddles into him, tucking her cold feet against his warm legs, and quickly falls asleep. He remains awake, his thoughts drifting to Anna and her dead daughter. He can't help wondering whether Jojo had Anna's dark eyes, or resembled the Senator. To stop his thoughts, he slows down his breathing, feeling each breath fill his belly, then slowly leave his nostrils.

It begins to work. He is a child again, back at the Golden Temple in Amritsar. He and his mother have entered through the gate by the tall clock tower, and the din of the city fades away, replaced by the sound of water lapping against the edges of the sacred lake. He lags behind his mother, watching the Sikh men in loincloths wade into the lake, carrying their small knives tucked into the folds of their turbans.

He looks at the men's faces. Some of them have grizzled gray beards and bellies, but others are young and muscled, their beards as black as night. Do any of them look like his father?

He strains to find an image of his father's face, but all he can remember is the medal in its square box. *Pitaji* had died the year after he was born, and that date is inscribed on the Param Vir Chakra medal. Sometimes he'd open the box and stroke it, feeling its cold, metallic surface, and then read the words inscribed on its back: *To Major Khalsa Singh, for valiant courage in the face of the enemy.*

Ranjit's friends say that he should be proud, and he is, except that each time he comes to the temple and sees these men, he starts wondering about his father. Would he be a graybeard now, or would his hair still be dark?

Mataji turns to him, gesturing to him to hurry up. She has volunteered her services at the *langar,* the communal kitchen. As she walks she hums a verse from the Guru Granth Sahib:

> Even in a gale of torrential rain, I would go
>> to meet my Guru
> Even if an ocean separates them,
> A Sikh would go to meet his Guru
> As a man dies of thirst without water
> A Sikh would die without his Guru . . .

Ranjit watches a bather enter the waters of the sacred lake. Rings ripple through the water, growing larger, intersecting with others. He forgets all his troubled thoughts and merges with the peace and silence.

Deep into the night, he wakes suddenly, his heart hammering in his chest, ears straining to hear a sound. He hears Preetam's slow breathing and the crashing of the waves down below.

He has been dreaming again. He sighs, turns on his side, and closes his eyes.

Then he hears it clearly.

The sound of a car crunching over the gravel driveway, coming to a stop in front of the house. He is suddenly wide awake.

Floating down the hillside is the muffled sound of voices.

CHAPTER NINE

He lies very still, listening intently.

He cannot make out the words, but the voices are male, harsh and confident. They probably think that nobody is in the house, because his truck is hidden behind a stand of trees.

Tensing, he waits for the shattering of glass, the sound of the door being forced. Instead there is a click, followed by the *beep beep beep* of the alarm being turned off. The intruders are inside the house.

They have a key and the alarm code. *Is the Senator back?*

Ranjit pulls on his jeans and his army surplus sweater and walks to the base of the stairs, hearing the voices drift down.

"Hey, look at this place."

"Yeah, it stinks of money."

Not the Senator's deep rumbling voice. These are two white men. *Plaid-shirt and his brother. They have tracked him down.*

141

Returning to the bedroom, he slides his sheathed knife out from under the mattress. He remembers the dog lunging at him through the darkness, its fangs bared. *This time he'll give those bastards the fright of their lives.*

He puts a hand over Preetam's mouth and shakes her awake. "There are two men upstairs. Don't make a sound. Put on your clothes and wait here."

Her eyes are liquid with panic. "Ranjit, call the police."

"No police. I'll take care of it. Get dressed."

He slides open the glass door and walks silently out onto the deck. Stars twinkle in the night sky and the air is as sharp as a blade. It must be three or four o'clock.

The darkness is on his side as he takes the exterior wooden stairs up, three at a time, heading for the top deck. *First rule of combat: identify the enemy.*

Lights are blazing in the living room. All the men can see is their own reflection in the sliding glass doors, but he can see them clearly. They are definitely not Plaid-shirt and his brother.

Both men wear dark business suits. One man is dark haired and muscular, the other taller, with long hair so pale that it seems

142

almost white. They stand with their backs to him, studying the glass case of dolls.

Ranjit stays back in the darkness. *The men look official. Did the Senator send them? Whoever they are, they can't find him living here illegally.*

The taller man turns, and Ranjit sees high cheekbones framed by wings of long, white-blond hair; gold cuff links gleam in the sleeves of his white shirt, and he wears a black knit tie.

He turns to his dark-haired companion, his voice strangely garbled. "Patience, Joey. Don't go grabbing the first one you see —"

"Yeah, yeah."

"Look in the bedrooms. Downstairs."

The men head for the circular stairs in the corner, and Ranjit thinks of Shanti, fast asleep on the floor below. He skids down the flight of wooden stairs that connect the two decks, turns the corner, and knocks softly on the sliding glass door of Shanti's bedroom.

She sleeps on. He pulls out his knife, slips its thin blade into the doorjamb, and feels the lock pop. As he steps into the room the blast of cold air wakes Shanti.

"Hey, we have to go. Code Red."

"What, again? Seriously?"

"Seriously. Go."

She stumbles to her closet, pulls on her new pink jacket and her boots. She grabs something from under the covers and stuffs it into her backpack. Under a minute. *Good girl.*

"Take the outside stairs to my room. Your mother is waiting there. Take her to the truck, it's under the trees. Got it?"

Shanti nods, tosses the hair out of her eyes, and is gone.

He pulls up the bedcovers and throws her clothes into the closet, hearing footsteps coming down the corridor, the voices getting louder. He steps out onto the deck and, just in time, pulls the glass door shut behind him.

Hunkering down behind a deck chair, he waits.

The door to Shanti's room opens and a pale hand fumbles for the light switch. The blond man steps through the doorway and stops. For a moment Ranjit thinks he's been seen, but the man is looking at his own reflection in the glass door, and brushes a stray strand of hair from his forehead. He is so close that Ranjit can see his manicured fingernails and his finely tailored pin-striped suit.

The dark-haired man enters the room and yawns loudly. "Jesus, I'm beat. What do we

144

have here?" He hitches up his pant legs and crouches in front of a shelf of toy dolls. "This is fucking stupid. Which one is it?"

But the blond man isn't listening. He crosses to the bed and puts his palm flat on the bedcover.

"Joey. It's warm. Somebody's been sleeping here."

"What is this Goldilocks-and-the-three-bears shit? There's not supposed to be anyone here, man."

"Shut up. Feel this."

The blond man is already walking toward the glass door. He notices the splinters around the lock and reaches into his jacket. There is a gleam of metal.

The door slides open and Ranjit shrinks behind the deck chair, gripping its heavy metal frame with both hands. A white-knuckled hand appears, clutching a handgun.

There is no choice now, no place to hide. Lifting up the deck chair, Ranjit brings it down hard, and the gun clatters onto the wooden deck. There is a shout of alarm.

Ranjit turns and runs down the wooden stairs. There are frantic footsteps above.

"Get him, stop him!" The dark-haired man peers through the stairs, arm outstretched, trying to get a shot through the risers.

Ranjit vaults over the deck rail onto the terrace. He sprints around the empty swimming pool and across the brown grass of the lawn, heading for the dark outline of the shrubbery.

He's halfway there when there is the hum of an angry wasp and the dirt ahead of him explodes.

A silencer, he thinks, *they're using a silencer.*

He runs faster, the cold air searing through his lungs, then he's through the shrubbery. The branches scrape his face, and the tall bushes close behind him like a wall.

Another shot thwacks through the bushes, going wide, but he doesn't look back.

He's running up the hill, out of breath now. Did he park the truck facing inward or outward? *Please, Guru, let it be facing out.*

Lungs burning, he sees the truck, pointed toward the driveway, the pale face of Shanti in the front passenger seat. She sees him and turns the key in the ignition. *Good girl.*

The engine rumbles, chokes, and dies.

Ranjit gets in, twists the key again, and the engine roars to life. From the backseat Preetam is screaming something that he can't understand.

The truck roars into the first sharp curve and almost goes over. He fights the wheel, slams the truck around the next curve, and heads up the hill, into darkness.

CHAPTER TEN

The winding road through Aquinnah is a blur. Ranjit's truck is pushing eighty but the blue tungsten headlights in the rearview mirror never fall back. He senses a powerful car hanging behind him, biding its time. As soon as there is room to pass, it will surge past and cut him off.

The truck roars through the sleeping towns of Chilmark and West Tisbury and turns onto the Edgartown–West Tisbury Road. The road widens here, with a wide bike path running alongside it. The car behind growls and accelerates, preparing to pass. *Good.*

Ranjit skews the truck sideways onto the bike path and screeches to a stop, his seat belt tightening against his chest. He reaches out and kills the headlights.

A boxy white van hurtles past. At the speed it is traveling, it'll take a few minutes to stop and turn around.

He quickly backs the truck and turns onto a deeply rutted dirt track. Driving without lights, he takes each left fork, heading deeper and deeper into the brush. The few houses here are dark, their high slatted fences showing the outlines of sleeping horses.

Soon there are no more houses and the truck's tires slip on sandy soil. Stunted pines close in, their twisted branches scraping against the truck, and then the land suddenly opens up, and water gleams in the distance.

He reaches a large sign that says LONG POINT WILDLIFE RESERVATION — MAINTENANCE STAFF ONLY. A padlocked gate bars his way, but he just drives around it, crashing through the undergrowth. He'd come here with Jõao during the summer to do some illegal fishing and learned some poacher's tricks.

The truck jolts onto a dirt track, and he follows it, stopping under a stand of trees at the edge of Tisbury Great Pond. When he turns off the engine the *lap lap lap* of the enclosed pond fills the air, and beyond that is the dull roar of the open Atlantic.

Hah. They'd need a helicopter to find him here.

He looks around, suddenly aware that

Shanti is gripping her seat belt, a line of blood on her lower lip where she has bitten herself. Behind him Preetam is sitting stock-still, the hood of her new coat askew over one shoulder, crying silently, tears running down her cheeks and soaking into its plush collar.

As the adrenaline rush fades, Ranjit tries to think. *Had the Senator sent those men to retrieve something from the house? But why would they carry guns with silencers? Are they thieves, after Anna's doll collection? She had said they were valuable antiques.*

With the engine turned off, cold seeps into the truck. Preetam is still crying, and he turns to the backseat.

"Preetam, let me explain —"

She draws in her breath sharply. "Why did we have to run from that house? Why?"

He thinks back to the gun in the blond man's hand, a greenish-gray .45 Colt automatic. With the silencer, Preetam wouldn't have heard the shots.

She leans between the seats and looks directly at him, her face streaked with tears.

"I knew it was too good to be true," she says. "I knew it all along."

He tries again. "Just let me explain. There are these burglaries happening on the island —"

"If those men were burglars, why did we have to run away? Why didn't you just call the police?" When he doesn't answer, she continues. "No more lies, Ranjit. What are you trying to hide? That you took us to live in someone else's house? And they came back and thought *we* were intruders? Now they will call the police and you will be in jail. Again."

"Please, not in front of Shanti —"

"No. I *will* speak. All those years you were in prison, when everybody was spitting on your name, do you know what my father said? *Divorce Ranjit, he's useless. You're young, you can get remarried.* But I wouldn't listen to him. It was my duty as a wife to stand by you, so I *waited* for you, for three long years."

"Preetam, please —"

"Then, when you wanted to come to America, I did my duty as a wife, and I came with you, leaving my whole family behind. All of this, for *you,* so we could rebuild our lives. Then you go and take us to live in some stranger's house . . ."

He tries to reach out and hold her hand, but she pushes him away.

Shanti is shivering, her big eyes focused on Ranjit. "*Papaji,* you were in *prison*? Why?"

The army prison. He remembers the cold concrete floors and the smell of old sweat. Preetam had visited him just once, when Shanti was less than a year old. Despite the dark circles under her eyes, she had dressed up for the occasion in a white *salwar kameez.* Sitting across the scarred wood table from her, he could smell her perfume, and wanted to touch her.

She asked him again what had happened up there, and when he told her, she insisted it was a mistake. She asked if her father, the Colonel, could help in any way. He just shook his head. *Don't come back here,* he said. *Don't ever visit me here again.*

When they finally let him out, Shanti was almost four years old. She was singing to herself and playing in the garden, her dark curls bouncing. Seeing the tall, gaunt Sikh coming through the gate, she ran to her mother for protection.

Now Shanti looks up at him, and her voice trembles. "*Papaji,* why did you go to jail?"

"Something bad happened. Men died. I'll explain it to you when you're older."

"But it was a war, right? Men die in wars?"

Not like this, jaan, *not like this.* "It was a mistake. All a mistake —"

"Ranjit." Preetam's voice is tired and

152

faint. "I don't think I can stay here anymore."

"I think that's a good idea. You two go back to Boston for a while, and I'll sort out this mess —"

"That's not what I mean."

He feels suddenly sick to his stomach.

"I'm going to Lallu *Mama*'s in Boston, but I cannot go on like this. I cannot live with you any longer. It's just one lie after another."

"What . . . what are you saying?"

"I think we should live separately. I'm taking Shanti with me. I have to think about what I want to do." Preetam leans back, her lips pressed into a thin line.

"Papaji!" Tears spill from Shanti's eyes.

He holds his crying daughter, feeling the hot tears on his chest. He rubs her skinny, long back and tries to comfort her.

"Enough of this, Ranjit. Drive us to the ferry in Oak Bluffs."

The pink light of dawn is filling the sky and a gentle breeze makes waves on the surface of Tisbury Great Pond. There is a cry and a pair of loons flashes up into the sky, twisting and turning.

It is going to be a cloudless, sunny, beautiful day.

CHAPTER ELEVEN

The sun is still low in the sky when Ranjit drives up to the ferry terminal at Oak Bluffs. He has argued and pleaded with Preetam, but she returns again and again to their flight from the house, convinced that the owners had returned. There is no way he can tell her about the man with the gun.

Before she gets out of the car, she turns fiercely to him.

"I don't care how you do it, but I want you to get my wedding jewelry from the Senator's house. Don't bother bringing it to Boston. Call my uncle and he will come and get it."

She slams the door and walks away down the wooden pier, leading Shanti by the hand.

"Wait —" Ranjit swings down from the truck as they walk away. "Preetam, please listen to me. Just listen —"

The few walk-on passengers turn and

stare at him, then at Preetam. She walks onward, dragging Shanti along, her eyes red, the collar of her black coat stained with snot.

Ranjit knows what they are thinking: *Look at these foreigners.* He does not want to make a scene, and so he stays by the truck, his hands balled into fists.

Without a backward glance Preetam vanishes into the dark mouth of the ferry. Shanti pauses and gives him a small, solemn wave. Then she too, is gone. The last few cars drive into the ferry and the bow doors swing shut. With a loud toot, the boat surges away, leaving behind a wake of plowed ocean.

When they first boarded the ferry to come here, he held Shanti's hand, and they watched a school of tiny silver fish nosing through the water. He felt the warm, salty breeze on his face, heard the clanging bells of the buoys, and felt free. The island was his last hope. *He cannot let things end like this.*

One of the Brazilian ferrymen looks up from coiling hawsers, sees him still standing there, and says, "Mister, the next one is in three hours. You come back later, okay?" The man seems to be in a bad mood as he wrestles with the thick rope.

"The ferry was pretty empty today, wasn't it?" Ranjit says, just making conversation.

The ferryman stops his work and looks up. "Of course it's empty. Who the hell travels on Christmas Day?"

Ranjit nods. "Oh yes, of course." *Christmas.* He had forgotten all about it.

He returns to the truck and drums his fingers against the steering wheel as he formulates a plan.

If the men were professional thieves, the dolls are all probably gone by now; once they have what they want, they'll leave the island. He can go back and move his family's possessions out of the Senator's house, then mess it up to make it look like another break-in. Senator Neals is sure to have massive insurance coverage, rich people always do. And once he has found another place to live, he'll drive to Boston and convince Preetam to return. *Yes, that is what he'll do.*

He parks the truck in the brush along Lighthouse Road, scrambles down a steep stretch of hillside, and lies behind the tall shrubbery, watching the house.

It seems empty, its tall windows glinting blindly in the mid-morning sunlight; from here he can look right into the empty living room and even see the tall display case. Ten, then fifteen minutes pass, and his back feels as stiff as a board, but there is no movement inside.

The thieves have left the front door unlocked, and it opens with a push of his hand. Inside it is silent and dark, and the air is still scented with cumin from last night's dinner. He edges into the living room and stops abruptly. The cabinet is full of dolls, and he walks closer, seeing that there are none missing. *So what the hell did they come to steal?*

Running down the curved stairs to the lowest level, he enters their bedroom: it is as they left it, the sheets rumpled, Preetam's faded nightgown thrown on the bed. He pulls open the bottom drawer of the dresser and sees her flat red jewelry boxes; when he opens them, heavy gold necklaces and bangles fall onto the bed. *What kind of thieves leave jewelry behind?*

He sits on the bed, exhausted and confused, and just then his cell phone buzzes. *Preetam has cooled down and realized that she's made a mistake. Maybe she and Shanti are on the return ferry.* He quickly flips open the phone.

"It's okay, just come back and —"

"Ranjit? Hey, Ranjit?" It is a familiar coy, mellifluous voice.

"Celia? Sorry. I thought you were someone else."

"I haven't seen you for so long. Did you forget about me when you moved up-island? How is life as a bachelor?"

He slumps back on the bed. "Bachelor? Why do you say that?"

"My cousin works on the ferry, he saw your wife leaving." Her voice is low and teasing. "What happened, you two had a fight or something?"

He presses his thumb and forefinger into his eye sockets. "How many cousins do you have, Celia? They're everywhere."

"A lot."

"Well, your cousin is imagining things. Preetam's on a short holiday. What do they call it here? Vacation. Yes, she's going to Boston for Christmas."

"Oh, Boston." Her laugh is high and silvery. "That's what I thought. She always goes to Central Square in Cambridge, right? Her uncle has a store there? Well, listen. You're alone, and I'm cooking a big Christmas dinner. Roast turkey, *bacalhau, farofa.* You should come over."

Ranjit can imagine Celia sitting in her small office at Mike's Tow, her feet up on her desk, her short skirt riding up her long legs. He wants to shout, *Leave me alone,* and hang up, but he controls his voice. *Normal. Everything has to appear normal.*

"Thanks, but I'm working today."

"Oh, *working.* Even on Christmas Day, you're *working.* You need to relax, Ranjit. You'll have a heart attack."

"Listen, I have to go —"

"Hey, when you get a big new job, don't forget to thank me." Her voice is playful.

"What do you mean?" He shifts on the bed, feeling one of Preetam's wedding necklaces dig into his thigh.

"Two men came by this morning looking for you. They told me they need a caretaker for a big place up-island. I said that your wife had left for her uncle's place in Boston, and I wasn't sure if you went too, so I gave them your cell number. Now, when you make big bucks —"

He sits upright. "Men? What did they look like?"

"I don't know. Rich. Nice suits."

"Was one tall, with blond hair? Almost white?"

There is a short silence. "Yes. Hair like a *fantasma,* how do you say it, ghost? Why?"

"Oh my God." The thieves are looking for him. *In heaven's name, what do they want?*

"Ranjit? Hello?" Celia's voice is confused.

"What else did they ask you?"

"Only if you had a green card, if you were legal. I said to them, *Ranjit is hired by Senator Neals, of course he's legal.* Did I say something wrong?"

He takes a deep breath. "Celia, those men aren't looking for a caretaker. They just wanted information about me. If you see them again —"

"Oh my God, Ranjit, are they from U.S. Immigration? I'm so sorry, me and my big mouth . . . do you think they'll come back? Jõao has his green card, but me, no, I came here on a visitor's visa, and —"

"Just don't tell them anything. I'm sorry, Celia, I have to go now."

He hangs up. *Why would the thieves care about his immigration status?* He looks at the empty drawer and realizes with a sickening lurch that their battered red pouch is missing. Maybe it's in another drawer. He hunts through Preetam's faded underwear, his turbans and sweaters, but there is no pouch, and he stands stock-still, staring at the mess.

Inside the missing red pouch are three blue Indian passports with black-and-white photographs: in them Shanti is still a baby, Ranjit is wearing his army uniform, and Preetam is a young woman with a shy smile. Stamped inside each passport is a wavy red-

and-blue U.S. tourist visa, valid for a stay of exactly six months, and all these visas have expired.

The men who took that pouch now know exactly who Ranjit is. They also know that he and his family are illegal.

Think, Ranjit snarls at himself, *think.*

The missing passports can only mean one thing: that the thieves want to track him down. Why would they go to such great lengths? Breathing deeply, he remembers the men standing in front of the glass case full of dolls; then they had gone to Shanti's room to continue their search.

He runs up the stairs and peers into her pink bedroom: the bed has been stripped, the mattress turned over, and all the dolls from the shelves have been thrown to the ground.

Crouching down among them, he smells the sweet smell of old plastic: there are round-headed baby dolls, Barbies in miniskirts, even male Ken dolls with the smug expressions of small-town Romeos. Each one of the dolls has been stripped naked, then discarded. Pink plastic dolls lie on top of each other, their limbs entangled. *It looks just like . . . don't think of that now. Not now.*

He sinks down on Shanti's bed. Whatever the men were looking for, they thought it

161

was in this room.

What are the men going to do now? Celia has told them that Preetam has gone to her uncle's place in Boston, and that he has perhaps gone there too. The next logical move for them would be to follow him to Boston. And if they left this morning, they'll have a head start on him.

He looks at his watch. The ferry docked at Woods Hole an hour ago; Preetam and Shanti will now be on the mainland, driving away in Lallu's car.

He calls Preetam's cell phone and she must recognize his number, but she doesn't pick up, and he gets a recording.

"Preetam," he says. "Please call me back right away. You're both in danger. Call me, it's important."

Damn her stubbornness. He can take the ferry across, but what if the men are watching for him, either at the ferry terminal, or on the mainland? He rapidly dials Celia.

Her singsong voice answers on the second ring. "Hell-lo, Merry Christmas, Mike's Tow, you wreck it, we fix it. Can I help you?"

"Celia? It's Ranjit again."

Her voice turns warmer. "Hey, so you are coming over? You're not mad at me? You'll love my *farofa,* I make it with butter and bacon —"

"Listen. I have to get off the island today. Are you guys taking any wrecks across?"

She pauses, puzzled. "Today? Of course not, it's Christmas, Ranjit. Tomorrow, maybe. We have an old Cadillac that needs to go to the junkyard."

"I need to get to the mainland now. I can't just drive my truck onto the ferry, those men might be watching. Please. It'll take Jõao a couple of hours. Here's what I'm thinking . . ." He lays out his plan for her.

"Wait. Let me talk to Jõao." She speaks rapid-fire Portuguese, and when she returns to the phone her voice is flat and matter-of-fact. "Yes. Jõao will take you on the two o'clock ferry. I'm so, so sorry I talked to those men, Ranjit, I had no idea —"

He hangs up. Whatever happens, he has to get their stuff out of the house. He takes the duffel bag from the closet and fills it with all their clothes. Then he methodically cleans the house, wiping telltale black hair from the bathrooms. He scrubs the kitchen and sprays air freshener everywhere.

When he leaves, there is no trace that they ever lived there. The smell of cumin has been replaced by the artificial scent of peonies.

The sun is bright in the sky as Jõao's tow

truck drives slowly up the ramp of the ferry and into its dark maw. Swinging behind it on a hook is a red 1970s Cadillac Coupe deVille, its rear fins still gleaming, its chrome front grille staved in by a massive impact.

The ferrymen don't give the truck or the wreck a second glance. They shout Christmas greetings to Jõao and direct him deep into the dark hold. Ranjit lies on the floor of the wreck's backseat, covered by a prickly wool blanket.

When the tow truck is parked, Jõao switches off the engine, and Ranjit hears him clamber down and head to the top deck for a beer.

Lying still, Ranjit can feel the ferry rising and falling with the waves. His entire body aches and he wants to get out and walk around, but he can't risk it. He pulls the blanket off his head and breathes deeply, inhaling the strong smell of dried blood. Leaning forward, he sees that the driver's seat of the Cadillac is soaked a rusty brown, and its shattered speedometer is stuck at a hundred and ten miles an hour.

Engines deep below the deck begin throbbing and the ferry pulls away from the land.

Lying in the darkness, he thinks through his next steps: the ferry will get him to

Woods Hole in time for the afternoon bus to Boston, and he'll go straight to Lallu's store and make sure that his family is safe.

He feels his heart race as adrenaline begins to pump. Life suddenly loses its shapelessness and takes on the sharp velocity of an arrow in flight. It is a strangely familiar feeling, and then he remembers: this is the way he used to feel when he began a mission.

CHAPTER TWELVE

At twenty-one thousand feet on the Siachen Glacier the night sky is blue-black, closer to space than to the earth.

The Captain and his men have pitched their tent high up on the ridge, packing snow around it so that it is almost buried. The machine-gun fire that killed Dewan has been replaced by artillery shells that hammer down for hours. Suddenly, past midnight, they stop. It seems that even the Pakistani gun crews have to sleep sometime.

The men huddle around a map, listening to the Captain speak.

"This is the quickest route to the top." His finger traces a line up the steep eastern face of the Sia Kangri. "There are several places where we'll be exposed to enemy fire. We could take a longer route, but we might run out of rations. Personally, I'd rather take a bullet than freeze to death."

There is a murmur of assent, but after the

Captain has put the map away, the men can't even look at one another. Dewan was the mascot of the group, and losing him has spooked them.

Sergeant Khandelkar is huddled in the corner, his long priest's face etched with pain. He turns to the Captain and speaks softly, so that the others cannot hear. "Dewan was alive, Captain. He was still breathing when I cut him loose."

Khandelkar knows — as they all know — that Dewan is now dead, having drowned in snow, the icy fragments filling his nose and mouth.

The tent is full of the dead boy's presence. The Captain has to do something, fast.

He digs deep into his backpack and takes out a small bottle of Old Monk rum. Alcohol is forbidden at this altitude, but what the hell, they might not live long enough to regret it. He unscrews the top and raises the bottle, the amber liquid gleaming.

"To Dewan," he says quietly. "He sacrificed himself for us. We will find his body on the way back and take him home."

The rum goes down with a burn.

The men pass around the bottle, taking controlled swigs, wiping their mouths, saying *Aaaah.*

"To Dewan. May he fly on wings to

heaven."

In unison now, five voices speak, hoarse with exhaustion, blurred by alcohol.

"To Dewan. To Dewan."

The soldiers sit back, bleary eyed, but the mood has lifted. The tent fills with the thick fumes from their kerosene stove, mingled with the stink of unwashed bodies.

The bottle reaches Khandelkar. He drinks, grimaces, then turns to the Captain, his breath hot with rum. "We'll find the boy? We'll take him home?"

The Captain nods and gulps down another mouthful. "I promise you, Sergeant."

Khandelkar lowers his voice. "Sir, one more thing. We're the first Indian team to probe this area, right? But the Pakis seemed to be prepared. First the machine-gun post, then the artillery. It's almost like they were ready for us."

"Are you saying that the mission has been leaked?"

"Why couldn't they tell us what the target is? Who the hell was running the briefing, anyway? The officer at the back?"

The Captain thinks back on the briefing, run by two men from the Special Frontier Forces. They were young and arrogant, wearing uniforms with no insignia, dealing out satellite photos like magic playing cards.

Hidden at the back of the darkened auditorium was an army officer who had left halfway through the briefing, a flash of light illuminating the row of medals on his chest.

"I don't know who that officer was, Sergeant. Let's not worry about it now. Get some sleep."

But the Captain cannot sleep, either. He feels around in his backpack and finds a small photograph wrapped in plastic. By the faint glow of the kerosene stove he can make out the smiling oval face of his wife, a curly-haired baby in her arms. The photograph had arrived in a rare mail drop, and was six weeks old by the time it reached him.

The Sergeant's voice comes out of the darkness. "Don't worry, Captain. You'll see them again."

The Captain hurriedly puts the photograph away. He dozes for a few hours and wakes the men before dawn, before the artillery shells begin again.

Like ghosts, heads covered with white hoods, they begin the final climb. Their faint plumes of breath are the only trace of their earthly existence.

■ ■ ■ ■

II
MAINLAND

■ ■ ■ ■

Countless rulers who commit tyranny.
Countless cutthroats who commit murder.
Countless liars, wandering lost in their lies.
Countless sinners who keep on sinning.
Countless barbarians who eat their ration of
    dirt . . .

           — Guru Granth Sahib, Jup

CHAPTER THIRTEEN

The Peter Pan bus from Woods Hole to Boston is nearly empty. Ranjit sits by a window, watching the fields and woods fade away, replaced by strip malls and brightly lit fast-food places. As the bus lumbers over the Bourne Bridge to the mainland he glances at his watch: at this rate he won't get to Boston before dark, and if those men get there before he does . . .

To distract himself he flips through a crumpled copy of *The New York Times* lying on the seat next to him. As usual, the world is in disarray: Somali sea pirates have hijacked another oil tanker, the Palestinians and Israelis are at it again, and a predator drone in Afghanistan has killed the wrong people.

A small graphic on an inside page catches his attention. It is just an abstract triangle of gray with a dotted line below it, but he recognizes it instantly and grips the newspaper tighter. The triangle is the Siachen Glacier, and the dotted line under it is the northern border between India and Pakistan, ending suddenly at coordinate point NJ9842. When the border was hastily drawn in 1947, no one had bothered to extend it into the uninhabited, frozen wasteland to the north.

That wasteland, hotly contested now, is the highest battlefield in the world, its slopes and peaks changing hands as battles are fought and men die.

The headline over the graphic says "Global Warming Comes to a War," and the article continues:

The Siachen Glacier is claimed by both India and Pakistan. For over a decade, the two armies have fought each other here at altitudes over 20,000 feet. Soldiers on both sides have died in skirmishes and artillery battles, and been killed by avalanches and frostbite. Many others have suffered from high-altitude pulmonary cerebral edema, a leakage of brain fluid that leads to hallucinations and death. Now, adding to the list of killers is global warming.

Unseasonal temperatures have led to a sudden melting of the snow along the glacier, opening up a treacherous network of crevasses. Our correspondent in Leh reports that at the southern mouth of the glacier, the melting snow has swollen the Nubra River, which is threatening to overflow its banks . . .

Ranjit stops reading. *Sergeant Khandelkar had said that the snow on the glacier was melting. If he was just a hallucination, how could he have known that?*

Ranjit shivers as he shuts the newspaper. The past, long buried, seems to be coming alive, and there is nothing he can do to stop it.

The bus station in Boston is built in the air over the tracks of South Station, and as the bus climbs an elevated ramp, Ranjit has an airplane view of the city. The sun is setting, and the redbrick buildings of Chinatown and the glass skyscrapers of the Financial District glow in the fading light; beyond them is the gray loop of the Charles River, separating Boston from Cambridge. That is where Preetam and Shanti should be, in the apartment above Lallu's store.

Seeing the city again, he thinks of the two miserable winters he spent in that small, run-down apartment. It had snowed endlessly, and the city, crowded with ancient brick buildings, had seemed like a bad dream, populated by pale-faced inhabitants who spoke in a harsh, flat accent. When he left, he had sworn never to return, and yet here he is.

The bus lumbers up the ramp, and just as it wheezes to a stop Ranjit's cell phone begins to chirp. He grabs it, sure that Preetam is finally calling back, but when he checks the caller ID, he sees a restricted number. Hitting "Ignore," he waits for the call to go to his voice mail, but there is no message. The phone begins to ring again, loud and insistent, and he quickly silences it.

Who the hell is calling him? Remembering that Celia had given those men his cell phone number, he feels a surge of panic. What if they are waiting for him at the bus station? Quickly unwrapping his turban, he pushes it deep into his backpack and covers his topknot with a battered Mike's Tow baseball cap. He's now wearing a greasy blue mechanic's jacket that he borrowed from Jõao, but the cap and jacket are not much of a disguise. He will stand out in the empty bus station, and his only weapon is the thin sliver of steel in his boot.

"Hey, buddy. Last stop." All the other passengers have gone, and the bus driver sticks his head around the door, his face red with annoyance. "Move it, will ya? Some of us gotta get home. It's Christmas Day, for Chrisssake."

Nodding, Ranjit steps down from the bus. The glass doors of the bus station are straight ahead, but glancing around, he notices a metal door marked DRIVERS ONLY, wedged open with a folded newspaper.

The bus driver turns his back and starts talking to an old lady struggling with her suitcase. Ranjit takes a few long strides, goes through the "Drivers Only" doorway, and finds himself in a bare concrete stairwell littered with cigarette butts. He runs down the stairs and emerges at ground level, facing Chinatown.

A uniformed bus driver leaning against the wall and smoking is surprised to see Ranjit. "Hey, what the hell. That stairwell is only for drivers."

"No English."

Ranjit shrugs, smiles, and walks away, hearing the driver mutter *"Goddamn foreigners."* He crosses the road and heads down Beach Street toward Chinatown. Remembering that the trains will be running on a holiday schedule, he curses; instead of twenty minutes, it will probably take an hour for him to reach Cambridge.

Walking under a tall gate with a green-tiled pagoda roof, he enters Chinatown. After the emptiness of the Vineyard, he is shocked to find its narrow streets crowded with people, its restaurants open for business and full of customers.

He passes Cantonese restaurants, their windows hung with eyeless roasted ducks, and seafood places with tanks of sluggish white fish. Smelling roasting meat, he feels a stab of hunger, but there is no time to eat. Walking on, he passes sidewalk fruit stands where old Chinese ladies in Mao jackets hawk piles of kiwis, mangoes, and star fruit. The crowd thickens, elbows jostle him, and when an old man suddenly spits, Ranjit dances aside, the thick gob of phlegm narrowly missing his boots.

At the corner of Washington Street he sees the transient hotel that Jõao told him about, the one that does not check identification. The Garibaldi is a sooty yellow-brick building, its entry flanked by wrought-iron standards that once held glass light fixtures. Looking into the gloomy lobby, he sees a fake Christmas tree, its flickering lights illuminating a few men sitting on battered couches. Other slump-shouldered men stand on the steps and share a cigarette,

178

paying no attention to Ranjit as he passes.

He feels safe amongst the crowds of Chinatown, but he knows that the rest of Boston is different. The city is divided along racial lines: South and East Boston are working class and white, the Hispanics all live in Jamaica Plain, and the blacks are confined to Roxbury. A brown-skinned, bearded man in the wrong neighborhood will certainly stand out.

He enters the Chinatown subway station and walks to a far corner of the empty platform, tugging down the brim of his baseball cap. He looks down the dark mouth of the tunnel, hoping to see the lights of a train, but it is quiet, and the only sound is the squeak of mice scurrying across the tracks. Leaning against the cold wall, he wills himself to wait.

It is dark when he comes out of the subway entrance in Cambridge. Central Square is deserted on Christmas Day except for a few homeless people who stand in front of a 7-Eleven convenience store, scratching forlornly at their lottery cards. Next to it, a light burns in the shop window of Kohinoor Foods and Spices, illuminating a headless mannequin in a dusty yellow sari. Lallu's only concession to Christmas is a strand of purple tinsel strung across the doorway.

When Ranjit peers into the shop window he sees that it is empty, the cash register manned by Ricky, Lallu's nineteen-year-old son. As always, Ricky is nattily attired in baggy jeans and a tight red polyester T-shirt that matches his crimson turban. He strokes his wispy beard as he peers into a thin silver laptop, its cover pasted over with the stickers of indie bands; Ricky lives and dreams computers, and should be in college, but his father insists that he go to night school and spend his days at the store.

A thin woman with blond dreadlocks and a silver nose ring swishes past Ranjit and enters the store, her long cotton skirt dragging on the ground. She saunters through the aisles and examines the packages of incense, smiling shyly at Ricky, entranced by his turban and bulging muscles. *Some things never change.*

Ranjit still has his keys to the store and enters through a door in the alley, taking the stairs down into the dank basement. Having slaved down here for two years, he navigates easily through the darkness, walking past huge jars of mango pickle and sacks of rice. The musty smell reminds him of the hours he spent down here, sifting through the rice to remove dead insects. He'd often

180

find dragonflies, and once a mummified frog, transported all the way from India.

He climbs the stairs leading up to the shop and stops, listening for Lallu's booming voice, but there is only Ricky's unmistakable accent, half Punjabi and half American.

"So, yeah, this sandalwood incense is *real* good for meditation. If you like, I can come by sometime and show you how to meditate. It's *deep.*"

"Really?"

"I used to do yoga in India, you know. I used to meditate for, like, hours."

"Seriously? That's so cool. What kind of yoga do you like? Hot yoga or Hatha yoga or . . ."

Ranjit pushes open the door. He passes the humming refrigerated cases stuffed with frozen *chapattis* and *kulfi* and walks to the cash register.

Ricky looks up, stunned. "Ranjit *Mausa.* Ohmigod."

"Finish up with your customer. I need to talk to you."

Ricky hurriedly rings up the girl, giving her one last longing look. "*Mausa,* what are you doing here? Preetam *Mausi* says that she's leaving you and going back to India."

"That's just talk. She's angry. Now listen. Are they upstairs in the apartment?"

"No, no, my father took them to my house to get some clothes. They came here with nothing. Preetam *Mausi* won't tell me what happened —"

"I'll explain everything to you later. Right now I just need to talk to Preetam, calmly. I'll wait in the apartment upstairs. Do me a favor — don't tell your father I'm here. The last thing I need is for him to get involved."

Ricky smiles uncertainly. "Dad said that if you showed up, I wasn't to let you in. He was really angry. He said —"

Ranjit leans over the register. "Ricky, please. Your father didn't like me leaving the store, but I was dying in here. And what the hell are *you* doing behind the counter? You should be in school, full time."

"I know, I know. Sometimes my dad is a real pain, but what to do? He's my father and all . . . Okay, I'll keep my mouth shut. They should be back soon. You wait up-stairs." Ricky sighs and hands over the apartment keys.

"Thanks. You're a good kid." Ranjit reaches across the counter and pats the boy's shoulder. Returning to the staircase, he takes a flight of creaky wooden stairs to the small apartment above.

He enters it, smelling old carpet and mold and dust, and walks through the darkened living room to the bedroom at the back. It has one window looking out onto a brick wall, and a sagging bed with Shanti's new pink backpack lying on it.

Feeling exhausted, he sits down on the bed, moving the backpack aside. It is surprisingly heavy, and he pauses, trying to figure out what Shanti could have in there. He unzips it, seeing only a folded sweater, and almost zips it back up, but a glint catches his eyes. Pushing aside the sweater, he pulls out an old porcelain doll.

It is the ugly doll that Shanti found in the pink bedroom. He examines its dark painted eyes, its flat nose and exaggerated lips, and remembers how Shanti had pushed something into her backpack before they ran from the house.

The dark-haired intruder had squatted in front of the shelves in Shanti's room, staring at the collection of children's dolls. *Is this what he was looking for? Has Shanti inadvertently picked up something old and valuable?*

The doll scowls up at him. As he sits there, he hears the doors slam in the store below, followed by Lallu's loud and boastful voice; it sounds like he is coming up here. Ranjit's mind is a jumble of thoughts, and he shoves the doll into his own canvas backpack, tightly pulling the straps shut.

Just as he's leaving the apartment, he catches a glimpse of a calendar that he pinned to the wall when they lived here. It is illustrated with a picture of Guru Nanak in battle, seated on a rearing white horse, the curved sword in his hand dripping blood. Now the picture looks like a warning, and Ranjit wonders if he made the right decision by leaving the safety of this place. He hears Lallu's brash voice below, and a flare of anger goes through him. *Yes,* he decides, *better to do battle with the world than to hide from it.*

He hurries down the dark stairs and stops at the door to the store. Preetam and Lallu seem to be engaged in a long conversation, and he can't help listening.

Preetam's voice is so different, light and silvery with happiness. ". . . all these new clothes were not necessary. Really, Lallu *Mama,* you're so kind. I mean, we already owe you so much money . . ."

"*Aare,* it is nothing, my wife was happy to give them to you. And after all, you are my favorite niece, no? If that good-for-nothing husband cannot take care of you, I will."

Ranjit opens the door a crack and sees Lallu standing by the register, and Preetam preening in a new turquoise sari. Shanti stands sulkily to one side, a bright green *salwar kameez* draped over her arm.

"Shanti, thank Lallu *Mama* for your new clothes —"

"I don't want them. I like wearing my jeans."

"You ungrateful little girl. Thank your great-uncle."

Shanti shakes her head. "I won't wear them. They're ugly. I hate this green and —"

Preetam turns suddenly. There is the sharp sound of a slap, followed by Shanti's angry cry.

Ranjit feels the blood pound in his temples and pushes open the door a little more. Ricky spots him, looks terrified, and shakes his head, *No.*

Ranjit points to the alley outside and mouths, *Meet me outside.* Gritting his teeth, he leaves through the basement and walks into the dark alley. From inside comes the sound of more shouting, then Shanti's footsteps running up the stairs.

He forces himself to stay calm, though his fists are clenched, his nails digging into the palms of his hands. He has asked Preetam over and over not to hit the child, but when she gets angry, her hands fly out of their own accord. *What's a small slap?* Preetam

185

will say. *You want Shanti to grow up like these American children who show no respect for their elders? Better to be feared than to live without respect.*

The alley is dark and piss-smelling, its walls dense with looping graffiti. To calm down, he leans against the wall and tries to decipher the convoluted letters. A few minutes pass before Ricky steps out into the alley, wringing his hands, his smooth, handsome face clouded with pain.

"Ranjit *Mausa,* what the hell is going on?"

Ranjit steps forward and grips the boy's shoulders. "Ricky, can I trust you?"

"Of course. But what can I do? Preetam *Mausi* is pretty mad at you —"

"Listen to me. Someone is threatening us. Make sure that Preetam and Shanti stay upstairs, in the apartment. If two men come into the store — one of them is tall, very blond — don't say a word about them being there, just call me on my cell phone."

Ricky gulps. "Are you serious? Ohmigod."

"I'm counting on you to take care of them."

The boy nods uncertainly. "Yeah, okay. I've got the baseball bat behind the counter. Hey, where are you going?"

"I'll be nearby, don't worry. As soon as your father leaves, I'll come back and talk

186

to Preetam."

He squeezes Ricky's shoulder and walks away, the doll weighing down his backpack. Crossing the street, he looks back at the store, seeing lights go on in the apartment windows. Shanti is no doubt in there, her cheek red, crying her heart out.

At least they are both safe in the apartment. The only way up to it is through the store, and Ricky will be behind the counter till closing time.

He feels the weight of the doll in his backpack and wonders if the intruders were really after this old doll. If they call him again, maybe he can swap the doll for their passports. Senator Neals probably doesn't even know the doll is valuable, otherwise it would have been in the case, along with the others.

Now all he has to do is wait for the men to call.

Two hours pass, but Lallu does not leave the store. Ranjit sits in the Burger King across the road. He forces himself to eat a chicken sandwich, and drinks two cups of acidic, burnt coffee, but no one leaves the Indian store.

Burger King is about to close when he finally sees Lallu's shiny new Toyota pull out from the alley and drive away. Taking a deep breath, he walks across the road. Preetam has a terrible temper, but it usually burns itself out; if he can just convince her that the men were common thieves, maybe she'll agree to come back to the Vineyard.

He is almost to the other side when two white Chevy Tahoe SUVs zoom past him and pull up in front of the Indian store. They have navy-blue stripes across their sides, and gold federal eagles painted on their front doors.

Without thinking, he ducks into the 7-Eleven convenience store.

The door tinkles and slams shut. Inside, it smells of incense, and there are two Arab men behind the counter, an older one with bristly white hair and a dark-haired man in a sleek blue tracksuit. They both look curiously at Ranjit as he pushes past the newspaper stand and peers out of the plate-glass window. All he can see is the slice of sidewalk outside Lallu's store.

"Hello, my friend," says a voice behind him. "You come into my store, you buy something, okay?"

It is the old Arab. Without answering, Ranjit grabs a Snickers bar and slams it on the counter. Outside, men emerge from the vans, wearing bright blue uniforms with

188

black shoulder patches.

The young man in the tracksuit says something in guttural Arabic and slides out from behind the counter. All Ranjit can understand is the word "immigration."

"My friend." The old Arab's voice is soft and insistent. "You going to pay for this Snickers?"

Ranjit half turns, distracted, and the old man is looking straight at him with troubled brown eyes.

"My friend, your family runs the Indian store?"

"My wife's uncle. He owns it."

The man gestures outside. Ranjit turns, and a shout rises in his throat. Preetam is being pulled from the store, her turquoise sari slipping from her shoulders, two uniformed men gripping her by the elbows. Another man emerges holding Shanti's hand, and she follows him meekly, her head hanging down, a red bruise marking her cheek.

Ranjit's vision narrows to a dark tunnel. He reaches into his boot, feels the rough grip of the knife. Palming it, he heads toward the door.

He can take the two men who are holding Preetam. *But there are more in the vans, and what about Shanti?*

"My friend." The old Arab's voice is still soft. "What are you doing? If you walk out of here with a knife in your hand, they will shoot you down like a dog."

Preetam and Shanti are almost at the open doors of the van. *There are still a few seconds left* —

"That is the United States government out there. You understand?"

Ranjit stops at the door. The men out there have handguns, automatics. He'll die on the sidewalk with a sliver of kitchen steel in his hand.

The old Arab continues. "My friend, this is not the way. Get a lawyer and fight it in the courts. They think we are all terrorists, but there is still the rule of law in this country."

Ranjit's hands are trembling as he pushes the knife back into his boot.

The back doors of the SUVs are closing, the men climbing in beside Preetam and Shanti. *Guru, help me, help me now* —

Ricky runs out onto the sidewalk, weeping, a piece of paper clutched in his fist. "Hey, wait up! Listen to me. I'm an American citizen, I'm getting a lawyer —"

The uniformed men ignore him. Doors slam, and the SUVs pull a sharp U-turn and squeal back down Massachusetts Avenue, their red taillights growing smaller as they speed away.

Ricky stands shivering on the sidewalk, the piece of paper clutched in his hand.

The Arab man's voice is gentle. "Maybe you should exit the back way. That's where my brother went. His papers are not in order, either."

Ranjit looks around blindly. The door at the rear of the convenience store is swinging on its hinges.

"May God be with you." The old man's resigned brown eyes say that he has seen all this before.

Nodding wordlessly, Ranjit heads through the back door. He finds himself in a narrow brick alley lined with trash cans that stink of rotting meat.

His phone begins chirping, and this time he answers it.

It is a confident, calm voice, the words slightly garbled. "Mr. Singh. So you're answering the phone now?"

It is the voice of the tall blond intruder. Ranjit stops by the rear entrance to a butcher's shop and forces himself to speak. "Yes, I'm here."

"We just had your wife and daughter picked up by Homeland Security. As we speak, they're being taken to the Norfolk

County Correctional Center. They'll be held there, and thanks to the new laws, deported in ten days."

Through the screen door of the butcher's shop Ranjit sees a burly arm with a cleaver descend, splitting apart a shank of purpled flesh.

"That . . . that was not necessary. I was going to give you the doll —"

"You should have taken my last call, Mr. Singh. We're not fooling around here. If you hand it over, we can have the charges dropped against your family. They'll be released right away. You won't get an apology, of course. Those people never apologize."

Who in the Guru's name are these men? Stall them.

"I . . . I don't have it with me. I can give it to you tomorrow morning."

There is a silence, then a deep sigh. "We're not fools, Mr. Singh. I hope this isn't some bullshit delaying tactic."

"No, no. I'll give it to you. I don't want my family deported —"

"We know that you're in Boston. We'll call you at nine A.M. and tell you where to meet us. Or else your family goes back to India. And from what we've learned, you don't want that, right?"

192

"What do you mean?"

There is a faint chuckle. "We did some research, Mr. Singh. We know all about your illustrious military career in India. You certainly don't want your family to go back there, do you?"

Ranjit's head spins. *How the hell had they found out about him?*

"Oh, and one more thing. Don't try to contact the Senator. He's a busy man. We don't need to fill his ears with fairy stories, do we?"

There is a dry chuckle and the phone goes dead.

Breathing hard, Ranjit walks slowly down the dark alley, thinking about what will happen to his family if they are sent back to India. *"Sergeant,"* he whispers, *"help me. What do I do now?"*

A faint breeze blows down the alley, rustling stray newspapers and stirring up the smell of old urine.

"Is this my answer, Sergeant? Have you left me alone in this battle?"

The breeze blows stronger, and Ranjit lifts his head and sniffs the air; mixed in with all the other smells is something hard and clean, like the steel blade of a knife. It is going to snow soon, not just a snowstorm, but a blizzard.

As he emerges from the alley, still sniffing the air, he almost runs into a group of teenagers in dark hooded sweatshirts and combat boots. A tall boy with tattooed arms mimics Ranjit, raising his nose to the air.

"Hey, bro," the boy says, "you gotta stop sniffing glue. It'll rot your brain. Get some Colt 45 like the other bums."

The kids crowd around Ranjit, stamping their feet and slapping each other on the back. They have seen his grease-stained jacket and dirty baseball cap and assumed that he is one of the winos who hang around the 7-Eleven.

"Get the hell out of my way." Ranjit's voice is harsh, his hands balled into fists.

"Yo, we were just kidding. Relax, man . . ."

The kids step aside, and he walks away quickly, his face burning with anger. He walks fast all the way down Massachusetts Avenue, and by the time he reaches the Massachusetts Institute of Technology, he is freezing, the scar on his thumb beginning to throb. He needs to stop, to figure out what he's going to do next. After walking up the stairs of MIT's white neoclassical building, he enters its vast marble lobby. Slumping down on a bench, he tries to think through his next move, but all he can remember is coming here with Shanti.

She'd stood with him in this lobby, staring at the fluted columns soaring four floors to the curved dome above. They had walked through the long corridors, and he had pointed out the brightly lit computer labs crowded with Chinese and Indian kids. "When you grow up," he'd told her, "you can study here, become an engineer or a doctor. You don't have to work in a store like me."

Now she is gone, snatched away, and all he could do was watch. *What is he going to do now?*

One thing is clear: if those men have the power to deport his family, they can easily have him deported, too. As soon as he hands over the doll, he is finished.

He needs to get off the streets, to disappear. Thrusting his hands deep into his coat pockets, he heads back out into the cold. He crosses the Massachusetts Avenue bridge across the dark Charles River and heads toward Chinatown.

CHAPTER FOURTEEN

The overheated fifth-floor room at the Garibaldi Hotel costs thirty bucks a night. It barely has room for a metal-framed bed and a scarred wooden dresser, but at least it has a window with a view of Chinatown's rooftops. When Ranjit tries to heave it open, he discovers that many coats of white paint have jammed it permanently shut.

Giving up, he looks outside: as he predicted, it has started snowing. A thick layer already coats the rooftops, and the tall brick chimneys look like sentries, each wearing a white helmet of snow. Down below he sees a sliver of sidewalk, bright with reflected neon, where a group of elderly Chinese men wait for the evening bus to the Foxwoods Casino. They stamp their feet to keep warm, and their harsh, excited voices drift up to him.

He prays that there is a window wherever they have taken Preetam and Shanti. He has heard stories about the deportation centers, mainly old prisons, where two or three families are crowded into a single cell. There is only one break a day to go outside and see the sun, and as deportation looms, suicides are common.

Anxiety begins to bubble up, but he pushes it aside. He has to stay calm and think this through. After all, he has the doll, and the men desperately want it.

It sits on top of the dresser under a bare bulb, casting its looming shadow on the wall. He picks it up and examines its staring painted eyes, flat nose made of two whorls of porcelain, and cheeks puffed out like pillows. It is made to be a caricature but still manages to have the shrewd expression of a survivor.

When he pulls off its clothes, the brittle lace skirts leave faint crumbles on his fingertips. Its arms and face are painted dark brown, but the body underneath is shining white porcelain. *Could this ugly thing be valuable?* Unlike the dolls that Anna had shown Shanti, this one has no maker's mark, or any other clue to its origin.

He remembers the piece of paper clutched in Ricky's hand and decides to call him. He needs all the information he can get before he formulates a plan.

197

He's about to dial when he suddenly hears a cough, so loud that it seems to be coming from his own room. Mystified, he looks around: the room is tiny but high-ceilinged, and the scalloped plaster molding at the tops of the walls ends abruptly at the back wall. He realizes that this was once a much larger room, now subdivided, and that the wall by his bed is just a thin Sheetrock partition. Anything he says will be clearly audible next door.

Taking out his cell phone, he walks to the window and dials.

Ricky's querulous voice answers after eight rings. "Ranjit *Mausa*? Ohmigod. You don't know what happened after you left. They . . ."

"I saw it all." Ranjit keeps his voice flat. "Now listen. The men from Homeland Security. Did they leave a deportation notice?"

"A what?"

"I saw a piece of paper in your hand. What did it say?"

"Ohmigod, what are we going to do? Why is this happening?" The boy's voice quivers.

"Ricky. Get a grip. Find that piece of paper and tell me what it said."

"Okay, okay, it's here . . ." There is a shuffling noise. "It says, 'You are deportable under section 237 (a) 2(A)(iii) —"

"Skip that part."

"Okay, okay. '. . . you have been charged with illegally overstaying a tourist visa. The Department is serving you with this Final Administrative Removal Order without a hearing before an Immigration judge. You will be remanded to the Norfolk County Correctional Center and may be represented — at no expense to the United States Government — by counsel, authorized to practice in this proceeding. If you wish legal advice and cannot afford it . . .' "

"Does it say how soon they'll be deported?"

"Let me see . . . let me see . . . Oh yeah, here, 'You have the right to remain in the United States for fourteen calendar days so that you may file a petition for review of this order to the appropriate U.S. Circuit Court . . . If you fear torture in any specific country or countries . . .' "

"Enough." *The man on the phone had lied to him when he said ten days.* Not that another four days are going to make a difference.

In the background, Ranjit can hear Lallu talking on another line, using his outraged, bullying tone.

"Your father is back? What is he doing?"

199

"He is talking to his lawyer. You know, that guy, Mike Donohue, downtown."

Ranjit closes his eyes. Donohue is a small-time immigration lawyer who obtains specialty visas for cooks in Indian restaurants. He won't be able to do a damn thing.

"*Mausa? Mausa,* are you there? What are we going to do?"

"I need to think this through. Don't tell your father about this conversation. I'll call you as soon as I figure something out."

Ranjit hangs up and stares out of the window. The snow is falling faster now, erasing the sky, and powerful gusts rattle the windowpane.

He's safe here for tonight, but tomorrow the man with the strangely garbled voice is expecting him to hand over the doll. *Then what?* A bullet in his head, or a call that has him bundled into one of those white SUVs.

The only path of action left is to involve Senator Neals. If the Senator isn't aware of the value of this doll, he'll be glad to discover it now. He should call the Senator, explain the situation, and ask for help. *But it will mean telling the Senator about living in his house, and that part isn't going to go over well.*

No choice. He hunts through his wallet and finds the Senator's crisp business card.

200

He calls the number on it and a woman's voice answers instantly.

"Senator Neals's answering service."

"This is Ranjit Singh, the Senator's caretaker from Martha's Vineyard. I need to talk to him. Urgently."

"This is his *answering service.* Do you want to leave a message?"

"Please, I need to talk to the Senator. There is a huge problem with his house."

"What is the problem you are referring to?"

"I have to see the Senator personally. Tell him it involves his valuable doll collection."

The woman says, "Please hold."

He listens to the buzzing silence. When the woman comes back onto the line her voice is sharper. "Where are you now?"

"I'm in Boston."

"Wait." Silence again. Outside, snow is piling up on the windowsill, and Ranjit has the urge to force the window open and sweep it away with his hand.

The woman's voice clicks back in. "The Senator has a few minutes tomorrow before his official schedule begins. Seven-thirty A.M. Come to the JFK Federal Building on Cambridge Street. Check in at the lobby. I'll put you on the list."

"Yes, thank you, I appreciate —" The

phone goes dead.

He sits down on the creaking bed. Somewhere on the other side of the wall the coughing starts again, interspersed with gasping breaths.

He will just hand over the doll, tell Senator Neals the truth, and ask for help; surely a U.S. Senator has some influence with the immigration authorities? But will Neals believe his story, or think that he is crazy, and have him arrested for trespassing?

There is no choice now. Best to get some sleep and be ready for tomorrow.

He puts the knife on the floor beneath the bed, noticing that its rope handle has darkened with the dead dog's blood. Taking off his cracked boots, he strips to his undershirt and slides under the threadbare blue blanket. His long hair, unwashed now for three days, is beginning to smell musty.

He tosses and turns, listening to the person coughing next door. From other rooms down the hall he can hear the faint wail of music and the murmur of a television talk show. It occurs to him that once again he is alone, and in the company of men. When he checked in, he'd seen some men sitting in the lobby, playing cards by the light of the flickering Christmas tree, and they had looked up, their faces pale and listless. He's talked to such men in Central Square, and their stories all followed the same arc: drugs, jail, or divorce estranged them from their families and left them alone on the streets. It frightens him how easily families fragment in America, leaving the survivors isolated.

He lies on the hard bed, replaying the same scene over and over: the SUVs screeching up, the anguished look on Preetam's face, the terrified way that Shanti hung her head. *I will find a way to free them,* he tells himself, *and we will be together once more.*

The coughing in the next room continues. Past midnight he just can't take it anymore and bangs on the wall. The coughing stops briefly, and during the few moments of silence he slips into a deep, troubled sleep.

CHAPTER FIFTEEN

The sun is rising over the Siachen Glacier when the Captain and his men reach a sheer ice face. The Captain climbs alone, and his men wait for him to reach the top and lower a rope down.

No one else has ever climbed this route, but he doesn't let that thought cloud his mind. He focuses on the enemy target, which is very close now, somewhere up there.

It is so cold that his beard freezes from the moisture of his breathing. He wills himself to become an automaton, an extension of his two ice axes and the toothed crampons on his feet. He lifts one foot, drives the crampon deep into the ice, swings an ice ax, and anchors it above him. Pulling himself up, he finds another foothold, then swings the second ice ax and repeats the motion.

The carabiners in his belt tinkle with each

move. Every hundred feet or so he stops and checks the ice, and if it is firm, he chips a hole and twists in a long ice screw. Clipping a carabiner to the screw, he slips his climbing rope through it, and establishes one more point of connection to the mountain. If he falls from this height, the last belay point will catch him and leave him dangling in the air. In theory, he will be saved, but he knows he is too tired and frozen to scrabble back to the cliff face.

His mind grows mercifully blank. There are no thoughts of Private Dewan or of the mission, nothing except him and the mountain. He climbs to the howling of the wind and the *chip chip chip* of his ice axes.

It takes him over three hours to reach the top.

He is the first man to climb this route, but there are no flags to plant, no pictures to be taken. Hauling himself over the edge, he lies on his back, and the sun shines into his face and blinds him. His awareness of the mission returns, and he wishes that he could leave this mess behind and just keep on climbing upward, climb right into the thin blue sky . . .

Twisting his body, he looks down the other side of the mountain. On a ridge directly below is the enemy post, very close

to the coordinates given to him at the briefing.

After all this secrecy, he has expected the
enemy outpost to be something elaborate,
but it is simply a long slit trench covered in
gauzy white camouflage netting. At one end,
sandbags surround a long-barreled artillery
piece, and at the other end are three fiberglass igloos and a lavatory tent. From up
here he can see men scuttling around the
gun, and then it recoils. It takes a second
before he hears the boom and sees the shell
arcing out into the air.

So this is what the fuss was all about: a
hidden artillery position.

The Captain sits up and hammers both
axes deep into the ice. He hauls up a thick
rope and knots it firmly over the ax heads,
tugging to make sure that the anchor point
will hold. Using this guiding rope, the men
climb up slowly, arriving one by one. Two
hours later, the last man is Sergeant Khandelkar, blue-faced and wheezing.

The Sergeant squints through his binoculars and then lowers them disgustedly. "Too
far away, sir. Can't really see those bastards.
Should I radio in for confirmation?"

The Captain knows that all their radio
frequencies are monitored by the Pakis.
Within minutes of breaching radio silence,

the post below will be alerted. And if they manage to swivel that gun around before the jets arrive . . .

"That post is the only damn thing in the sector they gave us. Call in the air strike."

Khandelkar pauses. "Sir, permission to take the radio and climb down two hundred meters before calling it in. If they pinpoint the transmission, at least they'll be firing too low."

"Sergeant, I can't allow that, it's too dangerous."

"Sir, we cannot risk losing you. You are the only one who can get the men back down. Me, I'm expendable."

The Sergeant is right, as always. "All right, but don't get too close. The planes will bomb the whole ridge."

The Sergeant climbs down slowly, the radio strapped to his back, and soon his snowsuit merges with the white of the mountain.

On the post below, the enemy soldiers are oblivious. One of them heads to the latrine tent, and the Captain's men chuckle when they see this.

"Poor bastard," a soldier says, "one moment he's taking a shit, the next moment, he's dead. Hope he's done by then. I'd hate to die in the middle."

"They killed Dewan, they deserve it," another says quietly.

They wait, heads down, watching the post through binoculars.

Above them snow blows off the ragged peaks of the Sia Kangri and clouds flit through the sky, casting patches of shadow that alternate with sparkling sunshine. Existence up here is reduced to light and dark, to something elemental; no wonder the Hindus believe that these mountains are the abode of the gods.

Their reverie is broken by the hum of engines. Two planes fly in from the east, silver specks high in the blue sky.

The men grow tense. Knowing Sergeant Khandelkar, he will have crept as close as possible to the enemy position, and the Captain prays that he will be spared by the falling bombs.

The Jaguar jets are now clearly visible, long-nosed missiles slung under their stubby wings.

The enemy base below seems unconcerned. Their encampment merges easily with the rock and snow, hiding them from high-flying planes; jets from both sides probably fly over them regularly, unaware of their existence.

Without warning, the Jaguars launch their

missiles. The men at the post stop and stare upward. A man runs out of a tent and waves his arms above his head, signaling, *Air attack, air attack.*

The missiles swoop straight down, guided by invisible lasers.

The Captain and his men press their faces into the snow. The first missile misses the target and detonates against the mountain, making it rumble.

The second missile hits. There is an enormous wallop and the men can't breathe for a second. When they lift their heads the post below is a charred mess. A giant's hand has picked up the artillery gun and bent its barrel, and the lavatory tent has plunged into the depths. The Captain wonders what happened to the man inside it.

The jets circle like hawks, then break free and streak off over the horizon.

It has taken less than a minute, and when the smoke clears, the mountains gleam serenely.

The Captain rises, shaking off snow. His men arm their weapons and they climb down cautiously, finding Khandelkar crouched in a hollow, dazed and deafened, but alive.

"We got those bastards, Captain. Wiped them clean."

The Captain nods, but he is taking no chances. One surviving Pakistani could machine-gun them all. He sends the three men around in a flanking maneuver, and Khandelkar joins him. They advance slowly, assault rifles held ready.

"I've never seen a dead Pakistani up close," the Captain says.

"They look like us," the Sergeant replies, "no different."

Right by the scorched gun — the Pakis must have been trying to turn it around — are a pile of corpses. They have been killed by the massive impact, twisted and thrown like rag dolls, men lying on top of other men. Some are barefoot, their boots blown off, while others stretch out their arms in grotesque gestures of welcome.

Khandelkar stops first, the Captain right behind him. They see it at the same time.

The grizzled face of an old Sikh, turban unfurling, graying beard clotted with blood. His snowsuit has been torn open at the neck, and inside is a khaki uniform. He is a Sergeant in the Second Kumaon Battalion of the Indian Army.

Khandelkar's face crumples, like that of a child about to cry.

The Captain walks forward like a sleep-walker. He turns over the other corpses, finding more Indian Army uniforms.

"Our own people? How could it be?" Khandelkar demands an answer, but the Captain doesn't seem to hear him.

The Sergeant slumps to his knees, throws down his rifle, and shuts his eyes tightly, as if praying. The Captain walks on, mechanically counting the blackened bodies. Sixteen, all dead, no survivors.

He should have radioed, he should have checked. He's disobeyed the first rule of combat: *always identify your enemy.* When he looks back, Khandelkar is still on his knees.

"Sergeant, I . . . I . . . can't believe . . ."

The Sergeant reaches up and shoves the barrel of his assault rifle into his mouth.

The Captain starts to run.

One shot. Sergeant Khandelkar's head jerks backward.

The white snow is stained with red.

Chapter Sixteen

Ranjit wakes with a start in his room at the Garibaldi Hotel. Outside an amplified voice booms out, *"Snow emergency, snow emergency. All parked cars will be tagged and towed."* He gets out of bed, listening to the *scrape scrape* of shovels digging out.

The window shade springs upward with a snap and the room fills with blinding light. The snowstorm is over, and an orange snowplow moves slowly through the street below, pushing high banks of glittering snow to either side.

Looking up into the clear, cold sky, he remembers that Preetam and Shanti are gone. He takes a deep breath, and then another, fogging the panes of glass, till the world outside is obscured with mist.

There is no time for this. He must be on time to meet the Senator.

When he's dressed he takes a chair into the bathroom and looks up at its dropped ceiling. He lifts one square of ceiling tile from its metal grid and sees the original ceiling high above, the tops of the walls patterned with faded silver-and-blue wallpaper. Stashing the doll and his knife above the ceiling, he carefully replaces the tile. A cursory search of his room will reveal nothing.

Leaving, he hears the sound of coughing and glances through his neighbor's open door. A man sits on a metal chair in the corner of a windowless room, peering through steel-framed glasses at a thick book. He starts to say something, then begins to cough, spattering the open pages with spittle.

Ranjit stops in the doorway. "Are you okay?"

The man struggles for breath. "Yeah, yeah, I'm fine. I said, I hope I didn't keep you up last night. With all the coughing."

In the hot, stale air of his room, the man wears a white T-shirt that shows off a surprisingly muscular torso, and loose cargo pants. His iron-gray hair is long, brushed straight back, curling around his ears.

"It's not your fault. The walls are pretty thin in this place." Ranjit looks down at his watch: six thirty, an hour to go before meeting the Senator. He nods and turns to go.

"Hey. You're ex-army, right?"

Ranjit turns in surprise.

"How did you know?"

The man looks up at him, a smile creasing his round face. "Takes one to know one. Whose army? Not ours?" He takes a Snickers bar out of his pocket, unwraps it, and begins to chew.

Ranjit stalls. He looks around the man's room. It was once the rear part of his own room, with the same ornate molding high up on the walls. There is a bed in the corner, made with sharp hospital corners, and an open closet with a pull-up bar. On the dresser is a pile of library books, and a small golden Buddha, surrounded by sticks of incense and a single orange in a bowl. The air in here smells like stale incense, and something else, bitter and medicinal.

Still stalling, he leans against the door frame. "How about you? Were you in the American military?"

"Me? I was in 'Nam."

Ranjit nods. When he worked at the store, half the winos in Central Square claimed to be Vietnam vets, Marines or Special Forces; it was an easy way to get some sympathy.

"Oh, really, Vietnam? You were in the Marines, I suppose?"

The man smiles a twisted smile. "Marines?

Me? Hell, no. Eighteenth Engineer Brigade. We built ammo dumps, bridges, roads, we built the airfield at Qui Nhon. We weren't even supposed to see combat, but I got Agent Orange in my lungs. Not that it matters. The VC didn't take too kindly to me. They got my legs, too."

Looking down, Ranjit notices the man's legs hanging uselessly, and the folded wheelchair leaning against the wall.

"No big deal." The man smiles his twisted grin. "At least I got back to the World. Most of my buddies didn't make it. They're fertilizing rice fields back there . . . So where did *you* serve?"

Taking a deep breath, Ranjit answers.

"Captain in the Indian Army. Sixteenth Punjab Rifles, seconded to High Altitude Special Frontier Forces."

"Ah, a captain. Real bad boy, eh? So, were you in the shit? Or behind a desk, nice and safe?" The man doubles over, his body shaking with a series of rasping coughs.

Ranjit smiles. It sounds like something that Khandelkar would have said. "Oh, I was in the thick of things, no doubt about that." The man is still coughing, his face turning purple with the effort. "Hey, you're sure you're okay?"

"Sure, sure, I'm fine." The man gasps for

breath. "Just out of candy bars. There's a machine in the basement, but the fucking elevator is out. Shouldn't complain, though. At least the developers haven't bought up this place, turned it into condos. Then where would I be?" He laughs a raspy laugh.

"Nice talking to you. I'm in a bit of a hurry right now . . ."

"Go ahead, Captain. Sorry to have kept you waiting." With a hurt expression, the man picks up his book and starts to turn the pages.

Ranjit pauses. "Listen, the vending machine is probably expensive. I can stop by a drugstore later. What kind of candy do you like?"

"Snickers, the super-size ones. A bag would be great. Thanks, man." The man starts to take money out of his pocket, but Ranjit waves it away.

"On me, but I need a favor. Can you keep an eye on my room? I don't want anything stolen."

The man nods slowly, his eyes magnified by the bottle-thick lenses. "I know everybody in this joint. They're punks. They won't touch your stuff if I'm around."

Ranjit raises a hand in farewell and heads down the stairs. He is halfway through the lobby when he realizes that he didn't ask the man his name.

Outside, a cold, thin sun is shining down, and the silence is broken only by the whine of cars trying to get out of snowed-in spots. Ranjit moves quickly through the narrow, icy streets, passing old Chinese ladies who have cleared small patches of snow and set up their fruit stalls. With their scarves wrapped around their heads and plastic bags on their feet, they remind him of Indian peasants.

It is freezing today, at least ten below zero. His blue mechanic's jacket isn't insulated, and as he nears the Park Street subway station, he craves a cup of steaming hot *chai*. Ducking into a Dunkin' Donuts, he waits in line with Bostonians who order coffee and jelly-filled donuts. When he reaches the counter they are out of teabags, so he gets coffee and a cruller instead. He hungrily eats the sweet dough, but the acidic coffee disgusts him, and after a few sips, he throws it away.

Tremont Street turns into Cambridge Street, which leads to City Hall Plaza. He knows that old Bostonians still call this area Scollay Square, but the old neighborhood was demolished in the 1950s and replaced by a vast, windswept brick plaza circled by government buildings. He walks across the empty plaza, passes the concrete city hall, and heads for the JFK tower. The Senator's office is up there, on the tenth floor of the squat, weathered high-rise.

Waiting to cross the street, Ranjit watches traffic creep around a telephone pole that has fallen into the street. A Verizon van pulls up and three men in fluorescent safety vests arrange orange cones around the tangle of wood and wire.

The light changes and he crosses to the JFK tower. It was built in the sixties, back when wide-open glass lobbies were modern and daring, but the threat of terrorism has now surrounded it with a maze of concrete blast barriers. Weaving through them, he enters a large echoing lobby and steps through the portal of a metal detector, thanking the Guru that he'd left his knife behind.

The guard manning the metal detector is an African, his cheeks marked with parallel tribal scars. He examines Ranjit's backpack thoroughly, then stares at him, taking in the greasy blue jacket and baseball cap.

"What's your business here? Which floor you going to? Homeland Security?"

Following the guard's pointing finger, Ranjit looks at the board across the lobby and realizes, with a shock, that the offices of Homeland Security are indeed on the sixth floor.

"No, sir. I have an appointment with Senator Neals."

"Senator Neals? You on the list?"

Ranjit spells out his name, and the guard tells him to wait. He stands to one side, watching bureaucrats swarm through the turnstiles, identical in cheap gray suits, their polished black shoes squeaking on the granite floor.

"Singh, you're on the list," the guard says grudgingly, motioning Ranjit through. "Take that elevator, in the corner."

Ranjit walks over to an elevator marked PRIVATE and punches the button for the tenth floor. As the cab lurches into motion he rehearses what he'll say to the Senator. *Sir, something strange happened. You have to believe me when I say . . .*

The elevator slows at the third floor and two men in badly cut gray suits get on. They have the pink, over-barbered look of career government officials. Glancing at Ranjit, they move into a corner and continue their conversation.

". . . so how are the numbers looking?"

"This year? Tough, always tough. You know how it is."

The floor numbers above the door ding as the elevator speeds upward. *Five, six, seven.*

Ranjit thinks of the Senator's face darkening with anger when he learns that there is nothing wrong with his house. *Eight, nine.*

The elevator starts to slow when the bureaucrats in the corner move toward Ranjit. He steps back politely, glancing downward, and notices that the two men are wearing thick-soled brown work shoes, encrusted with mud.

He looks up and discounts the suits. He sees that both men are powerfully built, that they are still talking to each other, but their eyes are trained on him. *Is he imagining things?*

Ten. A slight jerk as the elevator stops.

The elevator doors open, and a man blocks his path, a tall man with blond-white hair curling over his collar.

Ranjit stares in shock. The two men in the gray suits grab his arms and jerk him back into the elevator. The blond man steps into the elevator and jabs a gun hard into his side.

"Nobody will hear the shot, Mr. Singh. Your body will muffle it. To be precise, your kidneys." His voice is arrogant and slightly muffled, the same voice Ranjit heard on the phone last night, the same voice he heard at

220

the Senator's house. *What the hell is this man doing here?*

"Do you hear me?" The barrel of the gun pushes into Ranjit's kidneys, and he gasps as his arms are twisted behind him.

"Yes. I hear you." The blond man presses a button for the basement and the elevator falls like a stone.

Ranjit stares at the man: he has the Nordic cheekbones and icy blue eyes of a ski model, but his white-blond hair and translucent eyebrows give him a strange, ill-defined air. Today he wears a black double-breasted blazer and a pink silk tie.

"The Senator," the man says slowly, "asked me to tell you how disappointed he is. He is a big-hearted man, but when you move into his house and take his possessions, well, he doesn't like that at all."

With his free hand the man tugs a strand of hair over his ear, and Ranjit glimpses the curled pink plastic of a hearing aid. Suddenly the man's garbled, deliberate diction makes sense: it is the voice of a person who can barely hear himself.

Ranjit's voice is ragged. "You work for the Senator? I don't believe you."

"Is that so. The Senator told me about that smart little daughter of yours. He said she was going to be a lawyer one day . . ."

Ranjit feels a sudden sickness in his stomach.

". . . and we did a little research on you, too. A former Indian Army captain shows up in the Vineyard, makes his way to the Senator's house. I told him he shouldn't have hired you without a background check. But he was tired, he made a mistake."

"I have no idea what you are talking about —"

"Look, Mr. Singh, I don't give a rat's ass who you are working for. We just want the contents of that doll back, okay?"

Ranjit suppresses a flicker of excitement. *There is something hidden inside it.*

The elevator slows, and the doors open onto a dark underground car park. The men push Ranjit out, still gripping his arms, and sensors click, turning on blue fluorescent lights.

"Search him. Thoroughly. I'm sure he brought it."

One of the gray-suited men holds Ranjit's arms while the other rifles through his backpack and his pockets.

"He doesn't have it."

"You're smarter than I thought. Where the hell is it?"

Ranjit knows he needs to get out of the

garage. "At my hotel. Ten minutes from here."

"We'll go now and get it. Which hotel?"

"The Marriott, in Copley Square." Ranjit chooses the biggest hotel he can recall, and makes his voice soft with defeat.

The blond man turns to his men. "Where's the van?"

One of the gray suits answers, "There was too much snow. It's parked on the street."

The blond man turns to Ranjit. "You can walk up this ramp, or we'll just break both your legs and carry you up. Your choice."

"I'll walk."

The blond man is ahead of Ranjit as they walk up the spiraling ramp and the other two flank him. Their footsteps reverberate against the raw concrete walls, and motion-activated lights flare on ahead, then blink out behind them.

In a few minutes they emerge out into a loading bay, cut off from the road by a high bank of snow. Across the road, a white van pulls up behind the Verizon truck and puts on its hazard lights. *The same van that chased him on the Vineyard. Once he gets into it, he's dead.*

"Ah, there it is. We're crossing the road. All of us, together." The blond man's gun hand disappears into his pocket.

When the streetlight turns red, they all clamber over the bank of snow and start to cross the icy road.

There is a sudden whirring sound and the telephone pole lying in the road begins to rise, hoisted up by the long arm of a mechanical winch. It is soon upright and wavers in the sky, casting its long, purple shadow across the white snow. Three workers pull on thick ropes attached to the pole, stabilizing it, while a fourth bolts it into the sidewalk with long metal angles.

And right by the pole there is a sudden shimmer of light. Sergeant Khandelkar appears and raises one thin hand, pointing three fingers downward, making a tripod. His image quivers for an instant, then disappears.

What the hell? Ranjit blinks, but then he understands what to do. There will be a few seconds when the winch disengages, and the pole will be held in place by the three men with their ropes. The force of each man will counterbalance the others, making a perfect tripod.

They reach the other side of the road and walk alongside a high snowbank. The blond man is walking behind now, so close that his breath is warm on the back of Ranjit's neck. One gray suit walks ahead of Ranjit, and the other is alongside him, pushing him against the snowbank.

The piled snow gives way to a shoveled-out patch where the Verizon crew is at work. Just as they draw alongside, the winch holding the pole upright disengages with a whine and the three workers grunt as the strain is transferred to the ropes they hold.

Ranjit lunges sideways, slamming into a burly worker in a safety-orange vest. The worker falls, the rope slipping from his hands.

"What the . . . fuck, watch out!"

The telephone pole leans sideways and the other two workers are jerked forward. All stability gone, the pole begins to fall, its dark shadow hurtling down.

One gray suit walks right under it. Ranjit hurls himself out of its path, falling onto the blond man behind him. The pole slams into the second gray suit's shoulder, sending him sprawling. It hits the ground with a sickening thud, inches away from Ranjit.

Under Ranjit the blond man curses and scrabbles to free the gun in his pocket. Pushing him away, Ranjit levers himself up, his feet sliding in the snow. Two security guards are running across the road from the JFK building, and the fallen pole blocks his path ahead.

He turns and runs down Cambridge Street.

Cold air sears his lungs and his feet slip and slide. He sprints through an intersection, a blur of motion, rapid thoughts running through his head: the street is too wide, too open, lined with office buildings.

He turns suddenly up a steep cobbled street into residential Beacon Hill. Sprinting up the brick sidewalk, he passes gas streetlamps and tiny, elegant brick row houses with black shutters. The nineteenth century has been preserved up here, the cobbled streets so narrow that the sun hardly reaches them, and the brick houses are crowded together, their granite steps dimpled by centuries of use.

Turning right and then left, he makes his way up the hill. He listens for footfalls behind him, but there is silence, and by the time he reaches Pinckney Street he slows to a walk. The doorways in this exclusive neighborhood bristle with the snouts of security cameras, and a running man will soon be spotted.

Where can he go? From far down the hill he hears sirens, ambulances or police cars, moving toward the JFK building. Best to head toward the river, where there is a subway station and the huge Mass General

Hospital. He walks rapidly down the street, passing an empty Laundromat and then a tiny corner store, his heartbeat slowing. A white van barrels across Pinckney Street and slams to a stop.

Damn it.

The blond man jumps out and sprints toward him. Ranjit takes a deep breath and runs again, ducking into a side alley. It turns and twists, and soon he is completely disoriented, the blond man's footfalls right behind him. Slowing to look over his shoulder, he skids on a patch of ice and his feet slip under him. He falls, and the blond man catches up. A fist hits out, knocking off Ranjit's baseball cap, and fingers like talons sink deep into his topknot, grabbing his hair. The hard muzzle of a gun jams into the back of his neck.

"Enough of this bullshit."

Yanking Ranjit's hair from behind, the blond man pulls him to his feet.

Ranjit complies for an instant, then lowers his head and twists away. He feels a sharp pain as his hair rips from his scalp, and the blond man falls backward, clutching a handful of long black hair. His shoulder slams hard into the cobblestones, and a flesh-colored hearing aid spills from one ear.

Ranjit kicks the gun from the man's hand,

and it skitters away into the darkness.

The blond man lies on the ground, his pink silk tie skewed across his chest. His shoulder is unnaturally high — dislocated or broken — and he looks up at Ranjit, stifling a moan of pain.

"You're dead. You and your fucking family are *dead*."

There are sirens coming from below, and the sound of shouting. Ranjit looks around for the gun, but it has vanished into a tangle of old lumber and discarded window grates.

"You think you can run? We'll find you —"

Ranjit doesn't wait to hear the rest. The sirens are getting louder now. He picks up his baseball cap and jams it onto his head. He runs again, arms pumping, feet slithering on the ice.

By the time he reaches Louisburg Square at the top of the hill he can barely breathe. It is bright up here after the narrow streets below, and the tall, bay-windowed town houses face a rectangular park surrounded by high iron railings. A white-haired woman in a fur coat stands inside the park, cooing at a small Pekingese, and as Ranjit slows to a walk, the dog runs to the railings and barks at him.

The woman reaches down and scoops the

dog into her arms. "Shush, Princess, shush. That scary man can't get in here."

Scary man? What is she talking about? Touching the back of his head, his fingers come away red and sticky; his scalp is bleeding badly.

He runs again, diving into the network of back alleys that meander down the other side of the hill. Turning into an alley just wide enough for a person, he follows its twists and turns, looking for a place to hide, but all the parked cars are locked, and the houses are all alarmed.

He stops at the rear of a town house marked with a Realtor's sign. The door into the walled backyard is alarmed, accessible only by a keypad, but he recognizes the bright blue security company logo; it is the same firm that monitors the Red Heron Estate. Maybe the override code will work here as well. Praying under his breath, he punches in BLUESKY.

The alarm light blinks off and the door opens with a click. *Thank you, Guru.* He enters the postage-stamp backyard, dead brown grass crunching under his feet. The house seems deserted, the shades down in all the windows.

Making sure the door is shut, he crouches down, just in time. Footsteps outside race past, then return, and a hand tugs on the door. After a pause, the footsteps clatter away, dying out somewhere down the hill.

As the adrenaline wears off, the shock hits Ranjit, and he begins to shake. The blond man isn't a thief, but an employee of Senator Neals. Ranjit is being hunted by a powerful man with enormous resources.

But why? What the hell is hidden inside the doll?

He crouches in the deserted yard, listening intently. Minutes pass, but all he hears is the cawing of crows and the swish of traffic on Charles Street. The sun is high in the sky when he opens the door a crack and peers down the alley. It is empty except for a tabby cat stretching leisurely in the weak sunlight.

Sticking to the alleys, he makes his way down the hill and emerges onto Charles Street. The Starbucks coffee shop across the road looks empty at this time, and he ducks into it, heading for the restroom at the back.

Locking the door, he washes blood off the back of his neck. The blond man has torn out a chunk of hair at the back of his head, and he jams paper towels into his baseball cap to absorb any further bleeding.

The door handle rattles, and an irate Bostonian voice says, "C'mon, c'mon. Step on

230

it, for Chrissakes. There are people waiting out here."

Ignoring the voice, Ranjit glances into the mirror, and his own gaunt, bearded face stares back at him. *This will not do.* The Senator's men will be looking for him now, taking his description all around the city. If the Senator can manipulate Homeland Security, he can easily tell the cops that Ranjit is a criminal or a terrorist.

When he emerges from the restroom, a bald man waiting outside glares at him. Ranjit walks quickly down Charles Street, looking for a drugstore, and finds one a block away. He buys a disposable razor, shaving cream and scissors, and, remembering the coughing man, adds six large Snickers bars to his purchases.

Clutching his plastic bag, he heads down Charles Street, passing a row of antique shops, art galleries, and trendy clothing boutiques. The young mothers wheeling their babies in three-hundred-dollar strollers see his greasy blue mechanic's jacket and baseball cap and give him a wide berth as he passes.

As he walks toward Chinatown, he is alert for the wail of a siren or the screech of a car stopping. He relaxes only when he reaches the open expanse of the Boston Common.

231

CHAPTER SEVENTEEN

It is midmorning by the time he enters the Garibaldi, inhaling its smell of stale body odor and cleaning fluid. He's passing the battered reception counter when the hotel manager waves him over.

"You in room five-nineteen, right?"

Ranjit fights the urge to run. "Why, is there a problem?"

"If you stay past noon, you need to pay for another night."

"Oh yeah. Sure, sure."

The manager looks as beat-up as any of his guests, with reddened, pouchy eyes and close-cropped white hair. Ranjit hands over the money and the man grins lopsidedly and points to the radio playing in the background.

"You hear about it? Telephone pole fell on Cambridge Street. Two guys in the hospital, they say. What are the chances, huh? Getting hit by a telephone pole?"

Ranjit just grunts and looks away.

The manager laboriously writes out a receipt and tries a different tack. "So . . . getting much sleep up there, next to old Jimmy?"

"The walls are pretty thin."

"Yeah, they subdivided this place back in the seventies. Used to be a grand old hotel. Babe Ruth stayed here, you know. Yeah, Jimmy's been coughing like that for two years. Amazing he's still alive."

"His name is Jimmy?"

"Don't call him Jimmy to his face. He hates that. Likes to go by James."

Ranjit nods and heads up to his room. The elevator is still broken, and by the time he reaches the fifth floor he is exhausted and soaked in sweat.

Clear, hard sunlight pours through the jammed window of his room. He sits on his bed and runs his fingers along the cold porcelain of the naked doll, feeling for the outlines of a hidden compartment.

Rattling the doll, he listens hard, but there is only silence. He holds its tiny skirt and then its blouse up to the light, looking for something sewn into the cloth, and sees only ancient brown stains, lipstick, or perhaps blood.

The doll lies in his lap, looking at him tauntingly with its painted black eyes. He remembers how Shanti had slept with it, her curly hair streaming across the pillow, her arm thrown around it. If only he had taken away the doll and not indulged her, none of this would have happened. *What the hell is hidden in here?* He imagines smashing it into a hundred jagged pieces, but if he does that, he might destroy whatever is hidden in it. There has to be a better way.

He thinks of Preetam and Shanti. *They have now spent a whole night in detention.* He can imagine them in a small cell, frightened and sleepless, waiting for help. And the key to everything is hidden in this damn doll.

He remembers passing the antique stores on Charles Street. They might be able to tell him something about the doll, but first things first. He can't walk around Boston looking like this.

The fluorescent light in the tiny bathroom buzzes and blinks into life. Touching the back of his head, he feels his hair matted with blood; at least his scalp has stopped bleeding.

Taking off his shirt, he stands bare-chested

in front of the small mirror. The glass has lost most of its silvering over the years, but the murky image that stares back at him is unmistakably that of a bearded Sikh.

He unknots his hair and it falls to his waist. There are glimmers of gray in his beard that weren't there a few days ago. It does not matter now.

He remembers walking through the Golden Temple with his mother. *Mataji* had pointed at the men bathing in the glittering waters of the *sarovar,* the sacred lake.

"Ranjit," she had said, "a Sikh never cuts his hair. Our ancestors were warriors who would rather face death than be defiled. Your turban is part of who you are. If you lose your identity, you lose yourself. You must never betray the Gurus."

He had looked at his reflection in the water, proud of his turban, proud to be a Sikh, and he had promised her that he would never betray his faith.

He can hear his mother praying, her voice melodious and strong.

Even in a gale of torrential rain
I would go to meet my Guru
Even if an ocean separates them
A Sikh would go to meet his Guru

As a man dies of thirst without water
A Sikh would die without his Guru . . .

Now, standing in the gloomy bathroom, he opens his eyes and looks at himself one last time. Taking a deep breath he raises the gleaming scissors to his head.
Forgive me, Mataji.

His arm aches and the bathroom floor is inches deep in thick black hair. When he's done with his scalp, he begins cutting into his beard and mustache, and soon there is only stubble. He soaps his face and shaves, using the cheap plastic razor. He is clumsy and cuts himself, and the white lather on his face turns pink.

When he's done, he runs a plastic comb through his hair, feeling the teeth bite into his scalp. Maybe he shouldn't have cut his hair quite so short. Now he'll have to buy some gel and spike it, like he's seen in the magazines.

He gathers up the drifts of hair from the floor and stuffs them into a plastic bag, all the while avoiding his reflection in the mirror. When he can delay no more, he is forced to look at himself.

A stranger's face stares back from the mirror. Short, spiky hair. A long face with a strong jaw, a sharp nose, and tired eyes. And there is the scar: a thick ridge that starts under his jaw and curves to his left ear. With his beard gone, it is exposed.

He turns his head away, shuts off the bathroom light, and heads to the trash chute down the corridor. Pulling open the metal flap, he throws the bag down its dark mouth, imagining the black ropes of hair mingled with chicken bones and bloody paper towels. *A part of himself will now remain forever in America.*

He returns to his room for the Snickers bars and walks over to his neighbor's open door, knocking loudly on the door frame. James looks up startled from his book and skitters backward in his wheelchair.

"Hey, it's me. Ranjit, from next door."

"Jeez," James gasps. "You scared the hell out of me. I didn't recognize you."

"Thanks for watching my room. Here is your candy. Snickers, right?"

James takes the bag, nods his thanks, and immediately wolfs down a whole bar, chewing hungrily through the sticky caramel. Ranjit watches him eat, realizing with a pang that there is probably no food in the room, other than the orange in front of the gold Buddha. The small room smells strongly of bitter herbs, and he sees that

James is brewing some kind of tea, a dark cup of it sitting on the dresser.

Finishing the candy bar, James looks up wonderingly. "*Hah.* Your own mother wouldn't recognize you. Whaddya do, knock over a bank?"

"Nothing like that. I just had a shave and a haircut."

"I'd fire that barber if I were you. You're all cut up."

Ranjit smiles. It sounds so much like something Khandelkar would say. He leans against the wall and watches James unwrap another Snickers bar. "What's that you're drinking? Smells awful."

"Chinese herbs, my friend. Stuff comes from the mainland, it's the real thing. Man, this Snickers is good. Thanks again."

"Hey, no problem. James, I have a question to ask you —"

James's wheelchair makes a slight arcing motion as he grips its arms. "*James?* You called me *James*? They're talking about me at the front desk?"

"They told me that you don't like to be called Jim. Or Jimmy. That's all."

James looks up, a faraway look in his eyes. "I was named James. I like to be called what I was named. It's only proper."

"Okay, James. Listen, I need to sell something, an heirloom. Do you know anything about the antique stores on Charles Street?" Ranjit thinks of the doll, now back in its hiding place above the bathroom ceiling.

James laughs as he reaches for another candy bar, peeling off the wrapper as though it were a banana.

"Selling your stuff? You must be in bad shape." Leaning back, he pauses, the candy bar halfway to his mouth. "Those places on Charles Street, they're thieves. Go down to Boylston, past the Steinway Store. There are a couple of places that have been there a hundred, hundred and fifty years. If it's old, they'll buy it."

"Thanks. I'll check it out."

"And while you're down there, keep a lookout for some gold cuff links. Engraved with the initials 'FX.' "

Ranjit looks puzzled. "Why, did someone steal them?"

"No, no. They're my father's. I sold them when I got back from 'Nam. Now I dream about them. I keep thinking I'll get them back one day."

Ranjit nods and leaves, seeing tears in James's eyes.

This country, he thinks, *it's just full of lonely old people.* If this were India, there would be someone — a nephew, a daughter — to care for James. When he dies at the Garibaldi Hotel, this small room will be his tomb; it could be weeks before someone realizes that he isn't coughing anymore.

CHAPTER EIGHTEEN

It is late afternoon and the sun is setting when he leaves the Garibaldi. Walking down Essex Street, he feels strangely naked without his beard, and his head feels light, shorn of the weight of his hair. Reaching the Boston Common, he walks along it, mingling with a string of office workers hurrying home from work, their breath steaming into the cold air. When he waits with them to cross Boylston Street, no one stares at him or moves away. A pretty, middle-aged white woman actually smiles at him, and he smiles back, surprised. So this is what it is like to resemble everyone else.

The antique stores are in a line at the far end of Boylston Street, their shop windows all lit, glowing like aquariums in the gloom.

The first window is crowded with antique musical instruments, slender oboes, tarnished brass trumpets, and saxophones with mouthpieces worn smooth by years of

241

spittle. The second window features carved Victorian furniture, but the third is full of bric-a-brac, old wind-up gramophones and silver tea sets, and he decides to enter it.

A man sitting behind a counter is reading *The Boston Globe,* and Ranjit gets a shock when he sees a photograph of Senator Neals's face staring up at him. It is the same image from the hostage release, the Senator with his arms raised triumphantly, like a prizefighter.

The gray-faced man hurriedly puts the paper away and is surprisingly deferential when Ranjit shows him the doll.

"Hmmm. A very curious object. But not my line, I'm afraid. I deal in nineteenth-century ephemera. This looks older. Try Tim Hubley at the end of the street."

Ranjit thanks him and walks farther, spotting a battered tin sign that says HUBLEY AND SONS, AUCTION HOUSE, and in its window, behind china figurines, is a row of porcelain dolls. These seem newer than the ones in Anna's collection, and are made to resemble little girls, with button noses and shiny, synthetic hair.

A tinny bell rings when he enters the crowded shop. Along the walls are dusty glass cases of children's toys, and Ranjit can make out lead toy soldiers, battered metal trucks, even a hobby horse with a mangy mane, all marked with numbered tags. One half of the store is taken up by a small wooden stage with rows of empty metal folding chairs facing it.

A curtain ripples behind the stage and a youngish man with long brown hair emerges, a carton of Chinese food in one hand, chopsticks in the other. He gestures to the rows of empty chairs.

"The auction isn't till tomorrow morning. But feel free to browse. We have some wonderful nineteenth-century toy soldiers."

Ranjit takes the doll from his backpack. "Actually, I was hoping to learn more about this. I see you have some in your window."

The young man puts down the carton and wipes his hands on his baggy corduroy pants. Up close, he is not that young, with a receding hairline and dust in the creases of his face.

"Can you tell me anything about it? I think it's quite old."

The man lifts the doll, feels its weight, and his expression changes. "Dolls aren't my department, sir. Please wait a minute."

He turns and walks back to the heavy velvet curtains, pokes his head between them, and bellows, "Martha! Hey, Martha, come take a look at this."

An elderly lady shuffles through the curtains, wiping a speck of rice from the corner of her mouth. She has a high forehead and dyed black hair swept back with a Spanish comb.

"Hmmm. Hmmm." She picks up the doll. "What have we here?"

She stares at the doll, her face expressionless. Switching on a gooseneck lamp sitting on the counter, she examines it, turning it slowly with her long fingers.

"Where did you get this, sir?" Her voice is polite, but unable to hide a note of excitement.

Ranjit just smiles. "Oh, it was a gift."

The woman sighs. "Yes. Well. We'll give you five hundred dollars for it."

"I was told it was very old. Worth much more than that."

The woman nods calmly, but her thin mouth is quivering with excitement. "Well, yes, pre–Civil War, but its value is purely as a novelty item. You see, these mammy dolls were usually made out of cloth, not porcelain."

"Mammy? I'm sorry, I don't understand . . ."

The woman speaks slowly, as though addressing a child. "Down south, a mammy was the black nursemaid who looked after

244

white children. This doll was part of a set. Black dolls and white dolls. The white dolls were pretty children. This one was the mammy."

There is a silence. The young man to the side watches closely.

"Did these kind of dolls have hidden compartments? Places to hide things?"

The woman's eyes are riveted on the doll, and her fingers caress its rustling skirt.

"Well, you have to understand that in the eighteenth century there were no banks and no safe-deposit boxes. There were hiding places in every house, in desks and under beds. In dolls, the usual method is a spring-loaded release — sir, I am willing to give you a thousand for this. My best and final offer."

"It's not for sale. Thank you for the information." Ranjit takes the doll and pushes it into his backpack. As he walks to the door, the woman looks like she is about to faint.

The long-haired man falls in step with Ranjit, his breath perfumed with sesame oil. "All right. Three thousand. Cash. No questions asked."

"Sorry, it's not for sale."

The bell on the door tinkles as Ranjit exits. The young man follows him out onto the sidewalk, shivering with cold.

"Five thousand, for Christ's sake. Right now. I'll go to the bank."

Ranjit shakes his head and starts to walk away.

"Where did you get it?" The man grips Ranjit's shoulder, his voice a growl. "The only other doll like this is at the Smithsonian. Is it stolen?"

Ranjit is suddenly tired of being threatened. He stares down at the man, his voice soft and reasonable.

"Since you just offered to buy it, I doubt that's your concern. Now get your hand off my shoulder. Or else I'll remove it myself."

The young man snarls and stomps back into the store. Ranjit hefts his backpack onto his shoulder and hurries back toward the Garibaldi Hotel.

It is dark now. His room is cold and there is no sound traveling through the thin back wall; maybe James is asleep.

Ranjit clicks on the naked overhead bulb and takes out the doll, holding it up to the light. *A five-thousand-dollar doll.* And if the man had offered that amount, it's got to be worth much more. But that's not why the men had wanted it: the blond man clearly said there was something hidden inside it.

He sits on the bed and holds the doll, running his fingers absently over its porcelain head, its raised features bumpy against his fingertips.

The woman in the antique store had said something about a spring-loaded mechanism. Which means that a hidden spring would have to be pressure-activated, opening a door into the doll's body cavity. Yet there is no outline of any opening along the smooth, cool porcelain.

He puts the doll between his knees and presses his fingertips along its torso. He covers every inch of it, but nothing happens. *Damn it.* His fingers are slippery with sweat, and he wipes them on his jeans.

Leaning against the wall with the doll in his lap, he looks out at the snow-covered rooftops. Like a hunted animal, he can sense the space around him shrinking. If the Senator's men find him in this room, there is no fire escape and no back stair.

Still holding the doll's head in his right hand, he squeezes it in frustration. There is a sudden, faint vibration under his fingertips and he feels something give way behind its ears. *The spring mechanism is in its head.* He squeezes harder, but it's not enough; there must be another part of the release mechanism.

Still squeezing with his right hand, he uses his left to push at the nose, then the eyes.

Suddenly there is no resistance. With a click the head slides smoothly upward and he almost drops it.

He looks down and sees that the porcelain torso is hollow. Wiping his sweaty hands, he reaches inside it with two trembling fingers.

What the hell is this? He stares at the object in his hand: a thin, long rectangle of stiff cream cardboard, punched with columns of elongated holes. Inset in a corner is a small square of celluloid film. Holding it up to the light, all he can make out is a faint, elaborate geometry, as intricately constructed as a spiderweb. It is some kind of microfilm, but what do the columns of punched holes mean? They dance up and down, like abstract musical notation, and are saying something, if only he could understand it.

If only he had access to the Internet, he could find out what this damn thing is. In India there are Internet cafés on every street, but here everyone has computers at home. Then he remembers taking Shanti to the public library in Oak Bluffs, and seeing the row of computers against the wall.

James has a pile of library books by his bed, so there is probably one close by. It is now past five, and he will have to wait till tomorrow morning. His stomach growls, and he realizes that he hasn't eaten anything since the cruller early that morning.

Putting the doll back into its hiding place, he carefully locks his door and walks past James's room, seeing that his door is shut. The elevator is working now, and he rides it down, looking at the angular graffiti on its plastic walls: *Yankees suck. Kilroy was here, 1974,* and one that has been scratched deep into the plastic, *No one gets out of here alive.*

He enters the Dong Kanh Vietnamese restaurant down the street and orders a takeout container of fish ball soup. The small, steamy restaurant is packed, the sole waiter weaving between the tables with huge bowls of *pho* and plates piled high with bean sprouts and basil leaves. He watches a Vietnamese family eating at a round table, a father, mother, and a young girl Shanti's age, with shoulder-length gleaming black hair. He watches the mother reach out with her chopsticks and lovingly deposit a morsel of pork onto her daughter's plate, and he can't bear to see any more.

When his soup is ready, he pays for it, then heads up the block and buys a small bottle of Bacardi. Returning to his room, he eats on the bed, alternating the hot, fatty chicken

249

broth with sips of rich dark liquor.

Outside it is pitch black, and the sounds of Chinatown drift into his room: choppy conversation in Cantonese, the wail of music from a far-off radio, the whine of cars sliding through the slippery streets below.

Another full day has passed since they picked up Preetam and Shanti: twelve days left before they will be deported. He imagines them in a prison cell lit with stark fluorescent light, still wearing the same clothes. After forty-eight hours of prison, he knows the tricks that the mind can play.

During the first day they will have felt a faint glimmer of hope, but by now the outside world will have receded, and there will be only the bare walls of the prison. As more time passes, they will turn completely into themselves, like snails retreating into their shells. Once that happens, their isolation will be complete.

He has to get them out, but how? If Khandelkar were here, he would know. With unerring instinct, whatever the odds, the Sergeant always found a way.

"You saved me this morning, Sergeant," he whispers. "Please help me one more time."

He holds his breath, willing himself to see a flicker in the darkness. But there is only the darkness of the room and the stink of alcohol on his breath. Pulling off his boots and clothes, he crawls into the bed and chugs the rest of the Bacardi, feeling its warmth spread through him. Soon his consciousness fades, and the alcohol takes him down into sleep.

CHAPTER NINETEEN

The Captain wraps Khandelkar's body in a sleeping bag. They bury him in the snow, use his rifle as a marker, and leave him high up on the mountain.

The Captain leads his three surviving men down quickly, spurred on by confusion and shame. At seventeen thousand feet they run out of water, and when they reach the Indian Army outpost at Bilafond La two days later, the Captain is so dehydrated that he can hardly talk. The commanding officer there sees the frostbite on their faces and hands, and radios for a chopper.

Eight hours later the Captain and his men are at the mouth of the glacier, jolting in a three-ton truck to the hospital at Kumar Base Camp. The Captain sits silently as the truck rumbles past neat rows of barracks, tall flagpoles, and troops practicing drill formations. It all seems like a stage set.

He is taken away from his men and escorted into a deserted hospital ward with one small window high up in the wall. A dark-haired nurse examines the black blisters on his hands, clucks her tongue, and pushes an IV into his arm. Cold saline solution flows into his veins and makes his head swim.

"My hands," he asks, "are they going to be all right?"

"We'll see," she says. "With frostbite, it's all a matter of time. Take these blue pills, they will help you to sleep."

For one nightmarish day and night the Captain lies shivering, despite layers of blankets, waking every few hours to check for feeling in his hands, willing them to thaw out. He hears the nurse changing the heavy bottle of saline hanging above him, feels the cool liquid seep into him, and waits for the officers to arrive.

They come late on the afternoon of the second day, when a bright square of sunlight slants across the stone floor.

The Captain hears the clatter of boots, pulls himself up to a sitting position and salutes, though the movement makes him dizzy.

A General and a Major walk down the ward. Both wear olive-green dress uniforms with well-polished boots, and the rows of medals on the General's chest reach back to the sixties, to the original wars with China. The Captain knows that the top brass no longer fear the Chinese, who have now satisfied their territorial hunger by taking Tibet. No, now they fear and hate the Pakistanis, for they have the bomb, and one day will use it.

As they come closer, the Captain stiffens when he recognizes the short, barrel-chested General with the thick graying mustache. General "Bear" Handa is a legend, the man who single-handedly started the entire Siachen war.

Back in 1980 the glacier was simply a blank spot on the map, bereft of any people, tactically useless to the Indians and the Pakistanis. Bear Handa, a legendary climber, had taken an army expedition out onto the virgin glacier, climbed many peaks and skied down their icy slopes. Along the way he had found the debris of an unknown climbing expedition, and noticed among it an empty packet of Pakistani Gold Leaf cigarettes.

Everyone knows the story that then unfolded: Bear had taken the cigarette packet to his superiors as evidence of Pakistani trespassing. Fearing that the Paki military would grab the glacier, the Indian Army had scrambled to get troops up there. They had secured all the high passes hours ahead of the Pakis, and both sides dug in at high altitudes. What was once a wonderland of ice had become a battlefield.

There is a screech of metal as the two officers pull up folding chairs and take off their peaked caps. The Captain knows that this is the preliminary to a court-martial.

Outside he can hear the chanting of a drill sergeant as troops march past. *Left, right, left, right.*

The Captain wants to get it over with. He wants the blackened, torn bodies of the dead men brought down. He will tell them where Dewan died, and they will find him, too; this is all he can do, now, before they lock him away for good.

General Bear Handa sits silently, his square face emotionless, turning his cap round and round in hands the size of spades.

The Major does all the talking. He has a smooth complexion and hair slicked back with sweet, pungent coconut oil. As he speaks, all the Captain can think about is how easily coconut oil freezes; to maintain his sleek hairstyle, the Major must heat up a bottle every day.

The Major asks about the Captain's

health and that of his surviving troops and then he gets to the point.

". . . so, Captain Singh. Regretfully, we have to ask you about what happened on the glacier. Sixteen men killed. Why didn't you confirm it was an enemy position before calling in the strike?"

The Captain tries to focus. "Sir, the post was within the sector given to me by the Frontier Forces people. And we were told to maintain radio silence . . ."

Suddenly he is exhausted. He wants to get this over with, and his voice comes in a rush.

"I take full responsibility for what happened. All I ask is that the bodies be brought down, now, while the weather holds. My Sergeant is up there too, along with a Private killed earlier . . ."

The Major pauses before choosing his words carefully. "Captain, I know how you feel. I admire you for your loyalty to your men, but it is not in our best interest right now to go back up there."

Through the fog in his head the Captain tries to understand what has just been said. "Sir, I don't follow. We must get the bodies of those men down . . ."

General Handa leans forward. His face is deeply weathered, his voice low and gravelly.

"Captain Singh, I had the honor to serve with your father. We were both awarded the Param Vir Chakra for the same action."

He points to a familiar round medal hanging from a faded purple ribbon.

The Captain is stunned. He remembers holding his father's identical medal, feeling the cold, heavy disc in his hands. Suddenly *Pitaji* is alive again, and he wants to ask, *You knew him? What was my father like?*

General Handa anticipates the question. "Of course, you were just a baby, you don't remember him, do you? The Sardar, as we called him, was a brave man. I was with him in '71, at the battle of Longewala. With one company of infantry, he held off sixty-five Pakistani tanks all night. The last time I saw him, he was out on the battlefield in a Jeep with a rear-mounted RPG. He'd taken out five or six Paki tanks, and there were flames everywhere. I told him he had done enough, that he should leave, but he just grinned and drove back into the fight. He died, and I lived."

The Captain sits upright, imagining his father silhouetted against the glare of firelight.

General Handa continues. "Things were different then. We lost half our men, we had to retreat. The Pakis were honorable, they

257

held their fire as we left, and we had time to retrieve your father's body. Not like the dirty war we are fighting now."

The Major leans forward, light rippling across his wavy, well-oiled hair.

"The General is trying to make a point. We are fully aware of our responsibility to your deceased troops. But there are other considerations. A Japanese television crew is filming on the glacier. They are escorted, of course, but still . . . It's not a good time to tell the outside world that we just killed sixteen of our own men."

The Captain looks pleadingly at General Handa. "Sir, we can easily bring the men down now. The weather up there can change in a second, you have to understand, avalanches, rockslides . . ."

There is silence. Bear Handa leans forward, the medals on his uniform tinkling.

"Captain Singh, you are from a military family. What happened on the glacier — was unfortunate. If you face a court-martial, you will be convicted. But there is another way."

The Captain waits. *Is the General trying to save him as a favor to his dead father?*

General Handa's voice drops to a whisper. "The Japanese film crew is here, and we need support for this war. Public opinion is turning against us. The glacier is seen as an

258

environmental catastrophe. *Pah!* The environment!"

He makes a chopping motion with his large hand. "You know as well as I do, Captain, that we need to draw the line *here*. We need to send the message to the Pakis that we'll *never* give up our land. And we need experienced men like you to run our missions. Dedicated, skilled. We need you back out there, not rotting uselessly in a prison."

The Major leans in again, the smell of his hair oil making the Captain nauseous. "Things would be completely different if the world finds out that the *Pakistanis* wiped out our outpost. If the general public gets to see the footage of the dead men up there —"

"Enough." General Handa is getting to his feet slowly. "Captain Singh is not stupid. He understands fully. Captain, I know you will do the right thing. The Major will return for an answer in the morning."

As they leave, the Major looks back, and his stern expression is unmistakable: *Either you are one of us, or you are not.*

The Captain lies in the empty hospital ward, the IV pumping cool fluid into his arm.

He closes his eyes. He sees Dewan falling

into the snow far below, his thin chest heaving, the cut rope fluttering around his waist. He sees Sergeant Khandelkar as he kneels in the snow like a monk performing a religious ceremony, the rifle barrel shoved deep into his mouth.

"I promised them," he mutters. "I promised."

The dark-haired nurse appears, takes his temperature and feeds him more pills. He can barely swallow them, and his mouth fills with their bitter taste.

CHAPTER TWENTY

The next morning, Ranjit spends twenty minutes trying to comb his unruly hair, then gives up and pulls on his baseball cap.

He needs to ask James where the nearest library is and is relieved to find his neighbor's door wide open. The small room has already been tidied up, and the blanket on the metal bed is stretched taut. James is doing pull-ups on the bar in the closet, his wheelchair locked under him.

"Hey, sorry to disturb you. I can come back —"

"No, no, have a seat. Forty-two, forty-three . . ." James's muscular torso rises and dips.

Ranjit sits in the metal chair, seeing that all the library books stacked beside him are about Vietnam: histories, memoirs, biographies.

James speaks through clenched teeth. "People say we could have won the war.

Bullshit. The politicians lied the whole time we were there. Turned the war into statistics, body counts, and KIAs . . . Forty-six, forty-seven . . ."

Ranjit picks up a large hardcover and opens it at random, seeing a double-page black-and-white photograph. Vietnamese civilians are lying dead in a ditch, some bodies sprawled out, others curled into tight balls, as if they could ward off the bullets. The bare white soles of a man's feet protrude into the lower corner, but the rest of him is cut off by the frame of the photograph.

The My Lai massacre. They had studied it in officer training college. Ranjit's face is pale as he snaps the book shut, but the image remains: bodies huddled together, caught in the moment of death —

"Fifty." James drops into his wheelchair, his white T-shirt soaked in sweat. "The least we could have done was behaved with dignity — hey, are you all right?"

Ranjit's head is whirling and he leans back in the metal chair. *Bodies, lying in piles, high up on the mountain . . . not now, not in James's room . . .*

Too late. There is a shimmer in the far corner of the room and Sergeant Khandelkar appears. His white snowsuit is stained with what looks like rust, and his mouth is a hole in a mask of stretched skin.

Trust this man, Captain. He can help you.

Ranjit can't tell if the Sergeant's words are in his head, or were spoken out loud.

Sergeant, what are you doing here?

I have no strength left, Captain. I cannot come anymore. This man can help you. Talk to him.

He's sick, he's going to die soon.

He will stay alive if he is needed. Trust him. He's one of us.

The image shimmers and vanishes. Ranjit stares wildly around the room, and James follows his gaze.

"Hey, what the hell are you looking at?" A shiver runs through James's wide, muscular shoulders. "Jesus, I feel as though someone just walked over my grave."

Ranjit slumps forward and buries his face in his hands. There is the squeak of James's wheelchair coming toward him and a strong hand squeezes his shoulder. When he opens his eyes, James's pale face is inches away, so close that Ranjit can see the whorls of fingerprints on his thick lenses.

"You okay? Is it a seizure?"

Ranjit shakes his head and opens his mouth, but no words come.

James's voice is softer. "Voices? You hear

them too? I know you're not crazy. It's just that . . . the men who died. They come back sometimes."

Ranjit nods. "I . . . can't control it. It just happens."

They sit in silence. When Ranjit finally speaks it comes out in a rush.

"James, I am in big trouble. My daughter took this doll from a house I was looking after, and now she and my wife are going to be deported —"

"You're married? You have a kid? Jesus." A shadow passes over James's face.

"They have nothing to do with this mess. It's all my fault."

James takes his hand off Ranjit's shoulder and wheels his chair a few feet backward, waiting for more. "Why don't you tell me about it?" He shrugs. "I've got plenty of time."

When Ranjit is done with his story, James leans back in his wheelchair.

"You're shitting me. Senator Neals, the guy who brought that journalist home? He's a hero, man. People say he might run for President."

Ranjit takes out the piece of cardboard. "I'm not making this stuff up. This was inside the doll."

James just stares at it. "What the hell?" He reaches out and takes the card from Ranjit's hand. "I didn't know they made these anymore."

"You know what it is?"

"Yeah. This was inside a *doll*?"

"It's some kind of microfilm, right?"

"It's an aperture card. We used them back in 'Nam, when I was in the Eighteenth Engineer Brigade." James holds it up to the light, his eyes magnified by his thick lenses. "Used to store blueprints on them. This window here is microfilm, it holds the image for one drawing. The punches are code, they note the order of the drawing within a larger set. When we built the airfield at Qui Nhon, we had thousands of drawings. The exact order is important."

"Why would someone have this? Isn't all this information digital nowadays?"

James smiles. "Sometimes, my friend, the old ways are the best ways. You know what the life span of a CD is? Ten years. One of these cards can survive a hundred years, even in hot, humid weather. And if you use digital images, the viewing technology changes every few years. This aperture card exists outside technology, it's mechanical. Just pop it in a viewer, and there's all your information."

Ranjit nods. "So what's on it?"

"It's microfilm. You need a viewer to enlarge it."

"What about the code?"

James shrugs. "I was an engineer, not a programmer. See the columns of holes? Some sort of ID punched in here. Know any computer programmers?" He leans forward and returns the card.

Computer programmers? Ranjit shakes his head, then stops himself. *Ricky Singh. Despite his flashy turbans and tight T-shirts, the kid knows a lot about computers.*

"Thanks, James. You've been a big help. I have to go now."

"Wait." James wheels himself rapidly to the door. He slams it shut and turns around to face Ranjit.

"I need to know what you're up to."

Ranjit is silent.

"This place" — James gestures at the corridor — "this whole place is full of men hiding from something. Druggies here, and plenty of ex-cons. But you, Captain, you're different. You show up with a turban and beard, then it's gone. Now you have some sort of microfilm. And last night the elevator was working, so I went down. Two men were in the lobby, asking the night manager questions. They showed him a picture, an

266

old picture, but it was you, wearing an army uniform."

Ranjit stands stock-still. *His passport photograph. Game over, they've found him.*

"What . . . what did you tell them?"

"Nothing. And the night manager hadn't seen you." James's voice is steady, the eyes behind the smudged lenses boring into Ranjit. "But in my experience, cheap suits always mean law enforcement. You told me quite a story, Captain. But maybe it's a bunch of bullshit. Like maybe you want to blow something up here, like a tall building?"

"James, it's nothing like that, I swear, on my daughter's life."

"You know, folks here are always talking about their wives, their daughters. Most of the time, there isn't anyone, it's all in their heads. You don't strike me as a married man, Captain."

Ranjit takes out his cell phone. He scrolls through the menu, finds an image, and passes the phone to James. "Look. That's my daughter."

James stares down at the image. It was taken on a sunny summer day in Vineyard Haven, and Shanti was eating a red Popsicle, her mouth stained red as she smiled up into the camera.

"And this is her with my wife."

He scrolls to a photograph of Preetam standing in the front yard of the old house, under a tall oak tree. Shanti has climbed up into it, and smiles down from a branch above her mother's head.

"And this is me with her."

Another picture — blurry this time, because Preetam had taken it — of Shanti helping him to rake the yard, red and gold leaves stuck into her hair.

Ranjit's voice is softer now. "I'm not lying to you, James."

James takes a deep breath and hands the phone back. "She looks like you. Same eyes. Tall, too."

Ranjit closes his phone with a click. "Think about it. Last summer, people said the Senator wouldn't even be reelected. Then he goes to Korea, comes back a hero, and suddenly he's on top again. It's strange."

There is a silence, then James nods his head. "People will do anything to stay in power. And absolute power corrupts absolutely. I saw it in 'Nam, when they bombed the crap out of Laos and Cambodia and lied about it. If politicians can lie about dropping incendiaries on thousands of people, they can do anything."

He takes off his glasses and wipes them on his sweat-stained T-shirt, looking up at Ranjit with naked eyes. "Okay, I'll believe you, for now."

"Thank you." Ranjit gets up and heads for the door.

"Wait." James gestures at the cardboard strip in Ranjit's hand. "The aperture card. It's not for a building. Or a bridge. To design those, you need hundreds, maybe a few thousand drawings. This is part of a huge set, tens of thousands of drawings. It's some kind of machine, a very intricate machine. Go in peace, Captain. I'll pray for your family."

As Ranjit walks through the door, he hears the click of a lighter and smells incense. Glancing back, he sees James bent over in front of the golden Buddha, his eyes closed and his palms pressed together.

The sound of James's mumbled prayer follows Ranjit all the way down the corridor.

Ricky sounds very frightened on the phone. He can't get away from the store till later that afternoon, and they agree to meet at a coffee shop inside MIT's student union. Ranjit arrives early and sips a *chai* latte, looking out of the window at the students passing by. Most of them are clad in just

T-shirts and jeans, even in this freezing weather. Kids in this country revolt by underdressing for the cold, something he will never understand.

For once, he feels at ease; there are so many foreigners at MIT that two brown men here will easily go unnoticed. Across from him, a group of Chinese students sketch complicated diagrams on napkins, and in another corner a table of men in leather jackets are talking in some Eastern European language.

He takes a sip of what passes for *chai* here, and wishes he could just step around the counter and brew his own, flavored with cardamom and cloves.

Just then Ricky enters the coffee shop, wearing a crisp white turban and a tight green T-shirt with BROOKLYN written across it. He sees Ranjit and a stunned expression crosses his face.

"Ohmigod. *Mausa,* you cut off your hair? You dishonored yourself?"

The hiss of the espresso machine masks Ricky's loud voice, though some girls lined up for coffee stare at him.

"Keep your voice down, please. I had to do this. Those men who came for Preetam and Shanti are looking for me, too."

Ricky sits down and leans forward, his

eyes wide with fear. "I can't believe this shit. I didn't even recognize you."

"Have those Homeland Security men come back?"

"No, but they turned the store upside down. They even went through the bins in the basement. We had to close for a day, just to clean up. Dad can't sleep anymore. He spends all his time calling his lawyer, and the lawyer calls Homeland Security and gets a recorded message. We're going crazy, we don't know what to do."

"Did you tell anyone I was at the store?"

"No. Dad thinks you're in the Vineyard, and that the immigration people will pick you up, too. He says you deserve to be deported. He says you are a —"

Ranjit holds up his hand. "Enough. I know what your father thinks." He pushes his mug of tea aside. "Did you bring your laptop? And the scanner?"

"Yeah, I always carry it. But how is this going to help Preetam *Mausi*?"

"Listen, you have to just trust me. The less you know, the better."

Ricky's pale, handsome face takes on a stubborn look. "What the heck can happen to me? I was born here. I'm American."

Ranjit sighs in exasperation. *You could end up on a flight out of this country, bound and*

271

gagged, he wants to say. *You could wake up in a cell in Yemen or Egypt with a bag over your head.* Instead, he hands over the card and watches Ricky's eyes gleam with excitement.

"*Cool.* What the heck is this? Hey, it looks like a punch card for one of the old mainframes. I recognize the code, it's Fortran."

"I just need to know what it says. Do you know how to read it?"

Ricky laughs, his fears forgotten now that he has a technical problem to solve. "You don't just *read* it, *Mausa.* It's got to be decoded by a machine."

"Do you know someone who can do that? Quickly?"

"There are some Sikh guys from MIT who come into the store. They're cool, but kinda losers, they always want me to set them up with girls. I've done some programming with them. I'll e-mail them."

Ranjit watches as Ricky takes out a pocket-sized scanner and feeds the aperture card through it. He attaches the scan to an e-mail, addressing his message to a string of people with names like "BigbearSikh" and "PunkSingh." He types rapidly, then signs off with the traditional Sikh greeting, *Sat Sri Akal.* For these American-born kids, Sikhism is just one aspect of their lives.

Their beards and turbans are just style, something that makes the girls pay attention.

The e-mail vanishes with a small beep.

"What now?" Ranjit asks.

"Now," says Ricky, standing up, "we wait. I'm going to get some coffee."

Half an hour passes. Ricky is on his second half-caf double-whip mochachino. Ranjit is tense, watching the students entering the coffee shop, blue with cold, stamping their feet and shivering.

"I miss Shanti," Ricky says quietly. "She's such a cool kid. She's got a great sense of humor. I don't get it. Why would they want to deport a kid?"

"They're just enforcing the rules. Our tourist visas have expired, but nobody would have found out. Someone deliberately tipped off Homeland Security."

"Who? Who would want to do that?"

"I have an idea of who it is, but I told you, I don't want you involved in this."

Ricky wipes a line of foam from his mustache, a gesture that reminds Ranjit of Shanti. "My dad said that he offered to sponsor you for a green card if you kept working at the store. But you turned him down. Why?"

Ranjit looks out of the plate-glass window. The temperature must have dropped, because the kids outside are walking faster, their hands thrust deep into their pockets.

"Ricky, I couldn't take the store anymore. Maybe I should have listened to your father, but I . . . look, what's happened is all my fault. I know that."

"I'm not blaming you. I hate working there, too. It's bullshit. If I were a programmer, I'd be pulling down some real cash, but Dad says I have to help him. What should I do? With you gone, there's only me, and —"

The laptop beeps. They both look down, and Ricky opens the e-mail, his eyes scanning the screen.

"*Mausa*, is this a joke?"

"Why?"

"One of my friends replied. He's at the Draper Lab at MIT. Look at this." He turns the laptop around and Ranjit reads from the screen.

Dear Dickhead, the e-mail says.

Nice joke. Didn't know you could code in Fortran. And the aperture card gag is a good one. So this is #11,078 in a set of 23,010 engineering drawings for the Agni developed by IGMDP? Ha ha. Very funny. Though I did enlarge the image of the circuit, and it looks pretty real. Almost got me. Are you up for going bowling in Allston Saturday? Can you get that cute yoga chick to come, the one you told me about . . .

Ricky looks puzzled. "What does *Agni* mean?"

"Let me have your computer for a second."

Ranjit opens a new window and types into a search engine, then clicks his way through several Web pages. He drums his fingers as a military Web site slowly loads, reads from the screen, then closes the window.

"So what's it all about? What is an *Agni*?"

Ranjit ignores the boy's question. "Can you find out what's on that microfilm?"

"Yeah, probably." The boy's face creases in thought. "My friend said it was some kind of circuit, but he's a programmer, not an engineer. I can post an image on a bulletin board, and someone will know what it is. But then it'll be out in the open. You want that?"

Ranjit remembers the abstract geometry embedded in the microfilm. *It doesn't matter exactly what information the drawing contains.* He realizes he has a powerful bargaining

275

chip, good enough to cut a deal.

He stands up abruptly. "Tell your friend that your e-mail was a joke. Delete the whole exchange, and don't talk to anyone. Thanks, you've been a great help."

"That's it? You have to tell me what's going on." Ricky's mouth is open as he stares up at Ranjit. "C'mon. This military stuff sounds cool."

Ranjit puts both hands flat on the table. "*Cool?* This is serious, Ricky. You might have been born here, but you are still a brown man in a turban. You tell anyone about this, and you'll be in big trouble —"

"Hey." Ricky pulls back. "You sound like my dad. You know how many fights I got into in high school because of my turban? You know how often the cops pull me over?" His eyes are bright with anger. "You think I don't want to cut off my hair, like you? Just be a normal guy? Huh?"

"Sorry. Sorry, I didn't mean to lecture you." He pats Ricky's shoulder. "You've been a great help. I'll call you when I know more."

Just then two Indian kids walk into the coffee shop, both wearing thick black-framed glasses and tight T-shirts under plaid shirts.

"Ricky! Hey, man, what are you doing

here? What's goin' on?"

They head over to the table, and Ranjit squeezes Ricky's shoulder and walks away. When he looks back, the kids are high-fiving Ricky, who stares in Ranjit's direction, a worried look on his handsome face.

As the sun fades from the sky the temperature drops rapidly. Ranjit crosses the bridge over the Charles River and notices a thin crust of ice beginning to form over the dark water. He takes a left onto Commonwealth Avenue and heads down the landscaped strip in its center, walking between two rows of trees wrapped in tiny white lights. The sky turns black and the twinkling lights come on, illuminating tall statues of Revolutionary War generals, abolitionists, and mayors.

He walks quickly, shrouded in wisps of his own breath.

The Web site he accessed on Ricky's computer said that IGMDP stood for the Indian military's Integrated Guided Missile Development Program. In 1989 the IGMDP designed and built a long-range missile to carry a nuclear warhead.

In Hindi, "Agni" means fire or flame. It is also the code name that the Indian military had given to their first homegrown missile.

Memories flash through his mind. He was a child when the black-and-white TV showed footage of India's first nuclear test, deep under the Thar Desert. He watched transfixed, as a bomb perversely named "Smiling Buddha" was detonated, heaving up a mountain of sand and leaving a deep, dark crater.

India had the bomb, but they still needed some way to deliver it. The missiles they had, British- and French-made, were erratic, their guidance systems shorting out, the missiles plunging into the sea.

It had taken Indian scientists another fifteen years to build an accurate missile. He remembers that Republic Day parade in Delhi when the homegrown missiles were revealed: first came the marching troops, then the tanks, and finally the missile carriers, the missiles lean and sharklike, their tips painted a patriotic orange. The crowds had seen them and cheered, as though greeting a Bollywood film star.

Thrusting his hand into his jacket pocket, Ranjit feels the stiff rectangle of cardboard. He can hardly believe that this battered cardboard strip with its window of film is a blueprint for some part of the Agni missile. *How has it ended up inside a doll in Senator Neals's house?*

Walking through the twinkling darkness, Ranjit remembers Neals's flushed face after three beers, boasting about his trip to India to negotiate a nuclear truce. The easiest explanation is that the Senator somehow got his hands on the microfilm during his trip to India.

He had hidden it inside a doll that belonged to his dead daughter, in a bedroom that lay unused in his summer house. In the dead of winter, he had sent the blond man to retrieve it. If Ranjit and his family hadn't been living there, no one would ever have known.

How long did the microfilm lie hidden inside the doll? And why did the Senator need it *now,* right after he returned from North Korea?

Ranjit walks on through the twinkling lights of Commonwealth Avenue, something niggling at the back of his mind.

North Korea. He remembers something he had read a few years ago, in an article about the Pakistani nuclear scientist A. Q. Khan. Concerned about the burgeoning international trade in nuclear information, the Americans had traced the source to Pakistan. It turned out that Khan had been selling information on uranium enrichment and centrifuges to the Libyans, the Iranians, and the North Koreans.

The international sanctions against the North Koreans were designed to prevent them from getting their hands on any nuclear information, but thanks to Khan, no one knows whether they actually have the bomb or not. The uncertainty around it helps to prop up their decrepit regime. *Like Khan, is Senator Neals selling nuclear secrets to the North Koreans?*

Khan is one thing — a renegade scientist in a corrupt country. But Senator Neals is rich — he certainly doesn't need the money — and powerful, his popularity soaring after he returned from North Korea with the hostage.

Ranjit stops abruptly, remembering again that evening in the Senator's house.

Shanti had walked up to the Senator, still sipping on her orange soda, and asked him why the North Koreans had let the hostage go. He'd replied patronizingly, asking her if she knew what a negotiation was. When she shook her head, he had said, *They wanted something, and I wanted something, and we worked it out.* Undeterred, Shanti had asked, *Huh, what did you give them?*

Ranjit walks on, passing a tall statue of Alexander Hamilton, now reduced to a dark, looming silhouette, surrounded by twinkling lights.

His clever, too-curious daughter had asked the right question back then. It all makes too much sense: the Senator's trip to India and the negotiations with the Koreans are a decade apart, but the microfilm hidden inside the doll may be the link between the two deeds.

Had the Senator offered the North Koreans this microfilm in exchange for the hostage? If his guess is true, the Senator will be under tremendous pressure to get the microfilm back, will even kill for it. Ranjit shivers when he thinks of what he might be involved with.

He realizes that he has walked the length of Commonwealth Avenue, and now stands across the road from the ornate wrought-iron fence of the Boston Public Garden. His fingers and toes are blocks of ice, and he stamps his feet and slaps his arms as he waits to cross Arlington Street.

Entering the garden, he walks down its winding paths, deserted now, lit by soft globes of light. The huge weeping willows are brown and drooping, and the pond in its midst is frozen solid, covered with a dusting of snow.

He remembers coming here with Shanti on a summer day. The garden had been

281

crowded with tourists and full of excited children. Shanti had been captivated by the swan boats, long paddleboats that puttered across the pond, each decorated with a large wooden swan. He'd taken her on a ride across the green pond, past the water lotuses with their shocking pink flowers, and she'd giggled at the real swans turning themselves upside down, their webbed feet sticking comically up in the air.

If only Shanti hadn't taken that damn doll . . . but there is no use thinking like that. What the hell is he going to do now?

The important thing is that he knows what is on this microfilm. He can use it to trade for his family's freedom, but it is too dangerous to approach the Senator directly. There has to be some other way.

Anna. She said that she was returning to Boston. She cannot be mixed up in this mess: he thinks of their discussions during the summer, how she seemed disgusted by the world of power and money. He doesn't have to tell her much; all she has to do is set up a meeting with the Senator and make sure that the blond man isn't there.

Despite the freezing cold, the narrow iron bridge across the pond holds a pair of lovers, mouths pressed into each other. Averting his eyes, Ranjit walks past them, emerges on the other side of the garden, and cuts across the empty expanse of the Boston Common.

As he heads toward Chinatown, he passes the old colonial graveyard at the edge of the Common, its marble tombstones sticking out of the snow. The stones have been worn smooth by centuries of weather, and all he can make out are a few words: *eternity, peace,* and *rest.*

He walks faster, heading down Essex Street, and is glad to enter the crowded swirl of Chinatown.

Stopping in the lobby of the Garibaldi Hotel, he asks the white-haired day manager behind the desk for a phone book.

The man stares blankly at Ranjit. "Nobody uses those. They show up and we throw them out."

But miraculously, there is a battered copy under the counter, from five years ago. And that is probably a good thing, because Ranjit is sure that Senator Neals's address is not listed anymore. But there it is, in black and white: Clayton Rivers Neals, 51 Rutland Square, Boston.

"Where is this place?" Ranjit asks the manager, who squints down at the small print.

"South End." The man chuckles. "Back in

the old days nobody would set foot there. The place was full of junkies. You could buy a house from the city for a dollar. Now it's all gays and yuppies and wine bars. Take the Orange Line, then walk down Mass. Ave. and . . ."

Ranjit leans on the counter and copies the address onto a scrap of paper. The rich and powerful of Boston live on their estates in Wellesley and Lincoln, but not Senator Neals; the kid who grew up in hardscrabble Roxbury has stayed close to his old neighborhood. Anna is just a few miles away from him, and he will go and see her tomorrow.

Walking up to his floor, Ranjit hopes that James is in his room, but his neighbor's door is shut. Entering his own room, Ranjit takes down the doll from above the bathroom ceiling, replaces the aperture card, and stashes it up there again. He retrieves his knife and puts it on the dressing table, wishing he had been able to take the blond man's handgun.

Taking a deep breath, he reminds himself that he has the upper hand: he knows what is on the microfilm now, and the Senator badly wants it back. When he thinks of Anna, he feels a familiar flush of shame, mixed with desire. *What is he going to say to her when he sees her?*

CHAPTER TWENTY-ONE

The next morning, Ranjit walks down Columbus Avenue in the South End. Even with the trees bare and gray crusts of snow piled on the ground, Anna's neighborhood stinks of money.

He turns onto Rutland Square, passing rows of Victorian brick town houses with curved bay windows, their high brick stoops rebuilt with faux-antique iron railings. Land Rovers and Saabs are parked in the tiny service alleys, and through the windows he sees high-ceilinged rooms with chandeliers and tall, dark pieces of furniture. *The richer Americans are,* he thinks, *the older they like their houses.*

The Dunkin' Donuts near the subway stop was still out of tea, so he bought a cup of hot chocolate. He sips it as he walks, noticing the street numbers painted in gold leaf on the high transoms. Number 51 is at the center of the square, and a motion-activated security camera above its front door whirrs to life as he approaches.

Cursing under his breath, he hurries past. He really should have planned this better. *What is he going to do, wait for Anna to emerge? Or should he just ring the doorbell and hope that the Senator isn't home?*

He pauses in front of a brick town house on the other side of the square. It has been gutted and is being rebuilt, its windows empty holes, its interior swarming with workers in yellow helmets. He smells freshly cut lumber and hears the *crack crack crack* of compressed-air nail guns.

Moving closer, he stands on its stairs, hoping that in his blue mechanic's jacket and boots he will fit in with the construction workers.

Minutes pass, and soon the hot cocoa is down to a chemical-tasting sludge. He looks for somewhere to throw his cup, but there seem to be no trash cans in this neatly manicured world. He is looking up and down the block when Anna emerges from her front door and pulls it shut.

He recognizes her long-limbed, confident stride right away. She's wearing her blue-and-gold running sneakers and silver down jacket, her short hair hidden under an orange knit hat.

Anna, it's me, Ranjit, please, can I have a minute . . . The words are in his throat as he starts to cross the road. And then he stops.

A black Land Rover emerges from the alley and pulls alongside her. The rear window hisses down and he gets a glimpse of the dark, shaved head of Senator Neals.

Stupid. Seeing her has made him stupid. Ranjit walks casually back to the construction site.

"Hey, you!" A bearded face peers down at him from a high window of the gutted house. "Yeah, I'm talkin' to ya. Ya with the Sheetrockers? Where's the rest of the fucking crew?"

Ranjit nods. "They'll be right by. They're looking for parking."

"Parking? In this neighborhood? Stupid crackhead motherfuckers." The man's head disappears.

Across the road Anna leans into the car. Ranjit hears scattered words above the crash of construction.

". . . nice today . . . going running . . . thanks . . ."

The Land Rover roars ahead and Anna sets off toward Massachusetts Avenue at a rapid walk. He quickly follows, expecting her to break into a run at any second. *When she starts jogging, what is he going to do,*

287

chase her?

She doesn't look back, just walks on rapidly, swinging her arms. Maybe she's heading to the Esplanade, the park that runs along the length of the Charles River. It's at least a fifteen-minute walk from here.

He crosses the road toward Anna, but just then she turns and runs lightly down the stairs to the Massachusetts Avenue subway stop. Following her, he slams through the turnstiles and takes the stairs to the open-air track below. It is rush hour, and the platform is packed with office workers. Just then an Orange Line train pulls into the station, disgorging more passengers, and he loses sight of her.

He stands, peering at the sea of people, swamped by the gray overcoats and dark business suits. Just as the doors begin to close, there is the flash of an orange knit cap, and he sees Anna pushing her way into a car at the rear of the train.

He runs for the car nearest to him, seeing the doors sliding shut. *Damn it.*

A hand appears between the doors, and they jerk open. He jumps in, hearing them hiss shut behind him.

"Made it, huh, buddy?" A black man in faded blue janitor's overalls retracts his arm and smiles at Ranjit.

"Thanks," Ranjit manages to gasp. "I was late for work."

"Yeah, I know how that is."

The man cracks open a *Boston Globe* and there is a photograph of Senator Neals on the front page. *Damn it, the man is everywhere.* The headline above the photograph says SENATOR NEALS SPEAKS AT HARVARD TODAY: HOW TO DEAL WITH A DANGEROUS WORLD.

The train hurtles down a dark tunnel and Ranjit wipes sweat from his eyes, leaning into the motion of the train. He'll move back to Anna's car at the next station, but he suddenly feels wary about talking to her. It's clear that she isn't going running. *Why the hell did she lie to the Senator?*

Looking out of the window, he watches the dark walls of the tunnel swallow up the train.

The train jerks to a stop at Back Bay and he quickly changes subway cars. There is no sign of Anna and he pushes to the middle of the car, feeling the panic build, then spots her sitting in the far corner. She has taken off her hat and her hair is longer now, its dark wings framing her face. Her summer tan has faded, and in the dull light of the train her skin is beige; she seems edgy, her black eyes flicking about the train, her slim body swaying with its jerky movement. He's always thought of her as strong, but just now she seems brittle, diminished by the crowds and the darkness.

Taking a deep breath, he is about to walk up to her when a well-barbered gray-haired man steps in front of her, raising the wooden handle of his umbrella in greeting.

"Why, Anna Neals. I had no idea you took the T."

Her face brightens artificially. She is instantly gracious, dimples appearing as she smiles. "Oh, Walter. I'm just going to the gym. How are things downtown?"

Ranjit curses and steps back. *So she is going running after all, but inside, at a gym.*

He sees the back of the man's neck redden, sees how animated he is in Anna's company. From what he can hear, they're talking about a dinner party, then a new play at the American Repertory Theater.

". . . wonderful," Anna says. "What presence. But a little histrionic, don't you think?"

The man leans closer. "Well, it is a play by Pinter. My understanding is that he had a tumultuous life himself, I mean, the marriages . . ."

The man talks on and on, and Anna

smiles and makes a show of listening, looking now and then at the phone in her hand. Ranjit does not understand what the hell they are talking about and feels dread settle into his bones. This is Anna's world: Rutland Square, gyms with treadmills, going to the theater with men like Walter. He had probably only seen her summer personality, the one that goes with her cotton dresses and straw hats.

The stations hurtle past, taking him back the way he had come: Tufts Medical Center, Chinatown. *How far away is her gym?*

As they roll into Downtown Crossing, he sees her pull on her hat and ready herself, but Walter misses all her cues and is still talking as the train screeches to a stop. She hurries off the train with a small wave, too distracted to notice Ranjit a few steps behind her, and they are both instantly swallowed by the crowd.

She strides toward the turnstiles, pushing past teenagers in baggy jeans, men in cheap leather jackets, and secretaries wearing bright lipstick. He is right behind her when a man in a puffy black jacket cuts in front, blocking his view. In the few seconds it takes to get through the turnstiles, she is gone.

He stands on his tiptoes, peering into several exits leading in different directions.

Has she gone to the Red Line on the lower level? Or on to Oak Grove?

There is a flash of her orange hat going up the stairs, and he moves, following her up to a long, narrow concourse. She strides past the Africans selling incense and scarves from wooden carts and ducks into an entrance for Filene's Basement, its door plastered with signs for discount clothes.

Is she using this as a shortcut on her way to the gym? He enters behind her, inhaling perfume-scented air, and finds himself in the women's section. Despite the early hour, the low-ceilinged basement is swarming with women who scour the racks of brightly colored clothes with methodical precision.

Anna's closets in the Vineyard were full of brand-new clothes with designer labels. Surely she isn't shopping here, among the remainders and clothes left over from previous seasons?

Right in front of Ranjit a busty redhead is trying on a new pink silk blouse over her white one. She looks up at Ranjit and glares. *Clearly, the women's department does not welcome men in construction boots and stained mechanic's jackets.* He walks on, eager not to lose Anna.

The subterranean basement is vast, with exits to the street and to the department store above. He remembers coming here with Preetam, and how she was confused and stepped onto the escalator to the main department store above. He remembers that the store detective had treated her like a criminal, his flat Bostonian voice rising to a shout.

Ahead of him, Anna walks unhurriedly. She fingers a thin dress of orange silk as bright as a flame, then runs her hands across a pile of pink cashmere sweaters. Her desultory progress allows him to move closer, and he sees a dreamy, unfocused look on her face. Seeing her like this, a strange feeling comes over him, a sense that something is not right.

She soon reaches the back of the store and stops by large wooden bins piled with mismatched luggage. Pulling a red Samsonite suitcase from the pile, she rights it, and rolls it back and forth.

He feels a rush of relief. *She came here to get a cheap suitcase, that's all; even a senator's wife likes a bargain.* He rehearses the words he is going to say, and is striding toward her when there is a blur in his periphery. A white-blond head moves down a side aisle, heading toward her.

The blond man steps into view, walking fast, his face flushed. His brown tweed coat is draped over his shoulders, and under it his right arm is in a bulky sling. *In the name of the Guru, what is he doing here?*

The man stops a few feet behind Anna and looks around. She is still rolling the red suitcase back and forth, a pensive expression on her face. She must sense something, because she turns, and when she sees the man her eyes widen, and her mouth opens as though to say something.

Ranjit ducks down behind a shelf of cashmere sweaters. He crouches there, his face half pressed into the soft wool, listening to the murmur of their voices.

"What happened to you?" Anna asks. "Your arm looks bad."

"Oh, a car accident, nothing serious. The whiplash messed up my shoulder."

Ranjit risks a glance, seeing that Anna is listening intently, her dark eyes shining with some peculiar emotion; fear, he thinks, from the way she grips the suitcase handle.

The man holds Anna by the elbow and moves her farther away, and their conversation is reduced to a murmur.

Ranjit crouches behind the shelf of sweaters, straining to hear, but it is no use. He hears footsteps behind him and sees a woman in a short dress glancing through a rack of spangled cocktail frocks.

Any second now she will notice him, and he can't remain crouched here. There is a cash register, at the back of the store, closer to where Anna is. Straightening up, he throws a sweater over his arm and walks quickly over to the register, manned by a plump, gum-chewing woman, her thick arms resting on the counter.

"Could you tell me how much this is?" He gestures at the label, a mess of colored markdown stickers.

The woman scowls, pulls on reading glasses, and mutters to herself as she peers at the label, as though interpreting divine scripture.

"Nineteen ninety-five," she says definitively. "Ya want it?"

Behind Ranjit, the blond man is still talking. He leans closer, still holding Anna's arm, and murmurs. If only Ranjit could hear what they were saying . . .

"Hey, it's a good price for cashmere. Ya want it or not?"

Ranjit turns his attention back to the register. "*Um,* I don't know . . . Pink? What do you think?"

The woman stares at him disbelievingly. "You know that it's a woman's sweater, right? Right?"

Anna and the blond man are walking

slowly toward the cash register. In a few seconds, they will see him.

Ranjit shakes his head, *No,* thrusts the sweater at the woman, and walks on toward the entrance, hearing the woman snort loudly behind him.

He has no time to see if they are behind him. Heading through the turnstiles, he boards the first train he sees, a Red Line train to Ashmont. The doors slam shut, and he ducks into a corner just as Anna emerges alone onto the platform.

The train speeds out of the station and a voice intones the stops: *South Station, Broadway, Andrew, UMass, Savin Hill, Fields Corner . . .*

Ranjit breathes hard. *Stupid. He could have been caught.* He replays the image of Anna talking to the blond man, trying to place the expression on her face; it was a mixture of fear and something else, something he can't pinpoint. *If the blond man is watching Anna, it will be hard to get to her.* He sits in the rocking train, trying to figure out what to do.

The subway car has emptied out by the time it rumbles aboveground in Dorchester. Outside, impoverished neighborhoods flash by, the wooden triple-decker houses crowded close to the tracks, their yards piled high with snow. A yellow dog on a back porch barks as the train goes by. White sheets hung out to dry are frozen solid, hanging in a line like distress flags.

At the next stop the doors slide open and a breeze flutters the discarded newspapers that litter the floor. *The newspaper from this morning,* he thinks. *The one with the Senator's picture on it.*

He searches for the front page of the *Globe* and finds it, rereading the headline he'd seen earlier this morning: SENATOR NEALS SPEAKS AT HARVARD TODAY: HOW TO DEAL WITH A DANGEROUS WORLD.

The Senator is giving a speech at Harvard tonight. He will be talking to a group of African-American students at the Barker Center about American foreign policy, and given his hero status, it will be very well attended. If the speech is as important as the newspaper says, surely Anna will accompany him.

With all the attention focused on the Senator, it might be easier to get to her. It is always easier to hide in a crowd.

The elevator at the Garibaldi Hotel is broken again. Ranjit climbs the stairs, breathing in the now-familiar smell of Lysol, and the dank odor of men living together at close quarters. Reaching his floor, he sees that the door to James's room is open. Lit only by a bar of fluorescent light, the tiny space seems frozen in time, like a waiting lounge at an airport.

James looks up from the book in his lap and gestures Ranjit in. He is freshly bathed and wears a new white T-shirt, his long gray hair wet and combed straight back.

"Come in, come in. Tell me about the world." He is sipping from a cup of dark tea and the steam fogs his glasses.

Ranjit closes the door and turns to him. "I found out what that microfilm is for. It's a missile. Part of one, anyway. I don't know what the hell it was doing in the doll —"

James motions Ranjit to sit and wheels his chair closer. Still clutching the day's newspaper, Ranjit tells him about his theory: that the Senator was giving the North Koreans the microfilm in exchange for the hostage.

"It makes perfect sense." Ranjit pauses. "Look at the timing. People were saying that he wouldn't be reelected. So he goes to North Korea, does something that even the President couldn't do, and comes back a hero. He must really want this microfilm, right? I've got to find a way to approach him, trade it for my family —"

"Hold it right there." James frowns.

"You're just going to give this scumbag the microfilm? What happens if those North Korean bastards build a missile? World War Three, man. Go to the newspapers. Blow this thing wide open."

"Who is going to believe me?" Ranjit spreads his arms wide. "I'm an illegal. I can't even talk to the Indian Embassy. As soon as they dig up my record, I'll have no credibility. I'm on my own, James. No one can help me get my family back."

James is silent for a moment. "You got a copy of the aperture card?"

"My nephew scanned it, so he has a copy on his computer."

"Okay. When your family is safe, you give me the copy. I'll take it to the *Times,* the *Globe,* the *Post,* whatever."

Ranjit can't see the mainstream media believing a paraplegic veteran, but he humors the man. "Okay, James, if that's what you want to do."

"Damn straight. I hate these fucking politicians." James nods in satisfaction.

"So, look. I know the Senator's wife, I did some work for her last summer. I might be able to get to the Senator through her . . ."

Ranjit tells James about his plan to approach Anna at Harvard tonight, and when he is done, James is silent.

299

"It's risky to approach the wife in public," he finally says. "It's risky, but I see how it could work. Good tactical move." He points at Ranjit's blue jacket. "But if you're going to Hah-vahd, you gotta get some new clothes. Get rid of that crap."

Ranjit looks down at his stained blue jacket, his jeans and cracked brown boots.

"That's how it is, man. Ya leave the army, but ya just keep on wearing the uniform. Army kills the need to wear clothes. Look in there." James waves at the wardrobe in the corner, but Ranjit hesitates.

"Go on, look inside it. Nothing's going to jump out and bite you."

Ranjit opens the wardrobe doors and the sharp smell of mothballs brings tears to his eyes. He blinks, seeing a row of clothes hanging inside, all neatly encased in plastic: starched cotton shirts, jackets with silk linings, heavy wool topcoats.

"Take what you want. I don't wear any of it. Couldn't bear to part with them when my wife — ex-wife, now — kicked me out of the house."

Ranjit fingers a thick black wool overcoat.

"They should fit you. Believe it or not, I used to be your height. I got no ties to give you, those got left behind. Go to the Salvation Army and get yourself some nice silk ones. A man in a suit without a tie is like a rooster without . . ."

Ranjit hesitates, then chooses a cream-colored shirt, a dark blue suit, and the black overcoat. He turns to James.

"Thank you. I wish I could pay you, but I don't have much money right now —"

"I don't want your money, Captain." James looks away as he talks. "Foolish to keep those clothes. Pride is the last thing to go, you know. When I kick, they'll end up in a Dumpster, anyway."

The clothes are bundled over Ranjit's arms. "James, don't talk like that. I saw you doing fifty pull-ups —"

James smiles. "It's okay, Captain. Dying doesn't bother me. Over in 'Nam, they're all Buddhists, they say that death is a release from the endless suffering of life. I've done bad things in my life, but now I pray and meditate." He gestures at the gold Buddha sitting on his dresser. "My soul is prepared. It's the body that I'm worried about. The cancer is in my lungs now, and it's spreading."

"Surely you can do something? Chemo?"

"I don't believe in that crap. I have my Chinese herbal teas, and when the pain gets bad, I get some acupuncture . . . it's just that I worry about dying in this goddamn

301

room, stinking up the place. No dignity in that." He stops and looks away.

The clothes are heavy in Ranjit's arms. "What can I do to help?"

"I've paid for the cremation. I just need someone to take my ashes to the ocean. Put me in there. I don't really care where, just so long as it's the open ocean. Not a lake or a pond. I hate still water."

Ranjit thinks of South Beach in the Vineyard, the way the waves roar in, landing on the sand with a crash. He thinks of ashes mixing with the water and instantly dispersing, sinking down into the green-gray depths.

"You're going to live for a while. But if that's what you want, I'll do it."

Holding the bundle of clothes, he thanks James again. As he gently closes the door, he hears the click of a lighter and smells again the sweetness of incense. He leaves James murmuring to his Buddha.

Life is suffering. Anna had said the same thing.

He drapes the clothes over his dresser and, heaving hard, he opens the window to air them out.

A few hours later, his room is freezing, but at least the smell of mothballs has faded from the clothes. He tries on the cream shirt with the dark blue suit. The shirt is hand-stitched, the lining of the jacket a deep maroon silk. The pants are a little loose, but otherwise, the clothes fit surprisingly well.

Looking at himself in the bathroom mirror, a distant memory tugs at him. Then he realizes that the suit resembles his officer's uniform, and turns away from the mirror.

CHAPTER TWENTY-TWO

It is four o'clock and already dark as Ranjit walks through the snow-covered quadrangle of Harvard Yard, looking for the Barker Center. *I have to talk to Anna tonight,* he tells himself. *Preetam and Shanti have been locked up for three days now.*

From his own experience, he knows that seventy-two hours in jail is a long time. The empty days and nights blur, and there is nothing but the moans and shouts of other people. Shanti might do better, able to retreat into her own fantasy world, but confinement will destroy Preetam's already fragile sense of self.

He's so deep in his thoughts that it takes him a few minutes to realize that he's lost. Glancing at his watch, he realizes that the Senator's speech starts in fifteen minutes.

Redbrick dormitories surround all four sides of Harvard Yard, their windows glowing with light. As he walks past an arched entry, a door opens and a shaggy-haired student emerges, wearing a hoodie and headphones, his head bopping to music. Ranjit wants to ask the boy where the Barker Center is, but something stops him.

When he worked at Lallu's store, one subway stop away, some of the Harvard kids would come in, pile their shopping baskets full of spicy snacks, and ignore Ranjit completely as he swiped their gold and platinum credit cards. Now he is afraid that this boy will just stare right through him.

Maybe the Barker Center is on the east side of the yard. He walks past the wide steps of Widener Library and crosses a narrow road, and just as he reaches the other side, a Harvard police car drifts past him. It stops and backs up.

The window of the car rolls down and a voice drifts out, polite and low-pitched. "Looking for something, sir?"

Ranjit feels his throat constrict with panic. He speaks slowly, making his voice a little absentminded. "Ah, yes, Senator Neals's talk at the Barker Center. I seem to be a little lost."

"You're in the right place, sir. It's right over there, next to the Faculty Club. You can't miss it."

Ranjit thanks the cop, who raises a hand

in salutation and drives off.

He takes a deep breath. If he'd still worn a turban, he's sure that the cop's voice would have been steely, with an implicit undertone of threat. But the short hair and dark suit seem to be working, along with the silk paisley tie and black Oxford shoes that he bought from the Salvation Army.

Walking through a low gate, he sees the tall white portico of the Barker Center right ahead. A stream of well-dressed people is making its way up the stairs, and just inside the doors a harassed-looking security guard is checking ID cards.

He merges with a group of elderly African-Americans, the men wearing double-breasted suits, the women in pearls and embroidered shawls. Going up the stairs, he is shoulder-to-shoulder with a white-haired lady whose high heels suddenly slip on the icy stairs. Without thinking he reaches out and holds her elbow, steadying her.

"Oh, why thank you. Really, the facilities people should do a better job. And you are?" She peers at him over the rim of her stylish red-framed glasses.

"I'm just visiting from India," he says as he guides her up the stairs.

"India is a fascinating country. Are you with the Scholars at Risk program? What is your area of expertise?"

"I'm a historian. Military history, mostly."

The security guard at the top of the stairs recognizes the small group and smiles as he waves them in. The old lady lets go of Ranjit's arm and unwraps her embroidered silk shawl, emitting a cloud of lavender perfume.

"Another historian, how fortuitous. My husband, Alfred, will be fascinated to meet you. He's Professor Emeritus of history. Do you know people here? No? Then you must sit with us, we have reserved seats."

They pass through a tall atrium lit by a giant chandelier made of stag horns, each upturned point bearing a glittering burst of light. The lecture is in a wood-paneled room next door, one wall dominated by a huge stone fireplace, the others lined with marble busts of philosophers. A podium has been set up at one end, with sofas pulled to face it, and beyond are rows of folding chairs, already full, the few empty seats reserved with piles of coats.

The crowd is mainly African-American, some students with high Afros and ragged army-surplus jackets, but many others in blazers and ties. More faculty pour in, the men gravelly-voiced and assured, the women in twinsets and pearls, patting their

307

straightened hair. There is the strong sense of these people owning this room and its history.

For two years Ranjit had labored in the basement of Lallu's store, and never guessed that a world like this existed.

The old lady gestures him to one of the sofas, and he finds himself seated next to a tall, hawk-nosed man with bushy eyebrows. With his pale skin, the man could have easily passed as Italian, but the rich cadences of his speech are those of Dr. King.

"Ah," the old man says. "You're from India. I used to study Gandhi and non-violence and all that. Now tell me, why is your country hell-bent on starting a nuclear war?"

"The usual reasons." Ranjit thinks of General Handa at his court-martial, his thick shoulders hunched, eyes glittering with anger. "Pride, honor, arrogance. Here we are, a continent of people, and the Pakistanis sit in their narrow little country hurling insults at us. They're arming militants in Kashmir, backing the terrorists who shot up half of Mumbai. But mainly it's because we have nuclear capability and we're itching to try it out." He's listening to his voice as he speaks, authoritative and strong after so long.

"Ah. Human beings, eh? Hubris and ego —" The old man stops in mid-sentence, noticing a stir in the audience.

Senator Neals has just entered the room, wearing a dark suit and tie, a small American flag glistening in his lapel. Gone is the fatigued, slightly drunk man whom Ranjit had met. The Senator's smile is high-wattage as he shakes hands and banters with the students.

Walking next to him, wearing a deep orange suit, her hair freshly cut, is Anna. With a shock, Ranjit realizes that she's wearing makeup, her eyelashes darkened with mascara, a dab of color on each cheekbone. And right behind her is the blond man, his neck swiveling, his gaze passing over Ranjit without a hint of recognition.

Anna walks to within a few feet of Ranjit, so close that he can smell the musk of her perfume. She sits in the front row, the Senator next to her, his large hands clasped together. The blond man stands at the entrance to the room, rocking back and forth on his heels.

"Very impressive person, the Senator. Experienced with realpolitik in a way that other politicians are not."

Ranjit turns to the Professor Emeritus next to him. "What do you mean, sir?"

"It is a mistake to assume that the world is any different now than during the Cold War. Power is power. We need to move beyond ideology, all this good-and-evil nonsense, and support our own interests. All this talk about nation building. *Pshaw.*"

The man lectures on in his sonorous voice. As the minutes pass, more people pour into the room and the murmur turns to a dull roar. Ranjit glances at the back of Anna's head, seeing how stiffly she sits, her shoulders pulled back. Every few minutes she glances at her phone, then thrusts it back inside her small purse.

A tall man in a suit makes his way onto the stage and turns to the crowd, his round glasses gleaming.

"I'm Charles Dorr, head of the African-American program here at Harvard. And today we have a man of remarkable ability to deliver the first Huggins lecture of the season. The man who won the famous Harvard-Yale football game of 1968, a graduate of Harvard Law School, a politician who rose from the projects of Roxbury to the heights of Washington. Senator Clayton Rivers Neals."

There is loud applause as the Senator bounds up to the microphone. He leans forward, his large hands gripping the podium, and a hush falls over the room.

"Seeing so many young faces, it makes me feel old."

As the laughter fades away, he continues. "Professor Dorr here mentioned the football game, back in 1968. That's ancient history. It should be long forgotten. But even now, I run into Yalies from back then — I'll be in a restaurant in Washington, and some sixty-year-old will come over to me, and we'll shake hands, and then he'll ask me, *Speedy, how did you win that game? You guys were down by sixteen points, and there were just forty-five seconds left. How in God's name did you do it?*

"Some of them insist it was brute force. Well, I was a few pounds heavier back then, but that's not it. Some of them say it was speed — yes, I was so fast, I could stop on a dime. I was so fast, the Yale team had to practice by chasing a chicken across the field —"

The crowd erupts with laughter, and the Senator waits for it to subside.

"— but no, speed and brute force didn't win that game. I'll tell you what did. Other players, they saw that wall of defenders, but I saw the gaps, the holes, the opportunities. That game was won by *vision.*"

The Senator stops and takes a drink of water.

"Now, let me talk about our country, and its leadership. I've been a Democrat all my life. Three terms in the State Senate, been in the U.S. Senate ever since. I served with Ted Kennedy, and he taught me one thing I will never forget. Politics is politics. Forget about slogans, forget about trying to change the way that power works. Use the system. And if you have *vision,* you can do so.

"Now, I found a way to get the Indians and Pakistanis to back away from a nuclear war. Hell, I even negotiated a deal with the North Koreans, and those people are tough, let me tell you . . ."

The crowd claps loudly, and the Senator pauses. Ranjit sees a flash of orange as Anna rises and walks rapidly out of the room, stepping over the students sitting on the floor. A shadow crosses the Senator's face as he continues, his deep voice filling the room, but no one else seems to have noticed Anna's departure.

Ranjit sees her walking through the empty atrium, heading for the open stairway to the second floor. He hesitates for a few seconds. The blond man's eyes are still scanning the crowd, but then he turns to the podium, his fingers fidgeting under the wing of hair that covers his ear.

Murmuring an apology, Ranjit rises and follows Anna into the atrium, just in time to catch a glimpse of her orange suit. The huge chandelier throws her shadow against the wall as she climbs the open staircase and disappears through a door on the second floor.

He follows her, taking the stairs two at a time. Pushing open the door at the top, he walks down a dim hallway lined with mahogany doors, professors' names stenciled on them in gold paint.

Anna is at the far end of the corridor, silhouetted against a large Palladian window. She hears his footsteps and whips around, her teeth bared, clicking her phone shut in one movement.

"What the hell?"

"Anna, it's me. Ranjit Singh. From the Vineyard."

Her dark eyes stare at him. She blinks, recognizing his voice, but distrusting his appearance.

"I cut off my hair and shaved my beard. It's me."

She relaxes a little, but confusion still clouds her face. She is quivering with tension, the smell of her perfume mixed with the tang of fresh sweat. Up close he sees that her dark eyes are dull with tiredness.

The phone in her hand buzzes again, and she silences it with a jab of her thumb.

"Ranjit. What the hell are you doing here? Looking like this?"

"Anna, I have to talk to you . . ."

"Not in the corridor. Come inside."

Apparently professors at Harvard don't lock their offices, because when she tries a door handle, it opens. The room is large, one wall lined with books, the others painted a deep red and hung with African masks. A large desk is in the corner, a crystal ashtray on it holding a half-smoked cigar, and the small room smells of rich tobacco.

Anna sinks into an overstuffed leather armchair and kicks off her high heels.

"God, these things are killing me."

She tilts back her head, closes her eyes, and takes a deep breath. When she opens them, she looks directly at him, and despite himself, he feels the slow burn of desire.

"Ranjit. You chose a hell of a day to show up like this."

He leans against the closed door. From here, he'll be able to hear anyone coming. "Is something wrong, Anna?"

"I'm tired of all these bullshit speeches. Ever since he got back, all he's been doing is giving speeches. I think he wants to be

314

the next Secretary of State. He's even talking about running for President one day." She stops and catches herself. "But you, Ranjit. Clayton told me that something happened . . . that you'd stolen the dolls? I didn't believe him, I told him he was mistaken, but he insists it's true."

Ranjit leans against the door and unbuttons his suit jacket. The stale tobacco smoke that fills the room has a strangely narcotic effect.

"I came here to talk to you about it. I'm not a thief. Shanti picked up an old doll from the pink bedroom downstairs. I wanted to return it, but —"

"Betsy? Your daughter took Betsy? That was my doll when I was a child." Anna frowns in confusion. "Clayton said that you'd taken the Meissen dolls from the cabinet."

"Shanti just took that old doll. The others are safe, I promise you."

"So it's a mix-up, right? I'll talk to Clayton, I'll straighten the whole thing out."

He shakes his head. "Things aren't that simple. That man who works for your husband — the blond man downstairs — he's after me now, he won't stop." He pauses, then his words rush out. "You see, our visas had expired, and he called Homeland Security, and they've taken Preetam and Shanti away. They're both going to be deported —"

"*What?* Your little girl?"

"Homeland Security picked her up, in front of my own eyes."

Anna leans back, her face tight with anger. "Fucking Matti Kohonen. How dare he do that."

"Who is he? I was right behind you today at Filene's Basement when he showed up."

She laughs, an abrupt, bitter burst. "You were there? In the women's section? And I didn't see you?"

Ranjit nods, his cheeks reddening. "What does he do for the Senator?"

Slumped in the leather chair, she looks up at him. Underneath the orange suit jacket she wears a pale cream camisole. He can see the swell of her chest as she breathes, smell the heat rising up from her.

"Kohonen's ex-CIA, he washed out of SAD." She sees the confusion on his face and continues. "It's a euphemism. 'Special Activities Group' means covert operations. He was hired to head up security, but now he's Clayton's chief of staff."

She shakes her head in disgust. "He's very ambitious. Clayton spends more time with him than with me."

316

"What was he talking to you about? Today, at Filene's."

"He said he wanted to warn me about you. Said you were a thief, that you'd stolen all the dolls. I told him that I didn't believe him, but he was very insistent, said that you might try to contact me. But I don't understand. Why does that old doll interest *him*?"

Ranjit can hear raucous laughter from below, followed by loud applause.

He has to trust her.

"That doll — Betsy — has a hidden compartment. You have to push down a certain way, and the head comes off. And I found something hidden inside it."

She sits forward, her fingers digging into the soft leather armrests. "What are you talking about?"

"A frame of microfilm for an Indian Army missile. What was the Senator doing with it? Giving it to the North Koreans in exchange for the hostage?"

Rising abruptly from the chair, she walks to the tall window, its thin mullions casting a grid of shadow across her face. "Crap. That's what it's all about."

"You knew what he was doing?"

Her voice is soft and emphatic. "I knew but I didn't want to know. I've been so stupid." She pauses, and the grid of shadow

317

wavers across her face. "Ranjit, you have to promise that you'll . . . you'll trust my judgment on this, okay?"

He nods. Her voice grows softer, and he has to walk closer to hear her.

"Clayton has won every election since he ran for State Senator. He's survived so long because he knows how to cut a deal. When the nuclear crisis happened between India and Pakistan, they were looking for someone to go there and negotiate, and he was the perfect man for the job."

She laughs, a bitter, abrupt sound. "But the Indians just stalled him. Poor Clayton, he was so frustrated. He'd call me late at night from Delhi and rant about the heat, the diarrhea he was getting from the spicy food. It looked like he would fail. Then, a week later, he told me, *Kohonen says he can help, he still has some CIA contacts here.* And that was it. It took Kohonen just a month to break the deadlock."

"How did he do it?"

"Clayton was very proud of what Kohonen did. He's deaf, you know. With hearing aids, he can hear a little, but he's an expert at reading lips. During the breaks in the negotiations, the Indians used to huddle across the room and talk amongst themselves. Kohonen turned off his hearing aids

318

and just watched them. He realized that they were talking about a new long-range nuclear missile they had developed."

"The Agni. That's what it is called."

She pauses and frowns. "I think that's it. Anyway, this missile was so accurate, the Indians could hit many targets at once. They were now confident that they could win a nuclear war. Once Kohonen knew that, he got to work. I don't know how he got the blueprints for it, but he did, and Clayton showed them to the Pakistanis. It scared the hell out of them, and they backed off."

"The Senator just kept the blueprints? Gave them to the North Koreans, in exchange for the hostage?"

She looks at the closed door, and her voice drops to a whisper.

"No. That's not exactly what happened. I don't think he meant to —"

Through the thick door, Ranjit can hear the cadences of the speech below. *How much longer will it last?*

"Go on, Anna, I'm listening."

"You have to understand the context. When Clayton came back from India in ohtwo, he was a hero for a while. But then the new President was elected, and people became tired of politics as usual. No one remembered what Clayton had done. The voters wanted something different, and he began to realize that he might just lose his Senate seat."

Her voice is so soft that he strains to hear her.

"It was Kohonen — I'm sure it was him — who saw the hostage crisis as a great opportunity. The President of the United States couldn't talk to the North Koreans and get the hostage released, neither could the Secretary of State. But a senator could fly down to North Korea and call it a 'humanitarian mission.' "

"How did the deal work?"

"There is a trade embargo against North Korea, you know. They desperately needed grain, machine parts, medicine. Kohonen was going to have it trans-shipped through Dubai, it was all untraceable." She shrugs her slim shoulders. "Clayton told me that we do business through back channels all the time with Iran, Libya, Syria, and I was okay with it. I'm not a big fan of people dying of hunger or disease, just because of politics —"

"But once the Senator got there, the North Koreans changed their terms?"

"Of course. Clayton was expecting that. Maybe more machine parts, or more medicines. But as soon as he reached Pyongyang, he called me. The line was crackling, I could barely hear him, but he was cursing, calling them a bunch of two-faced fucks. *They want something else,* he told me, *or else they'll hang the hostage.* He knew that it would end his career to bring her back in a coffin."

Anna's voice drops to a whisper. "He told me I'd find an envelope in his desk in the Vineyard. I didn't look inside, I just took it to his secretary in Boston. The envelope was sent through the diplomatic pouch to North Korea. Two days later, the hostage was released." She pauses and takes a deep breath. "I suspected he gave them something he shouldn't have, but I never made the connection with India."

Downstairs, the speech seems to be winding down, but Ranjit needs to know more.

"If he gave them the microfilm, why was that one frame hidden inside the doll?"

She shakes her head as she rises from her chair. "I don't know. Clayton's been on tenterhooks ever since he got back. He's frightened of something." Her dark eyes scan his face as she moves closer. With her fingertips, she traces the scar on his neck. "What happened to you? I didn't notice this before."

He feels the blood rising to his face. "It's

an old wound. Anna, please, I need your help. I need to talk to the Senator soon, without Kohonen around. I'll give him the microfilm back, but I want my family released —"

She takes a deep breath. "We're planning to go back to the Vineyard this weekend. Come by the house on Sunday evening, and you can talk to Clayton alone. Just bring the doll, bring the damn microfilm or whatever."

"You're sure? That man, Kohonen, he's after me —"

"I'll make sure he won't be there. I have to go now, but —"

She holds his face with both hands. When she kisses him, he tastes the sweet, waxy taste of lipstick. Her body presses into his, and her scent is dizzying.

From down below there is the sound of clapping, and a voice shouts, *"Tell it like it is!"*

She pulls away. "There. I've wanted to do that since I saw you."

Digging into her small handbag, she pulls out a tube of crimson lipstick and deftly applies it. She smiles at him, the door clicks shut, and she's gone.

He can hear her heels ticking down the corridor and descending the stairs. Gradually, the smell of her musky perfume is replaced by the harsh odor of tobacco.

Leaving the office, he hesitates at the top of the stairs. The crowd is giving the Senator a standing ovation, and there is no sign of Kohonen. Ranjit runs down the stairs, slips through the atrium, and heads out of the main door.

It is very cold outside. There are two police cruisers parked outside the Barker Center, and he sees a pair of cops standing by them, sipping hot cups of coffee. As he passes them, more applause drifts through the cold night air.

One cop turns to Ranjit and grins. "Some speech, huh?"

"Yes, it seems to be well received."

"Yeah, we need a guy like that in the White House. He gets things done. Have a good night, sir."

The cop turns back to his coffee, and Ranjit hurries on. He turns from the darkness of Quincy Street onto brightly lit Massachusetts Avenue and heads for the subway station.

So he had been partially right: the North Koreans had blackmailed the Senator into giving them the blueprints for the Agni, all except that one frame of microfilm stuffed inside the doll. Ricky had said that it was some sort of circuit, and he wishes he knew exactly what it was.

A group of giggling girls in tight jeans and boots emerges from the Grafton Street Grill, and Ranjit steps aside to let them pass, smelling beer and perfume. He walks past the brightly lit Harvard Bookstore, seeing students browsing inside. More students sit inside ice-cream parlors and coffee shops, talking and drinking, cocooned in their own reality. Across the road, the homeless settle into the darkened portico of the Harvard Coop, swathed in coarse gray blankets.

Before Ranjit descends into the subway he glances over his shoulder. Massachusetts Avenue is empty and no one seems to be following him, yet he feels a shiver of fear, and the feeling intensifies as he waits on the freezing platform. He is going up against a man who has been playing a secret, high-stakes international game, a man who will do anything to fulfill his ambitions. And now Ranjit has agreed to return to Martha's Vineyard. If the Senator sets a trap for him, this time there will be no way out.

He has one more day before leaving for the Vineyard; enough time to find an army surplus store and buy a snowsuit and a pair of powerful binoculars. More important, he'll go to the Boston Public Library and research all he can about the Senator's activities. He is sure Anna is telling the truth, but that one hidden frame of microfilm unsettles him. *The second rule of combat: know everything about your enemy.*

A Red Line train pulls into the station, and he gets on, seeing only a pair of necking students and a few tired Hispanic workers. Finding a seat, he remembers Anna's lips soft and warm against his, her hard, muscular body pressing into him. He had thought all that was over, but her touch has awakened something in him, and he feels confusion, mixed with an urgent desire.

All that evening, alone at the Garibaldi Hotel, he feels her warm fingertips tracing the scar on his neck. Even a bowl of soup and another bottle of Bacardi will not dull his thoughts. He tries not to, but he falls asleep thinking about her.

CHAPTER TWENTY-THREE

The Captain lies awake all night in the long, empty hospital ward, its one window a dark rectangle high up on the wall. He falls asleep just as light begins to seep into the sky, and is still sleeping when the Major returns and shakes him awake.

Even at this early hour, the Major's uniform is immaculately pressed, and his wavy hair gives off the sweet scent of fresh coconut oil. He looks around the long, empty ward, clears his throat, and begins.

"Well, Captain Singh, you've had time to think about our conversation. I'm sure you understand it is for the good of our country."

The Captain stares up sleepily. "I was up all night thinking about it. I discussed it with my Sergeant."

The Major frowns and looks around. "Someone else has been here? We told you, Captain, this is top secret."

"It's quite all right. My Sergeant is dead. He shot himself in the mouth. I told you all about it, remember?"

"Captain Singh, you are not making any sense. You say the man is dead?"

"Yes, that's what I thought, too. But he was here, he was most definitely here."

The Major makes a chopping gesture with the edge of his hand. "Enough of this nonsense. I assume we can count on you? The Japanese TV crew is waiting to interview you. Keep it short. Tell them that you saw Pakistani planes destroying our command post. Be very clear about this."

The Captain shakes his head, as though trying to clear his mind of sleep. "My Sergeant came to me last night. He stood right where you are standing. We talked it over, and sorry, the answer is no. I will not lie about what happened."

"If you refuse to cooperate, Captain, you will be court-martialed for your failure. You will go to jail. Do you understand that?"

The Captain nods silently.

"Then why are you doing this?"

"The Sergeant said he's very cold up there. He wants to be brought down."

The Major's face turns red, and his voice trembles with rage. "Captain, think again. This is the biggest mistake of your life. You will be transferred to a prison and we will start court-martial proceedings immediately. Think about it."

"I have."

The Major walks away, his back stiff with anger. When he is gone, the Captain turns over and falls into a sleep as deep as a crevasse.

All day long he sleeps. Many hours later he jerks awake, convinced that Sergeant Khandelkar is standing by his bed.

The ward is dark, and there is no sign of anyone else. The feeling fades, and the Captain lies still, wishing he knew the time. From the silence outside, he guesses that it is late evening.

There are footsteps at the end of the ward, and he turns his head to see a hospital orderly walking down the aisle, pushing a cart of medicines. He doesn't want to take any more of the blue pills, so he closes his eyes and pretends to be asleep.

The footsteps stop by his bed, and he hears a squeak as the cart comes to a halt. He waits for the orderly to remove the clipboard from the foot of his bed, make a note on his chart, then move on.

Instead there is only silence, broken by the orderly's rapid breathing. When Ranjit opens his eyes, he sees that the man is preparing a hypodermic syringe, pulling back the plunger and releasing a small squirt of colorless liquid into the air.

"Hey, what is this?"

The burly orderly starts. "Oh, you're awake. Time for your injection."

"I don't have injections. What is this for?"

The orderly steps forward, smiling unconvincingly as he taps the glass of the hypodermic.

"This is something new. It will help with the frostbite . . ."

The orderly reaches out for the Captain's arm, and the needle comes down fast, but the Captain slaps away the hypodermic. It flies out of the man's hand and smashes on the wall.

"Stupid bastard."

The orderly reaches under his hospital smock and a blade flashes in the darkness. The Captain feels a hot sting across his neck.

The orderly's knife hand rises, preparing to slice down again. The Captain throws up both his hands, feeling the IVs rip away, grabs the bottle of saline hanging above his head, and brings it down hard.

There is the sound of glass hitting skull. The orderly falls sideways, stunned, and the whole IV stand goes over with a crash.

Lights come on at the end of the ward.

There is the shocking hot leak from the Captain's neck.

The orderly rises from the floor, staggers to the wall, and boosts himself out of the high window.

The dark-haired nurse comes running down the corridor just as the Captain slips into unconsciousness.

CHAPTER TWENTY-FOUR

The next afternoon Ranjit sits in a crowded room at the Boston Public Library. On the floor next to him is a bulky plastic bag that contains a Finnish army surplus snowsuit and an expensive folding pair of Zeiss binoculars that have eaten up the last of his money.

The Microtext Room, tucked away in a corner of the library, has a vast archive, and he looks through old issues of *The New York Times,* the spools of microfilm whirring across a bulky reader with a backlit glass screen. The freezing cold has driven many of the city's marginal inhabitants into the library, and next to him an old woman mutters to herself as she scans headlines from World War Two. Across from him, a homeless man grins as pinups from ancient *Jet* magazines flash across his screen.

Ranjit stares intently as the blurry black-and-white pages flash across the screen.

The North Korean crisis last summer started when the Korean-American reporter accidentally crossed the border into North Korea and was arrested as a spy. Ranjit reads about the outcry in the international press, the denunciations by the United Nations, and the tightening of the trade embargo, all of which just seemed to make the North Koreans angrier.

He stares at a grainy picture of the reporter peering out from a prison cell, surrounded by hard-faced Korean men with brutal army haircuts. Then come the reports from the trial, and an angry press release from the North Korean government announcing her death sentence. Senator Neals flies into Pyongyang at the eleventh hour, and after two days of negotiations, he emerges with the reporter, a wide smile creasing his face.

There are articles about the reporter, articles about the brutal and repressive North Korean regime, and interviews with a few dissidents and a human-rights group, and Ranjit reads them all, finding out nothing new. Anna's explanation makes perfect sense.

The steam radiators in the crowded room whistle and clang, and he feels a headache coming on as he feeds a new reel of microfilm into the reader.

This one is from *The Times of India,* and for the next three hours he scans the columns, reliving the tense year when nuclear war almost broke out between India and Pakistan.

He had been on the Siachen then, taking his patrols into Pakistani territory and earning a reputation as a gung-ho young Captain. As rumors of war thickened he had watched as troops massed along the Kashmir border, but it had all seemed unreal. On the Siachen, weren't they already at war with the Pakis? And this kind of war wasn't so bad, it was an adventure, with the satisfaction of climbing mountains that no civilian mountaineer could. Now, looking back at those months, it seems incredible that the year hadn't ended in the flare of nuclear missiles and the senseless deaths of millions.

He stares at photographs from December 2001, seeing images of the masked terrorists who rammed through the gates of the Indian Parliament, intent on killing the politicians within. The attackers were Muslim terrorists from Kashmir who had been armed and trained by the Pakistanis. In a flurry of recriminations, both countries went on high alert, moving troops to their borders, and the nuclear bluster began.

By May of 2002, the Pakistanis were threatening to launch their nukes if the Indians crossed the Line of Control in Kashmir. The Indian Defense Minister was quoted as saying that India "could take a bomb or two more, but when we are finished, there will be no more Pakistan."

As he whirrs through the reels, day by day the posturing and blustering slowly turned toward a real war.

Pakistani-backed Muslim militants attacked an Indian Army camp in Kashmir, killing the wives and children of soldiers. Pakistan began shelling the northern state of Jammu. An Indian Army pilotless drone was shot down over Pakistan. And just when war seemed inevitable, the Americans arrived.

He pops in another roll of microfilm, and there, at last, is Senator Neals. The black-and-white pictures of him are grainy, but there is no mistaking his brilliant smile as he poses at a conference table, surrounded by the Indian Army's top brass.

Ranjit zooms in closer and closer.

Neals's seersucker Brooks Brothers suit is crumpled, speaking of his mad dash from halfway across the world, but he is smiling broadly and radiating a calm competence. What a clever strategy to send a black man to India, sidestepping all the colonial impli-cations of white skin. Neals must have been giving his "I'm one of you, I understand what it means to be oppressed" speech to anyone who would hear it.

A week later, the threat of Armageddon is still hanging over the world, but here is the Senator at a formal banquet in New Delhi, a garland of marigolds hanging around his thick neck. There is a man sitting next to Neals, his face hidden by the shadow of the flash, but there is no mistaking the pale hands and neatly manicured nails. It is definitely Kohonen. Ranjit studies the picture intently, zooming in till it degener-ates into a blur of pixels.

Soon the microfilm heats up and the smell of hot plastic fills his nostrils; he turns off the reader and sits in front of the blank screen. *How had Kohonen obtained the blueprints for the Agni missile? And what the hell is that one frame of microfilm doing inside the doll?*

His head begins to throb, and his throat is parched. Walking to a water fountain in the corridor, he bends over it and slurps ice-cold water.

When he returns, the librarian looks up at him from her desk. She is a slim Hispanic woman, her eyebrows carefully plucked, her large silver earrings jangling as she speaks.

"Are you doing okay? Finding what you're looking for?"

"Thank you, yes. I'm just researching a paper."

Her smile is tentative. "Well, if you need anything, just ask. That's why I'm here. And just to let you know, we'll be closing early, because of New Year's Eve."

New Year's Eve. Of course. Christmas now seems like a year ago.

When he sits down, the librarian is still looking at him. Catching his gaze, she blushes and turns away.

Popping in another reel of microfilm, he fast-forwards, searching for more news about the Senator.

For six weeks going forward — till the nuclear crisis passes — Neals's pictures appear regularly, but Kohonen does not make another appearance. The Senator is shown speaking to the Indians, then the Pakistanis, shuttling back and forth between New Delhi and Islamabad. Never once does his smile slip, and he radiates a calm authority. Talks are always "frank and extensive," the Senator is always "hopeful for constructive dialogue." But Neals's presence is working: both countries withdraw troops from the border and diplomatic relations are reestablished. Warships sail back to base from the Indian Ocean. And just like that, the nuclear threat goes away.

So the Senator's plan had worked; showing the Agni blueprints to the Pakistanis had scared them off.

Ranjit's headache is growing worse. He needs to get out of this stifling airless room and breathe in some fresh air. He has found out nothing new except information that confirms Anna's story.

He rewinds the microfilm, and as the year rushes back onto itself, he watches ads zip by for saris, for farm equipment, for mosquito repellent. He sees all the garish Hindi movie posters for the romances and action flicks that he'd missed that year; Preetam, alone, had seen them all.

And just then, one last picture catches his eye. He stops the microfilm with a jerk. *How had he missed this?*

In the photograph, Senator Neals is getting off a jet and being received by the Indian military. Standing on the tarmac, waiting in line to shake the Senator's hand, is a familiar figure. A thick-set man with the gold insignia of a general, his chest dripping with rows of medals. He is bare-headed, as usual, holding his heavily brocaded cap in his square, large hands. There is no mistaking the bulk of General Bear Handa.

Ranjit feels his headache worsen. Neals, the envoy of peace, was meeting with the General who had wanted to prolong the war. *It makes no sense.*

The librarian is going around from carrel to carrel, saying that the library is closing.

"Please, ma'am," Ranjit says, "I need five more minutes. Just five."

The woman's face softens. "All right. But then I really have to lock up."

He spins back through pages of microfilm, looking for the General's face, for any mention of his name, but there is nothing else, and soon Ranjit's time is up. Putting the reels into their boxes, he drops them onto a re-shelving cart. As he's leaving the librarian walks up to him. She moves with an easy grace as she pulls on a belted overcoat.

"Did you find what you were looking for? By the way, my name is Juanita."

"I'm Ranjit, and no, I didn't find it. But it's all right. I understand you have to close."

"We have other archives, you know. If you come back on Monday, I could help you."

By Monday everything will have changed. "I might not be back next week," he says gently.

She blushes and looks away, biting her lower lip. "Oh. Well, I'm here most days."

"Thank you for your help. I appreciate it." He touches her lightly on her shoulder, gathers up his plastic bag, and walks quickly down the stairs.

Exiting through the massive library doors, he stops for a moment at the top of the bank of stairs. From the Copley Plaza Hotel he can hear faint music, and sees people hurry by, the men in tuxes and bow ties, the women tripping along in high heels. Now that he knows, it certainly feels like New Year's Eve.

His headache recedes as he cuts through the darkened expanse of the Boston Common. It has been transformed into a wonderland, with giant ice sculptures of swans, dragons, and castles, all glittering in the glow of colored spotlights. Groups of revelers are already out, swathed in scarves and thick coats, passing bottles to each other. From a far-off bandstand comes the crackle of an electric guitar.

Shanti would have loved to see this, he thinks, walking past children who run excitedly from one sculpture to the next.

"Happy Nooo Year," someone shouts out, but he ducks his head and doesn't return the greeting.

CHAPTER TWENTY-FIVE

He leaves the Garibaldi Hotel the next morning, stopping to give James a bag of Snickers and a manila envelope. For once, the streets of Chinatown are silent, the sidewalks littered with the red shards of exploded firecrackers and frozen pools of vomit, the remnants of last night's celebrations.

The first day of the new year is just like the old one, cold and gray, and the passengers on this morning's Peter Pan bus to the Vineyard are sullen and hungover. Ranjit looks out of the window as the highway unspools, grateful for the lack of conversation.

When he alights at the Woods Hole ferry terminal, a sign says that the "threat index" is elevated to Level Orange, but whoever is threatening Woods Hole seems to have taken the day off, because the rows of wooden benches inside the ferry terminal are deserted. He buys a paper cup of coffee from a machine and takes a few sips before tossing it into the trash, wishing for the millionth time that he could have some real *chai*.

It has started snowing again, and the afternoon light turns muddy. A few cars roll on board the ferry, a flat-bottomed freighter with an open hold, not the large, multistory ferry of the tourist season. He walks up the ramp and heads to the cabin behind the bridge. It is littered with beer cans and old newspapers, and he clears a seat by the window.

The freighter lets out a whistle and heads out in a straight line before starting its slow dogleg toward the island. The ocean grows rougher, and the cars on deck groan with each successive line of waves.

He picks up a copy of the *Vineyard Gazette* left on the seat next to him. On the front page is a headline that says BURGLARIES CONTINUE. The article below it says that there have been three more break-ins up-island. The locals are outraged, and angry questions have been asked at an evening community meeting with the police. An Officer Gardner is quoted as saying, "We have some very good leads, and are close to apprehending the suspects." When asked by the *Gazette* reporter why it is taking them so long to make an arrest, the officer replied that the suspects were hiding in different summer properties throughout the island. He advised the year-round residents to "be aware of any unusual signs of inhabitation, such as lights in windows, unfamiliar parked cars, or nighttime comings and goings."

Ranjit knows that Plaid-shirt and his brother have plenty of houses to choose from and can probably hide out for weeks. Shaking his head, he folds the paper shut. They will inevitably be caught, but even a life sentence will not bring back the old lady they had murdered. Justice, when it happens, is inevitably too late, and can never compensate for the crime.

There is no mention of the burglaries in the pages of *The Boston Globe,* but its weekend section has a long profile on Senator Neals, portraying him as a phoenix that has arisen from the ashes of the old political order. Ranjit studies a photograph taken at the Harvard talk: the Senator's muscular frame is leaning forward, gripping the edges of the podium. The American people, it seems, are hungry for a hero who can jet around the world and get things done.

The article says the usual things about the Senator's background: born poor in Roxbury, football scholarship to Harvard, his first childless marriage, and his remarriage to Anna Williams, the daughter of a patrician Vineyard family. The next paragraph makes Ranjit stop.

It describes the events of September 15, three years ago. "The Senator was devastated when his daughter, Josephine Williams Neals, aged four, drowned at his summer home in Martha's Vineyard. After a long period of introspection, the Senator decided to return to public service . . ."

There is a picture of the entire family sitting out on a deck, the glistening Vineyard Sound behind them. Senator Neals looks much younger, and in his lap is a little girl wearing a summer dress printed with flowers. She has Anna's dark eyes, and she is squinting up at her father and laughing.

Ranjit stares at the photograph. *Betty Green hadn't told him that Anna's daughter had drowned.* He looks at the picture again, recognizes the sloping lawn, and then he knows where it had happened.

The swimming pool that had lain empty all summer, gathering leaves, though he had offered to fill it. He remembers Anna sitting next to it, staring blankly at her book. *She had been keeping a vigil over the place her daughter died.*

He reads the paragraph again, and the

date of the little girl's death catches his eye. *September fifteenth. That was the day that Anna had come to him, taken his hand, and led him to her bedroom.* Left alone on her daughter's death anniversary, the pain must have been too much for her to bear . . . He thinks of the little girl who had drowned, and then of his own beloved Shanti. Closing his eyes, he says a prayer.

No power to speak, no power to keep silent
No power to beg, no power to give
No power to live, no power to die
No power to escape from this world
He alone has the power in His hands, he
   watches over us all
O, Nanak, no one, rich or poor, escapes
   your sight . . .

The freighter toots loudly and Ranjit looks out to see the white gas tanks of Vineyard Haven come into view. He presses his nose to the porthole, running through his plan. He'll retrieve his truck from Mike's Tow Yard and drive out to the Senator's house well before the time set for their meeting. This time, there can be no mistakes.

He lifts up his backpack, feeling the heavy doll inside it, and watches the land approaching.

■ ■ ■ ■

III
RETURN

■ ■ ■ ■

Even by thinking a hundred thousand
    times,
He cannot be reduced to thought.
Even by piling up loads of worldly goods,
    the hunger of the hungry cannot be
    appeased.
Hundreds of thousands of clever tricks,
But none of them will serve you in the end.
How can you reach the truth? How can the
    veil of illusion be torn away?
                 — Guru Granth Sahib, Jup

CHAPTER TWENTY-SIX

The Senator and Anna are arguing violently.

It is dusk, but Ranjit can see them clearly through the powerful binoculars pressed to his eyes. He's lying hidden behind the high shrubbery by the side of the Senator's house, his white snowsuit blending into the snow.

Watching the two of them is like watching characters in a play, but with the sound turned off.

The living room is dark, except for a tall floor lamp that casts a circle of light over Clayton Neals. He sits slumped in an armchair, wearing gray sweatpants and a red T-shirt. Anna stands over him, wearing a black tracksuit, leaning in so close that she is speaking right into his face.

Ranjit adjusts the magnification on the binoculars. He sees Anna's mouth open, the tendons of her long neck quivering as she shouts. The Senator suddenly throws up his arms and rises, his face contorted, his hands balled into fists. Ranjit stiffens, realizing that he is on the verge of violence, but Anna says something and the Senator slumps back into the chair, his mouth opening and closing helplessly. She continues to talk, striding in and out of the circle of light, and finally stops in front of the Senator's chair, blocking Ranjit's view.

When she moves aside a few minutes later, the Senator is sitting with his head tilted back, his eyes closed, his thick, muscled arms resting limply on the armrests.

Anna stalks away and disappears down the circular stairs in the corner. The Senator leans forward, resting his head on his knees, as if someone has punched him in the stomach.

The scene seems strangely familiar, and despite the insulated snowsuit, Ranjit feels a chill in his bones. When he first got out of prison he was drinking a bottle of Old Monk rum every evening, and at the halfway point Preetam would start screaming at him. Usually he'd just ignore her, but one night he reached the three-quarter mark and could not stand her shrieking voice a moment longer. He'd pushed her away, and she had stumbled and fallen, almost hitting her head against the edge of a marble table.

He was so frightened that he had begged her forgiveness and stopped drinking for a whole month.

He raises the binoculars to his eyes, watching Anna as she strides through the room wearing her silver down jacket and orange knit cap. She bends by the door to lace up her running shoes, and then he hears the front door slam. He swivels to see her stride into the snow, steam coming out of her nostrils.

She bends to stretch her back, then launches into a run, her stride lengthening, her arms pumping as she rounds the first curve of the driveway. *She is going running now?*

He scans the driveway, but she has crested the hill, and must be out on the long, flat stretch of Lighthouse Road. He imagines her moving through the darkness, chest heaving, breathing in air as cold as steel.

Turning back to the house, he sees the Senator's colossus-sized figure still sitting motionless.

Ranjit shifts uneasily, feeling the snow crunch under him. He sweeps the house again, taking in the darkened lower rooms and the empty decks. The snow around the house is devoid of all tire tracks except for the steel-belted radials of Anna's Mercedes;

it seems that she has succeeded in keeping Kohonen away.

He stands, feeling the hardness of the knife in his boot, brushes snow off his backpack, and walks slowly to the house. As he rings the doorbell he remembers waiting here with Shanti a few weeks ago, her small, warm hand in his, her bright eyes looking up at him.

He hears heavy footsteps, and the tall oak door swings open, letting out a blast of heat. The Senator's huge frame fills the doorway: he is barefoot, his eyes bloodshot, gray stubble running across his broad chin.

"Ran-jitt." He squints down, taking in Ranjit's short hair and clean-shaven face. "You've got a lot of nerve, getting Anna involved in this. I should just call the police and have you locked away."

All the charisma has leaked away, and what remains is a brutal man, his voice tight with anger.

Ranjit smiles, baring his teeth. "You do that, and you'll never find the microfilm. I know it's from the Agni missile, and I know you want it back. Anna said you would talk to me —"

"Anna. Of course." Without looking back, the Senator turns and strides into the house.

Ranjit enters the house, smelling something spiky and hormonal, and recognizes the stink of desperation. He studies the living room, knowing that desperate men are twice as dangerous: papers are scattered all over the sofa and a half-eaten pepperoni pizza lies on the granite island. The room looks foreign, as though Preetam and Shanti had never set foot in it, as though they had never eaten Christmas dinner by the bay window.

The Senator stands in front of the tall lamp, the light catching the sides of his shaved head, his face remaining in deep shadow. He's put on weight, and without a tailored suit to hide his bulk, displays the beginnings of a belly.

"Anna has really taken a liking to you." The Senator's lips bow in distaste, and his voice rises. "This is the first time she's had such poor judgment. How much money do you want?"

"I don't want your money —"

"Careful, my friend, don't think you can blackmail me. Anna is a grown woman, she does what she wants. Just give me the microfilm and get the hell out of here. Consider yourself lucky that you're alive."

"My wife and child. I want them free."

"You brought that on yourself, damn it. You play with fire, you get burnt."

"My daughter is nine years old — you met her, for God's sake. She has nothing to do with this —"

The Senator runs a hand over his face. "You left me no choice. Give me the microfilm, then we can talk about it."

Ranjit feels a surge of anger. "No."

He steps into the circle of light, so that the Senator can see clearly. He takes out the doll and slides its head off with a click, revealing the empty cavity within.

"I have the doll. The microfilm is elsewhere. You agree to my terms and I —"

The Senator reaches out for the doll. He holds it in his large hands and stares down at its dark, smooth face. "Anna was upset about this, she'll be glad to have it back." He looks up abruptly. "You don't even realize what the goddamn microfilm means. Give it to me, and I'll pay you for it. I have money, outside, I can —"

Crack.

A glass sliding door suddenly cobwebs and shatters. Shards of glass fly into the room.

The Senator jumps back, dropping the doll. A red dot flickers high on his chest, and he swats at it as though trying to kill a fly.

The dot flickers, searching the room, and settles onto Ranjit's stomach. He dives for

352

the floor.

The red dot wavers for a second, then swoops downward.

Time slows as Ranjit twists and rolls away.

Crack crack crack. Another glass door bursts apart. Pain like a burning knife slices into Ranjit's side and he screams.

The Senator is bellowing. Ranjit rolls behind a high-backed leather armchair and a rain of bullets thwacks into its thick leather padding.

There is a blur as the Senator sprints for the stairs, yelling in anger. A glint of his shaved head, and he's gone.

A trap. The Senator has set a trap. Kohonen is out there with a sniper's rifle, using a laser targeting scope. *A coward's way to kill.*

Slumped behind the armchair, Ranjit touches his side, feels the warm leak of blood, and knows that he'll pass out soon.

No. Not here, not like this.

The light. Kill the floor lamp. Kohonen could be using an infrared scope, in which case it's hopeless. Still.

He forces himself up on one elbow and tugs at the base of the tall brass lamp. It topples, its white silk shade buckling against the floor, and the lightbulb goes out.

Crack. A large mirror behind him shatters. Blind, panicked shooting. *Kohonen is firing like an amateur.*

Ranjit sits up, pressing against the back of the armchair. Its thick upholstery has saved him, but he has to stanch the blood before he passes out.

The silence grows, the echo from the shots giving way to the booming of the ocean. Is Kohonen reloading, or is he trying to fake Ranjit out? What if he has brought help, what if there are two gunmen?

The blood puddles inside Ranjit's snowsuit. If only he had a gun . . . his knife is in his boot, useless against a high-velocity hunting rifle.

He has to chance it. He forces himself up, crawling on hands and knees across the floor, his back tense, braced for the impact of a bullet. Crawling behind the granite island, he collapses against the kitchen cabinets.

No shots come.

He pulls dish towels down from a hook and pushes them into his bloody snowsuit. Reaching up, he opens a drawer and fumbles inside. Finding a long silk runner, he loops it around his waist and ties it tightly.

Stars blink in his head, a signal that he is about to black out. *Too much blood. He's losing too much blood.*

Think, damn it. Think. From the muzzle flashes, he can tell that Kohonen is out there, by the shrubbery. He'll come to the house to finish Ranjit off. *How long from there to here?*

He retraces the route in his head, counting strides. *Four and a half minutes, in a half-run, carrying a heavy hunting rifle.*

Where will he come from? The front door is farther back, and besides, it offers a poor field of fire. The best option is to enter from the deck outside, with a full view of the living room.

He reaches up, feeling the pain sear into him, and turns a dial on the stove. Then he strains up to the microwave and punches in four and a half minutes.

Everything depends on the timing. If there is more than one man, he's dead. If they flank the house, or come in through the front door, he's dead.

Clinging onto the edge of the granite island, he forces himself to stand, darkness gathering at the corners of his vision. Doubled over, he heads for the front door, unlocks it, and slumps against the wall. From here he can see the flickering green numbers of the microwave's LCD display. Bending down, he pulls the knife from the top of his boot and clutches it tightly in his

355

sweating hands.

His head swoons, and blackness comes.

It is the morning of his father's death anniversary. He is a child again, standing helplessly outside the bathroom door as his mother bathes. The sound of running water is mixed with her sobbing.

"Guru," she moans, "why did you take him? Why, why, why?"

He cannot stand it anymore. He runs from the house, to the gulmohar tree in the corner of the courtyard, blood-red blossoms drooping from its branches. He shimmies up the rough bark and climbs, the branches swaying as he climbs higher and higher. Soon he reaches the top, and the house is reduced to a small rectangle below. Up here is light and air and peace . . .

His eyes open and he staggers against the wall. He looks across the room at the green LCD draining time. Two minutes and eighteen seconds left.

Blackness comes again.

. . . he is up in the tree again. He watches bamboo-framed kites rise into the hot sky. Dark mynahs twitter from the treetops. It is so good to be up here, away from *Mataji*'s tears and choking voice. He will never come down.

But there is his mother, walking into the

356

courtyard below, her wet hair falling limply around her shoulders. Her tiny figure casts a long shadow as she calls his name, "Ranjit, Ranjit, where are you, my son? Ranjit!"

He is stubborn. He will not reply. He will stay in the tree.

But she will not go away, and keeps calling him . . .

His eyes open. Damn it, he cannot drift off again. He twists the improvised bandage tighter, causing a hot splinter of pain. *Aaah.* That will wake him up. In his clammy hand, the knife feels like a block of wood.

The green LCD of the microwave says twenty-three seconds left.

Stay awake. Twenty-three, twenty-one. Odd numbers. Always odd numbers. Is death an odd number?

He breathes in, breathes out. *Eight seconds left.*

A noise on the deck outside. A dark figure is advancing slowly. Rifle held high, ready to shoot. A hand fumbles at the latch of the shattered glass door. *Amateur. So much noise.*

Four seconds. Three.

The figure is inside the room, advancing, the muzzle of the rifle sweeping the room. Ranjit holds his breath, tenses his legs, willing them to move.

Two. One.

Beep beep beep beep. Triiiiiing. The stove and microwave timers go off.

The figure whirls and fires at the noise.

Ranjit hurls himself out of the front door, staggering, running, the cold air like a slap in his face. *Take the enemy onto your terrain.* He runs past the shrubbery, hearing the thud of feet behind him. The knife glints in his hand.

Run faster. Faster, to the cliff edge. And here are the stairs, curling down to the beach far below, each granite step gleaming and slick with ice.

He takes the steps two at a time. *How many steps?* Sixty-eight to the beach. *And the one he had been meaning to fix, which one was it?* It's after the middle landing, he knows that.

Behind him, Kohonen is snarling like a dog. *Why doesn't he shoot? Did he bring only a rifle to his assignment? Amateur.*

Here's the first landing. The Vineyard Sound is dark below, the strip of beach strangely empty. *Can't think of that now.* Which step is loose?

At a turn in the stairs he feels the granite under his feet rock back and forth. He bends and grips the step with all his strength, heaves, and feels it come loose.

Kohonen is right behind him.

Ranjit runs down four, five more stairs. Then turns, his knife up and ready.

Kohonen lands hard on the loose step and it rocks forward, catapulting him into space.

He falls, slamming a hand into Ranjit's stomach, pushing him off-balance. Ranjit pitches backward, his hand smashing on stone, the knife skittering away.

Kohonen is on top of him. Their two bodies slither and twist down the stairs. Each jolt is a flash of agony and Ranjit hears himself screaming.

They hit the last landing, and Ranjit tries to rise, but Kohonen's knees are on his chest, holding him down. Hands reach for his throat, thumbs burrow into his flesh, searching for his windpipe.

A galaxy of stars flashes above. Ranjit tries to pull the man's arms apart but there is hot breath in his face, scented with rot.

Choking. Breath gone. Blackness rushing in.

Oh. A sudden grunt. The fingers on his throat go slack. The man topples onto Ranjit.

Black as night.

"Ranjit, Ranjit, Ranjit."

It is his mother again, calling to him. He

359

will not answer, he will remain up in the tree, free of her tears. But she will not go away, she stands there, calling his name. Sadly, reluctantly, he starts down.

"Ranjit, wake up. Please wake up."

Anna Neals's dark eyes stare down at him. She holds a flat piece of granite, its edge dark and dripping.

The man lies sprawled facedown on the landing. The back of his head has been crushed.

Anna. Anna. Thank you, Anna.

He tries to talk, cannot, groans. Blackness crowds in again. He feels cold hands slapping his cheeks, shocking him into consciousness.

"Don't close your eyes. Stay awake."

". . . what are you . . . here?"

"Stay awake. You're in shock. You've lost a lot of blood. We have to get back up there."

"Kohonen. Shot me."

She shakes her head. Strands of hair have escaped from under her knit cap and are plastered on her cheeks. "No," she whispers, "not Kohonen. I know him. Jesus, I know him . . ."

She rolls the man over, grunting with effort, and pulls down the blood-soaked hood of his black sweatshirt. A pale face stares up, blue eyes open, mouth twisted into a

360

rictus of death.

"Who . . ."

"It's Norman Nash, he was there when we met that evening in the parking lot —"

Ranjit looks again. He pulls up the sleeves of the black sweatshirt and sees the tattoos on the man's muscled forearms: dark, swirling fish, their fanlike tails looping around to meet their open mouths. He remembers these tattooed arms pointing a shotgun at him, and his mind swirls in confusion. *What the hell is this man doing here, at the Senator's house?*

"Is he dead? Ranjit, is he dead?"

Ranjit doesn't need to feel for a pulse. He's seen enough corpses to know when the soul has evaporated into cold air, leaving a waxy shell. "Yes. He's gone. Anna, check his pockets."

She stares at him, then wipes her hands on her silver jacket, leaving dark streaks. She slides her hands quickly into the pockets of the man's sweatshirt, then his dark pants, finding only a rectangular box of ammunition.

"There's nothing here. Nothing else."

Something is bothering Ranjit, but he can't place the thought. He shakes his head to clear it, but the stars blossom again.

"Anna, I'm losing too much blood. We

have to move. Can you get me up there?"

She nods her head dully. "What about him?"

"Leave him for now."

When she pulls Ranjit to his feet, he howls in pain. The sound is lost in the crashing of the waves below.

He is dizzy as a drunk. She walks on the outside, surprisingly strong, her arm tight around his back, her legs straining to lift him up.

They stagger up one step. Then another.

"Don't think," she says. "Don't look down."

They are in lockstep. Time passes and he sees the toes of his own cracked boots, and her blue-and-gold running sneakers. The niggling thought lies in the recesses of his mind, and he tries to grasp it, but it evades him.

When they reach the top of the cliff, his knees buckle, and they both slump into the dead, rustling grass. He smells the salt of his own blood, hears her breathing in his ear.

"Where is Clayton?" she asks, as though remembering his existence.

"He ran away when the shooting started."

She stops and gulps. "I'm going to call an ambulance."

The thought that has been hiding in his fogged mind suddenly becomes clear: if the tattooed man is here, his older brother is sure to be close by.

"No time for that. This man's brother, they're always together. He has to be here. Bring the Mercedes as close as you can. We have to leave."

"Are you sure? I didn't see anyone —"

"Go. Now. Go."

Anna takes a deep breath and disappears toward the driveway.

He must have passed out because when he gains consciousness the Mercedes is parked at the edge of the driveway, the twin beams of its headlights shining down on him.

"Turn off the headlights. Turn off —"

A shot rings out, smacking into the grass a few feet from his head. The headlights go off, and it is pitch black, all Ranjit's night vision destroyed by the sudden glare.

Another shot, closer this time. He starts to crawl, and hears Anna's breathing as she stumbles toward him. She hauls him to his feet, and they make it up the slope, the firing wild now, peppering the darkness.

He half falls into the backseat of the Mercedes. "Can you make it up the hill without lights?"

Her breathing is ragged. "I think so . . . I run this route all the time."

The Mercedes surges into the darkness, the white gravel driveway a blur. She takes the first curve fast, almost goes over the next one, but makes the next two turns. The driveway straightens out, and they roar over the crest of the hill.

She is crying as she drives down Lighthouse Road, bawling like a child. "I've got to get you to a hospital. You're losing too much blood . . ."

He shakes his head no. He tells her to go to the Red Heron Estate. He tells her that the override code for the alarms is BLUESKY, and then he goes back under.

CHAPTER TWENTY-SEVEN

His mouth is parched. There is the sound of his own ragged breathing.

He lies in a vast bed, its sheets a dazzling white, stretching away on all sides like a field of snow. There is a large fireplace against the far wall, and a small figure sitting in a flowered armchair.

He is so thirsty that he thinks he will go mad. "Water," he whispers. "Please give me water."

"I can't do that, Ranjit."

"Please. Water."

"Listen to me. I've bandaged you. The bleeding has stopped. But if the bullet hit something inside . . . we have to wait. When you pee, we'll know it's okay."

"Need water. In the Guru's name —"

He passes out, into blinding whiteness.

Snow goggles. He's forgotten his goggles and the snow-light blinds his eyes. He can barely keep up with the line of men who march in front of him, their legs wading through the knee-deep snow. He tries to shout to them, but his tongue sticks to the roof of his mouth.

He must have water. Stumbling to a stop, he scoops up a handful of snow. It is like eating glass, and the sharp points of the snow cut into the insides of his cheeks. His tongue desperately seeks a trickle of water, but finds only numbing cold.

"Captain, you know that will just make you thirstier."

Khandelkar's long face looks down at him, frowning in disapproval.

"Well, damn it, tell the men to stop. I need to catch up."

There is a flicker of pity in Khandelkar's brown eyes. He starts to say something, then just tightens the strap of his assault rifle and walks away.

"Take me with you! Goddamn it. Don't leave me here!"

The Sergeant trudges on, deaf to Ranjit's cries. The figures of the men dwindle against the slope of the mountain.

Ranjit staggers after them, falling and getting up and falling again. Soon he's too tired to move and lies in the white snow as though it is a bed.

He wishes he could just fall sleep, fall into

blackness, but his thirst is terrible. He must have water. *Cool water pouring down into his gullet, his throat, coiling softly down into his stomach . . .*

Someone is dripping water into his mouth. The fire is out and early morning light floods the huge room.

"More. Please more."

"Take it slow. Small sips."

Anna tilts a glass into his mouth. He drinks, looks up to see her dark eyes peering intently at him. Her short hair is pinned back on either side of her head with metal barrettes, her small, shell-like ears exposed.

"You're all right. You peed. You can drink all you want."

He feels the warm wetness around him and shame flushes through him. "Sorry, so sorry . . ."

"It's okay. I'll clean you up."

Strong arms lift his legs, sponge him, slide clean pajamas up to his waist. He closes his eyes and feels the burn of fever.

Her cool hand rests on his forehead. "Your temperature is too high. I'm worried about infection. We have to get you to a doctor."

"No. No doctors. Too dangerous. Anna, listen —"

He mumbles into her ear, telling her about the house in Ocean Park, the tin box in the closet stuffed with vials of broad-spectrum antibiotics and syringes. He tells her to bring the rectangular case from under the bed.

Nodding, she straightens up. She is silhouetted against a backdrop of gauzy white curtains as she searches through his clothes, and there is the clink of his keys being picked up. He shows her the ones she needs, and she turns to leave.

"Anna. The alarms here . . ."

Her face is drawn and solemn. "Don't worry. They're all on. The gates, the perimeter, the cameras around the house. Nobody is going to get in while I'm gone."

"Please, hurry . . ."

He falls asleep. Wakes, seemingly minutes later, to the cold swab of alcohol on his forearm, a hard flick of fingers on his skin to raise the veins. The stab of a needle sliding in.

Good girl. Anna, Anna, Anna.

He wakes in the dark of the night, desperately needing a drink of water, but his mouth is too dry to speak. A fire is burning low in the fireplace, and a charred log of wood suddenly crumbles, the flames flaring up before dying away. In the firelight he sees Anna: she is sitting motionless in the armchair beside the fireplace, covered by a thick wool blanket. At first he thinks that she is asleep, but then his eyes adjust to the darkness, and he sees her staring into the dying fire.

"Anna," he manages to whisper, "Anna, water."

She stares into the heart of the fire and does not seem to hear him.

"Water, please," he whispers again, but she does not react. She seems to have gone from herself, leaving her body sitting in the chair.

A crystal jug of water is sitting on the side table by his bed, its cut-glass facets dim with reflected light. There is no way he can reach it, or lift the heavy jug. He turns his head away, banishing all thoughts of cool, clear water. He closes his mouth, and swallows, and somehow drifts back into sleep.

He wakes in a room full of late-morning light. Or is it the afternoon? *How long has he been asleep?*

He is wearing someone else's blue silk pajamas and lying in a large sleigh bed, the ends of it curving upward in arcs of polished wood. The bed is at one end of a long, high-ceilinged room that must take up the entire front of the house, and at the other end is the dark, ashy mouth of the fireplace. Tall windows line the outside wall, their gauzy curtains pulled open, revealing wide lawns that slope down to the gray-blue water of Tisbury Great Pond. Even now, in the heart of winter, this room, with its thin curtains and vivid floral prints, speaks of summer, of warm breezes and windows flung open.

Except that it is freezing cold, and by the side of the bed is a metal trash can, filled to the brim with used gauze bandages, cotton pads stiff with blood, and empty syringes. On the floor next to it are the remains of his snowsuit, scissored into ragged pieces.

It all comes back: the tattooed man on top of him, fingers like steel jabbing into his throat, and then the sudden blow, the man's skull smashed in. Then the hail of bullets as the other brother started shooting at them. He remembers the article he read on the ferry, how the burglars were thought to be hiding somewhere on the island, steps away from being arrested. *Had the Senator hired them to kill him?*

"Good. You're awake. I was getting worried."

Anna is coming through the doorway, wearing a man's black sweater and a pair of brown wide-wale corduroys that are too big for her, kept up with a thick leather belt.

Her hair is still clipped back with barrettes, and in her oversized clothes she looks very young.

She puts the tray she's carrying down on the bedside table. "Well, Ranjit. I seem to be always bandaging you up." He smiles wanly up at her, and she continues. "Don't worry, the alarms are on. There's no electricity here, but they are running on some sort of backup power. There are plenty of candles, though, and a woodstove, and the cabinets are full of food. I heated up some chicken broth for you."

She stacks pillows up against the headboard of the bed and helps him to sit up.

"Anna." His voice is a hoarse whisper. "How long have I been here?"

"Today is the second day. Two nights and one full day."

He does the math. Today is the ninth day that his family has been in detention. *What if Kohonen had been right, what if they'll be deported after ten days, not fourteen?* Panic rises in his throat.

She reaches for the bowl of chicken soup, but he gestures for her to wait.

"I'm trying to understand . . . what happened at the house."

Her face darkens as she sits carefully on the edge of the bed. "I don't know, Ranjit."

371

She picks up the bowl of soup in both hands. "You should eat this before it gets cold."

"When did you tell the Senator that I was coming?"

"Clayton didn't know till that evening. I told him right before you showed up."

"Did you tell anyone else?"

"No, Ranjit, no. I thought you would be safe there. When I heard the shots, I turned back, I ran as fast as I could, I was so frightened . . ."

"You recognized those two men in the parking lot. Does the Senator know them too?"

She shakes her head. "I barely remember them. We were in the same high school, but they both dropped out. Clayton doesn't know them."

"Maybe they did some work for you? On the house?"

"I'd never hire them. The whole island knows they're drunks."

His head spins and he leans back into the soft pillows. *None of this makes any sense.* "I was watching the house with binoculars, I saw you arguing with the Senator. What happened?"

She sits silently, holding the bowl in her lap.

"Anna, please talk to me."

She looks at him, and then looks away. "I'll tell you everything, Ranjit. But please don't hate me for it."

He nods silently, and she looks away, staring out of the window as she talks. "I told Clayton that I met you at Harvard, and that he was lying to me about the dolls. He was furious, he said I was a fool, that I had no idea what I was interfering with. He accused me of . . . all kinds of things. And I was tired of being bullied by him, so tired.

"When he screamed at me, something inside me snapped. I told him we had slept together, I told him I was going to divorce him. He begged me to stop talking, but I was so angry, I couldn't breathe. I had to leave the house. I put on my running clothes and got the hell out. I wouldn't have left if I'd known this would happen."

She stares out of tall windows at the thick, black-trunked trees, and her eyes fill with tears. Outside, a crow caws and rises up into the air.

"That man, Norman Nash. I killed him, didn't I?"

It is Ranjit's turn to be silent.

She grips the bowl in her lap. "I saw him on top of you. I picked up that piece of

stone, I smashed it down as hard as I could
—"

"Don't think about that now."

"I was nine the first time I shot a mallard. Clipped its wing and it fell out of the sky. My father said to me, *Finish it off, put it out of its misery. Come on, you shot it, now follow through.* I didn't want to. He said, *Damn it, don't behave like a girl.* I used the butt of my gun and its skull crumpled like an eggshell. It was looking at me when it died, looking right at me . . ."

Her voice trembles with hysteria. He has seen this in combat before. Once the fighting stopped and his men were back in safety, the shock of the battle hit them.

"We'll talk later. Just don't think about it now."

Wiping her eyes with the back of one hand, she gestures at the bowl of chicken broth. "You must eat. Get your strength back."

The chicken broth is very salty, and is now cold. She feeds him, her movements as regular as a metronome, and it seems to calm her down. He has no appetite, but he swallows every mouthful.

Death surrounds them now, and he knows that he can't continue the conversation. As he eats, a verse from the Guru Granth Sahib floats into his head:

Everything earthly is devoured by death
He sits and examines the accounts,
In the place where no one may enter with
    anyone else
Those who weep and wail might just as
    well bundle together stalks of straw . . .

When he finishes the broth, the fever has come back, and he closes his eyes, feeling the redness bloom behind his eyelids.

"Sleep," she says. And even though he doesn't want to, he does.

High up on the glacier there is the cawing of crows. They circle in the sky, small specks that swoop lower and lower.

He is still lying in the snow, looking upward, when a large black crow lands next to him. He wants to sit up and scare it away, but he is paralyzed. The crow hops around him, doing a strange jerky dance.

Go away, crow, go away.

It flaps its wings once and lands on his chest. Cocking its head, it looks at him, its beady eyes bright with a malignant intelligence. It opens its beak and says *Caaaaw.*

His eyes flicker rapidly, trying to see what it is doing. It lowers its dark head and he feels a sharp pain in his chest, a series of pecks that are moving upward.

The crow hops toward his face, its curved beak dark and dripping. He blinks furiously, shouting out loud, but no sound will come. Its beak flashes down, aiming at his eyes —

"Wake up, Ranjit. It's just a dream. Wake up."

A hand shakes him and the scream dies in his throat. He reaches out a hand and feels the bulge of his eyeballs under the hot, papery eyelids.

"It's all right, I'm here, I'm right here."

Anna lies down and presses into him, and he feels her heat seep into his chilled body. Preetam was always cold, always snuggling into him for warmth, but this woman is like a furnace. She must have been sweating in her sleep, because her white T-shirt is soaked through.

"Ranjit, you're drenched. You have to change."

He realizes that it's his sweat, not hers. His silk pajama top is sopping wet.

There is a flare of a match as she lights a candle. In its blue flame he sees that her short hair is sticking up in the back, and she's wearing a white T-shirt and black boxers. She sits him up, unbuttons his wet shirt, and slips a cool, dry T-shirt over his chest.

It has the musty scent of long-stored cloth-ing.

"Leave the candle burning. Please." The crow's wingbeats are receding, but he needs the light to banish its image.

"You were screaming. A nightmare."

"I'm sorry. Go back to sleep."

She props herself up on an elbow and stares down at him. "What were you dream-ing about?"

He feels her waiting for his reply, but he cannot speak. The candle behind her casts dark shadows underneath her eyes and nose.

As the silence grows, she leans in, her breath warm with sleep. "Do you remember the first time you came to my house?"

He nods, and she continues. "It was very hot, remember? You came with those Brazil-ian men, you were unloading the truck in the driveway. I was just returning from a run, and I was soaked in sweat. The Brazil-ians knew I was the Senator's wife, they dared not look directly at me, but they sneaked glances at my breasts, at my legs. I felt them looking.

"But you . . . you did not even glance at me. They helped you unload the granite, and when they left, you started to arrange it into piles. You were so . . . apart. Alone.

"I went into the house and drank some

377

water and watched you from behind the curtains. I watched you all afternoon as you measured and cut stone. Everything you did was so precise. I said to myself, this is not an ordinary man."

He lies in the darkness, feeling her hand stroke the back of his neck.

"I don't believe in God, or fate, or destiny, any of that. It's stupid. But that day I felt as though you'd been sent to me. And when I finally had the nerve to talk to you, it was worse, much worse, because I found out you had a wife and a child, and I had nothing. You understand how it hurt? So that afternoon in September . . . I . . . I was selfish, I wanted you so badly. You must have been very confused. I'm so, so sorry."

He can tell by her breathing that she is crying. He reaches up and pulls her face to his, feeling the hot tears on her cheeks.

"Anna," he says. He says her name like a prayer, over and over, *Anna, Anna, Anna,* till she muffles it with her lips.

She is slow and deliberate.

He lies on his back and she straddles him carefully, her muscular arms reaching upward to pull off her own T-shirt, her breasts rolling free. Their hard points push into his chest as she leans forward to kiss him.

Her hair brushes against his face, giving off the faint scent of sweat. Her breasts, when she feeds them to him, taste like water.

Crouched over him, she guides his hand to the wetness between her thighs.

"Like this," she whispers, "like this."

She moves against his hand, her palms flat on either side of him, her entire body taut as a bow. He watches her lower lip tremble, watches her eyes glaze over. Then she is kissing him hard, breathing into his mouth. His hand is cramping when she pushes down and says, *Yes.*

When she is done she topples beside him and hides her face in his chest. He pulls her to him with one arm, moving to cover her with the comforter, but she shakes her head and says, "No, I'm not done."

"Anna, I don't know if I can —"

"*Shhh.* No talking."

Lying next to him, she covers his mouth with hers, and her hand moves slowly down his chest, and despite the pain, he is aroused. The softness of her body is underlaid with muscle, and she is very strong; the hand that grips him down below will not be denied. She kisses his chest, then moves lower, licks and nuzzles. She knows exactly what she is doing.

He feels her breasts pressing against the

inside of his thighs, feels her mouth on him. She is eating him alive, but that is not all. She is devouring him and ministering to him at the same time, drawing poison out of his body, years of curdled desire.

Pleasure mixes with searing pain. There is a taste in his mouth from childhood, of mangoes sprinkled with coarse salt, both sweet and painfully salty.

He moans and collapses. It is as though she has drawn blood from him, blood he cannot afford to lose.

Her face moves up next to his. She sees his expression, grateful and bashful and pained, and holds his face in her hands.

"What are you thinking of? What is going on in that head of yours?"

The part of himself that remains detached watches himself lying in bed with her.

"Nothing."

They lie in the darkness, intertwined, till she rises naked from the bed.

He watches her crouch in front of the fireplace, placing more logs and arranging torn newspaper. She lights a match, the fire catches, and her face turns golden-orange. Her muscular legs and arms are a faded brown, her small, rounded breasts and stomach the color of milky coffee.

He thinks that she is the most beautiful

woman he has ever seen.

She comes back to the bed shivering, half warm from the fire, her back cold. He takes her hands in his and massages them, and soon they are warm.

The room heats up, and the air is scented with the smell of their lovemaking.

Her warm fingertips find the scar under his chin and she caresses it, as though trying to smooth away the raised ridge.

"Ranjit Singh," she says quietly, "where did you get this scar? I want to know, I really do."

Closing his eyes, he lies back on the soaked pillow. He is quiet for so long that his own voice startles him, as though he is talking in his sleep.

"I was high up on a glacier, between India and Pakistan. Most people don't even know it exists. It was beautiful up there, but there was a war going on. A war, and not a war. It was the strangest thing, like two men fighting in a room, but they mustn't make a sound, because nobody else is supposed to know that they are there . . ."

She props herself up onto an elbow. "Go on, I'm listening."

"There was this nineteen-year-old in my platoon. Skinny kid, his ears stuck out, he was a real jokester, used to keep the men laughing. He listened to this band all the time, I think it's called Guns and Roses. Always the same song, *Loaded like a freight train, flyin' like an aeroplane . . .*"

He can't help smiling, thinking of Dewan high up on the glacier, headphones clamped over his knit cap, nodding to his music. He'd listen to the same song till the batteries of his Walkman froze, then put them in his armpits to warm them up.

". . . and there was my Sergeant, Khandelkar. He had no family, and the army was his whole life. He'd gone into East Pakistan in 1971, fought counterinsurgency missions in Sri Lanka in the eighties, but he had no hate. You'd see him darning his socks, and think that he looked like an old grandmother, but when the shooting started he was the calmest head around. He taught me everything I know about leading men, about war. He was like a father to me."

Anna's face is so close that he cannot see her expression. "I'm listening, Ranjit. What happened to them?"

He breathes deeply. "They're dead. They're both dead. Only I survived."

He talks into the night, filling the silence with his words.

It had been a cloudy day when he disembarked from an army transport plane and saw the Kumar Base Camp for the first time. With its parade grounds of crushed stone and red-roofed regimental buildings it had looked like any other camp, just more desolate, and strangely silent.

When the clouds lifted, he was stunned. The rocks and rubble of the glacier gave way to a tongue of snow that swept endlessly northward, and to the west were the towering peaks of the Saltoro Ridge. The sky was a deep blue he had never seen before, and as he watched, a lone white cloud floated through it, casting a patch of shadow that flitted across the barren mountains.

There was a sudden, chattering roar as the Cheetah helicopters began to fly, taking advantage of the clear weather to evacuate the wounded from high up in the mountains. They looked like bumblebees, scarcely more than a glass bubble canopy and a skeletal tail, and behind them came the M-17s, large lumbering choppers that parachuted in heavier supplies. White silk parasols bloomed in the air, and he gasped, thinking that he had never seen anything more graceful.

And the mountains! They were dazzling,

taking on the pink and orange of the setting sun, their snow cones a stark white even in the darkness. Mountains without names, some only with coordinates, twenty-four thousand feet high, and unclimbed. Unlike Mount Everest or Kanchenjunga, whose every inch had been mapped, these mountains were mysteries.

As darkness fell, the Cheetahs came clattering back. They unloaded men, some walking, some on stretchers, their hands and feet blistered with frostbite. He was not dissuaded by the sight, and even remained cheerful the next day, when an avalanche on the mountain buried an entire outpost, and dog teams were helicoptered out to find the bodies.

The main thing was that there were mountains to climb, heights he had dreamed of scaling since he was a boy.

His first command was a two-week watch in the command post at Bilafond La Pass. As they climbed toward it, he saw for the first time the damage that the war had done. The pipeline built to transport kerosene oil up the glacier leaked continuously, staining the snow black. The high pass was littered with the dried-out corpses of dead mules, their grinning skulls stripped by the crows. And as they climbed higher, he saw strange, tall pillars jutting from the glacier, almost as though giants were standing motionless in the snow.

Getting closer, he recognized the beautiful parachutes he had seen, fallen to earth and frozen into high plumes. Near them were tall columns of garbage, discarded jerry cans and human excreta. The cold of the glacier, which preserved everything, held in its grip all the detritus of the war.

When he finally reached the command post he could not believe what he saw: a cluster of fiberglass igloos at one end of the ridge, linked by a trench to a machine gun post and a toilet platform. The Pakistanis were on the neighboring ridge, and if he forgot to duck as he walked along the trench, he'd get his head blown off.

Each day up there passed in a haze of exhaustion and fear. Pakistani artillery shells boomed in at all hours, thrown off course by the howling winds, but close enough for a freak hit. The igloo was heated by a kerosene stove, and at night they breathed in its thick smoke; after a few days, like the other men, he began to cough up its black residue.

Two weeks passed up there, and when he came back down he went straight to the commanding officer and volunteered to climb higher, into the death zone, if necessary. The CO pulled his file, saw his climbing record, smiled and said, "We just had one officer retire, I think you'll be an ideal replacement for him."

That was the first time he met his men. Initially Sergeant Khandelkar just watched him, not saying a word, but after he led the men on their first sabotage mission, climbing a sheer cliff and two ice walls, the Sergeant put a hand on his shoulder and said, "Sir, not bad. Not bad at all."

With Khandelkar's help, he recruited real climbers. Not the showoffs who hacked their way up with spurts of machismo, but the boys with the faraway look in their eyes, the ones who climbed for the sheer love of it. They found Dewan one morning, scaling a cliff with no crampons and no rope, and watched open-mouthed as he made his way down, grinning with excitement.

The mountains were real and he climbed them with respect and skill, leaving behind the death and the waste and the stupid politics of the war. He took his men, again and again, through situations that were thought to be impossible, emerging like ghosts on top of the Paki posts, and then setting up mortars or calling in the jets. The Generals took notice of the tall Sikh Captain who spoke little, who came back mission after mission with all his men, filing terse reports: "Indira Col is now clear of enemy combatants," "Two positions taken and destroyed," "Eastern approach route now usable."

When they asked him to go on that final mission, he felt a rush of excitement — he knew that no one had ever climbed the eastern face of the Sia Kangri — and agreed without hesitation.

The fire is dying. The flames in the fireplace flicker up wildly and then collapse, leaving only the glow of red-hot embers. Drying sweat has made Ranjit's skin feel clammy, and he huddles close to Anna as he tells her about that last mission.

"My men had already been out on three missions that month. They should have gone down below and rested. I ignored the fact that my best climber — the kid I was telling you about was pushed to his limit. Other men found it difficult to acclimatize to those altitudes, but I could only breathe freely when I was up there. If I hadn't been so greedy to climb, my men would have lived."

Her breath is warm on his cheek. "Don't blame yourself. People die in a war."

He moves away from her slightly. "That is

not all. I made a much worse mistake. I thought we had found a Pakistani outpost within the sector they had given me. I didn't bother to check." He pauses and looks away. "I called in an air strike and killed sixteen of our own men.

"The scar you want to know about? My own people tried to kill me. After I came back from the mission, this General Handa, he wanted me to cover up my mistake and blame the attack on the Pakis. He wanted to prolong the war, but I refused to lie.

"The General tried to have me killed, but he failed, and I went on trial. The story got out and it made headlines in the papers. Suddenly the Indian public learned about a dirty war going on up there. There were questions in Parliament, editorials, and the journalists descended.

"The army sentenced me to three years in jail, and it was worth it. Now there is a cease-fire on Siachen, but my men are still lying up there. They're still there."

Anna takes a deep breath. "That's a terrible story, Ranjit. So that's why you ended up coming to America, to the Vineyard?"

He nods, and the silence between them grows. The room suddenly feels very cold.

"Death," she says softly, "always death, everywhere . . . The Buddhists say that death is a release from the suffering in this life, but still . . ."

She stiffens in his arms, a dark mood settling over her. He cups her face in his hands and kisses her, but she does not kiss him back.

He speaks softly, trying to comfort her. "You know, I like it here, on the Vineyard. The space, the feeling of being cut off from the crazy world. I wish I had come here twenty years ago. It must have been a very different place."

She thinks a moment, and her voice brightens. "Yes, it was different. No traffic, no presidential visits, no multimillion-dollar houses. It was wilder, a magical place."

"You grew up here, right?"

She nods. "I'm the third generation in the Vineyard, you know. People are always shocked to find out that we've owned that land in Aquinnah for over a hundred years. But the island has always been a refuge for people like us . . ."

She is deep in her memories now, and he feels her body soften in his arms.

"I grew up in Oak Bluffs — my grandfather had a big dry-goods store there, and that's where Daddy had his law practice — but I always loved going up-island. Every weekend Daddy would load up his old station wagon — with sandwiches, beer for him, orange soda for me — and we'd drive up to the shack in Aquinnah. For two days we wouldn't bathe or change our clothes, but I didn't care.

"Up there, free from the town, my father was a different person. He'd shoot birds mostly, but in season, he'd hunt deer. By the time I was twelve, I could skin and butcher a deer; I'd show up for school on Monday morning in bloodstained jeans. Oh, the other girls teased me mercilessly. Bad enough being the only black girl in the school, but to also dress like a boy . . ."

"That's when you learned to shoot?"

"Oh, I could shoot soon after I could walk. Daddy taught me. But he stopped hunting when I was in middle school. He had some bad luck, he lost a string of cases, and suddenly his Harvard degree was no use; he became just another uppity black man. We'd still go up to the shack, but he would start drinking the minute we got there. By nightfall, he'd be too drunk to hunt, and he'd stay that way all weekend. After a while, I stopped going and stayed in town. He'd go alone." She pauses. "He wasn't an angry drunk, he never hit me or anything. But drunk, he became sloppy, he stopped hiding things from me."

"What do you mean?" In the darkness he cannot see her face.

"When I was a kid, he would sometimes get a babysitter for me and go out, on a Friday night — he was a handsome man when he cleaned up, and a great dancer. I remember him coming back late, leaning into my bed to kiss me, smelling of cigarette smoke and scotch. He always came back alone, no matter how late.

"But drunk, he'd bring women home. I woke up one Sunday — I must have been fourteen — and there was a woman's dress thrown on the bathroom floor. I was so mad, I screamed at him and he made her leave. He was deeply ashamed, I know, and soon the women stopped. All he did was drink."

His voice comes out of the darkness. "And you — how did you handle it?"

"Handle it? I was a teenager, Ranjit . . . well, you wouldn't know about that, you didn't grow up here. You know those kids, the ones who hang around behind the ferry terminal?"

He nods.

"Well, I was one of them. Not a skateboarder, though, back then the style was punk: ripped jeans, purple hair, the whole deal. Oh, I got quite a reputation. People would call the cops on us, but the police knew Daddy, they'd always let me off with a warning."

"And then?"

"Well, my father had gone to Harvard, so I guess I was a legacy, they had to take me. All those nice preppy black kids from New York and Connecticut were a real shock, but I soon got used to it. I stopped coming back to the island. Every summer I'd stay with friends in New York, Taos, San Francisco. Then I got into law school, and I was busier than ever. By the time I moved to Washington and started working in Clayton's office, I wasn't even talking to my father anymore.

"The poor man died all alone out in the shack, and a hunter found him a week later. Clayton came back with me to the funeral — it was closed casket — and on the ferry afterward, he proposed, and I said yes. There's nothing else to tell, really. We built the house out in Aquinnah, and it was as though I had never left."

She says nothing about her daughter. Ranjit's arm under her head has become numb, and he shifts a little, his voice gentle in the darkness.

"Anna, I know about your daughter. I know what happened."

There is a sharp intake of breath. "Who told you?"

"Betty Green, I ran into her in the post office —"

"Betty Green. That woman is a real bitch. Even when I was a teenager, she used to gossip about me, spread rumors that I was sleeping around —"

"Anna, it was even in the paper. A few days ago."

"Oh." She turns to face him, her head rising from the pillows. "I told Clayton — I goddamn told him — that with all this publicity, they were going to bring it up again. What did they say?"

"Only . . . only that she drowned. Here. On the Vineyard."

She sits up abruptly. "Ranjit," she whispers, "there are times when I can't remember my baby's face. I'm losing her all over again."

"You're tired now, Anna. Let's get some sleep. You'll see, when you're rested, you'll remember. Come here."

He pulls her under the covers, and she cuddles into him.

They lie entwined in the darkness, and soon her chest is rising and falling and she is asleep. He stays awake, thinking of Shanti. He can see her clearly as a baby, lying gurgling in her stroller, but he has to reassemble her nine-year-old self, using her big eyes from one memory, her heart-shaped face from another. Finally her face is complete, and she smiles up at him, showing her small, even teeth. *What would happen if he couldn't see her for years? Would he be able to remember her then?*

The question haunts him as he drifts into sleep.

CHAPTER TWENTY-EIGHT

He wakes late the next morning into glittering winter light. Anna is gone from the bed, the place where she had lain cold and empty.

Sitting up, he feels a sharp ache in his side, and remembers again the red dot moving through the darkness of the Senator's living room. He sees it swerve from the Senator's chest to his, hears again the shattering of the glass. Something about the scene bothers him, and he replays it again and again, getting nowhere.

Panic washes through him as he looks around the huge bedroom. *This is the tenth day that his family is in detention. They will be deported soon, and here he is, with Anna. He has to do something.* Gritting his teeth, he slides his legs over the side of the bed. He takes slow, halting steps to the bathroom, holds the edge of the sink, and peers into the mirror. His face is hollowed out, his eyes cloudy, and a bristly beard has begun to grow back, the hair on his chin a shining gray.

"Ranjit, you're up? I heard a noise, I thought you'd fallen —"

Anna is in the doorway, her hair damp, her eyes bright. She's wearing the same brown corduroys as the day before, but with a man's electric-blue dress shirt.

"I just need some help getting dressed. Are there any clothes that will fit me?"

She gestures to an armoire in the corner. "That's full of clothes. But are you sure you can walk?"

"Yes," he says, but suddenly the room spins. She comes into the bathroom and grabs his arm.

Half an hour later, he is dressed in a thick cream cable-knit sweater and a pair of too-short gray corduroys that match the ones Anna is wearing. She supports him and they walk slowly down the stairs and along the ground-floor hallway. Its windows look onto the front porch, and he sees the pastel rocking chairs outside moving silently, back and forth, caught in a gust of wind.

They walk past the doorway of a dark sitting room, its furniture hidden under heavy canvas dust covers, and enter the kitchen.

Anna has started the potbellied woodstove

in the corner, and it is warm in here. Ranjit slumps into a straw-backed chair at the wide-plank table and looks around the room. Polished copper pots and pans cover one wall, sparkling with morning sunlight, and hanging bunches of dried basil and marjoram give off faint, woody smells. Despite the hominess of it all, the eight-burner stove and dishwasher are of industrial quality, clearly meant to service a house full of demanding guests.

He slumps into a chair, feeling the waves of heat radiate from the stove, and watches as Anna pulls cans and packages from the white wooden cabinets. He knows that the bottom cabinet in the corner, identical to all the others, holds the security system for the house.

"Voilà!" She returns to the table and piles up her finds. "Baked beans, sardines, caviar, wheat crackers, and umm, pickles."

In the glint and gleam of the kitchen, she looks rested and happy, far from the anguished creature of the night before.

"Did you sleep well?"

"Thanks to you, I did." She brandishes a can opener. "Now, what do you want to eat?"

"The beans and crackers for me, please. Is there any tea?"

She turns back to the cupboard and finds a green tin. She opens it under his nose, and he sighs as he inhales the rich aroma of Darjeeling. There is even a can of condensed milk, sticks of cinnamon, and some cloves — now they can make *chai.*

He guides her as she carefully measures out water, milk, tea leaves, and spices, boiling them together in a copper-bottomed saucepan.

"*Mmmm,* this smells good," she says, inhaling the steam. "I thought you had to make *chai* out of a mix."

"Ah, that's just American nonsense. They turn everything into a can or a mix."

She pours the boiling liquid into two thick pottery mugs, and he takes a large sip.

"*Aaah.* Now *this* is real tea."

"It must be a magic potion. You look a hundred times better already." She smiles at him as she heats up the beans on the woodstove.

Sunlight shines on his face, and his palms wrapped around the warm cup of *chai* soak in its heat. After last night, every emotion seems newly minted; even the dull ache in his side reminds him that he is alive. He watches Anna at the stove, her dark hair silvered with sunlight, the electric-blue shirt bright against her dark skin.

She catches him looking and smiles shyly, deep dimples appearing in her cheeks. When the beans are hot, she spoons some onto his plate, but their sweetness makes him nauseous. After a few bites he eats only crackers, dipping them into the hot tea.

"Isn't this house amazing?" She sits across from him, eating oily sardines on crackers. "I came over here last summer, you know, to have tea with the First Lady. It turned out to be more like cocktails. The President was there, too. People think he's so stiff, but he isn't really, he's quite funny when he's relaxed. She was egging him on, and he was imitating his enemies. He said, *Hell, the amount of times I've had to go to church to prove that I'm not a Muslim. Maybe I should just eat a pork chop on prime time. That'll show them, once and for all . . .*"

She captures the President's calm, professorial voice, and he can't help smiling.

"It's amazing that he can joke about it." Ranjit takes another sip of tea. "Being able to laugh at yourself is probably a sign of sanity. You know, in India they're always telling jokes about Sikhs. Even Sikhs tell Sikh jokes."

Anna looks up at him. "Well, I'm waiting. Tell me one."

"Okay." He thinks for a moment. "How

399

do you make a Sikh laugh on Sunday?"

"I don't know. How?"

"Tell him a joke on Wednesday."

"*Ha.* That's not very nice." But there is a smile on her lips.

"Hmm. Okay. Here's another one. How do you defeat a submarine full of Sikhs?"

"Stumped again."

"Just knock on the door, and they'll open it."

She laughs like a man, with deep, hearty guffaws. Soon they are both laughing, each burst of laughter tied to a twinge of pain in his side.

"It's not your jokes," she gasps. "Your jokes are awful. It's just so nice to see you happy —"

There is a sudden loud beeping.

His eyes jerk toward the cabinet in the corner, and she rises and throws it open. A green light flashes, and beside it a small television screen shows a grainy image of the boundary wall.

"Something set off the motion detector," he says, walking over to her. "Swivel the camera."

She uses a small joystick and the image flickers and moves. Bare black trees, more snow, and the stone wall stretching into the distance, casting a short blue shadow. Then they see a blur of motion, disappearing behind what looks like a woodshed.

"Did you see that? What was it?" Anna bites her lower lip, and he raises a hand for silence.

He squints at the other screens, scrutinizing the front gate, the porch with the rocking chairs, the lakefront, and the dock. There is just sparkling light and snow and emptiness.

"Anna, the leather case from the house in Ocean Park? Where is it?"

"Upstairs, in the bedroom. Want me to bring it?"

He nods, and she runs up the stairs, returning in a minute. He clicks open the locks and her eyes widen. She reaches in, her fingers caressing the varnished walnut stock and the whorls of silver engraving on the receiver.

"Here. Let me assemble it. It's a Holland and Holland, right?"

"You know this gun?"

"Twelve bore, side by side. I've always wanted one of these."

Her hands fly across the pieces without hesitation. She swiftly slides in the side-lock and tightens the screws, then attaches the barrels. She cocks the gun, breaks it open again, and pushes in two fat yellow cartridges.

"This load would take down a bear," she says softly. "I'll go outside and check it out. The east wall, right, by the lake?"

He forces himself to stand. "I'm coming with you. You carry the gun."

"But Ranjit, you can barely stand —"

"I'm coming with you," he insists. "Can you find me a coat?"

They make their way slowly through the snow, Anna holding his arm tightly and supporting him. Underneath a blue padded coat and a red hunting cap with earflaps, he is sweating heavily from the effort of walking. She is wearing her silver down coat and orange watch cap, pulled low on her forehead.

The section of wall they are heading toward has a drift of snow piled high against it, but from this distance he can see no footprints, and the triple strand of barbed wire on top is intact. The woodshed is about a hundred feet in, obscuring a section of wall.

He bends, picks up two large pine cones, and his voice drops to a whisper. "He will have heard us coming. I'll take the left side of the woodshed and lob these over. You

402

move in from the right. Only fire if you have to. I want him able to talk."

Anna squints into the whiteness as she slides off the safety catch. They split up, and she walks toward the woodshed, the muzzle of the gun up and ready. The only sound is the faint crunch of their footsteps in the deep snow.

He reaches the woodshed first and sees her frozen motionless at the other end, waiting for him to act. Leaning against the rough planking, he wipes salty sweat from his eyes. He peeks through a small window, trying to see through to the other side, but the glass is dusty, and all he can make out is a quick, dipping motion; there is definitely someone by the wall.

Gripping the pine cones, he lumbers to the corner and throws them over the woodshed, hearing them thud against the low roof, then spiral into the air. Ducking back, he hears Anna rounding the far corner, her feet crunching in the snow, hears her shout.

There is the galloping of feet, and suddenly a large deer bounds out from behind the woodshed, a buck with huge, spreading antlers. It lifts off in mid-gallop and soars into the air, clearing the stone wall and the barbed wire. There is the crashing of brush on the other side, a flash of its white tail, and then it vanishes into the tree line.

He forces himself upright and lurches around the woodshed. "It's me, Anna, it's me."

She is standing in the deep snow, her mouth open, the shotgun still raised. "Jesus Christ. Did you see that?" With a quick movement she breaks the shotgun and drapes it over the crook of her arm. "Another second, and I would have shot it."

He bends to examine the deep footprints and pain arcs down his side. He staggers then, and she runs to his side. "Hey, hey, are you okay? Can you make it back to the house?"

His head is spinning. "I just . . . need to sit for a moment."

She tries the door to the woodshed, but it is locked. He gestures to an upside-down rowboat, a hundred yards away at the edge of Tisbury Great Pond. Arms entwined, they walk there, and she sweeps the snow away with her gloved hands.

They both sit, breathing hard, listening to the soft *lap lap lap* of water. The clear blue sky above is bereft of clouds, but there is a knife-edged chill, and he knows that the weather is going to change very soon.

"Are you okay?" Anna peers at him and puts a concerned hand on his forearm. "It was just a deer."

"Yes, but next time it could be someone else. And in my condition —" He wipes his face, now slick with sweat.

"I've got the gun. I can handle it."

"I'm sure you can." He forces a smile, but the deer has proved that they cannot rely on the alarms and cameras. They need to get out of here. *What is the next move?* He shivers as a chill wind begins to blow.

"We better be getting back," she says, but he keeps on sitting.

"There is snow coming. A storm, perhaps a big one. Look at those clouds."

She squints at the gray clouds that have blotted out the sun. They part a little, and a single beam of light breaks through. "Looks pretty to me."

"Yes, it does." He suddenly thinks of James, back at the Garibaldi. "You know, a friend of mine wants his ashes scattered in water. This might be a good spot for it."

"That's pretty morbid." She moves closer and takes his arm. "What's on your mind? You have that look on your face. The look you get when you're thinking."

"I'm trying to figure out what happened." There is a silence and he can see her dark eyes staring at him from under her orange hat. "I've been thinking about those two men, back at your house."

"Ranjit, we should get you back inside. You're soaked, and —"

He turns to look at her. "At first I thought that the Senator hired those men, but I was watching him after you left. He didn't move from the chair, he just sat there. Even if he called them, there wasn't enough time for them to get into position. They were waiting for me."

He takes a deep breath. "It has to be Kohonen. He warned you at Filene's that I would approach you. And he knew that you and the Senator were coming to the Vineyard, right? But there's something else that is bothering me."

He closes his eyes and it all comes back to him: the darkened room, smelling of fear and desperation. The red dot wavering in the darkness, moving from the Senator's chest to his own. He sees again the Senator's eyes widening with shock as the glass door shattered, his frightened escape down the circular stairs.

"The Senator was just as surprised as I was when the shots came. I've had it wrong all this time. The shooter wanted us both dead."

"Why . . . why would Kohonen want to kill Clayton?"

"I don't know. And those two men were amateurs . . ." He remembers the gunman's shooting. Used to hunting deer, he had counted on the panicked movements of an animal in flight, not the reasoned tactics of a human adversary. ". . . while Kohonen is a professional."

They both stare out at the water, watching the wind ruffle its surface, throwing up small, choppy waves. Clad in an unknown man's coat and hat, Ranjit can smell the man's scent, something old and sour about it.

"Anna. This Kohonen — has he had a falling-out with the Senator?"

Picking up a piece of smooth, black driftwood lying next to the boat, she begins to doodle in the white crust of snow. "Like a fight? No, nothing like that." She cocks her head and thinks. "There has been a strange . . . tension, yes, I think that's the word for it, ever since they got back from North Korea. I thought Clayton would be happy with all the press, but he seemed frightened of something. We'd be in a restaurant or something, and he would look around, like he was afraid. And several times, I've heard him on the phone with Kohonen, yelling. That's unusual, the two of them have always been tight."

407

Using the stick, she makes convoluted loops in the snow. "What are we going to do, Ranjit? Go to the police? Tell them I killed that man? What will happen then?"

He thinks about Officer Gardner of the West Tisbury police. The man was upset at the sight of a dead dog. What is he going to make of a corpse lying on the cliff face?

"No police. And we can't stay here too long. If it is Kohonen, he knows I'm a caretaker, he's smart enough to get a list of my clients. And if a deer can get through that wall . . . we have to assume it's just a matter of time before he finds us." He takes a deep breath. "If I'm right about what happened at the house, I have to find the Senator, talk to him. He's in as much danger as I am. Where could he have gone? Back to Boston?"

She begins to doodle in the snow again. When she speaks, her voice is dull. "What happens when you find him?"

"I don't know. That really depends on him."

Despite the cold, her cheeks are burning with anger. She gestures out, beyond Tisbury Great Pond, at the ocean. "I think he's on the boat. The day you arrived, he'd spent the morning loading up supplies. He could live on that thing for a month."

Ranjit remembers the glimpse he'd had from the stairs, the dark line of the jetty stretching out into the water, strangely empty. *Of course.* The sloop that was moored there all summer was gone. He remembers its name painted in gold lettering on the bow: OSPREY.

"Come on," he says. "Let's go."

"Wait, where are we going?"

He turns and gestures to the horizon. The gray clouds are moving faster now, pushed along by an invisible hand. "There's a storm coming. Wherever the Senator is, he'll be forced back to the island. Vineyard Haven Harbor is the only anchorage deep enough to ride out a storm this big."

Without waiting for her, he stands. The pain shoots through his side, and he stumbles and almost falls.

"You're in no shape to go anywhere." She drops the stick of driftwood and grips his arm tightly. "If the bleeding starts again, I don't know what I'll do. You rest today, and we can look for him tomorrow, okay?"

He is forced to accept the truth of her words. As they walk away, he glances back at the rowboat: the patch of snow in front of where she had sat is now a forest of lines and swirls.

Leaning on her, he walks back to the

house, using the deep footprints they made on the way out.

Exhausted, he changes into dry clothes and falls asleep. When he wakes, the sun has set and he can hear the storm brewing outside, the wind whipping through the trees and making their branches creak. Anna starts a fire, lights a ring of candles, and they stay in bed, eating canned tuna, pickled onions, and crackers.

When they are done, she brushes the crumbs from his chest.

"Anna, the alarms, we have to be sure —"

"They're all on. Don't worry, we'll be able to hear them from up here."

He begins to say more, but she silences him, covering his mouth with hers.

They kiss, tentatively at first, then deeper, and soon the fishy taste in their mouths gives way to the sweetness of saliva.

Their lovemaking this time is slower, buffered by their knowledge of each other's bodies, more of an exploration, and less of a devouring. He holds her breasts in his hands, marveling at their firmness, his thumbs circling the thick nubs of her nipples. When she can stand his touch no more, he lowers his head and takes them into his mouth. And when she sighs and turns away from that pleasure, he kisses the salty back of her neck, feeling the curly hairs, moving lower to implant a line of kisses down her long back.

But he tires easily and sinks exhausted back into the pillows. It is her turn, her quick hands exploring the hard musculature of his legs, stroking the hair of his thighs till he is aroused and ready. She twists onto her side, and he wonders what she is doing, till her groin is near his head and her wish is explicit. He rests his head on her warm thigh and uses his tongue, and at the same time feels her mouth close over him.

In the darkness and the flickering candle-light he is no longer human, but has reverted to some sea-state that he has long forgotten, a world of membrane and brine. For a long time there are only pulse beats, slowing and quickening.

Then they are done, and pull away from each other. He's on the verge of sleep when her voice cuts through the darkness.

"I wish we could go away, Ranjit. Away from all this. Somewhere warm. Where would we go? India?"

"No." He thinks. "Not India. Brazil. I think we'd like it."

"What would we do?"

"Oh, drink wine. Eat grilled meat on the

beach. Walk around. We would fit in, I think."

"Yes, Brazil." Her voice is a sigh. "I can see us, at some market. We're buying fruit, and then we'll go home and peel them and eat them. Mangoes, and papayas . . ."

Her voice fades away as sleep overtakes him.

He wakes a few hours later, his consciousness sharpening for an instant, and he knows Anna is not in bed. She is sitting in the chair by the fireplace, her face blank, staring into the ashy fireplace with unseeing eyes.

CHAPTER TWENTY-NINE

All night there has been the swaying of trees. The next morning the storm is upon them, a soft snow pattering onto the ground. Anna is silent as she helps him get ready. He hesitates before he tells her to bring the shotgun, just for insurance.

He waits in the hallway downstairs, and she returns with the gun cradled in her hands. "You don't know Clayton. If you point this thing at him, you're going to have to use it."

"I don't plan on using it unless I have to. I know he's your husband —"

"He's nothing to me now. *Nothing.*"

The venom in her voice shocks him. They walk slowly to the Mercedes, and she lays the shotgun on the floor of the backseat.

As they head down-island the sunlight takes on a sudden, hard brilliance, even as it is being leached from the sky. The winds buffet the silver Mercedes, and Anna drives absentmindedly, speeding up and braking, barely slowing at the snow-covered forks. She leans on her horn, narrowly passing a slow-moving station wagon, and Ranjit sinks down into his seat and winces.

"Sorry, sorry," she says, but she doesn't slow down.

Tree branches along the road sway wildly as the wind grows stronger. A storm this strong can bring down trees and power lines, rip the shingles off houses. There is no doubt that the Senator will have to return to the deep, sheltered harbor at Vineyard Haven.

He needs to talk to the Senator and trade the microfilm for his family's release. *But then what?* All the old patterns have shattered, and none of the pieces fit together anymore.

Outside, the sky darkens and the air smells of newly whetted steel. They roar down the road to Vineyard Haven, heading for the ferry terminal.

The radio in the car fades in and out. Just as Anna pulls into the ferry terminal, it gives one final crackle and lapses into pure static. The snow is so thick now that Ranjit can barely make out the arms of land that encircle the deep harbor, or the stone breakwater that cuts across its mouth.

He takes out his binoculars and starts systematically sweeping the harbor, east to west.

Shanti loved to come down here in summer, buy an ice-cream cone at the Black Dog bakery, and walk with him along the wharf, watching the white sails of the yachts slipping across the calm, blue-green water.

Now the few sailboats anchored behind the breakwater are rising and falling with each massive swell, tugging at their anchors. The buoys in the harbor bob up and down on frothing waves, their bells clanging.

He adjusts the magnification on the binoculars and focuses on two specks coming in from the Vineyard Sound. They turn out to be fishing trawlers, identifiable by their tall superstructures.

"Nothing," he says, lowering the binoculars. "Maybe the Senator made landfall on the Cape after all."

"No." Anna's voice is firm. "He can't swim, he's scared of the ocean. He wouldn't be able to sail that far."

The waves break against the seawall, their spray spattering against the car windows. There is nothing else to look at, but Anna takes up the binoculars and peers out into the murk.

"Where the hell is he?" she mutters, her face flushed with anger.

Ranjit has seen this same look on some of his men before they went into battle. They were the ones who would be shot to pieces, while the scared, sober ones survived.

"Damn it." Anna thrusts the binoculars at him and reaches for the door handle. "The harbormaster's office is in the ferry terminal. They have a list of all the boats."

Without waiting for him, she steps out, staggering as a blast of wind hits her. Ranjit sighs, pulls on the red hunting cap, and they weave across the empty parking lot, soaked by the salty spray.

The harbormaster's office is a small, cramped room at the back of the ferry terminal. Anna pushes open a door and a white-haired man in shirtsleeves scowls up at her. His office is a mess, and papers are strewn across his desk, along with rolled-up charts and cups of congealed coffee.

"This office is private, young lady."

With a whine, a skinny greyhound rises from the corner. It's so thin that its ribs look as though they're carved out of balsa wood.

Ranjit stays behind Anna as she walks into the room and shakes her wet hair, sending

416

flakes of snow flying. She smiles sweetly, her dimples showing.

"You might remember me. I'm Anna Williams. Douglas Williams's daughter."

The man stares at her. "Williams? The hunter fella? Out in Aquinnah?"

She nods, and the man scratches his head. "I'll be damned. I remember you. You married a senator or something?"

Her smile grows brighter. "That's me. And I need a favor. We're not sure if a friend made it into the harbor today."

The greyhound comes over to Anna. She scratches its head, and it closes its eyes tightly, growling with pleasure.

The harbormaster's face softens. "Yeah, I can tell you that. What kind of boat? Name?"

"The *Osprey*. She's a sloop."

"*Osprey? Osprey?* What kind of damn name is that? These days, everybody names their boats this crap. Do you know I have five boats in the harbor — five — called *Carpe Diem*?"

The man swivels in his chair and turns to a clunky computer terminal. Muttering under his breath, he tilts his head back and reads from the screen.

"Sloop, you say? Yeah, your friend is safe. Came into the harbor yesterday evening, late, around seven."

"Why, thank you. Sorry to have disturbed you."

She smiles and rubs the dog's head, and it whines in protest as they leave.

Back in the car Ranjit blasts the heater and the fog slowly clears from the windshield.

"Anna, if he came in last night, he could have sailed anywhere. There are a million private harbors. He could be back at the house, for all we know. We have to get back now, before the snow gets any worse."

She bites her lower lip and starts the ignition. As they pull out of the parking lot, Ranjit sees that the Stop and Shop supermarket across the road is still open, and an entire Brazilian fishing crew is running in to it. If they are laying in supplies, then the storm is going to last a while.

"We should get some food," he says, and waves toward the supermarket. "I can't eat beans and crackers anymore."

He remains in the car, and ten minutes later, just as the lights in the supermarket go out, she emerges, carrying three bags of groceries.

Slamming the door shut, she brushes wet snow from her shoulders.

"Tea," he says. "Did you remember to get

418

more tea?"

She throws her head back and laughs.
"What is it?"

"Look at us," she says softly, "like an old
married couple," and leans forward to kiss
him with her cold lips. "Yes, they had tea.
And I even found a bottle of Indian pickle."

The anger in her seems to have leached
away, replaced by tenderness. She drives
slowly, holding his hand the whole way.

The snow is falling faster as they reach the
gates of the Red Heron Estate. Anna alights
and punches in BLUESKY. At the house, she
does the same, deactivating the alarms and
motion sensors. They have been gone barely
three hours, but the house seems colder.

He props the shotgun in a corner of the
kitchen and watches her unload the grocery
bags. Rice. Pink lentils. Jalapeño peppers.
Fragrant coriander leaves — how do they
get those in the Vineyard, in the dead of
winter? Onions, potatoes, and garlic. A
bottle of Indian mango pickle, the expira-
tion date reading two months ago. He is
suddenly aware of being ravenously hungry.

"I'll make you the best meal you've eaten,"
he tells Anna.

"He cooks, too," she says under her
breath, then smiles up at him.

"Well, I only know how to make one dish."

"Uh-oh," she says, mocking him. "Just don't put tea leaves in it, okay?"

Anna peels the onions and potatoes and washes the lentils and rice, and half an hour later, the hot, fragrant *khitchri* is done. He scoops two bowls full, and adds a dab of mango pickle to each.

"Eat it while it's hot," he says, handing Anna a bowl. They sit at the long plank table and eat silently, blowing on each spoonful.

"This is delicious," she says. "What is it?"

"*Khitchri.* We used to make it up on the glacier. It used to take five hours to cook, that's why we had to have four men at each post: two men on guard duty, one man to shovel snow, and one man to cook the *khitchri*."

"Well, I want more." She refills her bowl. "I really need to get the recipe for this."

"You just made it. You did everything. I just threw it all into the pot."

"Yes, but what about the proportions?"

"You just throw it together. There are no proportions."

"No proportions? Then how do you cook it?"

"Americans always want to measure

things. Just use your judgment."

She guffaws loudly.

"What is so funny?"

"It's just that . . . at times you're so Indian."

"What do you mean? I *am* Indian."

They look at each other and her laughter grows louder. Still chuckling, she gathers up their empty bowls and takes them to the sink, washing them with hot water from a kettle.

It is almost dark. He should get up and light the candles, but instead he just watches her washing up, her head bent over the sink, the back of her long neck exposed. She suddenly lowers her head, and a muffled sound escapes her lips. He thinks she's still laughing, and he's smiling when he addresses her.

"Now what's so funny?"

She just stands silently at the sink. When he puts a hand on her shoulder and turns her around he sees that her chest is heaving, and tears streak her face.

"What? What happened?" His hand grips her shoulder tightly.

"It's not fair," she says, her voice choked. "I'm . . . I'm so happy. Here, with you. Cooking together, eating together. And it's all a dream, right?"

She pushes hair from her eyes. "Ranjit, I

meant what I said last night. We don't have to go through with all this madness. Clayton has a slush fund hidden somewhere in the house. It's not a lot, but enough to get us far away from this mess. We could really go to Brazil."

He has a vision of the two of them: she is wearing her yellow dress and sitting on a shaded veranda. When he comes in from the heat, she smiles at him and hands him a cool glass, and he drinks deeply from it, tasting the tartness of fresh lime juice.

"Anna." He lowers his hands from her shoulders. "I need to get my family out of prison . . ."

Her dark eyes are fixed on his.

". . . I need to finish this. I've been running for too long, I don't have the strength to run any more. This has to stop. Somehow I have to make it stop."

"Then we'll go away when it's over. You and I." He feels her gaze focused on him. "We can take Shanti with us."

"Anna, if I leave Preetam" — he cannot bring himself to say *divorce* — "she'll make sure I never see Shanti again."

"That's absurd. There are courts, there are ways to handle that. Your daughter is a sweetheart, but your wife makes you so unhappy. Anyone can see that. Why do you stay with her?"

He thinks of Preetam, beautiful at twenty-one, the two of them in a movie theater, holding hands; and now, the woman who lives in a world of black-and-white nostalgia. *It is all his fault.* He was the one who took her out of India and into this strange world.

"I owe her," he says softly. "I owe her too much."

Anna turns back to the sink and turns the faucet on and off. "You *owe* her. How stupid of me. Of course." She gives the faucet another wrench. "I wonder if that's why Clayton stays with me? Because he *owes* me?"

In the silence Ranjit can hear water dripping. He wants to say, *In another life, Anna, we could be together. But this one is so crowded, so full of ghosts. There is barely a place for me, where could I put you?*

Instead he says nothing. She slips past him, walks down the long corridor, and turns into the darkened living room.

"Anna, please . . ."

He follows her. She pulls open the drapes and looks out of the French doors. The wind is roaring over the lawns, shaking the tall oaks at the periphery.

Standing beside her, he imagines a tree falling. The shock of it as it hits the ground,

423

its roots grasping at empty air, branches sprawled like broken limbs. When a thing that large dies, it takes an entire world with it.

"I am so grateful, without you I would be dead. But right now, I —"

She turns and puts her warm hands on his cheeks.

"*Shhh.* Don't say another word."

Taking his hand in hers, she leads him down the long corridor and up the stairs.

The bedroom is cold, and smells of the ashes from last night's fire. She bends to light some candles, and in the flickering light she undresses him with deft hands, taking his sweater off, then the long-sleeved T-shirt underneath. The bandage on his right side, which used to stretch across his stomach, is now a smaller rectangle of gauze; the black, sticky residue from the older bandage is still visible on his skin.

The cold air of the room knifes into him, and he moves toward the bed, but she motions for him to wait. She pulls off his trousers, and then steps quickly out of her own clothes. Naked, she pulls them both in front of the oval mirror that hangs over the dresser.

"Look at us," she says.

His own face stares out at him, shadowed by pain, his nose like a blade. His hair is still short and unruly, spiking up from his head.

"Look," she whispers. "I want you to remember us."

He cannot bear to look at her, but he forces himself, taking in her round breasts with their dark nipples, her narrow waist, the flare of her hips.

In the mirror, her raven-black eyes hold his gaze, and he sees that they are glistening with tears. They stand side by side, their bodies growing cold, but she will not let him go. Only when a shiver runs through him does she turn and lead him to the bed.

They take it very slowly, starting and stopping and starting again. Their gestures in the dark fight against time, against the loss of each other. They stretch out the minutes in wet and liquid ways, engaging and then pulling apart.

He tries to remember it all: every curve of her, the way she closes her dark eyes when he kisses her. The end is not a triumph but a surrender to nerves that are stretched taut, to muscles that scream for release. They lie in the darkness, their bodies chafed and raw.

The storm rages outside, claps of thunder

as crisp as artillery fire followed by the crack of tree branches breaking. Anna wraps her arms and legs around him and holds him tight. He hears her breathing slow, feels her drifting into sleep.

"Hey, are you awake?"

"Hmmm." She half opens her eyes. He needs to keep her up. If they fall asleep, the night will end, and tomorrow . . .

"If . . . if we went to India together, I know where I would take you. The Golden Temple in Amritsar. I used to go there with my mother, when I was a boy."

She sighs and moves in closer. "*Mmmm.* Tell me about it."

"We used to go once a year, on my father's death anniversary. Later, we went every day. My mother said it was the only place where she felt at peace."

"Your father . . . what was he like?"

"I can't really remember. All we had was a framed photograph, enlarged from his identification card, but it was so blurred that he looked like any other Sikh. But I knew he was a hero, because they awarded him a medal after he died. My mother hid it away under her saris, and sometimes I used to take it out and hold it. It was round and heavy, engraved with a three-headed lion.

"Anyway, we started to go to the Golden

426

Temple every day. My mother volunteered at the *langar,* the dining hall where they fed thousands of pilgrims every day. She'd roll up her sleeves and work like a demon, peeling mounds of onions, chopping hundreds of potatoes. There was no space for me in the kitchen — there were huge cauldrons full of scalding oil — so she'd send me outside to play."

Anna sighs and nuzzles into his chest.

"I used to just walk around and around the lake, stopping along the way at the sacred trees. Pilgrims and learned graybeards would sit in the shade and chant the scriptures. I liked the way their words sounded, like a song. And then, in the evening, walking back through the bazaar with my mother, I started remembering snatches. Never the whole *kirtan,* just phrases, and I would sing them to her. She was so happy, she was convinced I would become a priest.

"Later, she was so disappointed when I went into the army . . . Anyway, that is where I would take you. The Golden Temple is a beautiful place. You would like how peaceful it is . . ."

His voice trails off as he feels Anna's slow, steady breathing. She is fast asleep.

CHAPTER THIRTY

He is woken by the silence. There is faint dawn light in the windows and Anna is on the far side of the bed, buried under the comforter.

Getting slowly out of bed, he parts the white gauzy curtains, seeing only the whiteness of snow, marked by a dark tangle of downed trees and branches. The storm is over, and the wind has died down.

He thinks of the *Osprey,* docked somewhere on the island.

Today is the twelfth day since Preetam and Shanti were picked up. Each day has been like a decade, and yet he hasn't been able to help them. He thinks of the nights he has spent here with Anna, and the guilt rises in his throat like bile.

She sleeps on, an arm thrown over her eyes. He dresses and goes downstairs slowly, wincing with each step. Finding some lined paper in a kitchen drawer, he writes her a note, asking her to keep all the alarms on and to wait for his return.

The binoculars go around his neck and the Holland & Holland shotgun is cold in his hands. Walking slowly outside, he sees that a large, jagged branch lies less than ten feet from Anna's Mercedes. For once, he's been lucky.

As he drives away, the rising sun dyes the snow pink, and the trees cast long violet shadows across his path.

As he pulls into the empty parking lot of the Vineyard Haven ferry terminal, the first ferry of the day heaves into sight. Walking to the seawall, he raises his binoculars and scans the flat, calm water.

A sailboat has been swept onto the stone breakwater, and lies at a jaunty angle, its exposed keel shining in the early morning light. The masts of other vessels have been snapped in two and drag into the water, heavy with rigging. There is no sign of the *Osprey*. How the hell is he going to find one sailboat hidden amongst the island's many bays, coves, and private docks?

Two burly, tanned men walk past him, heading toward the water, talking in sing-song Portuguese. They climb into a rowboat and head slowly out into the harbor, making for a fishing vessel. The Brazilians now work in every seafaring trade: they run the ferry terminal, the docks, even crew the fishing boats.

Celia. She has cousins who work on the ferry, and others who are fishermen. She might be able to help him. Her big mouth has gotten him into trouble once before, but he can't think of another way right now. Sighing, he gets back into the Mercedes.

Even though it is seven in the morning, João's tow truck is gone. Ranjit walks through the open doors of the garage and crosses the oil-stained floor to the tiny office at the back. Finding it dark, he stands by the stairs leading to the second floor and shouts up a greeting. There is a shuffling noise and Celia peers over the banisters above, clutching a faded yellow housecoat closed with one hand.

"Ranjit? What are you doing here?" She is wearing glasses with thick black frames, and her face, devoid of makeup, has lost its usual sharp definition. "*Opa!* Your hair is so *curto . . .* short. What happened to your turban?"

He smiles his widest smile. "It's a new look. Do you like it?"

She peers at him through her owl-like

glasses. "What a terrible haircut! But you look so handsome. You could be Brazilian!"

Even in her housecoat and glasses, she can't help flirting, and he returns her smile.

"I need to talk to you. Just for a few minutes."

A shadow crosses her face. "Those men said that if I saw you again, I should call them. Otherwise they're going to deport me."

He climbs up the stairs while he talks. "They lied to you, Celia. They're not from Homeland Security, they're just common thieves. They tried to steal something from Senator Neals's house, and I got in their way —"

"Thieves? But I don't understand . . ."

The rickety wooden stairs groan as he reaches the top. Celia looks down at her housecoat and backs away.

"But I am a mess! A total mess! You should not see me like this! I look like an old woman!" She makes a shooing gesture. "You wait for me in the office downstairs. Please."

He smiles, backs down the stairs, and returns to her tiny office. Despite its exposed concrete-block walls, the room is neat, its shelves lined with colorful, labeled folders, and one wall is covered by a bright

431

poster. It is the iconic view of Rio, the massive concrete statue of Jesus high up on a hill, his arms spread out in benediction; below him, gleaming white skyscrapers step down to a tranquil blue bay.

He can imagine himself there with Anna, just walking the crowded streets, eating meat grilled on skewers, drinking rum, and sleeping together through the hot afternoons. In Rio a brown man and a black woman wouldn't draw a second glance.

"Ranjit! So, you leave here in one of Jõao's wrecks, and come back in a Mercedes?" Celia enters the room, gesturing at the silver-gray Kompressor parked outside.

She reaches up and kisses him on both cheeks, her lips bright crimson now. A smudge of lipstick stains her front teeth, and she's wearing a short lime-green dress.

"It's a long story, Celia. But the main thing is, you don't need to worry. My rich client — Senator Neals — he's helping me with this problem. It's his car I'm driving."

"Are you sure? Because those men . . ."

"Celia. If you have any doubts, you just call the Senator." Ranjit takes out Neals's business card, now creased, and thrusts it into her hand.

"United States Senate," she reads slowly, and then pins the card carefully onto her bulletin board.

"Celia, the reason I came to you is that the Senator and I need your help. His boat has been stolen, and I need to find it. Perhaps the ferrymen or the fishermen have seen it?"

The business card with its golden eagle seems to have convinced her. She gets out her cell phone and dials, her long nails skittering across the keypad. Leaning back in her chair, she chatters away in Portuguese. At the end of four calls she shakes her head sadly.

"Nobody has seen such a boat. Not in the water, and not in the harbors. Sorry."

Where the hell can you hide a boat? Ranjit looks through a window at the wrecks in the yard. A battered green Land Rover sits by the window, awaiting repair, its side gashed open, showing shining metal. *Of course. Why hadn't he thought of it before?*

"Celia, where do they repair boats? Or store them?"

"Storage? Only one place. Vineyard Haven Shipworks. Biggest place on the island."

"Do you know anyone who works there?"

"No, they won't give jobs to Brazilians. They check papers."

"Okay, thanks."

The shipyard is a ten-minute drive from

here. He's itching to go, but he listens as Celia tells him again about her plan to open a beauty parlor on the island. She kisses him on the cheek before he leaves, and runs her fingers through his cropped hair.

"Ranjit, when I get my parlor, you come to me, I'll fix your hair for you, okay?"

He laughs and disengages, but she follows him outside and waves at the Mercedes as he drives away.

The Vineyard Haven Shipworks is right on the harbor. It has its own jetty with a row of winches, and its large yard is lined with tall metal racks on which shrink-wrapped boats are stored, three high, like giant toys. At the rear is a row of massive metal sheds.

Ranjit parks the Mercedes farther down the road and walks back, entering through an unlocked gate in the high chain-link fence. He heads to a smaller shed whose door is propped open by a wooden tackle block. From inside comes a loud hiss, interspersed by pops and crackles.

Pulling the door open, he sees a man kneeling in the middle of the shed, clad in suede pants and jacket, his face hidden by a welding mask. The electric wand in his hands emits a blue bolt of electricity, and sparks fly as he expertly fuses together the parts of a large curved piece of metal.

"Excuse me, sir —"

The man wheels around. "Jeez, you scared the shit out of me." His voice echoes hollowly from within the mask, and he slides up its thick Plexiglas visor.

"I'm looking for a sloop. The *Osprey*. I believe it is in this shipyard?"

"Yeah, it's in the back. What is it, more pizza?"

Ranjit is confused, but decides to play along. "Pizza? Yes, that's right, it's in my truck."

The man pulls off his mask, revealing a thin face streaked with soot. "He's in the rear shed. D-3, all the way in the back." He shakes his head. "What does he think this place is, a shipyard or a motel?"

"I'm sorry?"

The man gestures with his welding wand. "The guy's crazy. Renting an entire storage shed for one little boat. Sleeping in there, getting food delivered. As soon as I get this damn propeller fixed, he's going to have to leave." Muttering, he pulls down his visor and turns to the twisted piece of metal.

Ranjit returns to the Mercedes and watches the entrance to the shipyard. Two excruciatingly long hours pass before the welder emerges, gets into a truck, and drives away in the direction of Vineyard Haven.

Ranjit lifts the shotgun from the backseat of the Mercedes, feeling the bandage on his side pull tight. The Senator is an angry man, and this time, he cannot make a mistake.

As he walks to the welding shed the light is fading fast, and an ominous chill spreads through the air. With one swift kick, he pops the lock on the door. Entering, he flicks on the overhead lights and sees the welding outfit folded neatly over a chair. He pulls it on, slips the welding mask over his head, and picks up the electric wand; it is too heavy for him to use as a weapon, and he'll have to move fast. Carrying the wand in one hand and the shotgun in the other, he walks to the rear of the boatyard.

. D-3 is a cathedral-like corrugated metal shed. Ranjit props the shotgun next to the door frame and bangs on the door, making a loud, booming sound. Hearing footsteps, he slips the visor down over his face and steps back, allowing himself to be seen.

The door opens a crack, and the Senator's voice shouts out. "Chris? What do you need now?"

"We need to talk." Ranjit's voice is muffled by the welding mask. "Problems with the propeller."

"Damn it, Chris, I need it fixed."

The door swings open, and Ranjit steps through. Senator Neals is wearing a thick blue down jacket, his bald head now sprouting dull gray fuzz. Behind him, propped upright on giant trestles, looms the *Osprey,* its wedge-shaped keel exposed, a gaping hole where the propeller should be. Under the boat are a crumpled sleeping bag, an electric heater, and a pile of cardboard pizza boxes.

The Senator walks past Ranjit and gestures up at the *Osprey.* "You said it'd be a quick fix. What the hell is the trouble now?"

"Well, it's the propeller —"

Ranjit swings the welding wand hard against the back of the Senator's legs. He goes down with a grunt, falling to his hands and knees.

Ranjit steps back into the doorway and grabs the shotgun, aiming it in one smooth motion.

"Senator, stay on the floor. I just want to talk to you. I think that Kohonen wants us both dead. The man who was shooting at us is a local deadbeat, the police are looking for him —"

"What the fuck." The Senator pushes himself off the ground with his fists.

Ranjit pulls off the welding mask with his

left hand, his right holding the shotgun steady.

"Look, I don't want to hurt you. I just need to talk. You need to *listen* to what I have to say."

Neals pushes himself up slowly, grimacing with pain. "You," he gasps. "You tried to kill me at the house."

"I had nothing to do with it. I'm trying to tell you, Kohonen —"

"Bullshit," Neals gasps. "You —" With superhuman strength, he jerks upright and lunges.

Enough of this. Ranjit reverses the shotgun and slams the stock against the side of the Senator's skull.

This time he stays down.

CHAPTER THIRTY-ONE

As Ranjit pulls out onto State Road the Mercedes sits lower, weighed down by the Senator's unconscious body in the backseat. He is covered by an oil-stained tarp, hands tied behind his back, his breathing rapid and rough.

Ranjit remembers the sickening thud as he hit the Senator, and prays that he hasn't fractured the man's skull. All he had wanted to do was talk, not beat the Senator half to death. It was a huge effort to drag the unconscious man to the Mercedes, and the wound in Ranjit's side now throbs with pain. He is driving slowly up-island, lost in his thoughts, when a black shape swoops toward his windshield. Instinctively, he slams on the brakes.

The Mercedes fishtails. It screeches to a halt at the side of the road, one wheel resting in the deep snow. Breathing hard, he peers up into the dark sky, seeing a massive pair of wings, then a flash of white under-belly. A huge bird flies out into a darkened field and lands on top of a tall telephone pole crowned by a jumble of twigs.

An osprey. His heartbeat slows. Is it the same bird that Shanti had seen? How has it survived the snow and the storm?

The osprey folds its wings and vanishes into the outline of its nest. Ranjit strains to see it, and starts when he hears a moan from the backseat.

". . . where? Where are you taking me? Money, I have money, I can pay you . . ."

"Senator? Are you awake?"

The mumbling voice falls silent, and Ranjit curses under his breath. The Senator is probably concussed, drifting in and out of consciousness. *Damn it.*

Ranjit starts the car and pulls out onto the road, feeling the jolt of wheels hitting asphalt.

The roads up-island are deserted and he makes good time back to the estate. He plans to take the Senator to one of the guest cottages and talk to him there; having Anna present will only complicate the situation.

Pulling up to the tall stone pillars of the Red Heron Estate, he leaves the engine running and rapidly punches in BLUESKY. Blowing on his cold hands, he waits for the

440

green light to flash.

A red blinks instead, and the LCD display says DENIED ENTRY.

Frowning, he punches in the code again. A red blinks, and it still says DENIED ENTRY. A third failure will alert the local police and send a signal to the security firm.

He can hear the Senator moaning in the backseat. *No choice.* With rapidly numbing fingers, he reaches into the control box and dials the main house on the touchpad. There is a soft buzzing, and a small television screen flashes to life.

"Anna? Anna, it's me. Ranjit."

Her face peers out at him, distorted by a fish-eye lens.

"The code isn't working. Open the front gate, please."

Her black eyes blink rapidly. "Where were you? I waited for you all day."

"I have him with me. The Senator."

She frowns, and her lips press tightly together. Anger, he thinks, and shame, and something else.

"Okay, I'm opening the gate now. Ready?"

With a silent swish, the gates start moving, and he drives through, watching them shut behind him. He relaxes as he travels the long, curving driveway, knowing that he is safe now, protected by the electrified fences and cameras and motion sensors.

The low, gray-shingled house comes into sight, the wind pushing the rocking chairs on the porch back and forth. He parks right by the front steps and removes the tarp from the backseat, seeing that the Senator is half awake now, breathing through his mouth; gathering up a handful of snow, he rubs it into the man's leathery face. A large purple bruise spreads across the side of his skull.

". . . *huh*. What the hell . . ." The Senator's eyes open and stare blearily at Ranjit. "Where am I? Where have you brought me?"

"It's a private estate. Don't even think of running. It's two miles to the gate, and the fences are electrified."

"Untie . . . untie my hands." The Senator shrugs his wide shoulders, feeling the ropes that immobilize his arms.

"I'll loosen the ropes now, so you can move. There is no need for any more of this. We need to talk, you understand? The man who works for you, Kohonen, he wants you dead, and me too. I need to know why."

The Senator takes a deep breath. "All right. Loosen the ropes, I can't feel my hands."

Ranjit puts an arm around the man's shoulders and heaves him upright, reaching behind him to create some slack in the rope.

442

The Senator scuttles to the edge of the seat, but pitches forward as he tries to get out of the car. Ranjit grabs him under his armpits, feeling a jolt of pain. He guides the Senator up the icy stairs, his free hand holding the shotgun.

The front door is open. *Good thinking, Anna.* Ranjit pushes the Senator down the long, dark hallway toward the kitchen.

"Anna," he calls out. "I'm bringing the Senator with me. Where are you?"

"I'm here."

There is a flicker of motion at the end of the corridor. Anna is standing behind the long plank table, her hands resting on its top, her dark eyes fixed on the Senator's advancing figure. Behind her the alarm cupboard is open, the screen showing the Mercedes parked outside.

The Senator stops his steady shuffle. He turns abruptly to Ranjit.

"She's with you? I knew it. Bitch. *Fucking bitch.*"

"Just keep walking, Senator." Ranjit pushes the barrels of the shotgun into the Senator's back.

As they pass the dark entrance to the living room there is a soft footfall behind Ranjit. Something hard and metallic is thrust into the back of his neck.

Everything freezes.

The Senator is in mid-stride, the shotgun jammed into his back. Ranjit is behind him, the unmistakable, icy barrel of a handgun pushing into the skin of his neck.

"Drop the shotgun. Do it." A careful, slurred voice.

The shotgun falls from Ranjit's hand and clatters onto the floor.

The Senator turns, and relief floods through his dark face. "Kohonen. Thank God."

Kohonen articulates each word. "Keep walking, Mr. Singh. Into the kitchen. Slowly."

The Senator is the first into the kitchen, and walks over to the wall with the copper pots, while Kohonen pushes Ranjit into the middle of the kitchen. Anna is still standing, hugging herself tightly as she stares at a piece of paper lying on the table. She glances from it to the Senator, her eyes red and angry.

The Senator's voice is a rasp. "Matti. Thank God. Untie me. This bastard tried to kill me at the house. I got away on the boat —"

"Senator, that's not true, I —"

"Shut up! And Anna's with him. She's working with him."

444

"I know. I know." Kohonen steps through the doorway. He's smiling, his teeth white and perfect. He's dressed for a weekend at an English country house, in gray tweed trousers and a quilted green Barbour jacket. The only discordant note is the sling that starts at his shoulder and wraps around his right hand: an army-issue Colt .45 automatic pokes out of the sling, and Ranjit's shotgun is in his left hand.

He walks over and puts the shotgun down on the table, right in front of Anna.

"No!" the Senator shouts. "Anna's with him! She told him about Korea, he knows —"

"Clayton." Anna's voice is soft and quivering. "Why did you lie to me?" She points at the piece of paper on the table. "It says six inches of water."

"I don't know what you mean." The Senator's face takes on a hunted look. "Kohonen, untie me. Anna, you're crazy. I don't know —"

"I'm the crazy one? I'm crazy?" Her hands are a blur as she swings the shotgun to her shoulder.

A blue muzzle flash. A deafening roar fills Ranjit's ears.

The Senator rises onto his toes, picked up by an invisible hand. He slams backward,

445

clanging against the copper pots, then slides to the floor, polished copper cascading around him. Like a magic trick, blood wells from his chest, oozes from a dozen puckered wounds on his face.

Anna lowers the shotgun. Kohonen walks up to her and in one quick motion she hands the shotgun to him, then falls back into a kitchen chair.

What?

Kohonen tucks the Colt into his waistband and puts an arm around Anna's shoulder, the shotgun aimed at Ranjit's head.

No, this cannot be happening. Not Anna. No.

The Senator lies slumped on the floor. His hands are still roped together behind his back and dark blood puddles around him, filling the white joints of the stone floor.

Ranjit waits, motionless, for the end.

Time stands still, as it used to in combat. Seconds like hours. But all the frantic calculations he does only come back to one thing: Anna. *In the Guru's name, why?*

The woman he had made love to sits behind the table, her eyes extinguished. She has gone, has retreated into her dark hiding place.

Ranjit keeps his voice steady. "Anna.

Listen to me. Clayton is bleeding to death. We need to get him to a hospital."

She does not reply. The shotgun in Kohonen's hand remains pointed at Ranjit.

"Anna, listen to me. He's losing a lot of blood. You were angry, you made a mistake, but you can save him —"

"Let him die. The bastard." She spits out the words. "He killed her."

"What are you talking about?"

Her voice is hollow, about to crack. "Josephine. She drowned. In six inches of water."

"Anna, it was an accident. It said so in the papers."

"*He* told me it was an accident. *He* told me that the pool was full. But it was almost empty. Look at the coroner's report. It said she drowned in *six inches* of water." She wipes a trembling hand over her face, as though trying to brush away a cobweb.

He can see the anger still burning in her; if she could, she would pick up the shotgun and shoot him again.

Ranjit takes a step forward. "Kohonen, you showed her that? You're sick, you're manipulating her."

Anna's face crumples. "He burnt all Jojo's photographs. One day I came home, and they were gone. He even took her picture

447

out of my pocketbook. He said I was stuck in the past, he said I needed to move on. Now I can't remember her face anymore. I can't remember my baby . . ."

Kohonen frowns. "No closer, Mr. Singh. That is enough, Anna." He squeezes her shoulder. "You didn't have to shoot him. That was stupid. But don't worry, I'll take care of it. Let's talk in the living room." He motions Ranjit toward the corridor. "And unlike those two fools, I won't miss at this range."

Ranjit can tell from the Senator's shallow, gasping breathing that he has fifteen, perhaps twenty minutes left. And it was he who led the Senator to his death.

The living room is dark, except for the fading light from the French doors. Ranjit sits in an armchair covered with a white dust cover, his hands resting in plain sight on its wide arms. Anna sits across from him, and Kohonen stands in front of the French doors, rocking back and forth on his heels, his injured hand caressing the silver engraving of the shotgun.

The two of them have been working together all this time. That day at Filene's Basement they were probably discussing how to lure him in. Then, at Harvard, Kohonen must

448

have alerted her that he was in the audience. He remembers that Anna had looked at her phone constantly; she had even left the lecture so he could approach her. *How could he have been so blind?*

He looks at Anna, sitting curled into the armchair, her dark hair tousled, her eyes blank, staring out of the French doors. He feels again her lips on his, her taut body against his, her words in the darkness mingling with his. It is as though he has been expelled from a warm, safe place.

"Anna, why are you doing this? Please?"

She turns her head away, and his disbelief gives way to a white flash of anger. "Damn it, Anna, all these days . . . you . . ."

Her voice is barely audible. "I asked you to go away with me. We could have left while there was time. You were the one who wanted to see it through . . ." She stares down at the floor and her voice trails off.

With a shock, he realizes that if he had agreed, she would really have gone with him to Brazil. He hears the wind outside, and has a mental flash of the empty rocking chairs on the porch, moving slowly back and forth.

He turns to Kohonen. "You're responsible for this, you can't just kill a United States Senator and get away with it."

Kohonen shrugs and smooths back a strand of long blond hair. "The Senator isn't really the issue. I talked to Anna" — Kohonen smiles at her — "before you got here, and we have a proposition for you. A business proposition."

Ranjit leans forward, his face red with anger. "You sent those two men to kill me. And the Senator."

Kohonen raises one hand, palm out, the gesture of a man trying to be reasonable.

"Yes, you're right. I hired the Nash brothers." He shrugs and smiles apologetically. "You did a good job of vanishing in Boston, Mr. Singh. I thought you might be back on the island, and I talked to a cop in West Tisbury. Nice guy, an Officer Gardner. He told me an interesting story about how you'd stumbled into some sort of robbery, identified two local hoodlums. He said they'd be arrested any day now.

"It was serendipitous, really. I found the Nash brothers, half starved out in Chappaquiddick, told them that I'd get them off the island if they did a job for me. They were glad to help me out. For some reason, they didn't like you very much, Mr. Singh. The Senator was extra." He shrugs again. "It would have looked like another botched robbery. If it's any consolation to you, I was going to let those two take the fall for it. They were going to spend the rest of their lives in jail anyway."

Anna's anguished voice comes from behind Ranjit. "I didn't know he was going to do that. He said that once you handed the microfilm over, he would let you go —"

A look of irritation passes over Kohonen's pale face. "Anna, pull yourself together. What's done is done. Mr. Singh, you're a military man, I'm sure you understand my logic. You were no good to me once you gave the microfilm back. The Senator — well, the Koreans want him dead. He really pissed them off." His voice is still reasonable. "My point is, Mr. Singh, you have the microfilm, and I need it. I'll pay you for it. How does ten million sound?"

"That one frame of microfilm is worth ten million dollars to you?"

Kohonen glances at Anna. "She didn't tell you the full story, did she?"

"No. She didn't." *Come closer, Kohonen, come closer, keep talking.* Ranjit's shoulders tense. He can dive from here, tackle him . . .

But Kohonen backs up, his fingers caressing the silver engraving on the shotgun.

"Back in India, I was the one who did all the hard work, I used all my connections to get the microfilms for the Agni missile. Of

451

course, the Senator was the hero, he got all the glory."

Kohonen gestures at the next room. "That's the problem with Clayton Neals. He thinks that if he says something enough times, it's true. You heard all those stories about growing up poor in Roxbury, how his father was an undertaker? That's bullshit, his father *owned* a string of funeral parlors." His face is flushed now.

"Now me, I did grow up poor. You know how I lost my hearing? Measles. Where I grew up, they didn't inoculate the kids. And you know how far a deaf man can go in the CIA? Once I washed out of there, what was I supposed to do? Security details for rock stars? I don't think so . . . but I'm digressing."

He smiles, showing his perfect white teeth. "Once we were done with the negotiations, we were supposed to destroy the microfilms, but the Senator kept the whole set, in case we had to deal with the Indians again. And that started me thinking. We had the microfilms, nobody knew about it, and the damn things were worth a lot of money. You know how much the Iraqis would have paid for them? Or the Libyans? But the Senator, he would never do something like that. The son of a bitch wouldn't even tell me where he hid them. He's an honorable guy, right?

"Then the North Korean hostage situation showed up, and it was perfect. I talked to them, and negotiated a pretty good deal: they would return the hostage — and give me a nice finder's fee — if I gave them the Agni microfilms. Sure, they were almost ten years old, but, hey, the missile worked, it did the job.

"Of course I didn't tell the Senator that. I told him that they would trade the hostage for medicine and machine parts, and he jumped at the deal. And once we were there, I said that the Koreans had reneged, that they wanted military information, something big. So now the Senator was really in a bind. Either he came up with the microfilms, or he returned with a dead hostage. Once his ass was on the line, it wasn't a hard decision."

He chuckles. "I gave the North Koreans the whole set of microfilm, they gave us the hostage, it was a done deal. I got paid, Neals was supposed to go home and get reelected. Everybody was supposed to be happy. But the Senator" — he gestures at the next room — "he went and fucked it all up.

"On the plane ride back he told me what he'd done. *Matti,* he said, *I couldn't go through with it. What happens if those bas-*

tards actually build that missile, point it at South Korea? We'll be sucked into a nuclear war. He'd kept the microfilm for the wiring of the guidance system. Without it, the missile is useless, it won't track. Can you imagine pulling a stupid stunt like that?

"I mean, even with the microfilm, the North Koreans can't build the damn missile. Half of them are eating bugs, they have no food, no medicine. How in God's name are they going to precision-engineer a missile?

"But even *they* finally figured out that one frame was missing. They asked nicely for it, but Neals wouldn't budge. He said he'd burnt the microfilm, but I knew he was lying. He always likes to have an ace hidden up his sleeve." Kohonen sighs, and waves his free hand. "The rest is mundane. The Koreans were after my ass, so I searched the house in the Vineyard, top to bottom, couldn't find a damn thing. Then Anna remembered the doll, but when we went back for it, there you were, Mr. Singh. You and your pesky little daughter."

Anna is sitting motionless behind them, her head held in her hands. As Kohonen talks, he draws nearer to Ranjit.

"What do you say, Mr. Singh? Ten million? I'm being generous here. That is the same amount Anna is getting."

Ranjit thinks of Neals dying in the next room and is suddenly exhausted at the stupidity of it all; ten million will barely buy a water view on the Vineyard. In any case, as soon as Kohonen has the microfilm, he will kill Anna too, and take all the money.

"All right," Ranjit says. "All right. You let my family go, and I'll give you the microfilm."

Kohonen shrugs, a small, elegant gesture. "Too late for your family, I'm afraid. The deportation procedures are under way. It was easy enough to tip off Homeland Security, but getting them to stop . . . well, if the Senator called, that would be another matter. But he's not really in great shape, is he?"

Blood floods into Ranjit's face. He thinks of Preetam and Shanti being escorted onto a plane, the General waiting at the other end.

"There's no need to worry. Ten million should be able to buy you plenty of protection in India. Now, where did you hide it?"

Ranjit fights down his anger. *Take the enemy onto your terrain, where you have the advantage.* He remembers Anna telling him about a hidden slush fund, and the Senator at the house saying, *Give it to me and I'll pay you for it. I have money inside . . .* And then he knows what he has to do.

"It's at the Senator's house," he says. "I hid it there."

"That's more like it." Kohonen gestures Ranjit to get up. "Anna, pull yourself together, you're driving. Let's go. And remember, we are all partners now."

They walk outside and Anna slides into the driver's seat of the Mercedes, with Ranjit next to her. Kohonen sits in the back with one ankle crossed over his knee, the shotgun pointed at the base of Ranjit's neck.

"Step on it, we don't have much time left."

She turns the ignition and the Mercedes jerks forward, gravel spraying.

As they go through the gate, Ranjit knows that neither of them has noticed. While leaving the house, Kohonen was focused on getting out quickly, and Anna walked as though in a trance. Ranjit had looked down the long hallway, one quick glance, but he was sure of what he'd seen.

Incredibly, the Senator was no longer slumped against the kitchen wall. Across the floor was smeared a trail of blood that led out of sight.

CHAPTER THIRTY-TWO

There are no other cars on the road. Anna drives blindly, taking the turns very wide, the intricate steering mechanism of the Mercedes instantly correcting. For long stretches of time she drives down the middle of the road.

Her foot presses down on the accelerator. *Seventy. Seventy-five.* The car surges effortlessly through the narrow stretch separating the waters of Menemsha and Squibnocket ponds. *Eighty, eighty-five.* Dusk is falling over the island, and if another car were to come toward them . . .

"Anna, please slow down. Please." Ranjit speaks softly.

"He's right." Kohonen's voice comes from the back. "Not so fast."

With a start, Anna eases off the accelerator and the car instantly slows. The details of her daughter's death seem to have taken her into so much pain that even pulling the trigger hasn't released her anger. Ranjit has to somehow bring her back to reality, otherwise both of them will soon be dead.

"Anna, I'm sorry about what happened to Josephine. Truly sorry."

She does not even look at him. "That's what they all say. Why are *you* sorry? You didn't know her."

"Mr. Singh, I didn't realize you liked to talk so much." Kohonen's voice comes from the backseat.

Ranjit ignores him and keeps talking, his voice soft and comforting. "Don't forget that I have a daughter. What was Josephine like?"

Anna glances at him from the corner of her eyes. *Does she recognize him now?*

There is a long silence. Houses blur by, their windows darkened. No lights shine across the road, no dogs bark. The very land, shadowy and uninhabited, is conspiring against him, just when he needs to fill her mind with thoughts of life.

There is a long silence, and then she speaks reluctantly, as though she has opened a door that was closed for a long time.

"Jojo was . . . always smiling . . . she trusted people." The car goes faster as memories crowd Anna's mind. "She would toddle up to dogs and want to pet them . . .

She was fearless. She would climb onto the back of the sofa, spread her arms, pretend she was flying, and jump off. She would shout, *Look at me.*"

Anna's eyes are shining now. Ranjit knows that her little girl is alive for a few seconds, moving and jumping.

"She liked to play with that old doll?" he prompts. "Betsy?"

"Clayton was always bringing her back dolls from his trips. She'd get excited, dress them up, but then, the next morning, she'd be back to playing with that old thing. She loved something about it. I had grown older and forgotten about that doll, but Jojo discovered its magic."

"Mr. Singh. Enough of your amateur psychology. Shut up and let Anna drive."

What is Kohonen going to do to him? Shoot him for talking? "Anna, why are you doing this? You don't need the money. Ten million is nothing."

She looks straight ahead and waves a hand toward the window. A flock of small birds is settling into a bare tree, swarming around it with quick strokes of their wings.

"What do you mean? Because of the birds?"

"Loons," she says. "And that's not all. Plovers, grackles, terns, ospreys."

She *has* lost her mind. "What are you talking about?"

The land is climbing now, and the car engine growls as she changes gears.

She continues. "Daddy must have shot hundreds of birds over the years. In the old days, people used to hunt osprey for their feathers, shoot grackles for grackle pie. But Daddy just killed them for sport, and a few years before he died, the birds stopped coming. Right at the end, he realized what he'd done."

"Anna, the birds are back. I saw an osprey just this afternoon —"

She ignores him and gestures outside. They are passing through old farmland, now covered with trees. "Daddy used to own all this land, all the way to the ocean. It would be worth how much now? Hundreds of millions? Maybe more?"

She laughs, her eyes emotionless. "I told you, he died up here, alone, in the shack. I think that he'd been searching the skies through his binoculars, waiting for the birds to return." A shiver runs through her slim shoulders. "And after the funeral, I found out what he'd done. He'd changed his will and left all the land — my land — to a nature preserve. All of it, in perpetuity."

"But you're not poor, you have the house

here, the town house in Boston —"

She shakes her head. "Oh, my father left me an inheritance, but that all went on Clayton's political campaigns. The house in Rutland Square is rented, and we took out a large loan to build the house here. They would have foreclosed on us long ago if Clayton hadn't been a Senator. You see, Ranjit . . ." Her hands tighten on the wheel. "Clayton took my daughter, and my money. And now I need money to get away. I'm going far away from this wretched island."

She turns down Lighthouse Road, and the entrance to the driveway appears. With a twist of her wrist, she enters the driveway, and Ranjit's seat belt tightens as the Mercedes swings wildly through the first hairpin turn. Soon the gray-black ocean curves into sight, its sullen waves receding in lines all the way to the horizon.

Kohonen jumps lightly out of the car, the shotgun in his hand. He has buttoned up his green padded jacket, and his long hair flutters in the wind.

Ranjit stands on the gravel driveway, looking at the tall brown shrubbery. He remembers the evening when he'd driven here with Shanti. The Senator's gray sweatshirt was soaked with sweat, and close to the shrubbery was the deep hole.

"Okay, Mr. Singh. Lead the way. Where is it?"

Ranjit points to a spot downhill from the shrubbery. "I buried it there."

"Anna, is he telling the truth?" Kohonen turns to where she leans shivering against the car. "Anna. Did you hear me?"

She stares down the hill at the kidney-shaped outline of the swimming pool, its blue canvas cover rippling in the wind. Her voice is faint. "I don't know."

"Well, Mr. Singh, let's get going. We don't have much time. The Koreans are sending someone to Woods Hole. We need to leave on the last ferry."

"I have to dig it out."

"You stay put. Anna, please get Mr. Singh a shovel from the garage."

She moves slowly toward the house. A stiff wind begins to gust, but Kohonen does not even blink. He holds the heavy shotgun uneasily, the weight of it clearly straining his injured shoulder.

Anna comes back with the Senator's metal shovel, hands it to Ranjit, and backs away. He hefts it in his hands, feeling the shaft of solid wood, the wide blade as sharp as a knife. *If only Kohonen would come closer . . .*

But Kohonen turns and walks about ten

feet away up the slope, the shotgun resting in the crook of his elbow. *The executioner's position.* Anna stands listlessly beside him, the cuffs of her oversized trousers flapping in the wind.

The shrubbery casts a long shadow. Ranjit closes his eyes and tries to remember where the hole was — four, no five feet from the gnarled roots. He slowly paces out the distance and rams the shovel into the frozen earth, pushing down with his foot. A sharp pain travels up his side, and he feels a slick wetness under his jacket. He prays that it is sweat, not blood from his wound.

The first few inches of earth are as hard as concrete, but after he breaks through the crust, the soil below crumbles easily. Further inland the ground is frozen solid, but the ocean moderates the temperatures along the coast.

He gasps as he digs deeper, the pain in his side worsening. *How far down does he have to go?*

The pale, sandy soil slowly grows into a mound. Ranjit is up to his calves in the hole, conscious that in another few minutes it will be completely dark. The sky is already dimming at its far edges; Kohonen's pale hair glows in the twilight, as do the whites of Anna's eyes.

The shock from each shovelful of dirt travels into Ranjit's arms and into his right side, translating into red-hot pain. He blanks his mind and concentrates on the motion.

Step on the edge of the shovel.

Feel it sink down.

Throw the earth to the side of the hole.

Repeat.

As the light fades, Ranjit can barely see his hands. *What if it's the wrong spot?* Kohonen is constantly turning his wrist and looking at his watch, anxious about meeting the North Koreans on the mainland.

The shovel clunks against something. Farther up the slope, Kohonen doesn't react. With his hearing aids, he probably can't hear over the howling of the wind — but Anna hears it, and tenses.

Ranjit crouches in the hole and pulls out a plastic-wrapped package the size of a shoebox. He digs his fingernails into the clear plastic and tears it open, revealing a polished wood box. It is sturdily made, its corners mortised together, and a deep scratch in the lid releases the pungent odor of cedar.

"What is it? Did you find it?" Kohonen aims the shotgun.

Ranjit pries open the wooden lid, expecting to find the Senator's slush fund, maybe a couple of hundred thousand. Certainly not enough to keep Kohonen happy — not when the microfilm is worth millions — but maybe enough to cause a distraction.

He stares down at a box full of photographs. A stack of faded color photographs, some with inscriptions on their backs. *Useless.*

He is dead now, unless he can lure Kohonen closer.

Climbing out of the hole, he holds out the open box. "Kohonen, here's the microfilm. Take it."

But Kohonen only smiles and cocks the shotgun. "You think I'm that stupid, Mr. Singh? Put the box down, next to the shovel. Anna, please bring me the box." The gusting wind clips the ends off his words.

That is it, then. Kohonen will probably shoot him first, then Anna. He imagines their bodies tumbling over the cliff, the cold ocean bubbling around them.

Ranjit places the box at his feet, inches away from the shovel.

"Anna." Kohonen shouts to be heard above the wind. "Get the box."

She walks shivering toward Ranjit, her hair blowing into her face. When she sees the box, she stops abruptly, a flicker of recognition in her eyes. She looks transfixed, reaches into it and pats the photographs gently.

"Anna! Is the microfilm there?"

Ranjit is inches away. "Anna," he whispers, "answer him. Tell him that it's there. Please. Or else he'll kill us both."

Kohonen's eyes narrow, trying to hear them above the howling of the wind.

Anna's eyes are shining brightly as she turns toward Kohonen. She nods. "It's here, it's in here," she says, in a loud voice.

"Good. Bring it over."

"Get him closer," Ranjit whispers. "Closer."

Anna doesn't move. A strange smile is on her lips as she looks into the box.

Kohonen steps toward them, his shotgun extended. "Anna! Give the box to me!" He takes another two steps and grabs for it.

Anna cries out and jerks the box away, and it tilts. A massive gust of wind blows just then, and the photographs scatter, swirling into the air.

"No!" Anna drops the box and reaches upward, her hands scrabbling. She slams into Kohonen, and for a second the shotgun tilts toward the sky.

Ranjit is a blur, reaching for the shovel.

Kohonen frantically elbows Anna aside,

trying to get a clear shot.

Ranjit lunges forward. The shovel's wide blade clangs against the barrels of the shotgun, pushing it away just as it fires.

The retort is deafening and buckshot spews into the sky.

Ranjit reverses the shovel and slams its wooden handle deep into Kohonen's midriff. The man gasps and doubles over, trying to aim the shotgun, but Ranjit wrenches it away. Grabbing Kohonen's injured arm, he twists it, and keeps on twisting till he feels it snap.

Kohonen screams and slumps to the ground, grasping his arm, and Ranjit kicks twice at his head, hearing the crunch of cartilage. Kohonen doesn't move again. He lies sprawled out, blood staining his face, his arm lying at a strange angle, like a chicken with a broken wing.

The gust of wind dies down. When Ranjit turns, Anna is scrabbling in the snow, gathering up the photographs. Then she turns and runs up the hill.

"Anna, wait. Wait!"

He tries to run, the pain shooting into his side. When he reaches the shrubbery, she is already in the Mercedes, the engine growling into life.

"Anna, stop . . . it's all over . . ."

Her face is a pale blur as the silver-gray car speeds up the driveway, faster and faster, cresting the hill.

Kohonen moans, and Ranjit walks toward him, hearing a muffled ringing noise. He searches through the man's pockets and finds a bulky cell phone that flashes as it rings.

He is about to turn the phone off, but then decides to answer it. The wind twists and distorts the voice at the other end, but it is unmistakably Asian, clipped and precise.

"We are meeting at the ferry terminal at Woods Hole, yes? You have it?"

Ranjit says nothing.

"Hello? Kohonen? Have you procured the microfilm? Hello?"

Ranjit makes a decision and talks into the phone, slurring his words slightly. "Yes," he says. "I have it. But I want more money."

"The line is bad. I can't hear you." The voice fades in and out.

"The deal is off. I want more money."

"We had a deal, Kohonen. Stick to it." Even distorted by static, Ranjit can hear the anger bubbling through the man's clipped accent.

"Sorry, the price has just gone up. Another ten million."

"We have already paid you, and you delivered a useless set of microfilm."

"Ten more. Or I burn it."

"You are dead, Kohonen."

There is a click, followed by the sound of static. Ranjit stares at the phone for an instant, then dials nine-one-one.

"There has been a shooting at the Red Heron Estate," he says. "A gunshot victim is in the main house. The gate is locked, you'll need to break in." An excited voice at the other end begins to ask questions, but he hangs up.

It has been close to forty minutes. The Senator must be dead in a pool of blood. *Damn it.* Ranjit feels an enormous weight settle on his chest. He has to go back to the Red Heron and see this through, no matter what.

Kohonen moans again, still unconscious, the blood drying on his face. He doesn't know it, but when he wakes up, he's finished. Ranjit retrieves the Colt from Kohonen's waistband and throws it over the edge of the cliff, along with the shotgun.

Where has Anna run to? He thinks of how her eyes came alive, and picks up the empty box, smelling the fresh scent of cedar. The photographs in it have all been carried away by the wind or scooped up by her.

His old truck is still hidden under the stand of trees by the driveway. He brushes snow off the windshield; the engine is cold, but it coughs to life after six tries. He drives up the hill, the pain jabbing into his side, praying under his breath that the Senator is somehow, miraculously, still alive.

CHAPTER THIRTY-THREE

Anna.

As the truck curves up the driveway and pulls out onto Lighthouse Road, he cannot stop thinking of her, alone somewhere out there in the darkness. The flare of anger that led her to pull the trigger will have worn off, and the full horror of what she has done will now unfold in infinitesimal moments, each leading up to the final second when the Senator rose up on his toes, then fell, pierced through and bleeding.

Where will she run to now? All the men in her life are gone, betrayers and potential saviors. Now he knows that she needs a man to be one or the other.

He drives along the top of the cliff, thoughts clouding his brain, the ocean roaring far below.

Seeing car headlights by the side of the road, he slows, thinking of Anna, but it is a red SUV, doors open, a blond teenage boy standing by the road with his arm around a long-haired girl. *They must have broken down.* He is about to speed up when he sees that their headlights illuminate the edge of the cliff: an entire section of the guardrail is missing, the gap framed in splintered white wood.

Feeling a sudden chill, he screeches to a halt, jumps out of the truck, and runs over. The teenagers hear his footfalls and turn, their faces white and staring. The boy wears a thin sweatshirt, and the girl's lipstick is smudged, her red sweater unbuttoned.

Ranjit stops when he's in the beam of their headlights. "What happened here?"

"We called the cops already, mister. Nothing we can do."

He looks over the edge of the cliff. There, four hundred feet below, lying overturned on the rocks, wheels still spinning, is the long shape of Anna's Mercedes.

No. Not this, Guru, not this.

The boy is behind him. "Someone moved in there. They're still alive."

He finds himself shouting. "When did this happen?"

"About five minutes ago? We were just parked here. We saw the headlights, saw the car swerve and go over the edge. Driver must be drunk."

The boy smirks, and the girl shivers dramatically. Ranjit wants to grab them and shake them.

He strains to see in the darkness. The car lies upside down on a thin strip of rocks, and the waves behind it move higher up with each ebb and flow. The tide is coming in.

The figure inside the car twitches. Anna is still alive, hanging upside down in the front seat.

"Who did you call?"

"The cops. But there's a delay. All the ambulances are in Menemsha. Some kind of accident at the Red Heron Estate."

"Call them again. Tell them she's trapped in the car and the tide is coming in. The Coast Guard needs to send a rescue boat. Got any rope?"

The boy shakes his head. The girl next to him whimpers as a wave below slaps against the car.

Ranjit walks back to the guardrail, seeing the tire tracks ending in midair, the soil at the cliff edge gouged deeply. He drops to his knees and looks down at the cliff face, its wet clay made slippery by the ocean spray.

No ropes. No one to belay him. *If he falls, he falls right onto the rocks.*

No choice. He rubs his hands in the dry, powdery dirt, turns, and swings his legs over the edge.

"Hey, mister. You can't go down there. That's crazy!"

"Don't worry about me. I'm a professional climber. Call. Now."

Twenty minutes later, he is spread-eagled against the cliff face, his arms quivering to maintain their hold. He's gone forty, maybe fifty feet down, the slick clay climb getting worse and worse. Now he holds on with every last ounce of strength.

He's losing circulation in his hands, and in another minute or so his fingers will be completely numb. He looks down to see the silver Mercedes lying on the rocks, the incoming tide lapping at it. Anna will drown. *She will die, as all the others did.*

The numbness sets into his hands. He closes his eyes tightly and prays. *Khandelkar, help me. Never again will I call you back. Please.*

He closes his eyes and crows hover in a cloudless sky above a landscape of powdery white. *Sergeant, tell me what to do. Help me.*

He hangs in the darkness, waiting for the priestlike face to appear. Minutes pass, and his arms are trembling violently, are about to give way. *Nothing.*

There are shouts from above. He raises his head, and is blinded.

The police have arrived and are shining a searchlight down the cliff face. The light sweeps past him, continuing its erratic journey across the cliff face, and he sees the colors hidden by the darkness, bands of purple and white and red clay that gleam for a second.

Then he sees it: fifteen feet to his right, the bright light illuminates a jagged shadow in the cliff face. He looks harder, seeing a deep crack running downward: there is a chimney in the cliff, hidden all this time by the darkness. If he can get to it, it might take him down.

He slowly moves one foot, searching for a toehold, then the next. He moves sideways like a crab, the waves thundering below him.

He is in the chimney, an endless slot that stretches down into darkness. Sheltered from the ocean spray, it is drier in here, the clay firmer. He has climbed in chimneys before, and knows that all his weight is going to be on his legs, the impact transferred to the wound in his side.

He jams one foot, knee high, into the wall of the chimney. The other leg stretches out behind him, braced against the opposing wall. Stretching out his arms to grip both sides, he becomes a human cork in a stone bottle.

The pain in his side is electric. He lowers one foot a little, then the next. He almost slides down, losing his grip.

Slower, smaller movements. He jerks downward, a few inches this time.

The pain is wrenching through him. *Turn it off. Turn off the mind. Don't think.*

Taking a deep breath, he slows his breathing.

He is at the top of the gulmohar tree, the wind rocking the branches. From here he can look down onto the flat roofs of houses, see the red ball of the sun setting over distant hills.

It is growing dark, and he must go down for dinner, or else his mother will come out and shout his name. He lowers one foot, searching for stability within the swaying of the tree.

Mataji appears in the garden below, her long hair tightly braided, her pale face searching for him. Even from up here, he can tell that the front of her *kameez* is spattered with turmeric and cooking oil.

There is pain, but somehow the pain is not his, it is the pain in his mother's voice as she calls his name.

I'm coming, Mataji. *Don't worry, I'm coming down.* The branches sway as he moves downward, the bark scraping against his knees.

He is soon halfway down, and the hills have disappeared. From this height, he can look into the window of an apartment building across the street. At one window, a Sikh family sits at a table, eating. In another, a white-bearded man prays silently in front of an altar, then places a garland of red flowers around a portrait of the Guru. He is so close that he can smell the incense, hear the tinkling of the prayer bell.

As he climbs down, he is reaching thicker branches, and they do not bend with his weight.

Ranjit, Ranjit, Ranjit, his mother calls. Her voice is bereft and heartbroken and worn with calling him.

He can see the ground now, and the low tattered hedges that flank the gate. He can see the wet patches of earth near the tube-well, crisscrossed by the tracks of his bicycle.

Coming, Mataji, *I'm coming. I'm almost there.*

Inch by inch he moves downward.

Taking a deep breath, he opens his eyes and

sees a slot of gray twilight at the base of the chimney. He lands on a jumble of wet boulders. Careful not to slip and shatter an ankle, he grips the cold stone and edges slowly forward.

The roar of the ocean gets louder. He clambers over the last massive boulder and lands on the rocky beach.

The silver Mercedes lies twenty yards away, the gray ocean lapping at its sides. *Guru, please let her still be alive.*

He runs up to the car. Its windshield has shattered into an opaque spiderweb, and inside, the slash of her seat belt pinning her upside down, is Anna. When he reaches her window she stares at him.

"Anna, I'm here."

Her eyes flicker. *Thank you, Guru.*

The door has jammed shut with the impact. He picks up a rock and slams it again and again into the windshield, which shudders and takes the blows, but does not break. Finally one corner falls inward. Taking off his jacket, he wraps his hands in it and tugs with all his strength, ripping the sheet of fractured glass from its frame.

He crouches down and peers into the car, seeing her clearly now. Her short hair hangs from her upside-down head.

"Anna. Help is on the way. I'm going to

478

stay here with you."

She opens her eyes and mumbles, "We should have gone away, Ranjit, we should have . . ."

He feels a surge of pain. "*Shhh.* Don't talk. Listen to me, listen to my voice. Can you move your head?"

She tries to, then gasps in pain, and her head flops sideways.

The tide is coming in fast. Water surges past the car, then retracts with a hiss.

"Don't . . . don't leave me in here. Get me out."

"Anna, I can't move you just yet. I think your neck is broken. If I move you —"

He feels the cold sluice of water around his feet. The waves are big enough now to tip the car, drop it from the rocks into the ocean.

"Please," she whispers. "Please. Get me out."

He looks at her hanging in the car. Maybe he can cushion her neck a little. He unbuckles her seat belt with one hand, the other steadying her head.

She moans as she tumbles forward, half out of the windshield, but she's still stuck. Then he sees the steering wheel jammed deep into her stomach. She smiles up at him, and a trickle of blood runs out of her mouth.

"It's okay. Get me out."

He heaves, and she comes through the empty windshield like a rag doll, arms and legs askew, head lolling backward.

Gathering her into his arms, he staggers to the base of the cliffs. With his back against a boulder, he lowers himself and manages to sit, cradling her head in his arms.

"Anna, hold on. A rescue boat is on its way."

She smiles faintly up at him, her teeth red with blood. "Josephine. I remember what she looks like. I remember her now."

"That's good. That's good. Tell me about her, Anna. Talk to me."

She coughs up bubbles of blood. Her head is warm and heavy in his arms.

He wills himself to forget her betrayal, to go back into the darkness, to when they lay naked together. "It's all right. I'll talk, you listen. Remember, that night, I was telling you about going to India? We'll go there, okay?"

She blinks up at him.

"Listen. We'll go to the Golden Temple in Amritsar. It's warm there. The sun is shining down and the marble is warm under your feet. You can hear women singing, you can hear their prayers floating across the water, and I'm with you —"

She begins to cough.

"— as we walk to the temple. All the women are there, singing *kirtans*. They are all wishing you well, they are praying for you. I am with you, I am with you —"

She clutches his arm. The blood flows from her mouth.

Then he is praying. He is saying every scrap of prayer he remembers. He is praying to the Gurus, he is praying to the universe, he is saying the words, over and over and over.

Give her peace. Give her shanti.
Om shanti om.
Shanti, shanti, om.
Om shanti, shanti.

He is still praying when the Coast Guard rescue launch pulls up close to the rocks. He hears the powerful thrum of its outboard engines, but does not open his eyes.

Men in gray uniforms hail him through a loudspeaker, then wade ashore. They find him sitting at the base of the cliff, Anna's head cradled in his arms. His eyes are shut, and he is speaking in a language they do not understand. They look at the Mercedes, now lying half submerged in water, and shake their heads. They look in awe at the tall, brown-skinned man, having heard of his climb down the cliff face.

"Sir," a voice comes through the fog. "We will take over now. You have to let us take her."

Arms pry Anna away, arms pull him to his feet.

They put her onto the stretcher and her head lolls. "Gentle," he cries. "Be gentle with her."

As they lift the stretcher, her jacket gapes open. Photographs scatter onto the rocks and are swept away by the waves.

He bends and scoops up three color pictures. They are stained with her blood, warped by the saltwater.

He looks down and a little girl with Anna's dark eyes smiles up at him. All the pictures are of her: she is on the beach, laughing, wearing a crumpled yellow sun hat. She is a plump baby, held tightly by her shirtless father. She is being bathed in a sink, a yellow rubber duck clutched in one fist.

Ranjit closes his eyes. He remembers the Senator digging a hole on that faraway evening. Anna had been wrong: her husband hadn't burned all the photographs of his daughter. Years after her death, he had put them into a cedar box and buried them, hoping that the pain would pass.

He had remembered his little girl after all.

CHAPTER THIRTY-FOUR

Two days later Ranjit stands in the doorway of a darkened hospital room. The shades have been pulled to keep out the afternoon light, what little there is of it, since the sky has been obliterated by falling snow.

As his eyes adjust to the darkness he can make out Senator Neals, lying like a fallen monument on the white-sheeted bed, his chest immobilized by a massive bandage. He seems unconscious, but then he moves his head, and his low voice fills the room.

"Who is it?"

Ranjit walks into the darkened room. The doctors said that the pellets from the shotgun had spattered through the Senator's chest, just missing his heart, shattering ribs and causing massive internal bleeding. Only a man built like an ox could have taken that blow and still crawled to the alarm cabinet. An emergency crew had found him slumped in a pool of his blood, hands still bound together, his fingers clamped over the red alarm button.

The doctors repaired eleven holes in his bowel, and then cut his chest open to remove the pellets close to his heart. They were worried that he wouldn't make it, but he had stabilized and woken this morning. Ranjit rushed over from Celia's apartment, where he was staying, under orders from the police not to leave the island.

He steps closer to the bed, seeing that the windowsill is crowded with vases of white flowers that he does not recognize. In India, the flowers of death are orange marigolds.

"Senator, I didn't know you were awake —"

"Open the blinds. It's too dark, I can't see."

Ranjit pulls up the blinds and a murky light shines into the room, casting shadows of the flowers onto the opposite wall.

"And tell the nurse to get rid of those flowers. I can't stand the smell, it's making me sick."

"Senator, I am deeply sorry. I tried to tell you about Kohonen, but you wouldn't listen. He was the one who —"

The Senator stares at Ranjit out of reddened eyes. Deep lines of pain bracket his mouth. "I kept losing consciousness in the other room, but I heard enough. Bragging about how he tricked me in North Korea, the bastard." He pauses and his breathing is ragged. "If Anna had been in her right mind, he never would have got through to her. She's a strong-willed woman."

The Senator has used the present tense, and for a few seconds Anna is alive and warm and beautiful, walking down the stone stairs in her yellow dress. Then reality reasserts itself, and Ranjit slumps down onto an upholstered chair. He stares at the shadows on the wall.

The Senator's voice breaks the silence. "They told me you climbed down the cliff, you tried to save her."

"There wasn't much I could do. Her neck was broken, her stomach ruptured. It was a matter of minutes."

"Did . . . she say anything? Anything at all?"

"She couldn't really talk. But she had these . . ." He takes the three photographs out of his pocket, warped and stained with blood and saltwater. ". . . she had these with her. There were more, but they were washed away."

The Senator takes the photographs with trembling fingers and his eyes widen. "Jesus. Where did she get these?"

Ranjit hesitates. "I dug them up. Kohonen wanted the microfilm, so I lied to him. I remembered you had buried something there, and I just wanted to distract him . . ."

"Jesus." The Senator turns his head away from the photographs and blinks into the dim light. "There is no forgetting, is there? I . . . I went into the house to take a call, I was gone not even five minutes. Jojo must have hit her head when she fell into the pool. I'd had it drained, there was just a puddle at the bottom. A puddle, I tell you. If she'd fallen on her back, she would have broken an arm or a leg, but she must have landed facedown."

Ranjit's mind fills with an image of Anna's little girl, her hair floating around her in the cool water, her breath bubbling up, until it stops.

The Senator tries to wipe away tears with his hands, but the IVs restrict his movements. "Anna was in so much pain, I told her the pool was full . . . I mean, what difference did it make? Jojo was gone." His voice thickens. "Anna could never forgive me. And then she started seeing other men. I knew about it, I thought she would stop, but it just went on and on. And those damn pictures, everywhere, it was like living in a shrine. Kohonen, that bastard, he saw what

487

she was doing, and he used her. I trusted him, I never thought . . ."

He is crying now, making no attempt to wipe away the tears rolling down his battered face.

"Senator, the Koreans think that he has the microfilm, that he's holding out for more money. They will track him down. He's not long for this world."

"No." The Senator's voice is thick. "Don't underestimate him. He's very resourceful, he has access to some far-reaching networks. I've put the word out that he's persona non grata, but still . . ."

Ranjit feels a pang of panic. "My family is still in detention. They'll be deported anytime now. Do you think he can get to them?"

"Ran-jitt." The Senator reaches out and grabs his sleeve. "When I called Homeland Security, we were after *you,* I never meant to involve your wife and girl, but Kohonen convinced me that it was the best way —"

"Please just get them out. I need to take them somewhere safe."

"I'll call my office, they'll take care of it. It'll take some time, these places have a lot of bureaucracy to get through." He lets go of Ranjit's sleeve and sinks back into his pillow. "And listen. Don't talk to anyone, okay? The police here have been told to back off, and we have the press under wraps."

"I haven't said anything." Ranjit thinks of the hours he spent in the Oak Bluffs police station. A phone call had come just as the cops started asking him questions, and they had stopped right away.

"And the microfilm? You have it?"

"Yes, it's safe." Ranjit thinks of the manila envelope that he'd left with James at the Garibaldi.

"I'm telling you, Kohonen isn't going to give up so easily. It's too dangerous to let it exist. Destroy it."

"I can do that, but it's not here, it's —"

The door opens and a nurse in pink scrubs peeks in, her olive-skinned face tightening when she sees the tears staining the Senator's face. "What in heaven's name is going on here? This man is in critical condition. Please end this visit, right now."

"I'm sorry, Senator, I'll come back later."

As Ranjit heads out of the door, the Senator is staring at the photographs, his blunt fingertips caressing his daughter's face.

Ranjit walks quickly across the icy parking lot and dials Ricky Singh's number. It rings and rings, but finally Ricky answers.

"Ranjit *Mausa*? Why haven't you called me? What is going on —"

"Ricky, where are you? At the store?"

Ricky's voice drops to a whisper. "Yeah, and my dad is here, he's restocking. He's going to hear us."

"Look, I don't have much time to explain, but I need you to close up. Drive to the Norfolk County Correctional Center. It's in Dedham, on I-95. Tell them that Senator Neals called on your behalf. They're going to release Preetam and Shanti in the next few hours."

"Are you sure? How can I —"

"Put your father on the phone. Don't worry, just do it."

There is a sigh. He hears Ricky calling out, and Lallu's brusque, loud voice comes onto the phone. "Ranjit? Where are you? How dare you try to get Ricky involved —"

"Lallu. Listen to me." He takes a deep breath. "I know you don't like me, I know you think that Preetam deserved better. You're probably right. But right now I need you to drive to Dedham and pick up Preetam and Shanti. They'll be released soon. I told Ricky where to go."

"Ricky knows?" There is a pause. "Okay, I will do it for her, not for you."

"Thank you, I —"

There is a click and Lallu is gone. Ranjit stares at the phone in his hand, then climbs into the truck and switches on the ignition.

They'll be released in a few hours, but Kohonen is still out there.

He drives aimlessly down the empty, frozen roads, turning at random, not sure where he is going. Finding himself near the airport, he takes the dirt road to the Long Point Wildlife Refuge and parks in its empty lot. Heading over the sand dunes, he walks along the beach, passing broken branches and tangles of lobster nets. As he walks he remembers the conversation he'd had this morning outside Mike's Tow. He was getting into his truck when a blue-and-white police cruiser pulled up. It was Officer Gardner from the West Tisbury Police Department.

The policeman rolled down his window. "Fine morning," he said, his forehead creasing as he squinted up at the snowflakes. "Where are you off to?"

Ranjit didn't see the point in lying. "The hospital."

Officer Gardner heaved his bulky frame out of the cruiser. "Ah. To have a chat with the Senator, no doubt. Give him my regards. He's lucky to survive being shot at such a

491

close range."

"Yes, he was lucky."

The officer stared up at the falling snow, flakes of it settling on the shoulders of his blue uniform. "It's pretty unusual to be found shot in the chest with one's hands tied behind one's back, isn't it?" His voice was slow and unhurried, the voice of someone discussing the weather. "And at the Red Heron Estate, where, coincidentally, you are the caretaker?"

Ranjit remained silent, the keys to the truck clutched in his hand.

"You wouldn't know it, but this used to be a nice place, before all the money washed in. Now there are people overdosing on cocaine, there are people falling out of speedboats — three this year — and the more money involved, the more calls we get from the mainland to be *cooperative*. I've had *cooperative* before, but never come up against *a matter of national security.*"

"I'm sorry, I'm in a hurry. Visiting hours are —"

Officer Gardner reached up and dusted snowflakes off his peaked hat. "Well, don't you want to hear about the body?"

"What are you talking about?" *Maybe he'd hit Kohonen a little too hard, perhaps a hemor-rhage . . .*

"A friend of yours, Norman Nash. You know, the guy who broke into the house in Lambert's Cove. He washed up on South Beach this morning, his pockets full of rocks." Gardner paused. "And we figured out, from the currents, that the body was thrown into the ocean around Aquinnah, where the Senator, coincidentally, has a house. And I'm not supposed to ask the Senator any questions. You can see the position I'm in."

"I'm sorry," Ranjit repeated. "I'm in a hurry."

Officer Gardner ignored him and continued in his calm, reasonable voice. "Last week I had a chat with the Senator's chief aide. He was asking me about you, said he was worried about your credentials as a caretaker. I told him that you had been a good citizen, told him that you had identified the Nash brothers. Now one of them washes up, dead. And the aide, apparently, he can't be found. So you see, Mr. Singh, the Senator gets shot, Norman Nash is dead, and the link in common is you. You sure you don't want to talk to me?"

Getting into his truck, Ranjit drove away, Gardner's final words echoing in his ears.

"*National security* may protect the Senator, but not you, Mr. Singh. You have to live here, work here, and I'll be watching you."

Now Ranjit walks down the beach, his mind whirling. So Kohonen had done some cleaning up after the shooting, had thrown Norman Nash into the ocean, but misjudged the tides. *Where is Kohonen now? Is there any way he can get to Preetam and Shanti inside the prison?*

Ranjit tries Ricky's cell phone but there is no answer. He just keeps on walking and dialing, and the tenth time he calls, Lallu Singh answers.

"Lallu? Are they out?"

There is a fumbling and the phone changes hands.

"*Papaji?* Is it you?" Shanti's high voice fills his ears.

He stops in his tracks, unable to talk. "Yes," he manages to say. "It's me. *Beti,* I am so —"

There is a scuffle, and the call ends with a click. He redials the number, punching in each digit with shaking fingers.

"What the hell is going on?"

Lallu answers. "Everything is all right, we are driving back to Cambridge. A man from the Senator's office was at the prison, he said it was all a mistake. He even made sure they got their passports back."

Ranjit sighs with relief. "Are they fine?

Let me talk to Preetam."

Lallu's voice is indignant. "After two weeks in jail, you ask if they are fine? Preetam is so thin, and the little one . . . Just a second."

There are muffled voices, then Lallu returns.

"Preetam does not wish to talk to you." In the background he can hear her voice, loud and strident. "She said to tell you that they're going back to India. They can take the night flight. I will pay for the ticket."

"No, Lallu, it's too dangerous. The General — Look, they must not go —"

"You are useless, Ranjit, I always said so. The poor woman wants to go home, and I support her."

Lallu hangs up. Ranjit stabs at his cell phone, calling back, again and again, but there is no answer. He stares out across the snowy beach at the empty, gray ocean.

As soon as Preetam lands in India, news will travel through the network of ex–military officers. All it will take is a man on a motorcycle, with a gun or a bomb. Anything can be written off as terrorism these days.

He runs down the beach, the cold searing his lungs. Starting the truck, he heads back to Oak Bluffs.

■ ■ ■ ■

The hospital is empty and his footsteps echo as he strides down the corridors. Pushing open the door to the Senator's room, he sees that the olive-skinned nurse is changing the dressing on the Senator's chest. Ranjit glimpses purple, pitted flesh before she turns and blocks his view, her face red with anger.

"Sir, visiting hours are *over*. It's seven o'clock." A wad of gauze is bundled tightly in her hands.

"Five minutes. Please, it's urgent."

The Senator tries to sit up. "I made the call, Ran-jitt. They should be out by now."

"Yes, they are, but —"

The nurse walks forward, her hands on her wide hips. "If you don't get out of here, I'll call security."

The Senator smiles his broad politician's smile. "Nurse, why don't you see to your next patient? I promise you this pest will leave soon."

The nurse backs away, glowering. "I'll be back in five minutes *exactly*. He better be gone."

When she leaves, Ranjit locks the door and walks over to the bed.

"Senator, I need to ask you one last question. When you went to India in oh-two, why did you meet Bear Handa? General Bear Handa?"

The Senator frowns. "Who? I met a lot of Generals back then."

"I did some research before I left Boston. There was a photograph in the Indian newspapers of you getting off a plane. General Handa was my commanding officer on the Siachen Glacier, and —"

The Senator pauses for a second. "The Siachen? Some sort of hot-shot climber? Short guy, built like a tank?"

"Yes, that's right."

The Senator laughs, then gasps in pain. "Yeah, I remember him. He was the worst. He kept trying to convince us that keeping his chunk of frozen ice was essential to India's security. Why?"

Ranjit looks down at the floor and his neck burns with shame. "He was my commanding officer. He asked me to do something . . . unethical, and I refused. That's why I had to leave India. My wife and daughter are flying back there tonight. If the General finds out, he'll destroy them. I need your help."

"My help?" The Senator stares at him. "I can't talk to our people in India. If I do, the

497

CIA is going to figure out that I —"

"Damn it." Ranjit leans over the bed. His eyes are burning with anger. "Even after all this, you're only concerned about your reputation? If my daughter dies, her death will be on your head." He is shouting now. "That's what you want? Can you live with it?"

"No, Ran-jitt, for God's sake, no." The Senator's voice is down to a faint whisper. "I still have some informal contacts in India. I'll make some calls, I'll see what I can do . . ."

The doorknob rattles and an irate voice says, "Hey. That was ten minutes. Let me in, or I'm calling security."

"They'll reach India tomorrow afternoon. There isn't much time."

Ranjit unlocks the door and walks past the furious nurse. He takes the stairs down to the parking lot, his footsteps echoing in the concrete stairwell.

Lying on a camp bed in Celia's office, Ranjit stares at the poster of Rio on the wall, at the hills and bays of a city he will never visit. For an instant Anna and he had dreamed of being together; now she is gone, and all he has left is his family.

Turning off the light, he stares into the

dark, watching a red digital clock on the desk draining time. He calculates and recalculates the hours before Preetam and Shanti arrive in India. If they go via Europe, it will take longer, but if they fly through Dubai, they will be there by midday.

The dead crowd around him now: Dewan and the Sergeant on the glacier. Norman Nash with his head smashed in. Anna's teeth stained with blood as she died in his arms.

He closes his eyes and prays:

There are so many beggars, but only the
    Lord can give
He is the giver of the soul, and the breath
    of life
When he dwells within the mind, there is
    peace
The world is a drama, staged in a dream,
    played out in a moment
Some attain union with the Lord, while
    others depart in separation
Whatever pleases Him comes to pass, and
    nothing else can be done.

He is still praying when his cell phone rings. The digital clock on the desk says that it is 2:13 A.M.

The Senator's voice is faint and exhausted.

"I talked to my people. They were in touch with the General till a few years ago, but he's vanished."

Ranjit can barely contain his impatience. "I know that. He's retired now —"

"No, not retired. Vanished. He tried to pull some sort of shit. Not clear what. The Indian military has frozen him out, they even axed his pension. He's disappeared off the face of the earth."

"What are you saying?"

"This guy is nearly eighty-five, and it looks like he's finished. You can go to India and bring your family back."

"It's too risky. You said that he vanished —"

"I worked out a deal for you. You can go back to India. Don't destroy the microfilm." The Senator's breathing is shallow and quick.

"What kind of deal? I can go home? Are you sure?"

"I need some time to figure out the details. Come see me tomorrow."

"Senator, there is one last thing. There's a friend of mine, a vet, living in an SRO in Boston. He has cancer, he's all alone. Can you get him into some decent housing?"

"Not a problem. We'll talk more tomorrow." There is a click and the Senator is gone.

Ranjit sits rigidly in the dark, still clutching his cell phone. It is stiflingly hot in Celia's office, and the close air smells like motor oil. He grabs his blue jacket and walks through the garage. Standing outside Mike's Tow, he looks across Masonic Avenue at the house where they once lived. The tall oak tree in its yard casts a dark shadow across the white snow. It is bone-chillingly cold, and so quiet that the silence rings in his ears.

On the other side of the world is the heat and noise of India. He imagines Shanti looking out of the plane window as it lands, her nose pressed against the glass.

Home. He thinks about Shanti when he hears that word.

CHAPTER THIRTY-FIVE

Home. Three days later, dawn is just breaking as the Air India flight descends out of the sky.

Ranjit looks down at the broad avenues of Chandigarh, interrupted only by regularly spaced gulmohar trees. As the plane flies lower, he sees rows of concrete houses, their rooftops crowded with antennas and potted plants. A few housewives hanging out wet laundry shield their eyes and wave as the plane flies lower, casting its shadow over the city.

His hands are sweating, and he wipes them on his trousers before taking out his passport, returned to him by the Senator's office. Slipped into it is a gift from the Senator: three laminated American green cards. And there is something else.

When he went back to the hospital, the Senator had whispered into his ear, "My people have talked to Indian Military Intelligence. Take the microfilm back to them. They've promised to protect your family if you return it."

Ranjit had left the Vineyard the same day.

Home. Almost there, and he feels acid rush into his stomach. The Senator assured him that he would be protected, but this is India; there are wheels within wheels, and levels of complexity that the Senator may not grasp.

His mind turns to Preetam. After two weeks in a jail cell, he can't blame her for running from him. But he has to try to save his family, and he has to see Shanti — he feels a physical ache as he remembers hugging her skinny body.

The plane's engines whine as it descends. As soon as the wheels bump against the tarmac, people jump up and begin unloading their bags, ignoring the repeated announcements to remain seated. Even before the plane rolls to a halt, the aisle is crowded with bodies.

Home. The doors hiss open and warm air floods in, smelling of wet earth mixed in with dust and heat and a million other odors. Ranjit grabs his backpack and joins the crush of passengers streaming down the stairs to the tarmac.

He walks past puddles of water reflecting

the bright morning sky, past tattered trees at the edge of the runway, the air full of twittering mynahs.

Home. He feels the heat soaking his bones.

Inside the terminal he stands in a long, irregular line, watching children run amid the shouting and laughing. In front of him is a family, stunned to be finally back: a Punjabi matron with her head covered, her husband anxiously scanning their immigration forms, and a teenage girl in jeans and a pink T-shirt. She turns to her parents and addresses them in an American accent, and her bright eyes and dark hair remind him of Shanti.

He is sweating as he approaches the khaki-clad immigration official, and can smell the sourness of his body, the odor of guilt. *I have nothing to hide,* he reminds himself. *I'm just another Sikh returning home.*

As the line inches forward, he looks down at his hands, noticing the dark crescents of American dirt still lodged under his fingernails. Life on the Vineyard suddenly seems so far away, and the immigration officials guard his entry into India. Everything now depends on the next few minutes.

When it is his turn, he steps up to the booth and presents his passport. The immigration official gives him an appraising look, taking in the crisp sky-blue turban and the dark suit. Under the turban, his hair is still short, but his beard and mustache have a clipped, military look.

"*Sat Sri Akal,* sir," the official says, and flips through his brand-new passport, taking in the issue date and the green card. "Ah, you are named Ranjit Singh. Like our great last emperor. But now living in America. Tell me, is it good there?"

"Mixed," Ranjit says, forcing a smile. The man distractedly taps information into an old gray desktop computer, squints at the screen, then stamps Ranjit's passport.

"Welcome home, sir."

It is that simple. After all these years, he cannot believe it.

Home. He walks through the baggage claim, sidestepping men dragging overstuffed suitcases off the conveyor belt. In a few minutes he is through the green channel and out of the exit doors.

Outside is the chaos of India. The arcade is crowded with touts who see him emerge and notice that there is no family to greet him.

"Mister! Here! Taxi?"

"No, no, here. Hotel, mister? You have dollars?"

Men and boys swarm around Ranjit, tugging at his backpack.

Ranjit strides down the arcade, saying, *No, no, no.*

He is busy keeping his backpack in sight when a lanky young man falls in by his side. The man's hair is shorn, aviator sunglasses cover his eyes, and he's wearing a white short-sleeved shirt and pressed khakis, the clothes favored by out-of-uniform army officers.

The Senator was wrong. The General is still powerful, and Ranjit will be dead within minutes. *Can he keep walking? Can he run?*

"Captain Singh?"

The touts crowd around Ranjit, blocking any escape. The young man turns and shouts at them in Punjabi, and hearing the authority in his voice, they scatter.

He turns to Ranjit. "Sir, I was sent by the Battalion. We were alerted of your arrival through certain channels. You have something for us? I was sent to collect it."

The microfilm. It's not the General after all. Relief floods through Ranjit, and he unslings his backpack and takes out a small manila envelope. Inside is the microfilm, retrieved from James on the way to Logan Airport.

"Here it is. I was promised protection in exchange."

The young man slips the envelope into his

506

breast pocket, then looks around, the blank aviator shades hiding his eyes. "Sir, we promised to protect your *family.* But if *you* stay here . . ." He shrugs his muscular shoulders. "Well, that is a difficult situation."

"What do you mean by that?"

"We cannot protect you, Captain. Your presence here will attract too much attention. Yes, we have resources, but even we have limits." He gestures to a jeep at the end of the arcade. "Can I drop you somewhere? I have transportation."

"Listen to me. The deal was for permanent protection —"

"I am just the messenger, Captain." The young man salutes smartly and walks away.

"Wait." Ranjit's voice is hard. "I served this country. I gave everything for it. I deserve better than this."

The man pauses by a pillar, then turns and walks back. His voice is halting now, losing its military crispness.

"Sir, I am speaking unofficially now. There will never be an official apology, but the military knows what General Handa did to you. You are an honorable man, Captain, and what happened to you was wrong."

Confusion spreads through Ranjit's mind. "What are you referring to? My court-martial?"

The young man takes Ranjit by the shoulder and leads him behind a pillar. "The court-martial was unnecessary, Captain. You were innocent all along. General Handa knew it was our own people up there. He deliberately sent you to the wrong sector. It seems that he wanted to prolong the war, even if it meant killing our own men and blaming it on the Pakistanis." The man's voice hardens with rage. "We only found out a year ago. We would have court-martialed the bastard, but he's a war hero, he's even been awarded the Param Vir Chakra. All we could do was force him to resign." His voice drops to a whisper. "Now he's vanished, but there are still officers loyal to him. They won't hurt a woman and child, but there is a price on your head. My advice to you, Captain, is don't stay here. Sooner or later someone will recognize you."

The young man salutes crisply. "Good luck, Captain." He walks quickly through the arcade, vaults into a jeep, and it roars away through the crowds.

Ranjit slumps against the pillar, stunned.

The briefing before his last mission. He has carried the memory of it with him all these years.

He is sitting with Khandelkar in a darkened auditorium at headquarters. Two men in plainclothes pore over maps, showing them the route. *Maintain radio silence,* they say. *No transmissions. No helicopter evacuations, no ammo drops.* And there is a darkened figure sitting at the back of the room, listening, and not saying a word. Halfway through the briefing the man leaves, and Ranjit sees, pinned to his chest, the flash of a round medal, something vaguely familiar about it.

Now he knows. That medal was the Param Vir Chakra. Both General Handa and his father had received the same medal for the same battle; the General had made it a point to tell him about it.

Ranjit stands motionless against the pillar, and the touts swarm toward him again.

"Mister, you want cheap hotel?"

"Nice girls, mister, nice girls?"

He shoulders his backpack and pushes through them to the taxi stand, choosing a round-bonneted Ambassador driven by an old Sikh in a crushed pink turban. When Ranjit gets in, he smells incense and realizes that the old man is praying. There is a small shrine set up on his dashboard, a photograph of the Guru flanked by two smoldering incense sticks.

Ranjit waits. When the old man is done

praying, he turns and looks back with clear eyes. "Where to, son?"

Ranjit gives the man Preetam's parents' address. He settles back into his seat and closes his eyes, feeling the thudding of his heart.

The General had deliberately sent him to kill those men. The disgrace, all those years in jail, his flight to America: they were all unnecessary, all the result of Bear Handa's secret plan. *Why had he done it?* Maybe fighting wars was all he knew. Maybe he had fought so much that war was his only reality, and peace a mirage that he refused to believe in.

Ranjit thinks of the Sergeant and Dewan still lying up there on the glacier. *"Sergeant,"* he whispers, *"if you can hear me, rest in peace. You were innocent, we both were."*

And then he is crying. Hot tears roll down his cheeks as he cries for Khandelkar, for Dewan, for Anna. He cries, for the first time, for someone else, a younger version of himself, a young man whose future had been snatched away.

There is the sudden blare of the taxi horn as it jerks to a stop. Through a blur of tears he sees a bullock cart roll slowly across the road.

"Son, are you all right?" the taxi driver

asks from the front seat.

Ranjit stares at the bullock cart. Beyond it, what were once green fields are now dotted with concrete bungalows. Huge garish signs line the road, advertising Japanese cars and washing machines.

"It has all changed so much," he replies. "I can hardly recognize this place."

"Son, you are returning from where?" Under the crumpled pink turban the driver's eyes are bright and clear.

"America, Uncle," says Ranjit, using the honorific.

"Have you been away long?"

"Yes, a long time. Too long."

"But you are still a Sikh. You have upheld our ways."

Ranjit hesitates. "Yes," he says.

The old man leans in and quotes a verse from the Guru Granth Sahib.

"God has his seat everywhere."

Ranjit finishes the verse. *"His treasure houses are in all places."*

The bullock cart has finally made its way across the road, and the traffic lurches forward.

The old Sikh smiles at Ranjit in the rearview mirror. "It's all right, son. You are home now. You are with your own people."

Ranjit looks wordlessly out of the window

at the streets swarming with people, sitting at roadside teashops and just loitering at each corner. He could be recognized by any one of them.

Home. The taxi drops him at the mouth of a narrow lane.

Ranjit pays the driver, adding a large tip. He walks slowly down the lane, between high walls with bright pink bougainvillea spilling over their tops. The noise of the main road ebbs away, and the silence here is broken only by the soft cooing of doves.

He passes bungalows on either side, hidden behind locked metal gates. His breath quickens as he reaches the tall iron gate at the end of the lane.

From behind the gate, there is a sudden shout in Punjabi. "*Oi,* you can't catch me, you can't catch me!"

Children scream with laughter.

"Yes, I can!"

It sounds like Shanti's voice, speaking fluent Punjabi. Ranjit presses his face against the metal bars of the gate.

But it isn't Shanti. Two little girls are running barefoot across the wide green lawn, the pale soles of their feet flashing. They have Shanti's curly black hair, and he recognizes Preetam's sister's daughters.

The little girl who is being chased veers breathlessly toward the gate. She sees Ranjit and stops, and the other girl bumps into her.

"Got you! Got you! Why did you stop running, silly?"

The first girl points, and both their eyes widen. They shout, "*Nani! Nani!* A man is here! A man is here!"

Preetam's mother comes out of the house and shades her eyes. "What is all this shouting about —" She spots Ranjit and her face crumples with relief. "Ranjit. Praise be to the Guru. You've come, you've come!"

Mrs. Kaur walks across the lawn, flicking the long *dupatta* of her *salwar kameez* over her shoulder. She reaches up, turns a key in a padlock, and the gate swings open.

"Preetam said you would never return," Mrs. Kaur says in Punjabi, waving her thick arms. "She said you were no good. There is something wrong with that girl. She came back here talking about divorce and whatnot."

"*Maji,*" Ranjit replies in Punjabi. "Many things have been my fault. Forgive me. I must talk to her." He bends down and touches his mother-in-law's feet, a mark of his respect.

"*Jeetay raho, beta,*" she says. *Live long, my*

son. Her face lights up with happiness and she gestures him toward the shady open veranda at the front of the house. "Come in, sit down," she says. "They are both out right now, but they will be back soon. Have you eaten?"

"I'm not hungry, but I am very thirsty."

They walk up the shallow stairs to the veranda and he lowers himself onto a wicker sofa. His two nieces peer at him, not recognizing him. The taller one was just a baby when he left for America.

"I'll bring water," Mrs. Kaur says. "When Preetam returns, you talk some sense to her. Please, you talk to her."

Mrs. Kaur goes into the house and returns with a metal tumbler of cold well water. Ranjit thanks her and drinks it in two swallows. Even water tastes better here. He stares at the girls running across the rich green lawn, at the sunlight filtering through the leaves of a gulmohar tree aflame with red flowers.

"How long are you going to stay? Are you taking them back to America?" Mrs. Kaur asks in Punjabi, wiping a bead of sweat from her forehead, her gold bangles jangling.

"I'm not sure," Ranjit replies. "I have to talk to Preetam. I was thinking that we could move to New York. She'll like it, there are plenty of Indians living there."

"*Aare,* you are the man, you make the decision. You are a good man. I've always said that, no matter what."

She is alluding to his years in prison. He aches to tell her what he has just learned, but he holds back. He must tell Preetam first.

Sitting back, he listens to the sun-dazed buzzing of flies, the exhaustion of the long journey clouding his head.

"Where have they both gone, *Mataji*? When will they be back?"

"Oh, Preetam has gone to see a film with one of her old school friends. Shanti was only just here, but she went to the bazaar. I was cooking and ran out of chilies, she wanted to go . . ."

"She went to the bazaar? Alone?"

"Yes, why not? She's a big girl now, and everybody knows us in this neighborhood. This is not America, Ranjit."

He feels a deep sense of unease at the thought of Shanti walking alone through the crowded streets. After all, she is a nine-year-old girl, easily snatched up and bundled into a car.

He rises to his feet. "The old bazaar, right? Down the road? Maybe I'll take a stroll there. My legs are cramped after the long flight."

"*Aare,* don't go out again! You look so tired, and Shanti will return in a few minutes. She's probably gone to the sweet shop with my change —"

"It's okay. I'll be right back."

He walks through the creaking gate and back down the lane, emerging onto the broad, sunlit street. Shielding his eyes, he looks for any sign of a curly black head, but there are only women returning from the bazaar, their shopping baskets overflowing with wet vegetables.

As he walks to the bazaar the air is warm and moist, surrounding him like a close embrace. Sweat trickles from his forehead, and he finds himself missing the cold of the Vineyard.

He smells the bazaar before he sees it, a mix of rotting vegetables and the gamey odor of fresh-killed chicken. Rounding the corner, he finds everything as he remembered it: rows of open-air stalls that line a large courtyard, each stall piled high with purple-black eggplants, wet bunches of spinach, pale green squashes, and fresh okra.

Which stall does Mrs. Kaur patronize? *The one on the far left,* he remembers, and walks over, pushing past two plump housewives who turn to stare at him.

The vegetable seller is sitting cross-legged above his piles of produce, busy weighing muddy potatoes on a handheld scale.

"Hello, Uncle?" Ranjit says.

The vegetable seller looks shocked. "Ranjit Sahib! But I thought you were in foreign! Across the ocean!"

"Well, I'm back for a visit. Have you seen my daughter? Shanti? She came to buy chilies. She's nine —" He pats the air to approximate her height.

"Mrs. Kaur's American granddaughter? Sure, she was here. She's not home yet?"

"When did she leave?"

The man shrugs. "Ten minutes ago, perhaps less. *Aare,* don't worry, she'll be home — children these days, they like to wander, especially with a little change in their hands."

Ranjit's chest tightens. He looks around the bazaar, and then remembers Bhupinder's sweet shop, just around the corner. Walking quickly, he reaches the corner, but just then a herd of dusty black goats thunders past, blocking his path. Sensing they will soon be slaughtered, the animals raise their bearded heads and bleat piteously.

The goats pass in a cloud of dust, and he

rounds the corner and sees the sweet shop dead ahead, its tall glass bottles holding myriad colors of boiled sweets. And there, reaching up to press a coin into Bhupinder's palm, is a familiar curly head.

"Shanti!"

She turns and sees him, her eyes widening. Then she is running to him, her sandaled feet kicking up puffs of dust, red sweets falling from the open paper bag in her hand.

He grabs her and presses her to him, unable to speak. She pushes her face into his shoulder and begins to cry.

"Hey, hey, don't worry. I'm here now. I'm here."

"Papaji," she sniffles, drawing back her tear-stained face. "I knew you'd come. Mama said that you'd stay in America, but I knew you'd come back."

"Hey, look at you. You look so pretty." He gestures at her pale pink *salwar kameez,* her wrists jangling with coral-colored glass bangles. Her hair is longer, the curls reaching her shoulders.

She hugs him again, and he lifts her up, feeling how much heavier she has become. All this in a few weeks? It feels as though he hasn't seen her in a decade.

"Come, *beti,"* he says. "Your grandmother

is waiting for us. You dropped your sweets. Do you want me to buy you some more?"

She holds his hand tightly and shakes her head. "Forget the stupid sweets. I don't even really like them. I wish they had Starburst chews here, like we get back home . . ."

Holding hands, they walk back along the main road. Shanti chatters on, so quickly that he can barely understand what she is saying.

". . . Mama was so scared in the detention center, she just lay on her bunk and stared at the wall . . . I told her you would get us out, but she didn't believe me. She wouldn't eat, you know how she gets, anyway, the food was horrible in there, and we had to sleep with the lights on. Then they told us we were going to be deported, and Mama was crying, she was so ashamed, but Ricky came to get us. And the plane ride, *Papaji,* we had to stop twice, in Amsterdam and Dubai, and then we got here, and it's so hot I can't sleep, and you know, *Nani* lets me run errands, but she's really strict, and sometimes I can't understand what she's saying, and . . ."

They turn into the coolness of the lane, and then stop, seeing a taxi at the far end. It begins to back up toward them, and they flatten themselves against the wall to let it pass. As they walk on, they see who its passenger was.

Preetam is wearing a sky-blue *salwar kameez* and silver high-heeled sandals, and she's holding a large shopping bag from a sari store.

"Mama!" Shanti shouts. "He's here! *Papaji* is here!"

Preetam turns and sees them, and her face goes pale.

He stands stock-still and clears his throat. "I just want to talk to you, give me a few minutes."

Without saying a word, Preetam reaches out, grabs Shanti's shoulder, and pulls the girl to her.

"What is there to talk about, Ranjit?"

Up close he can see that the time in detention has aged her. More gray strands run through her dark hair and her face is thinner. All the dreaminess is gone from her eyes, and they are sharp with anger.

"Can we please go inside, just for a minute? There is something important I just found out. It changes everything —"

Preetam pushes Shanti toward the gate. "Go inside. I need to talk to your father. Go."

"But, *Papaji* . . ." Shanti's face contorts, and she starts sobbing.

He bends and hugs her tightly. "It's going to be okay, *beti*. It's going to be okay. Listen to your mother."

Glancing backward, Shanti walks reluctantly through the gate and up the stairs to the veranda. When she enters the house, Preetam turns to Ranjit.

"What is it that you wanted to say?"

"Here? You want to talk here?"

She averts her face, and he has no choice but to continue. "Okay, listen. I just found out that I'm not guilty of killing those men on the glacier. It was all a setup: the mission, the court-martial, everything. This General set me up because —"

She raises a hand to silence him.

"This is what you wanted to tell me?"

Confusion clouds his thoughts.

"Yes, don't you understand? It changes everything."

"It changes nothing." Preetam closes her eyes for a few seconds, and when she opens them again, her face is calm, and she chooses her words carefully. "It changes nothing, Ranjit. Guilty or not guilty, you were my husband, and I waited for you all those years. I had faith in you, I believed you were a good man. But now . . ."

She pauses and then looks directly into his eyes. "In the detention center, I had plenty of time to think about things. You have lied to me, Ranjit, you have shown me such little respect. I feel as though I don't know you anymore."

Hearing her calm, considered words, he feels the panic grow.

"Preetam, please . . . look, it's not safe for me to stay here . . . I can explain it all to you, but we have to return to America. I have green cards for all of us, real green cards —"

When she does not respond, he reaches out and pulls her to him.

She does not resist, and he holds her, feeling how light she has become. He inhales the scent of her hair, and his grip tightens, but she still averts her face and remains passive in his arms. He might as well be holding a sack of straw.

Gently, she disentangles herself from him and steps back.

"You can do what you like, Ranjit. Return to America if you want, but leave us alone. I cannot go on like this anymore."

Before he can say anything else, she turns on her heel and walks down the lane, between the high walls. There is a flash of her sky-blue *salwar kameez,* and then the high iron gate slams shut. He hears the key turn in the padlock on the other side.

He is suddenly so exhausted that he cannot move.

Slumping against the wall, he closes his eyes. *It cannot end like this,* he vows. *Whatever it takes, I'll get my family back.*

But for now, he has to leave. All his frantic calculations return to the same conclusion: the longer he remains here, the more dangerous it is for them. Reaching into his pocket, he fingers the return ticket to Boston. The thought of returning there makes him sick; he'll change the ticket at the airport and fly back to New York. Maybe he can stay there till he figures out what to do.

He opens his eyes and walks down the lane, listening to the cooing of the doves. Soon the silence fades away, replaced by the raucous beeping of horns and the roar of traffic.

Squaring his shoulders, he walks out into the sunlit chaos of the main road. He looks around, but there is no one staring at him. He takes a deep breath and walks away, heading toward the taxi stand by the bazaar.

In a few minutes he is swallowed up by the crowd, and vanishes.

ACKNOWLEDGMENTS

Several works were crucial to the writing of this novel. *The Sikhs* by Patwant Singh (Doubleday, 1999) provided some of the quotes from the Guru Granth Sahib; others were adapted from the complete *Shri Guru Granth Sahib* (Forgotten Books, 2008). The haunting images from Martin A. Sugarman's *War Above the Clouds: Siachen Glacier: Photographs* (Sugarman Productions, 1996) provided insights into this hidden war.

A first novel owes many debts, and I am glad to acknowledge them here:

In Boston: Chris Castellani and Whitney Scharer at Grub Street provided invaluable support. Thanks to all those at "The Council," and a special thanks to Jenna Blum and Randy Susan Meyers for their unwavering guidance. Nicole Lamy for first publishing me. Bernice and Joel Lerner, Brother Tom Miller, and Miriam Stein for their kindness and insights. Tom Matlack, one of the best men I know. Alex and Whitney Van Praagh for many dinners and conversations.

In New York: Katia Lief and Matt de La Peña for early encouragement. My crew: Charlene Allen for always being there; Maija Makinen and Laura Chavez Silverman, who kept me on the path. I couldn't have done it without you guys. My talented agent, Stéphanie Abou, at Foundry Media, and my editor, Hilary Teeman, who made this a much better book.

In Martha's Vineyard: Wayne Elliott, whose stories about caretaking inspired this book; Karla Araujo for her insights into life on the island.

My fellow talented writers: Emily Russin and Chaiti Sen, for many conversations and support. Angie Kim for all her insights.

My family: Zig, Chippy, and Rehana for telling me stories. Doug and Carolyn Nash for their faith in me, and for keeping the 'chives. My parents, Ameer and Naseem; siblings, Karim and Naira, for keeping me company on this long road. My son, Amar, an artist in his own right, who drew many pictures while I wrote this book.

And this one is for my own dark-eyed girl, Jennifer Christine Nash, in the first decade

of our ongoing conversation: I owe you everything.

The employees of Thorndike Press hope you have enjoyed this Large Print book. All our Thorndike, Wheeler, and Kennebec Large Print titles are designed for easy reading, and all our books are made to last. Other Thorndike Press Large Print books are available at your library, through selected bookstores, or directly from us.

For information about titles, please call:
(800) 223-1244

or visit our Web site at:
http://gale.cengage.com/thorndike

To share your comments, please write:
Publisher
Thorndike Press
10 Water St., Suite 310
Waterville, ME 04901